Tango

Gleb lifted one hand and began ticking off
fingers as he spoke. 'The moment Lansky
brought Batista back to power Philby began
reviving his old Washington affiliations. The
moment Castro triumphed he was able to plant
inside the CIA a conspiracy to invade Cuba.
Listen:

'One, they believe it is their own brilliant idea
but, two, it can only fail and fail miserably . . .
costing them millions and us not a kopek . . .
while, three, it is guaranteed to smear shit all
over the Kennedy administration and the two
stainless young brothers who run it . . . and,
four, seat Castro even more firmly in Cuba's
saddle as the defender of the people . . . and
undermine in advance for all of Latin-America
any future proposal of goodwill Uncle Sam
might try to sell . . . and give Castro a
horrendous and powerful excuse to call upon his
friends, worldwide, meaning us . . . and hand
over to us in the name of Cuban security the
unrestricted licence to install whatever long-
range missiles we deem useful in protecting our
Cuban allies and dominating the land of the free
and the home of the brave . . . from a base just
offshore . . . and what is more, Kolya, to set up
for the CIA and have accepted in the highest
places of the American government *a model, a
pattern of illegal clandestine work which
routinely commits treason* against its own
people and its own country's best self-
interest . . .'

Leslie Waller, an American, lives in London. His
novels *The Banker*, *The Family*, *Mafia Wars* and
Deadly Sins are available as Mandarin
paperbacks. He also wrote the book for the film
classic *Close Encounters of the Third Kind*, and
the novel from which *Dog Day Afternoon* was
filmed.

Also by Leslie Waller

Fiction

Deadly Sins
Mafia Wars
Amazing Faith
Embassy
Gameplan
Blood and Dreams
The Brave and the Free
Trocadero
The Swiss Account
The Coast of Fear
Number One
The American
A Change in the Wind
New Sound
The Family
Overdrive
Will the Real Toulouse-Lautrec Please Stand Up?
K
The Banker
Phoenix Island
The Bed She Made
Show Me the Way
Three Day Pass

Non-Fiction

Half Life
Hide in Plain Sight
The Mob: The Story of Organized Crime in America
The Swiss Bank Connection

As Patrick Mann

Falcon Crest
Steal Big
Close Encounters of the Third Kind
Dog Day Afternoon
The Vacancy

Tango Havana
Leslie Waller

Mandarin

A Mandarin Paperback
TANGO HAVANA

First published in Great Britain 1993
by William Heinemann Ltd
This edition published 1994
by Mandarin Paperbacks
an imprint of Reed Consumer Books Ltd
Michelin House, 81 Fulham Road, London SW3 6RB
and Auckland, Melbourne, Singapore and Toronto

A CIP catalogue record for this title
is available from the British Library
ISBN 0 7493 1399 4

Printed and bound in Great Britain
by BPCC Paperbacks Ltd

Member of BPCC Ltd

For Sarah, Emily, Margaret and Julia

Author's Note

Secret agents usually die at the hands of secret police. It is the most normal thing in the world.

But when last I talked with Midge Boardman she was preparing for the wedding of one of her daughters. As for Victor Sanchez, he seemed quite at ease on his pleasant veranda protected only by palms and flowering shrubs from the turmoil of his home town, Havana.

Victor must be sixty years old. Neither the mafia, the KGB nor the CIA worry him any more. No wonder he produced one of his big, crooked smiles for me.

'Still on the Bay of Pigs?' He then uttered a Great Thought. These nuggets of wisdom are always brief. Consider Descartes' immortal: 'Doubt everything.'

Victor's was: 'Squeeze all blackheads.' He explained: 'A man had one behind his ear, hidden. It became a pimple, a cyst, a boil. He died on the operating table. Such blackheads created the Bay of Pigs. They blew open the head of an American president.'

'They?'

Victor's smile warped. 'Two blackheads, amigo. Meyer Lansky and Kim Philby.'

Chapter One

My name is Victor Sanchez. I was born Cuban. For sure I will die Cuban. But my mother, Maria Sanchez, tells me my father was a Yanqui. Well, after all, she should know.

I was her first and only child, conceived, she swears, the month after her first menstruation. She was not yet thirteen years of age. My Yanqui father, she swears, was perhaps sixteen, if that. It was the first time for two virgins.

'Which is why you grew up pure in heart, Victor.'

We must not believe everything my mother swears to, but I do remember being told that her designation in that place, at least until bearing a child stretched her, was House Virgin.

And I do know, from growing up in that place, what a premium men placed — still do — on violating a virgin. It wasn't the case with my father, my mother swears. His mates aboard his PT Boat had determined to, as the saying was in those days, 'bust his cherry'. Who better in all of Guantánamo to bust it than one whose own cherry was still intact?

Do you believe that? How could one be House Virgin and still intact? My mother refuses to play that game, except to observe that for sure there was a pearl at the bottom of it all.

'It may have been a burdel,' she recalls, 'but it was clean-scrubbed every morning, carbolic and pine oil, and we were inspected once a week by a real United States Navy medical officer. A Lieutenant Commander, at that. Victor, never forget: growing up on Gitmo gave you perfect command of English. Without that, where would you be today?'

Oh, from the mouths of mothers!

Where would I be? Dead, most likely. For sure dead-broke. Certainly not enriched by the highest levels of the mafia and the secret services of several lands. Surely not rich, famous and sitting here on my veranda. Nor, as it was last week, sitting on the reviewing stand while my beloved leader told the world what a great man I am.

Hijo de puta is what everyone is entitled to call me. I love my mother. Nothing connected with her can be an insult. But look at me: son of a whore, who took the dollar and the rouble, sitting in the bright Havana sunshine receiving honours the son of a saint would die to have.

And this despite the people I worked with, truly evil people, people who caused the deaths of many but were never punished themselves. No, never. Think of Charley Lucky, of J. Edgar Hoover, of Meyer Lansky, a brain so evil he guided a mafia of blood-crazed Sicilians and never even got his hands dirty.

Think of the plots hatched in that brain, crimes that made him and his partners feared, hated, hunted . . . and rich.

Still, it's a kick to be so highly praised. What would you expect from the pure-in-heart son of two virgins?

Of course, like anything a politician tells you, these public honours don't bear close attention. But close attention is what they now will get. And about time, eh?

Chapter Two

Of course I knew Victor. Lord, yes! In those faraway years both of us played the same games. He was and still is a handsome sonuvabitch, far more beautiful as a man than I as a woman but who says life is fair? For one thing, being tall is great for a woman nowadays. Then it was as welcome as cholera.

I grew from Baby Meg into a Vassar basketball centre five feet ten inches high, tagged with the name Midge, the way a tall man's called Tiny. Midge Boardman. I'm back to using my maiden name although Jim is my third husband. And last.

When they were considering hiring me at Defence as official

spokesperson and token female, they asked my age and what last name I wanted to use. I said my maiden name had some recognition value, the byline I used as one of the *New York Times'* correspondents, mostly in the Caribbean. It was the name under which I hob-nobbed with famous politicos and the infamous Meyer Lansky.

They already knew that a woman with grandchildren can hardly be less than in her 60s. Yes, nice of you to say that. I do keep a young look. If I slumped into frumpery what would happen to my credibility as a spokesperson? Up there vapouring on about surgical strikes and MIRV-headed ICBMs, I'd be perceived as a post-menopausal dodo who knew as much about Defence matters as a body louse.

Now, then. One fat para of potted bio and we're introduced. Margaret Ann Boardman. In Pieter Stuyvesant's day us Boordmaans settled upstate in the Hudson Valley, gentlemen farmers and smelterers of iron. On a European tour after Vassar I met my first husband, who worked for the Paris *Herald-Tribune*. When we divorced the *Trib* fired him and hired me. I also inherited his contract as a CIA spook. Later, I'm sure CIA clout got me hired by the *Times*. But only being able to speak Spanish got me the Havana assignment.

My favourite professor was a language buff, Dr Domandi, my Vassar faculty advisor. 'I'm high,' I confessed to him, 'on who, where, what, how and why.'

He gave me such a sad look. 'Any idiot can work out the first four. But as for why, forget it, Midge. There *is* no why.'

You would certainly say that about my Havana assignment. In the late 1950s Cuba was a nasty, vulgar little kasbah run by implausible US hoodlums who, if their right arms had been notched for each kill they either committed or paid for, would have resembled a zinc washboard.

The only why was greed. Its Grand Imperial Wizard was Meyer Lansky. The rest was mystery.

Which of us knew that the boy scouts in the hills would in time otherthrow this corrupt mobster and his brutish puppet regime? Who would guess this would upset the balance of power in the Caribbean, a mere ninety miles from our own national border at Key West?

Who, for that matter, including its own minions like me, could understand that the CIA had scuttled democracy and anointed itself a secret government all its own?

Why? Dr Domandi was right. Search for why and ye shall not find.

Reasons? What genius among us hungover hacks would ever foresee that a Cuba friendly to the Soviets would lead to the closest nuclear shave Uncle Sam has ever had and, second, to the successful murder of a very popular president?

Did I foresee it? Not I. Blame it on the rum, the men. Blame it on the elusive why. My years in the Caribbean, languorous palms, soft nights, went by in a blur of searching to find a reason. Nowadays, when Jim suggests a daiquiri I bow out. Lord, the rum memories are too poignant. And the reason's still elusive.

What? No, martinis. Very, very dry. Straight up.

'Why not your memoirs?' Jim asked me. Since he retired last year from his magazines, he's always trying to get me back into journalism. My Defence job wouldn't let me. Neither would the CIA, even though I left the payroll long ago. If you get gabby, they have a farewell gift. It's called termination with prejudice.

'Who needs some elderly broad's pillow talk?'

'Who?' Jim sounded offended. 'Our republic. Our frail democracy. Your granddaughters. What the hell, Midge, you were right there at the heart of it.'

He's right. That's a record for me, marrying somebody who gets it right. I *was* at the white-hot centre of the damned thing. I called Lansky Meyer to his face and Castro Fidel. 'But I still don't know why it happened.'

'Put it down on paper. The why'll show itself.'

I could picture Dr Domandi's dark, mischievous face explaining that there was no why. I did have a thing for him. I only wish he'd had one for me.

'It won't show itself because it doesn't exist,' I said. 'We're talking about huge events, hemispheric catastrophes, political massacres. Unless we know why these things happened they're meaningless.'

4

'Why?' Jim's voice got up there to an irritated bark. 'Why? Because people plotted and tinkered to make them happen.'

'But why . . . why were they so successful?'

'Is that important?'

'To find out would give aid and comfort to that frail democracy of yours. Just to find out why.'

'Because . . .' He stared balefully at me. We were sitting under the arbour of our back terrace in Alexandria, Virginia. The weather was balmy at dusk. The birds were settling in for the night. It was one of those magic moments when, all of a sudden, laden with years and experience that tell you you're wrong, you suddenly feel as if you might be able . . . might . . .

'I suppose . . .' My voice died away. 'Lord, what have I got to lose if . . .'

Jim, on his feet to stir up the hibachi charcoal, draped his arm around my shoulder. 'CIA Mata Hari,' he said, sketching with his finger in the air the imaginary headline he was writing, 'Strips Mystery from Cuban Cataclysm.'

'Grandma Bares All,' I added. We broke up, giggling.

Then I stopped giggling.

31 December 1958

Chapter Three

Just turned eighteen, I was the youngest of three young vaqueros hurrying down a narrow Havana sidestreet.

In daylight we might look innocent. At night, Havana's main thoroughfares were brightly lit by electricity. In those days there were even some of the old-fashioned arc-lamps that made you look like a corpse. But here the back passages and alleyways were often dark.

With only the passing flare of gas-jet or kerosene pressure lamp, we probably looked sinister, twisted close together for safety, six dark eyes roving sideways for signs of trouble.

The two muscle guys carried fat shoulder bags. I was taller, the leader, making notes in a small spiral-bound notebook. That's how you tell a leader: he doesn't carry anything heavier than a ballpoint pen.

As we passed even narrower alleyways we heard the night sounds of a city that rarely sleeps, the passionate sighs, belches, erotic moans, terrorised screams and gagging whimpers of Havana going about its business. Which is pleasure. Or was, in 1958.

All this would normally end around three or four in the morning, but not tonight. Tonight was the thirty-first day of December.

On New Year's Eve, Havana slept not at all. Everything would remain open, the lush casinos with their restaurants and flossy titshows, the bucket-of-blood gambling hells along these narrow, nasty streets, the brothels, the drinking places on the waterfront where ship captains still played the ancient game of shanghaiing seamen they had made falling-down drunk with cheap rum.

As with any island town, Havana had only a few exit

9

routes. I knew them all. Passed out on a trawler or freighter bound for the States with a plantation-load of cane, molasses or a great heaping catch of tuna, that was one exit. And you did pick up a puny pay packet afterwards.

The second was the tiny airport where every morning a DC-3 Dakota reached Mexico City in time for its courier passengers and their shoulder bags to be transferred to the Constellation day flight to Zurich. That paid better.

But the third exit was no way out and for sure no pay.

It was a few show highways Batista had caused to be built for a few miles of outlying shanty-town. They would then degenerate into narrow asphalt or spavined red-dirt lanes. There, if a peasant wanted, he could waylay and hijack a car to bring to the rebels.

To the East, up in the Sierra Maestra at the other end of the island, stolen autos or captured ammo or other loot were eagerly accepted by Fidel's men. Those who brought such gifts became friends and favoured colleagues of the rebel government that would – soon – topple the corrupt pervert Batista, pawn of Cuba's real owner, the Little Man, called El Pequeño.

Nobody realised how soon.

I like to remember myself as looking too clean cut, too out of place for the sleazy gambling club we now entered. The son of two virgins should at least *look* clean. But probably I looked just as degraded as the rest.

Is degraded the right word? Doesn't that mean all of these people were once higher before life degraded them? But none of them had ever been higher. Least of all an hijo de puta like me.

Let me say right at the start that if I had to choose, for sure I would always want to start life knowing who my mother was and what she did. What a calamity if later on, as happens to so many in a poor country, you learned much too late that your mother whored for a living.

The place we went into was run by one of the cliques that presented the January Sixth Three Kings Day parade. Behind the craps and blackjack tables – roulette was only for the big casinos – young women of the quarter would spend daytime hours repairing and brightening their skimpy Three Kings costumes.

But tonight no one was using valuable space to dilute the profitable main business of gambling. New Year's Eve all the locals, and even the few turistas who had wandered in by mistake, were being systematically milked for every dime, peso, franc, pound and yen in their pockets.

A short man with a small hump on the left side of his back nodded to me and my bodyguards. Through a room of smoke, sweat and cheap perfume, music from a tape player played a lazy and elegant version of 'Siboney' on two muted cornets.

'Noch', Bictor.' The hunchback liked to confuse his bs and vs, as most Cubans did. We know better but it gives you a feeling of belonging to call Havana Habana and Victor Bictor.

Manolo turned the dealing of his twin blackjack deck over to a young woman, one of his many daughters. Although they had many different mothers, they nearly all resembled the hunchback in being short and very plain. This did not stop the more mature ones from running a brothel across the narrow street.

Father, exploiter and pimp, Manolo led the three of us into a back room jammed with spangled, beaded costumes, hats, paper boots, cardboard tiaras glittering in the overhead electric bulb.

'I make it sixty gran' so far tonight, Bic.'

The hunchback's eyes widened. They locked into mine, which women have told me are green-brown, the colour of dark seas lying deep over coral. I smiled when delivering the insult: 'You are for sure the worst liar in all of Havana. Make it a hundred grand take. Es verdad, Manolo?'

Shamefaced — or faking it — Manolo produced wads of mixed currency notes and riffled them knowingly. 'Eighty-one, Bic. You with the X-ray eyes. Didn't nobody tell you X-rays can kill you?'

This was a man with decades of experience in both lying and in holding back take. But a boy raised in a whorehouse is already far older than anyone of any age. Even reporting eighty-one, Manolo, I was sure, held out ten grand for himself.

He would consider the cut due him for not trying to steal more.

I spread the thick stacks of bills out in fans. I have long fingers, like spider's legs, separating US hundred-dollar bills and other harder currency like British ten-pound notes. I stuffed them in the shoulder bag of Luis, my nearest body-guard. Then I entered the amount in my notebook.

'Hey, Big Bic, lemme give you a receipt to bring to the Little Man.'

The hunchback's joke caused all of them to guffaw.

In the noise, it was hard to hear the slight whirring hiss a throwing knife makes as it flies, blade first, toward its target. The handle is lead-weighted, giving it velocity. In the normal course of events, it would have buried itself to the hilt in my chest just to the left of my sternum, where my young heart thudded away, but my reflexes were just as young. I twisted sideways out of harm's way.

Luis snapped a single .22 shot – no louder than the bark of a chihuahua – into a dim shape hiding behind the Three Kings glitter. A young girl, another of Manolo's daughters, toppled forward, blood gushing from her throat's carotid artery. Not a pretty girl, but surely more attractive when dressed for the parade next week. Ay, que lagrimas. But Manolo has daughters to spare.

The chihuahua barked again. Luis put a bullet through Manolo's left shoulder, where the pack of hunchback gristle behind the joint stopped the slug and left it no exit. Manolo screamed in pain. Outside the room the muted cornets mimed his agony a third interval higher. They were playing a song made popular that year by Dizzy Gillespie called 'Tango Havana'.

'Good thought,' I said, trying to keep my breathing steady. 'The Little Man needs Manolo alive.'

'And taught a lesson,' Luis added piously, as if teaching was his profession.

Chapter Four

Everyone in Havana called him that. El Hombre Pequeño, El Pequeño. In some places this might be considered a put-down, since for sure he owned the town and everything in it. But in Cuba, where most of us are short, the nickname was only descriptive. And it was always spoken in an undertone, like a man naming his illness and confessing that it was (hush) cancer.

For that was what Meyer Lansky was to Cuba, feeding on our heart, eating us hollow from within. And I had by that night worked six months for him. I had first met him back in June.

'How could he not have hired you?' my mother demands. For her, Lansky was no more evil than any other man. 'Your looks. That's why he picked you,' she swears, 'with that tall, slim figure and that handsome face and your English.'

My mother is as partial to me as I am to her. But it was surely not my height that singled me out. I came recommended by an evil associate of El Pequeño who, without doing anything to earn it, shared a piece of the Guantánamo whorehouse with the Navy medico and Captain Jascek, aide to the commanding officer, Admiral Edward J. O'Donnell.

My mother knows too much about men to see how one of them can poison the earth with his wickedness. This is her mistake. It is like pissing in a swimming pool. How can it make any difference, being so diluted? How? Men like Lansky turn the seas to piss.

But she is right to place such importance on my speaking American English, the kind US sailors speak, with slang and curses and bad grammar. Like the English spoken by the Little Man.

'My English is perfect, Mr Lansky,' I said. I used the New York accent in which 'perfect' is 'payfic'. It was years later that I learned his accent had come originally from a town that was sometimes Poland when it wasn't the Ukraine.

'Nu,' the Little Man murmured, 'redden Yiddish?'

'Gibts nischt, Reb Lansky.'

He laughed very softly. That was his habit, speaking low, so that two things happened: you paid closer attention and, when he did have to shout it was a real shocker.

He had eyes as dark as mine and I swear they were nice eyes, even gentle. But for sure they could bore into you. Maybe he learned that from his Sicilian buddy, Charley Lucky. The Sicilians put a lot of faith in eye pressure. Still do.

'You and me, boychik, we'll get along.'

The incident at Manolo's happened while I was making my pre-midnight round to bring in the beginning flush of tourist cash. Visitors had started well before noon, mostly elderly Iowa couples off the cruise liners, used to being back on board and asleep by ten p.m.

In Havana of that faraway time the pace of life was easy. Yes, we were all slaves of El Pequeño. But even the whores took their time. The tangos and rhumbas were lazy, sensual. Like the pale soft rum, they stirred your body from within, a kind of private friction inside your veins and ears that teased you into going all night.

That's what the die-hard gamblers did. The Yanqui senators and governors and business tycoons – we used to call them blofistas – sent to Havana by the Little Man's mafia associates, all of them really didn't start at the blackjack and roulette tables till the Iowa tourists were snug in bed. Why take the chance of running into a voter from back home?

The town's sidestreets were filled with small clubs like Manolo's where you could also play poker, stuss, pinochle, rummy and craps. But most of the action was in big clubs like the Tropicana and the San Souci. That's why it took me and my crew a long time to finish our job, especially taking the time to make sure a doctor dug the slug out of Manolo's shoulder. Those .22s are vicious little bastards.

It took more time to dispose of the daughter. Even in a city most Yanquis would call lawless – for sure a stupid thing to say; because it was run by criminals why call it lawless? – there is still a right and a wrong way of doing things.

There is, for example, the right undertaker for a body hastily killed. The funeral must be the best in town and the cash paid in advance must buy a truly awe-inspiring ceremony. This girl's life may have been brief and cheap, her father may have abused and raped her regularly, but her parting had to be the best money could buy.

It took more time with my big casinos. Take the Tropicana: too much cash was at stake and too many crooks or IRS stoolies had their eyes open for a chance to dip their bill. Dipping was *my* job. We called it skimming.

Every casino was owned by the Little Man with silent partners among Havana politicos and mafia families in the States. He had started buying up Cuba in 1923 – first as a molasses broker – and laying down the simple rules of his regime. A percentage of nightly take was held as reserve against losses. The rest was salaries, supplies, a big chunk when you included pit staff, security gorillas, orchestra and entertainers, the restaurants and the bars.

The casino manager, his top two pit bosses and his head cashier would meet me in the strongroom where cash and chips were kept. Normally, older Cubans would take a kidding, fatherly interest in a teenager like me. But here we lived with too much fear.

They would show me their receipt tallies. In our heads, all of us would assign the take and agree on a skim figure. This was ticklish. I had to outguess their guess and announce a sum they would let me remove.

Here I couldn't override them, the way I had Manolo. These were men of respect, hand picked and trained by the Little Man. Moreover they had neatly totalled adding machine tapes to back up their lies. Still, we all knew they were lies.

A stink of fear-sweat perfumed those strongrooms, not from the customers who had lost their shirts but from hard guys on the payroll who knew that one false tally, no matter if it was a simple error, if discovered could cost them their lives.

It could for sure cost me mine. I had seen the way El Pequeño sentenced a man to death. He simply glanced sideways at one of his killers, nodded once, deeply, and went on talking of other things, as if a man's death was nothing. I was good at looking cool and unafraid. With a monster like Lansky one couldn't radiate panic. He would nose it as fast as a shark sensed blood.

That's a thought. Maybe the smell in the strongroom wasn't sweat. It had the sweeter charnel aroma of the slaughter house, where the scent of blood takes control of your nostrils. The air in those strongrooms . . .

The air spoke. Like the blood that spattered the Three Kings costumes, it told in a strangled grunt of secret watchers watching the watched, of triple betrayals, switchbacks, cons. Of a young daughter who had made a foolish mistake. Of someone her age who nearly had his heart pierced, not by love but greed.

It told of a discipline so brutal that a man didn't dare ask himself stupid, human questions like, 'Christ, what am I doing here?' A discipline without mercy, deadly as a hurricane and just as unpredictable.

Once collected, the skim had to be brought to the Little Man immediately. This is the essence of money stolen from oneself, reeking of larceny, tempting to be re-stolen, whisked quickly out of the eyesight of greedy underlings, government snoops and partners with big ideas.

There was for sure only one way to keep such pigs even remotely honest. It was Lansky's way, no mercy, no afterthoughts, no hesitation. Just death. And for the most filthy reason, money.

I know a woman reporter for the *New York Times* who had been to Vassar College. She would ask me to escort her around town on my night off, explaining how Havana worked. We got very friendly.

She told me why mierda, which is what we call shit, is the word we also use for trouble, for lies, for betrayal, for pretension, for money and for drugs, another form of money.

Without·shit we're lost. We can hardly speak. Don't give me that shit. Don't shit me. Pay me my shit. Sell me some

16

shit, you shit. She said it was all mixed up with when we were babies and had to depend on our mother to handle our shit.

Most of the shit I skimmed went inside air courier bags winging to Zurich, where the shipment of dollars and other currencies normally totalled twenty million dollars. A week. All together now: s-o-m-e shit!

If you think such a life was too choked with sudden death to be enjoyable, you would be wrong. If you think so because it often hung on twisting sideways before a knife reached your heart, remember, amigo: in those days Havana was heaven.

Especially if you were eighteen and the women called you guapo.

I had been seriously spoiled by women. Growing up where I did, how could I not know the effect on them of being able to control a little penis and undescended balls, to nuzzle and pet and suck, knowing the toys were clean and too small to generate semen yet ... There are all kinds of heaven, eh? Even heaven inside the hell Lansky ruled.

But this night, New Year's Eve, turned out to be quite different. When it was over, the whole world had changed. Once more my heart was targeted, this time by love. But I don't mean just my world changed. For sure I mean everyone's.

Chapter Five

Gangsters – and most men – separate women into madonnas and whores.

When I first met Meyer Lansky I was still at Vassar, but slumming in Manhattan. He had married a madonna called Anna Citron. Part of the price was a sexual itch soothed only by trying to pick up young shixehs like me, a full head taller than he was.

Dr Domandi, my faculty advisor, had suggested that what

my journalism writing needed was a dose of street-smarts. In those days it went by the generic term of 'personal experience'. He gave me a list of places when next I visited Manhattan.

One of them was a garment centre restaurant called Lou G. Siegel's filled with short, dark men speaking with add-ons in Yiddish or the Sicilian dialect. In those days the link between the two ethnic groups was pronounced. Sicilian mobsters like Salvatore (Charley Lucky) Lucania, renamed Luciano, born in Lercara Friddi, Sicily, was close friend and lifelong partner with Meyer Suchowljansky, renamed Lansky, born in Grodno, then in the Ukraine.

Lord knows, as I later learned, that other Sicilian mobsters and most Irish ones hated those they referred to as Christ-killers. But the Luciano-Lansky tie was strong throughout both their lives. When Lucky had to murder Meyer's closest friend, Bugsy Siegel, who was Jewish, he went to Meyer for prior approval and forgiveness. It was, after all, business. And got his OK to shoot.

'Cholent?' Lansky said as he stopped at my table the first time. 'A nice goyische maidel like you orders cholent?'

I looked up to see this dapper little man, elegant in clothing one era out of style. He had removed his grey homburg. Unshaded, his disturbing basilisk eyes bored into mine, demanding a fuck. I glanced down at the largely vegetarian casserole on my plate.

'Is this cholent?' I asked. 'If so, it's absolute tasteless.'

'May I join you?' he asked, sitting down first.

I pushed my cholent over to him. 'Take it all.'

For a young woman planning a career in journalism, knowing Meyer was a social advantage. In those days gangsters were still acceptable. Their exotic celebrity made them welcome in society and show biz circles. Lord, it still does.

And remember, I was dark-haired. If you are too, you've long ago noted that our American society, its movies and TV, assigns fun to blonde women. Men's fun, that is.

Serious is for brunettes, especially seriously bad women for whom the fun, if any, is angst-loaded and marred by betrayal of every kind. In movies they have the illegitimate children and the rotten boyfriends. Or they are the wisecracking sidekick whom the man never dreams of marrying.

However, brunettes have the advantage of contrast to frame their faces. In those years we all wore our hair long, mine with bangs. It needed no help to be full, richly black, springy, vital, with deep coal-blue lights. Ah, youth.

I suppose I had a name for mingling with the dark-haired – and a reputation among my acquaintances who used words like kike and wop – but being seen on the arm of a mobster was a daring posture honoured from Prohibition days down to the present. Fanny Brice and Nicky Arnstein; Arnold Rothstein, who fixed the 1919 world series, and a series of chorus girls; Jean Harlow and Abner Longie Zwillman.

Why not Midge Boardman and half a dozen hoodlum Hebrew heavyweights of the Lansky class? But never a Sicilian. They didn't romance women, they killed them. One of Meyer's earliest recorded arrests was for helping Charley Lucky beat up one of Charley's mistresses.

No, never. Meyer didn't appeal to me in a sexual way. And I am quite sure, after he bombed out with me, that it suited him to have a nightclub date without having to prove himself later. Some men, like Meyer's dearest friend Ben Siegel, must conquer or they suffer terrible insecurity. Not Meyer.

He was mean, filled with very controlled rage, uncanny in corrupting others. To say that he was callous misstates the case: for him there was no one else. Only his own interests mattered. And if they demanded inhuman evil from him, he suffered no pang of conscience doing it. For me he resembled one of those tiny snakes, called kraits, that carry the most dangerous venom on Earth.

I suppose there is something cheap and unredeeming about having spent that much time with a sociopath like Meyer. But I spent far more time with entirely different kinds of men. No, not someone worthwhile and academic like my dear Dr Domandi.

Usually a worthless fellow journalist who knew how to trade wisecracks, martinis and cynicisms. Since we often ended up in bed I nearly married them. I can't say these relationships were any more enlightening than mine with

Meyer. In fact, it's only this December-and-December marriage to Jim that's meant much. His urging me to recall this whole era has given my life a bit of an upward slant these days.

But Meyer . . . Meyer could be quite helpful, especially after I began covering the Caribbean for the *Times*. I suppose, even after he married his second wife, the tall manicurist he called Teddy, née Thelma, he considered me the one that got away. But it wasn't until I first reported to my CIA boss that I realised just how key Meyer had become.

It was a case of déjà vu. James Jesus Angleton, head of covert operations, was a short, birdlike, skeletal Anglo-Saxon Christian who also wore grey homburgs and affected a style of dress fully half a century out of date. This, as I found out later, was not the only attribute he shared with Meyer.

Was there, I wondered, something about being in a villainous line of work — murder, treachery, cheating — that made its leading villains try to throw off suspicion by dressing like part-time clerics?

'You're an upstate Boardman?' Angleton pried.

'I beg your pardon? Most of us are from Dutchess County.'

'Your mother was Katie Boardman?' he persisted.

'Still is.'

His hawk-like glance suddenly softened. 'Then we're second cousins, you and I.' His frame, joint by joint, relaxed cat-like into itself as if he had just eluded pursuers and squeezed inside an impregnable stockade.

'Are we?'

'Well, of course, I grant you everyone's some kind of cousin.' He was chirruping now in gossipy fashion, all smiles. 'I mean the Brit art specialist, Tony Blunt, who I'm now getting word may be a commie mole, is the Queen's second cousin. It's that kind of world, what?'

I got enough of the British pattern of ups and downs in his speech to understand that Angleton had contracted Anglophilia early in life. I wondered if he'd also contracted their weak gene, which let them tolerate traitors in their midst if only the traitor were a gentleman and 'one of us'.

'Is that why you asked for me, Cousin James?'

He actually grinned. 'And also to explain why it is you seem on such close terms with felons like Lansky and Luciano and Frank Costello.'

'You're saying it's a crime?'

This time that tight-skinned falcon's face actually burst open in a hoarse, cawing guffaw. 'If it were criminal,' he said, lapsing into the subjunctive as any good spy should, 'then our whole agency should be criminal.'

He sat very still for a long moment. 'I take it you've no objection to being seconded to me? While still on your cover work? Simply an odd job now and then. For instance, have your *Times* bureau chief send a note to Hoover at the FBI and ask him to give you an interview?'

'On what?'

'Women agents in the FBI? I simply want you to charm that charmless, thoroughly dishonest charlatan. It's not easy with a closet queen. He'll first check you out. He won't find your connection to us but just that you have prime security clearance. That'll help.'

'And then?'

'Cousin Midge, Hoover hates us because our funding is largely unreportable. He must occasionally appear before a congressional committee and report how many flashers he's sent to Alcatraz while letting the mafia run wild.'

'I understood he's amassed so much blackmail on so many congressmen and senators that no one dares withhold FBI funding.'

'That is one of our disadvantages we hope you can help correct.'

They're all dead now, Meyer, Angleton, Hoover. There is no way I can assess whether I or any other woman actually got close to Hoover. But he did use me as a sort of occasional 'beard' he would be seen with at dinner, he and Clyde Tolson, his, um, constant companion.

The dinners were all identical, a filet mignon, medium rare, a baked potato, a small Caesar salad. Lots of bourbon hi-balls, a quick spattering of the latest dirty jokes making the Washington rounds – he was a prude only when it suited him – and then a few gauzy hints of what matters interested him at the moment.

When, in the fullness of time and with the proper agent-craft, I would repeat these conversations to Angleton he would invariably say the same thing:

'My dear Midge, I do apologise.'

But there was no need. It was only by being trusted by Hoover that one could understand the key, pivotal role he played in unfolding Meyer's master strategy. And what a strategy it was.

Chapter Six

That New Year's Eve in Havana the three of us got back with our shoulder bags of skim to the Hotel Nacional about twenty minutes to midnight. There we took an elevator which made no stops on its way to the penthouse. The operator patted the bulging shoulder bags. He licked his lips and gave a kidding sexual moan but for sure he said nothing.

I have always liked the old Nacional, with its square twin towers, like the carillons of a double church, topped in red baked tiles and surrounded by penthouse terraces under our brilliant Cuban sky.

One penthouse in those days was a patio-garden without a real roof, shaded during the day by broad bands of beige-coloured canvas that could be rolled open or shut as sunshine shifted. It was off-limits except to people who had business with El Pequeño.

A small bar was backed up a smaller bandstand where a trio played, normally a guitar, accordion and soprano saxophone so antique that it didn't resemble a brass clarinet but had instead a narrow upcurved bassoon-like horn at the bottom.

The rest of that penthouse floor was a single apartment in which the Little Man lived when he wasn't in New York or Miami Beach. Windows gave him a good view during the daylight hours. Normally, at night, unless the weather was especially humid, he and his guests would relax under the stars, holding quiet conversations against a background of rhumbas and tangos in which the reedy tone of the soprano sax played a trumpet-like lead, but without the trumpet's ability to crack ear-drums.

When we got there I pointed my two bodyguards towards the bar for a hard-earned drink. But a waiter shook his head.

'Batista's inside with guests. El Máximo Lider,' he murmured sarcastically. 'Muy privado.'

'Leave it to him to choose the best place in town to celebrate the new year,' I said. I took the shoulder bags and ushered Luis and Cruz back into the elevator. 'Lo siento mucho, camaradas.'

Hanging a heavy bag on each shoulder, I went back to where the waiter had intercepted us. 'Que paso?'

A guilty look crossed the waiter's face. 'What else? He has some horny blofistas from United Fruit with him so, of course, the Yanquis demand the Havana Two-Shot.'

'They can't love shit as much as he does?'

'One develops a taste for it.'

Suddenly, from beyond the potted palms that set off the patio area, we heard the trio slump into a slow, Afro-Cubano beat, the guitarist drumming on his wooden instrument, the accordion producing slow, savage grunts, the sax moaning as if nearing orgasm.

Batista and his party, big, beefy Yanquis in tight-fitting tuxedos, their shopworn women in fantastic gowns decorated with feathers and spangles, sat with their backs to us.

A platinum blonde, hands tied behind her naked body, was being stretched over the backs of two naked black women, crouching as if to form a sacrificial offering, meat on an altar of meat.

'He never tires of it,' I muttered.

'Neither do his guests, especially the women.'

The stud arrived then, blacker than the rest, his oiled flesh contrasting wildly with the blue-white body of the platinum blonde. We Cubans come in all colours. He stroked his penis as if whacking off. Since it had arrived half erect it quickly stiffened and fattened to the size of the one-pound salamis El Pequeño imported from Lou G. Siegel's in New York.

Accompanied by fluttering lip-sounds of wonder from the women and hoots from the Yanqui businessmen, the stud shoved the blonde's legs apart at a cruel angle. Her peroxided muff seemed to glow phosphorescently. She screamed as he penetrated her with slow, steady slams. And screamed again as he began his excruciatingly deep thrust and draw. Underneath the blonde, her human altar swayed. The music reassembled all the players to the new tempo.

The stud had succeeded in drawing blood. It trickled down the blonde's pale left leg as she mimed ecstasy, horror, adoration and extreme pain. He sprawled over her, adding his weight to the torture. From behind the bar another black slave girl led an alert Alsatian dog into view. She produced a large sirloin steak which she gave to the eager Alsatian.

As well-trained as the rest of the tableau, he grasped the steak in his long pointed jaws and rammed it up against the stud's anus, slowly grinding the bloody meat up and down.

I turned away, angry as only an hijo de puta could be. 'For sure all blofistas are perverts.'

The waiter gave a shrug, meant to be philosophical. 'You can't imagine the kick they get when Mojo shits and comes at the same time.'

'Some kick.'

'I have seen fat capitalist pigs howl with envy, strip their women naked and try the same trick.'

'With whose prick?' I snapped. I picked up the shoulder bags and walked off towards the apartment entrance.

Chapter Seven

I admit it. Even that kind of dirty sex can get a man excited. I could feel that my face had flushed both with anger and erotic excitement. I rapped on the door of the Little Man's apartment. Maybe a little too hard.

24

The peephole slid open and a small eye regarded me for a long time. Then the door was opened by a short, jockey-sized man wearing a suit and tie, red suspenders and a snap-brim fedora. 'C'min,' he said past a much-chewed cigar butt. 'He's bin waitin' f'yeh.'

The Little Man's two-bedroom suite had its own kitchen and a living room that overlooked the north and the harbour of Havana. It is a harbour guarded to the east by three castle-forts at the very opening channel that leads from the ocean into the ensenada, or cove, where ships can moor.

Morro Castle crouched, guarding the entry channel, with the near side protected by the Castle de la Punta. Each, with San Carlos Castle further east, looked over its own dark history. Under Spain this maniacally protected harbour sent the loot of the Caribbean back home to Seville. And yet, despite such caution, it was here Spain lost everything when the battleship *Maine* was sunk.

On very clear days, so they told me, from the great height of the Nacional penthouse, with a powerful pair of racing binoculars you could just make out Key West, ninety miles away.

'Drop them there, boychik,' the Little Man said in his quiet voice.

With a quick brushing gesture he shooed the jockey type out of the room and sat back in an armchair, a *New York Times* on his lap while a lovely brunette manicurist attended to his fingertips. She was new to me.

At first I could see only the back of her long, black hair, loosely moving in great looping curls as she polished the Little Man's nails with a chamois-faced buffer. I parked the bags of cash on a settee and, at the same time, got a clear, hungry look at the girl's face. As much as I hated the scene outside, it had made me horny.

In Havana there were only young women you married or whores. Most men I knew had big problems because of this. They would find a 'good' woman and do their best to seduce her, thus changing her to my mother's status. But I had no such hang-ups. A woman could be a mother and a whore and it was all the same to me.

She turned towards me with contempt, as if to say 'Look your fill; it's all you'll ever get.' Her huge, wide-set eyes, darker than mine, flashed the kind of smoulder most men cannot fathom. Is it a get-away-from-me-filthy-one look? We find this on statues of the Virgin, which makes sense.

Is it a I-hate-you-but-the-other-side-of-the-coin-is-adoration look? We find this often on the faces of 'good' women because even they – especially they – understand that if they remain good forever there is no more human race.

For me, who has spent most of my life among women, their hooded glances are an open book. Never mind. This woman was different. I felt something sharp attack my heart, deadlier than a throwing knife. 'You want the total now, Mr Lansky, or – ?'

'The girlie is almost finished.' His words were hard to hear. 'How come you didn't join that bunch of schmutzig mishugenahs out there on the patio?'

'Not my taste. And the smell.'

He looked up at me, trying on an air of nobility, as if he wasn't a monster as bad as Batista. As if Lansky didn't license these orgies, as if they were a pus that oozed by itself without his permission. He was good at distancing himself.

I guess I was, too. If the mierda I had been handling all night didn't turn me sick, why was I making such a fuss about Mojo's shit? Better just to imitate the businesslike air of Mr Lansky, brisk, poking fun a little.

He produced a soundless cackle. 'For whose taste is it, I ask you?'

'For pigs!' the girl burst out.

Lansky withdrew his fingers from her grasp as if she had burned him. 'Schrei nit, girlie. This little half-hour I spend with you. You think I can't clean my own fingernails? It's supposed to calm my ulcers. You understand calm?'

'I'm sorry, Mr Lansky. I just get angry that our girls have to – '

'Enough.' He made a brushing motion that got her to her feet. Her long legs emphasised her high waist and firm breasts as she collected her manicure kit and left the room.

'Close your mouth,' the Little Man told me. 'I never saw a guy so smitten.'

'Smitten?' It was not a word any of the sailors used at the Guantánamo brothel.

'In the Bible, they smite each other. That cute little brunette has smote you something awful, Handsome.' His face went dead. 'What's the total?'

'Just under a three hundred grand.'

'Chickenshit. But I didn't want you out there after midnight hustling cash through a city of screaming schmendricks. Besides . . .' His quiet voice died away.

'Besides?' I repeated.

'Besides I'm expecting some news.' His voice chilled to the level of a mourner at a funeral.

'That reminds me. We had to ice one of Manolo's girls. After I leaned on him she tried to shiv me.'

Lansky smiled pleasantly. 'Manolo's OK?'

'Shoulder wound. He should be back dealing again in a month.'

Lansky nodded. 'Gives him enough time to see the error of his ways. And if not he doesn't leave the hospital till his wound kills him.' He held out his tiny, but neatly clipped and buffed fingers. 'Give me the tan bag first.'

It took him a while to count and recount the money in both bags. By then the New Year's Eve noise outside the windows facing north towards Key West had started to grow much louder.

The Little Man checked his watch. 'Ten minutes till midnight. Go find the girlie and buy her a drink.' He made the same brushing motion of dismissal.

She was in the kitchen of the apartment. She had cleaned and stored away her kit of scissors and creams. Now she was standing at the window, watching the city.

'He asked me to buy you a drink. My name's Victor.'

'I know your name. Big Bic.'

'And yours?'

She made me feel peculiar looking down at her. I never had the slightest hesitation speaking to women and telling them anything at all. But there was something hurt and hurting in

27

her smouldering glance. I still hadn't decoded that daunting look.

'Rita Melendez.' The hurt look deepened as if she had given away the key to her very soul.

'Rita. Does El Pequeño have a drink around here?'

'Try your shit-eating pals on the patio.'

'Pals they are not. Would anybody in his right mind choose to spend midnight with El Máximo Lider?'

She looked contrite. For the rest of my life I remembered that one time, so early on, when for a brief moment she had not seemed challenging, or betrayed. Just vulnerable. It was a look to treasure.

'Lo siento mucho. The two of us shouldn't quarrel. We work in the shadow of the same Satan.' She shrugged. 'Hell on the penthouse floor.' Her beautiful face grew even more sombre.

How long could she continue to smoulder? If she were a true Cubana, smiles had to come soon. We don't live for pouting. She opened the refrigerator and found a half-full bottle of dark, sweet rum. She poured an ounce into each of two water glasses and handed one to me.

Outside the horns were beginning to hoot. People were whirling noisy rattles overhead. 'Salud, guapo,' she said, deadpan. 'Y feliz año nuevo.'

I smiled so hard I forced an answering smile on her small, serious face. The sexual excitement surged back through me again. 'And may it be a lucky year for us both.'

'Viva,' she murmured softly, glancing at the closed door of the living room where the Little Man sat playing with money. 'Viva la revolucion.'

'Rita! You're crazy.' But I clinked my glass with hers and we drank.

'Not crazy. If you hate him, and his dog, Batista, you love freedom.'

I glanced at my watch. 'A minute to go.' I poured another small shot for both of us. We lifted our drinks and stood there, watching each other over the rims of our water glasses. The strong, sweet aroma of the rum filled my nostrils. It was the smell of our island, our Cuba, our lives.

A great shout went up outside the windows. Auto horns blended in a long, harsh honking. We touched glasses and drank again. The powerful spirit filled our mouths with chill heat.

I put down my glass and embraced her. As I lifted her off the ground, her breasts surged against me. I found her mouth. It tasted exactly like mine but hotter. We kissed for a long time, my tongue exploring the tiny wells of warm sweetness exploding in her mouth.

It took a while before we realised, in all the noise and the vivid tumbling of our own hearts, that we were not alone. The Little Man stood beside the open door to his living room. He held a telephone in one hand, its long cord disappearing into the room behind him.

'You're sure of it, Vito?' He nodded. 'Good boy. Stay on the line.' Lansky's pale, almost washed-out eyes regarded us. 'Happy New Year,' he said in a quiet, dry tone. 'Fidel and Che came down out of the Sierra Maestra tonight with at least five thousand troops. I expect them to be in Havana by next week.'

'Viva!' Rita burst out.

The Little Man frowned slightly. 'You Cubans, you're all meshugah. You think, girlie, they'll need manicures, these wild men?'

'You think I want to spend my life giving manicures?'

He suddenly smiled. 'She's loaded with chutzpah, Handsome.' He gestured to me. 'Help Sammy pack up the stuff. If I'm not out of here before Castro, I might just as well write my own obituary.'

'Obituary?'

'What is this, an English class? Get going!'

Chapter Eight

The start of it! And your correspondent, the Why Girl, almost missed it.

I'd been in Yucatan at the official unveiling of a Toltec dig.

About as exciting as watching oral plaque collect. As far as the *Times* was concerned, I could return to Mexico City, file the story and come back to life for tomorrow's New Year's Eve fiesta.

At Vassar, my pet prof, Dr Domandi, used to kid me about the V on my varsity basketball sweater. 'A Y Girl like you should've gone to Yale.'

The hack Tass had sent to Yucatan was a nice little fellow named Gleb Khsovko. He undoubtedly kept an NKVD beanie in his back pocket. No other reason for him using the only telephone booth not in the hotel as I approached at dusk.

'Well done, you!' he was saying into the phone with almost no trace of Russian accent. Veddy crisp, almost British.

'No, they couldn't get me on tonight's flight. You're on your own till tomorrow, old man. You and your pet skeleton.' He glanced idly about him and was shocked to see me within hearing distance. He produced a sweet smile. 'Yes, spelled T-o-l-t-e-c. Got it? Nyet. C not k. Da. Proshtchai.' He hung up and made a courtly gesture towards the phone. 'All yours, lovely capitalist colleague.'

'You were speaking to a Brit, you tricky man.'

Back at our hotel I left him at the bar and asked the concierge to book me on Mr Khsovko's flight. Which is how I found myself on New Year's Eve in Havana.

Lord, what a night! The Cubans are as fun-loving as the Brazilians, which means that even a funeral doesn't cool them down. But the news that Fidel had at last made his move and that Batista was in cowardly retreat added a sombre note of total uncertainty to the festivities.

Nobody could be sure Lansky would cut and run. He was known as a very devil of a bargainer. Maybe he could negotiate with Castro. None of us knew the liberator. All of us knew Lansky. You could get odds he'd sweet-talk Fidel into a deal to keep running the casinos.

I saw Gleb again that night but from a distance. I suppose that, like me, working two jobs simultaneously and as busy as a hooker with two beds, he had hired a taxi and was busily picking up useful titbits.

Out at the airport, for instance, I finally caught a glimpse of Gleb in the far distance, watching the Batista people embarking on a DC-4, its Aerovias Q insignia hastily painted out. I wondered if it would hop to Mexico City to let the whole pride of thieves transfer to the next Zurich flight. Neither Lansky, nor anyone connected with him, boarded the plane.

On the terrace of the Nacional, moodily sipping a martini, sat Angleton, lately made head of CIA's Covert Operations. With his hawk-like face and short, narrow body, he could well have been the pet skeleton Gleb had mentioned.

The man with him, a correspondent for a London newspaper, finished his martini and left. I instantly assumed he was the Brit Gleb had telephoned. Downstairs in the lobby Gleb sat reading a newspaper. They left separately, by different doors, but got in the same beige Jaguar and disappeared into the hugely pregnant night.

Who meets and who doesn't is a basic staple of intelligence work. It can disclose precisely what the opposition is trying to keep secret. But, of course, there are no secrets. You see, I knew the London man. He already had a mystery-man reputation and would one day become even more so.

I'd met him first in Washington, DC, when I'd just finished a cram course at Langley for new CIA contract people. When you have a legitimate job, as I did with a newspaper, you do not 'join' the CIA. There is a layer of separation. You sign a contract to snoop, rarely doing illegal stuff.

We contractees could often be very high up in the world. We could run AT&T in a Latin country like Chile, for instance, or be a busy banker in Britain or an engineer in the oil fields of Araby. But we weren't cleared for violence.

That was one of the few ways you could distinguish a co-opted civilian from a 'made' member of the CIA. You weren't a member of the killer elite. However, Cousin Angleton had already tucked me under his wing and encouraged me to cultivate my cover journalism.

When not in the Caribbean, I continued to be seen in all the best DC bars hob-nobbing with politicos, military honchos and other males interested in fucking tall females. I continued to ingest more than my normal requirement of steak and baked potato with Hoover. It was he, in fact, with his constant companion, Clyde Tolson, who first fingered the man from London for me.

This eatery not only served murderously generous bourbon hi-balls but dry martini cocktails in an unusually large triangular glass on a long, sturdy stem. I know from personal experience that if you ordered one straight up without ice, you got nearly five ounces of heaven.

It was at lunch with Hoover that he pointed out to me the Brit and Angleton in a robust four-martini lunch, examining the entrails of the world. Angleton had that hooded look of a falcon masked and gyved on the wrist of his master, a kind of blind menace more scary than if you had the direct glare of his yellowish eyes.

Angleton made no secret of being an Anglophile of the most depraved kind, the kind who wears well into July that imperviously thick Scots tweed that resembles being encased in Siberian sod. He's the one who sports a grey homburg slightly too big for his face, dark Cordovan boots made by Lobb to his own last, and diagonal-slant regimental ties.

It goes without saying there is a bachelor's button in his lapel and a four-pointed kerchief peeping above his outer breast pocket. It was not part of the Anglophilia that both he and the London journalist had such amazing heads for liquor. Nor was Angleton's ferocious appetite part of his love of things English.

'Hey, Clyde, look at that pansy chow down.'

How he ate! He often shamelessly scoffed up what was left on his companion's plate. Nevertheless, he always hovered at near-skeletal leanness.

Yes, I *have* avoided describing the Other, the man from London. I find it hard to draw his picture. He was pleasant looking, muy simpatico. You would say yes to dinner. I certainly did. He would listen to your problems with such interest that you often made up problems just to see how much he would believe.

'Hey, Clyde, next they'll be holding hands.'

The Brit would believe, in a word, anything you told him. He seemed as accepting as a vacuum cleaner but I assumed that, at some later point, he would sieve his dust to recover any nuggets therein.

The ideal confidante. Perhaps that was the secret of his friendship with Angleton. I never got the feeling it was a homosexual affair. But a spymaster like Angleton, whatever you may think, still needs a shoulder to sob on.

This was part of Angleton that at the time seemed not to bother his superiors. Without being gay he was . . . womanish. When he was with the Brit, he smiled a lot. At a lunch with others he deferred to the London man.

I had recently divorced my first husband and was acutely aware of how in marriage one partner can servilely defer to the other. In that era it fell to the woman to play the slave and put a pedestal under her man.

'Hey, Clyde, they really grow 'em in Dear Old Blighty.' This deference obviously hadn't escaped Hoover's notice. But it wouldn't, of course.

Was Angleton awed by the man's credentials? He'd been sent to the United States by the British equivalent of Angleton's bailiwick, the SIS or Secret Intelligence Service, often called MI6. Quite a gift package. He also dined with the FBI, this agreeable fellow.

Anyone as butch as the FBI director would jump to the wrong assumption. But that wasn't actually what was going on. It wasn't sexual, it was cultural. For Angleton to watch the Englishman's ready smile, to listen to his polished accent – he was a Cambridge man – was a treat. His American colleagues couldn't match the intellectual level of the plummy vowels. Nor could anyone else in the intelligence community with whom Angleton could feel easy.

So, even if he wasn't having a homosexual affair with the Brit, Angleton was having the time of his life. Then, at its very height it suddenly blew apart before his eyes, like a speared balloon.

But I'm getting ahead of my story.

Chapter Nine

I can never forget that first night, New Year's Eve with Rita. I never will. I moved as in a dream. We all did, the whole city, the island itself, we moved liked sleepwalkers.

For all its easy pace, Havana can quickly grow excited, especially on a New Year's Eve when you know, suddenly, that soon Fidel will make you free. So many things happening at once. So many rumours. So many changes in so few hours. But then a phantasm seemed to settle down over us. We weren't asleep but, for sure, in shock.

Cuba, Whorehouse of the Caribbean. We had been the cow of swollen udders on which the criminals of the Western Hemisphere sucked and grew fat. We Cubans existed only to pleasure the corruptors who ran the United States, to satisfy their filthy tastes and make them always richer.

Nice talk, from a young punk growing rich on the leavings of Meyer Lansky.

But, being in love with Rita Melendez did it. Not over a long period of time. Instantly! That night! Later, my mother told me I fell in love so quickly because Rita was the first honest woman I'd ever met. But it wasn't that. Like all of Havana, we were knocked for a loop.

Kneeling over her in her bedroom and licking her all over as if I were her dog. And she licking me, thirsty, unslakeable.

'I memorise your taste,' she told me.

By morning both of us tasted so much of each other that we no longer made a distinction.

I could tell she was new to it. But she learned in a night what had taken me years to know. I began to realise that all the secrets of the bed taught me by the girls in Guantánamo, and a lot of married women thereafter, were as basic as breathing, and so Rita found then.

In your teens you have nothing but juice and nothing better

34

to do than squander it on each other. We had such great luck that night, the privacy to enjoy our luck.

Rita's parents had gone west to her grandmother's tobacco fields in the Vuelta Abajo, so the apartment was for us alone. The Little Man and his jockey-sized body servant, Sammy, could have tracked us down to send me off on another skim. But they didn't.

No responsibilities, except to our bodies. No hang-ups about the two kinds of woman that drove other guys crazy. I knew guys – sensible, even bright – whose first worry would be: 'Hey, how can she enjoy this so much? Hey, she's been here before, huh? Hey, what kind of woman enjoys it like a man does?'

If you wonder why men are the crazy ones in this world, it's this stuff that drives us insane, if we let it. To keep sane, you don't ask a lot of nonsense, you just listen to your body do the talking. For sure. But that won't stop the woman from asking dumb questions.

'Why wait for Fidel and Che to arrive in Havana?' Rita asked.

We sat naked in her parents' kitchen sipping coffee at seven a.m. Neither of us had slept. Only I needed the caffeine; Rita was high on Fidel's coming victory. 'Why not go to meet the conquering heroes and volunteer for their cause?'

'Me?'

'Why not you? You know everything about Havana that Fidel needs to know. He will need men like you to safeguard his security. If I were a man, I – '

Her eyes glazed for a moment, those great, shining eyes, so dark but never opaque. How could black be so transparent? I could see inside them, down to the bottom of her soul, through fluid as clear as pure well water.

'I'm going with you,' she announced. Her full breasts seemed to rise and grow hard, the nipples in their wide magenta aureoles jutting like penises.

'Me?' I went around the table and knelt to suck at her breasts. 'Me?'

'They expect him to reach Matanzas in a few days.' She watched me at her teats. Then her powerful fingers dug into

35

my hair, clawed back my head and made me give up the nipple.

'Victor, I could easily sign up there and so could you. That we worked for El Pequeño will not be held against us. It will be an advantage, like a war wound.'

She was silent for a while. 'Did I ever tell you how much I hate that man? His fingers are too short. Like a doll's. A doll that kills.' To illustrate how powerful her own were, she squeezed a handful of my curly hair until it brought tears to my eyes.

We stared at each other across her hard, thrusting nipples. 'First we get married,' I heard my own voice say, out loud. 'Then we go to Fidel.'

Long after they left my mouth my words echoed in my ears like thunder. How insane can a man get? Of course, it was one good way of delaying the whole idea of signing up with Castro. Perhaps she hadn't heard me?

She let go of my hair by tossing my head back against her breasts. 'How much have you saved from the job with El Pequeño?' she asked.

'Not much.'

'How much is not much.'

But I was nuzzling at her again. 'Not enough . . . to support . . . a wife.'

'I support myself,' she snapped. 'I can't imagine that you didn't skim the skim, just a little.'

'A few dollars a night.'

'A few? Ten? A hundred?'

Those water-clear dark eyes could be piercing. Having her stare that way at you made you feel as if you were at the bottom of a well. Slowly her long slender legs jack-knifed apart and encircled my head. She buried me in her crotch as if to squeeze the truth from my lips.

'More,' I managed to say. 'A few hundred.' The silky inside skin of her thighs clamped against my ears.

'No lies.'

'On each skim.' I stared at her thick pubic muff, shiny with bluish highlights. In the shadows behind it, the lips of her vagina seemed to tighten and relax, tighten and relax like a

36

vertical smile. It was a dream made flesh, a desire I could touch.

What a terrifying thing lust was. Without any effort whatsoever she could make me give up secrets no one else knew, not even my mother. But, of course, I loved my mother in a very different way.

I kissed her muff. 'You know too much, already.' I freed myself from her thighs and went to the kitchen window. Outside the sun was rising brightly but the streets were deserted.

'Come for a walk,' I said. 'We must wish my mother Feliz Año Nuevo.'

She nodded firmly, as if recalled by good sense from the very edge of treacherous lust. She cleaned the coffee cups with a soapy brush and hot water, working with deft, economical movements.

I began to see that the Melendez family had money. Not much, perhaps. But my own mother's apartment had only cold water and she, among her friends, was considered a plutocrat for having running water of any kind and an indoor toilet, as well. So did Rita.

And this was the girl I'd asked to marry me. Think big, for sure.

Chapter Ten

I should have known the Melendez clan was higher up, socially. You had only to look at my beloved Rita to know what real class was. Her long, smooth legs? Well, I, too, had long legs, an unusual trait in a Cuban. But it didn't mean Rita's father had been a PT-Boat swabbie.

No, it was the mark of English pirate blood. Somewhere in the past Melendez corsairs had sailed with the freebooting English who murdered Spanish sailors for the Virgin Queen. It would be hard to choose who had been more deserving of pillage, the stinking Spanish or the lawless Limeys. We Cubanos hated them both.

But we classified those of some English blood as being fully as aristocratic as the Spaniards under Velázquez who murdered our Arawak ancestors, replaced them with African slaves and conquered our much-bloodied island.

To look at Rita's lovely face, with its high bones over almost hollow cheeks, the full, hungry mouth, the sharp teeth brilliant as crystal sugar, and that strong English chin, wilful, dominating, to drink in that face was to drown in pure, throat-tightening class. How funny then to listen to her left-wing thoughts, her unquestioning support for Fidel.

But in those days we all paid him respect. Anyone who promised liberation without sucking the public dry had to be honoured, if only with words. Ever since the Little Man had begun investing in Cuba we began praying for a liberator.

What made it clear was after Lansky had experimented with moderate-sounding puppets like Grau San Martin and Rio Jocarras. But they couldn't con the people into supporting them. Nor could they hold back the communists.

So the Little Man brought back our worst leader, Batista. He resumed his death-squad murdering and his fancy sexual exhibitions. Naturally, even a middle-class family like Rita's would despise him.

I say middle class but they were only a notch above poverty. Her father and his mother grew tobacco in the western end of Cuba where cane was not the major crop. They produced a line of cigars under the Melendez name, not one of the big houses that sold internationally, but popular enough in the domestic market to pay for hot and cold running water.

Without even thinking about it she and I moved dream-like towards a deserted Hotel Nacional on our way across town. Even here the streets were without people, without beggars, drunks, police. Empty of everything but old crêpe paper, abandoned rattles and spent confetti. The dream was over, but Havana still seemed in its grip.

It was already known that Batista and his crowd had cleared

out under Army escort. In two beat-up planes commandeered from Aerovias Q, he and his family and staff had scrammed.

We had been strolling along the Malecon, glancing at the sullen waters of the San Lazaro. At the Calzada de Infanta we headed inland on Rampa towards the Nacional Hotel. The January wind was chilly. Suddenly I realised where habit had led us, took Rita's arm and led her down a narrow side street.

'We mustn't pass the Nacional entrance. I don't want Lansky sending me off to do more work. Let someone else make the last casino run.'

'You think he's still in town?'

We walked more quickly down an alley behind the Nacional where its cartons of trash stood waiting for a pickup. 'The man has partners,' I explained. 'His first duty is to warn them of the disaster when Fidel takes command. His second is to save what cash he can, along with his ass.'

I had seen a Jaguar XKE only once before in my life, squat, streamlined, with cross-eyed headlights. This one was sand colour. I remember seeing it in front of the British Embassy a few weeks before.

Now it was parked in the alley behind the Nacional, as if waiting to pick up garbage. A tall woman sat behind the steering wheel, the one who had taught me about mierda. She was from the *New York Times*, also from the CIA. You would always notice Midge – because she was attractive and sophisticated – but also because she seemed so familiar.

In those days there was a Hollywood actress, Rosalind Russell. Midge resembled her, not only in looks but in savvy. The big difference was that Hollywood writers made up what Rosalind Russell said. Midge wrote her own lines.

Whenever she was in Havana I would escort her around town. I think Meyer introduced us. But, of course, those days were gone forever.

Being in love with Rita Melendez sent a stroke of fear through me. Midge Boardman had the power with a single word to expose my life before finding Rita. She would see how loose I had been, especially with foreign women like Midge.

But I was worrying too much. Midge didn't want to advertise our intimacy any more than I did. A stand-off. I was with my fiancée. She was with her boss. He sat in the front passenger's seat. I'd seen him at the hotel, a skeleton-like, hollow-cheeked bird of prey with burning, heavy-lidded eyes.

Another man lounged sleepily in the rear seat of the Jaguar. He seemed to have done himself too many injuries over the years, most of them with booze. His face had the look of a theatrical pro, a master of ceremonies, a magician, perhaps a concierge in a very expensive hotel, the man who can for sure satisfy your craziest wish.

He slumped down as if asleep. His blue, tropical-weight suit was badly wrinkled as if he had been drinking all night. Yet, in some odd way, he still looked . . . elegant. He wore pale blue suede shoes, now parked on the leather top of the front seat as he sprawled in the back. He wore no socks. But he still had class.

'Mawnin'' he drawled at us. 'How y'all doin'?'

I had heard every kind of American southern accent. He was faking his. Despite his drunken flush and wrinkled look, he was still too neat. When the Yanqui drinks that much, he goes entirely slob.

But the top button of his sky-blue shirt was still fastened. The dark-blue diagonally striped tie was firmly knotted in place. He might be drunk but he wasn't a North American. He was some kind of Brit, playing games.

Oh, my, yes. He was the greatest games player I have ever met.

'Victor is one of Meyer's stalwarts,' Angleton explained, as a way of introducing me.

'Victor,' said Midge, eyeing Rita out of the side of her big hazel eyes, 'is everybody's stalwart.'

What hung in the air was the way Angleton handled the s's in 'Meyer's stalwarts.' He sounded prissy, schoolteacherish. I saw that his eyes, too, were bloodshot but where the Englishman's face was slightly puffy, his was honed smooth, no suet around his beaky eagle's nose with its hungry nostrils.

I had seen him sipping drinks with Midge and El Pequeño late one afternoon on the open-air part of the Nacional's penthouse. This had been only a week ago, if that. Which was why Angleton remembered me and vice versa. Probably Midge told him my name.

The Englishman I had never seen before, but I was fated to see many times after that. I understood, later, that he came from far away, Beirut. He and Angleton had worked closely in Washington ten years before. Now, the dawn of 1959, 'they' had sent him back again to the Americas.

His blue irises seemed surrounded by coronas of fiery-red exploded capillaries. Vertically slashed across his temples were the veins alcoholics call the 'elevens'. You would not want to bet money on this man, not ever.

But I'm sure Angleton would. You only had to see that hawk's face and eye to know that Angleton was betting heavily on this man. Why? Why do gamblers gamble?

Maybe there was a sort of magic about the Englishman, as if he, too, was sleepwalking today, like the rest of Havana, sleepwalking through minefields. He smiled nicely at me, drunkenly but nicely. The smile said: *we are both living in the same dream.*

He was that sensitive to the atmosphere of the town and yet he hadn't said anything but fake-Dixie talk. But I got the feeling he could charm a wooden lamppost into being his true friend. And what he could do to women – !

I tightened my hold on Rita's lovely forearm, the soft, smooth flesh shifting slightly, as if any more pressure would produce some incredible juice or sap and we would all fall to our knees to lick up.

Midge saw the way I held Rita. She smiled but said nothing. We were nodding our goodbyes when Lansky himself rounded the corner, his little legs strutting fast. Suddenly, I got it.

The Jag had been waiting for El Pequeño. Behind him Sammy the Jockey struggled with two loaded shoulder bags, the ones from last night, but carrying much more money than before. I could see why the Little Man employed him; by comparison he made Lansky look tall.

Lansky stopped and gave us all the once-over, especially Rita and me. Before he could say anything the Englishman

41

came around to the trunk in the back of the Jaguar. It being a British vehicle, I suppose the trunk was a boot.

'Top of the morning, guv.' Even a yard away I could smell the booze on his breath. His movements were still precise, but greatly slowed down as he loaded in the heavy bags.

From where I stood, knowing how much evil Lansky controlled but not yet aware of what the other man could do, I had no idea I was looking at the two men who would destroy so many, corrupt so much and murder a president as attractive as a movie star.

The Little Man patted Rita on the cheek. 'These are the two star pupils in my English class.' I glanced down at his hands, really seeing them for the first time since I had worked for him. Rita was right. They were doll-like, not fit for a grown man, but not innocent either.

With those toy fingers he reached into his back pocket and brought out a roll of hundreds. 'Girlie, here.' He handed over what looked like five or six bills. 'Handsome, wish me luck.' He slipped me about the same.

'Schmul,' he said, paying Sammy off, 'sei gezündt.'

He hopped spryly inside the Jaguar. 'You could do worse than put Victor here on your payroll,' he told the bony man. It made my skin crawl to hear him praise me. Was I that evil?

'Victor,' Midge added, 'is value for money.' I could feel my face burn.

'Reliable, is he?' I got a long stare from those hooded Angleton eyes, examining me up and down, and Rita, too, as if we were unusually tasty cuts of meat in a butcher's window or plump field mice he could roar down upon and kidnap in his cruel talons. 'Drop by the Gatita Negra tonight around seven,' he told me.

'You never could resist crumpet,' the Englishman said as he closed the boot lid and got in beside Angleton. 'Onward,' he added. 'Time and BOAC wait for no man, however pequeño.'

'Meyer, meet Piers Plowman. A language scholar like you. A Cambridge man.'

Instead of shaking Lansky's tiny hand the Englisham tapped Midge on the shoulder. 'Dear one,' he said. 'Vamonos ahora.'

Midge started the car, tramped on the gas pedal. They roared off, leaving three hired bit players standing in the street. 'Only El Pequeño gets to ride, not you?' I asked the little jockey.

'He's godda geddem bags ouddada country. And oney the CIA guy can do it.'

'Angleton? And who's Plowman?'

'Juh'salong f'd'ride.'

I could tell, from the way Rita's lips curled, that she wanted no part of any of the three men who had just driven off. How she felt about Midge I had yet to learn. But I also knew that at seven tonight I would meet Angleton and take Uncle Sam's money to spy on Fidel.

No newly-married man would have done any less. To please Rita and soothe my conscience I would also take Fidel's money and give him an ear inside Angleton's plots. Why not? Poor people make do as best they can.

I had no idea this was the last time a desk man like James Jesus Angleton would be out in open air playing field agent scenarios with contract agents like Midge. I later learned that, as head of CIA covert operations, he was there to refamiliarise Plowman with the terrain. I suppose he needed the ego-building to say he had actually done at least one field job and got his pinkies dirty.

I also had no idea, looking at him and not knowing his middle name, that like me he had a madre latina, in his case Mexican. In an odd, spooky way, it made a bond between us. The link between the US and Latin America is filled with hatred, deceit, bloodshed and dollars. So it is a very strong link.

Those half-breeds among us who bridge both worlds are constantly having to answer ugly questions about ourselves that never bother other men. I wondered if he loved his mother the way I did mine.

I don't think so.

Chapter Eleven

You never do get used to surprise coincidences. No point in asking 'why?'. Life is stuffed with them.

That I was driving Cousin Jim Angleton to the airport in a Jag borrowed from the British embassy had been the original plan that morning. That he stopped to pick up the heavy-laden Lansky was the first of several surprises.

That I would run into Victor Sanchez was another. He was the most attractive escort in Havana, knew everybody and I didn't. But a *Times* correspondent should. Hence, Victor. He looked to be in his early 20s but had only just turned the age of consent. Not to be overly delicate, Victor was jailbait. Not in Havana, of course.

Another surprise of the morning was that he was so adoringly besotted with the jet-haired lady to whose arm he clung. I happened to know more about Victor than one usually does. His Guantánamo Bay connection didn't bother me. But he hardly seemed the kind to go for undying devotion.

But the sharpest surprise was the Englishman with the ludicrous Piers Plowman label and the palpable air of complicity. Like his friend Gleb, the man was not what he seemed. He was a whole lot more.

That was what a *Times* pal of mine learned after this affable, nice Brit had stolen his wife in Beirut. Then Plowman married her, I suspect, because he needed an American wife, or felt he did. I suppose I was damned lucky he hadn't tried to marry me.

Nowadays, with the feminist movement a very solid presence, an old-timer like me has no business reminding us of how we used to crumble when assaulted by the least likely, most destructive man of our acquaintance. When you assume, as I do, that Defence hired me as its female spokesperson because it was forced to by feminist currents in the political scene, you see I'm being ungrateful to my own sex. But, Lord, were we suckers!

His first wife? Back in 1933. A nice Austrian girl named Alice Friedman, called Litzi. I find that Viennese nickname endearing. She knew who he really was. But his second wife was British and, as I have said, his third American. Neither knew. Ah, but his fourth was Russian.

A perfect family man, husband, father, kiddies galore. But when he looked back on his magnificently long career – half a century of espionage tucked inside British intelligence – his Cuban adventure was his greatest triumph.

In 1952, when his brother moles, Burgess and Maclean, escaped to Russia, SIS rushed him home, snatched his passport and tried to make him out the Third Man. They couldn't prove it. In parliament, quite spectacularly, Macmillan had to give him a clean bill of health. He resumed journalism, got back his passport, became Beirut correspondent for two British publications, travelled a lot. Cuba? Of course.

Lord, what a Satan of Spies. But still, I'm not the Why Girl for nothing. His chumminess with Lansky was an early warning. Both were twisty, long-term haters. Both were brilliant strategists and tacticians.

But why . . . why did the Englishman's plots so neatly fulfil Lansky's blood feud with the Kennedys? And why . . . why does a patriotic American like me still ask why? Why we were such a fertile ground for such deadly mischief? And why – not how smart Lansky and the Brit were – how willing *we* were to fall in with their plans.

Why, in the end, was it so easy for them?

What? Yes, of course. Piers Plowman was Kim Philby.

Chapter Twelve

The Gatita Negra? Even when I was a boy it enjoyed the custom of 'in' journalists, entertainers, politicos, playboys, artists, gays and death-wish drinkers.

Since it served no food, it had never attracted foreigners like Hemingway, who spent his time between the Floridita and the Bodeguita del Medio trying to prove the foreign myth that food kept a straight diet of rum from rotting one's mind.

I got there at seven in the evening. There was no sign among the mostly male drinkers of the Angleton falcon with the hooded eyes. When I mentioned to Rita whom I was meeting at the Black Pussy she asked, she begged, that a friend of hers come with me. 'You don't have to drink with Ramos. He'll be your bodyguard.'

'And your spy?'

'Not mine. The revolution's.'

I knew Rita was in her heart a Fidelista. When he finally arrived in Havana, the conqueror at last, she would go to work for him in publicity. The Gatita Negra would become an essential place for leaking rumours. Even tonight, before Fidel's victory was known, rumours swept the huge room.

It was lit by cheap tallow candles and low-wattage electric bulbs, a cave of whispers, glances, subdued panic. But dark places like this were to me what an X-ray machine is to a doctor. Ramos, entering a minute behind me, proved to be the runtiest bodyguard a man ever had. He found a space three drinkers further along the mahogany-topped counter and ordered a beer.

Tonight the place had a high electric charge, something like the spot where at any second a lightning bolt will strike. I could feel it as if I were one of the electrodes. Even Ramos, behind thick, black-framed spectacles that made him look like a doctoral candidate in Advanced Grammar, seemed to have caught the charged atmosphere. He swivelled his head on its thin neck like an owl checking for its next mouse.

To make eavesdropping a harder game to play, two radios sat at opposite ends of the L-shaped room. One played the Spanish-language station in Little Havana, the Cuban exile community at the end of the Tamiami Trail along Calle Ocho in Miami.

Why does my Cuba produce so many exiles? They say one out of ten Cubans lives in Miami. It is not that the Calle Ocho is paved with gold, far from it. It is that ever since the

Spanish, we have produced incompetent dictatorships from which it is often necessary to flee. At the moment, the radio was blaring a big-band number called 'Tango Havana', ignited by a high, controlled scream from the Dizzy Gillespie trumpet.

You must know that the tango is not a Cuban dance. It is from the brothels of Argentina, which is why when they do it on stage the men are dressed as pimps and the women in bobbed hair with spit-curls. Never mind. If Dizzy wants to do a Cuban tango, let him. We gave the world rhumbas and mambos and meringues. Viva el tango!

The other radio was tuned to the earnest short-wave voice of Radio Libertad, the local pirate station that Castro had used for years to keep alive the idea that, one day, he would in fact lead us all to liberation. Between the two radios, you could lean close and murmur almost anything scabrous, traitorous or obscene without fear of being monitored.

A lot of people I knew were here, people who could be frank and fearless because of the noise. But they knew no more than anyone else at this point. The Castro radio gave away nothing about movements. Other sources reported that his forces had advanced, without opposition, moving in trucks and buses along the southern coast of the island, the Camagüey, cutting through areas supposedly loyal to Batista, like a razor through an eyeball.

They were, said some, now heading north to skirt the Escambray. Another report had them advancing along the northern shore. On only one thing did the rumours agree: Fidel would be in Havana by the end of the week.

While everyone knew of Batista's escape no one had marked the flight of El Pequeño, which suggested that among all these rumoristas I had better information than most, possibly even better than Fidel's man Ramos, now on his third beer.

Thirty minutes had elapsed without producing Angleton. I stopped nursing my glass of cheap, cheerful water-white rum called cane spirits, enhanced by chopped ice and lime juice. I finished it and started to push away from the bar. I had been

47

without my beloved Rita long enough. Behind me someone said: 'Can't fly on one wing, chappy.'

From the state of Piers Plowman's breath he had consumed many more wings since this morning. The sour-sick hydrochloric reek must have worried even him. He gestured loosely to the barman and indicated his empty glass and mine. Pedro made us new drinks.

'Salud,' I lifted the glass, whose heavy bottom kept the amount of actual rum quite frugal.

'Y pesos y tiempo para gastarlas,' Plowman finished. 'Wot, no viva for Fidel?'

'He does all right without my viva.'

'You Cubans are a cold-blooded lot.' He paid for the drinks and inhaled half of a bacardi daiquiri. 'Wah! He offers to free you from slavery. He removes the vampire bat Meyer Lansky from around your neck. But are you jumping for joy? You are not.'

'We have had liberators before, amigo.'

'True.' He stared gloomily at his half-empty glass. Standing side by side we seemed to be the same height, tall for this crowd. At that point he was old enough to be my father, but there was a loose jauntiness to him that made us seem of the same generation.

Men old enough to be my father would always be associated, in the minds of my own age group, with the giving of unasked-for advice, the voicing of dissatisfaction with us and our world, the pinched conservatism of view, the loss of joy and easy familiarity, the putting on of middle-aged masks of conformity, prudence, gravity.

Not Plowman. Perhaps it was the drinking that seemed to keep him looking at ease, unworried, as if he improvised his life while it rolled along. 'Nothing better than rum, is there? Muy sano. Eh?'

'An expert's opinion?' I asked.

'Cheeky little devil, aren't we?'

'Didn't Mr Angleton warn you?' I asked. 'Probably not. We don't actually know each other. He was supposed to be here half an hour ago.'

'Old Jim has not yet achieved Godhead. Can't be wombed

48

inside the Black Pussy when he's back in Fairfax, Virginia, at his desk.'

'Flew the coop, along with El Pequeño?'

Plowman smiled nicely. The feeling that he was a true friend was hard to fight off now that Rita wasn't here. Three drinkers away, Ramos had relaxed his vigilance; such a nice person could be no one of interest. He drained his beer and pushed the glass away, ready to follow me out.

'Old Jim felt like hell not getting to chat with you,' the Englishman said. 'But he did leave me a memento for your dark, soulful eyes only.'

He reached inside his wrinkled blue suit jacket and removed a long plain brown envelope. 'No glimmer what's inside, Sunshine, but I gather it could be the first of many. Old Jim's a sucker for tall, clean crumpet.'

I hefted the envelope. If Angleton, like Lansky, was using hundred dollar bills, there was a lot of cash inside. Later, they turned out to be fifties, ten of them. The envelope bore a telephone number with a Miami prefix and three words: 'PHONE BOOTH ONLY.'

I might be new to espionage but I could recognise a cut-out when I saw one. The Miami number would tell me only when and where to receive a return call from Fairfax, where Angleton roosted.

Made sense to run the cut-out via Miami. The Little Man, however, used New Orleans as his mainland base. Something to do with a long-standing feud with Santos Traficante, whose family ran all of Florida and most of Georgia, Alabama and Mississippi as well.

The rumour was Charley Lucky had sent Meyer to Cuba because he'd angered some tough New York cronies. He wasn't the kind of quick-fisted little guy who picks bar-room fights. He was the sort who savours revenge, often for years, before eating it.

That he quickly struck up a vendetta with Traficante, whose turf he proceeded to aggrandise, only gives you an idea that the mafia wasn't then, and still isn't, one stainless-steel monument to corporate discipline. Bad blood galore, but no such internal mafia conflict hampered the CIA.

The Englishman was watching me closely. Plowman's style was looking friendly, concerned, helpful, relieved when the envelope was pocketed without any rude questions. Then he glanced sombrely into what was left of his daiquiri. 'M'off tomorrow m'self,' he muttered, swallowing the last of his drink and wiggling a finger at the barman. 'Any message for Old Jim?'

'You're that close to him?'

Plowman cleared his throat, as if to brush away the mushiness starting to muffle his usually crisp speech. 'Our two nations have a spesure – special relationship,' he explained, smiling so dolefully he might have been crying, corners of the mouth turned down but eyes sparkling falsely. 'Many moons ago Old Jim needed help buh-badly. I was sent across the Atlan – ' He stopped as his new daiquiri arrived.

'To help him?' I asked.

'Do you hate gabby drunks as much as I do?'

I pushed away from the bar. So did the scrawny Ramos. There was one of those sudden silences that sometimes settles over a large, voluble crowd. In the tiny interval everyone could hear quite clearly the Miami radio:

'Early reports,' it said firmly in Spanish, 'make it clear that the advance of the guerrilla forces has bogged down at La Cienaga de Zapata, the swamp-like area east of the Bahia de Cochinos.'

'Thank you, CIA,' someone howled. 'Turn off the Yanqui mouthpiece.'

'Why would Fidel come by way of the Bay of Pigs?' someone else shouted. 'They must think we believe anything.'

A series of hoots and farting noises took over until the Miami station followed the bulletin with a Tito Puente recording of Lecuona's 'Siboney', more percussion than melody but to older Cubans almost a national anthem. Lecuona was, after all, Cuba's greatest composer and 'Siboney' his most popular composition, after his 'Malagueña', of course.

Slowly, noises of disbelief died away in rhythmic clicks and offbeat rapping of glasses. 'Agua,' someone shrieked in a fake religious delirium. 'Agua caliente por favo-o-or.' The place broke up in laughter.

The Englishman chuckled. 'Volatile, you Cubans. I'd give a sov for Old Jim to witness this. I keep telling him he needs a year in the field buh-before he can steer a desk.'

'Can you give Old Jim a message?' I asked.

'If it's a love letter, sweets, keep it decent.'

'Just tell him . . . um . . . we're on.'

The Englishman's dark blue eyes blinked pleasantly. He nodded, either in agreement or to signal that he had heard. Then his eyes looked suddenly empty, alcohol-soaked, the colour leached from their irises. He turned away with a slight frown. 'Bub-Barman,' he called, 'the rum walked through this diarrhea, dryeria, daiquiria wearing gum wuh-wuh-wellies.'

'Lo siento, compadre.' He splashed more rum into Plowman's glass.

'Sweet Lethe,' Plowman murmured, 'lead me through Hades to Fuh-Forgetfulness.'

He stirred his daiquiri with his longer middle finger. Instead of sucking it clean, as some might do amid the Black Pussy's unashamed sleaze, he removed a messy handkerchief from his breast pocket and tidily wiped his finger dry. Then he heaved a sigh of sheer heartbreak.

'Compadre,' he told the barman, assuming a Cuban accent, 'is t'irsty work bein' frien' of la humanidad.' He sipped his drink slowly. 'Buh-But someone has to do it,' he added as he slid down the front of the bar and came to rest beside the brass spittoon, mouth open, eyes shut.

I wondered whether to help him to his feet or get Pedro, the barman, to take care of it. After a few seconds I decided what my best move was. I turned and walked out of the Gatita Negra into the warm, humid, rumour-heavy night of Havana.

When Ramos didn't follow I turned back and peered through the window. The little bodyguard in the heavy spectacles had tucked his hands under the Englishman's armpits. Heaving mightily, he dragged Piers Plowman away from the spittoon and past standees to a small door at the rear.

It led to a former stable with a urinal and a place where drunks were often laid to sleep, a favour any friend might do. But what was a Fidelista doing, helping out a pal of the CIA? Was that how double agents operated? I was learning fast.

14 September 1959

Chapter Thirteen

Lord, what a summer. But the heatwave that embraced Washington DC showed little sign of cooling now that autumn was officially at hand. The *Times* and the CIA had given me maternity leave to have the first of my daughters. We were going to call her Susannah, so sure was I that she'd be a girl.

But it doesn't pay to be that sure. The sticky heavy air made pregnancy even harder to bear. My second husband, the expectant father, was an Air Force captain, which is why I was booked at Walter Reed Medical Centre.

Emory was a golfer. This made visiting me bearable because the hospital is near several good eighteen-hole courses. What? No, my first husband's hobby was drink. And Jim's – hard to believe – is billiards. Mine? Still martinis. What was I – ?

Susannah. She never arrived. She was one of those life-threatening fifth-month miscarriages. In those long-ago days, hospitals always saved the mother first and then didn't rush anybody.

The Walter Reed people gave me four days of lovely rest to get my ragged mind adjusted to not having Susannah. And, while the food wasn't much, the views south and west from my window were life-renewing.

I had them bob my hair short, cooling and not very motherly. I was trying not to be angry about Susannah. I had them body-wave my hair so it stuck out sideways like a Klimt woman's. It wasn't fashionable in those days. But I wasn't trying to be fashionable.

I was looking out at one of the District of Columbia's larger pocket parks, Rock Creek Park, through which the creek meandered sluggishly in such heat. If you picture the District as a diamond-shaped patch carved mostly out of Virginia and Maryland, Rock Creek lies near the uppermost corner of the diamond.

From long experience I also knew it was CIA's favourite place for staging a confidential rendezvous between people who were not to be seen together.

James Jesus Angleton, who had never been seen to perspire, would have preferred to hold this meeting in his Langley, Virginia, office. But two things changed his mind: first, the CIA building was imperfectly air-conditioned and his guest was a profuse, a fabled, a rank generator of sweat. Second, as a point of protocol, a civil servant, no matter how powerful, simply did not summon the Vice President of the United States of America to his office like a lowly file clerk.

There was a third reason but it didn't loom large in Angleton's mind. He had promised to visit me at Walter Reed that afternoon.

As to his chat with Richard Milhous Nixon in the park, one would not have expected the Vice President to serve as duty officer and White House intermediary for such a secrecy-ridden affair as the Castro problem. Never mind he was an unlikely choice for anything else you had in mind.

It could be said he had some little Navy experience. Other than that he had about as much military know-how as Dick Bissell, whom our CIA chief, Allen Dulles, had put in charge of toppling Castro.

Nixon has lurked in a corner of our eye for so many decades now, like a floating mote of dried pus, that we forget how he looked in those vice-presidential days, busy sinking Alger Hiss and other fiends. Thinner, collegy, if a half-shaven set of jowls can ever look freshman-like, with the sharp sideways glance of an experienced poker liar checking his effect on a patsy.

Nixon's Secret Service guards would approve all the trees and shrubs that provided necessary isolation. But they added a certain confused reminder that man's schemes existed in a great green world that rolled on whatever madness they created. Being here lent a fake sense of calm.

Calm Nixon knew not. We all noted that something had

kept him sweating on tenterhooks all this year, chivvying Dulles *and* President Eisenhower to intervene in Cuba and shove Castro from his brand new perch. Everyone had remarked on the fervour of his crusade. Odd.

Watching him close up in the dappled September sunshine, Angleton wondered how the American democracy spat up such specimens for public trust. He could have added himself to that list but the thought would never occur, since he'd never run for election.

But the vice president. I mean ... after all. He never was, and never would be, a pretty face, a polished thinker, a gregarious mixer. Nor was his political acumen ever higher than that of a ward heeler's naked appeal to ambition.

That face. Billboarding how true his lies were. Those arms. Working sideways and outward in not-me disclaimers. Those sincere drops in voice, heralding deeper larcenies. What was this nervy grab for action against Cuba?

Very odd. No matter how useful Nixon's anti-communist career had been – scaring up great chunks of campaign money from nervous West Coast industrialists – it couldn't yet stretch its demonic pantheon to include the Cuban leader.

Castro had been, in most ways, a model Socialist, making charismatic but well-bred murmurs at the United Nations, endearing himself to US citizens of Latin-American provenance and convincing the *New York Times*, for one, that he was, if not Mr Squeaky-Clean, then certainly Mr Reliable Enough.

The greenery of this part of Rock Creek Park, although it had lost its summer brilliance, had not yet turned autumnal. It made a fairly secure place for the meeting of plain, ordinary Jim and Dick, sitting on granite boulders by the bank of the stream exchanging top secret malice.

Anyone at her nearby hospital window with a long-range parabolic microphone – fear not, I wouldn't have known how to work the cursed thing – would also have to overcome the purling babble of the creek and, quite close, the underlying rumble and hum of high-speed traffic along the Beltway, US

495, and the north-south extension of Sixteenth Street. No, my eavesdropping was second hand. Still . . .

'It makes no sense,' Nixon was complaining, 'that your people have yet to report fucking huge unrest and dissatisfaction throughout Cuba.'

'I've left quite a team behind,' Angleton demurred. 'In Havana alone I have three good men, all natives. I have more scattered over the island. And our esteemed English cousin from SIS.'

'That's another thing,' Nixon added. His voice took on a peevish tone. 'By what right does this mystery Brit wander around as if he was a native-born American? I'm told he isn't even here, officially. He's on a holiday from Lebanon.'

Angleton tried to keep his voice unemotional. 'You recall that when Truman phased out the wartime OSS in 1947? We had a gap of a year or so before he authorised the CIA start-up? And I'm sure you remember we didn't want OSS veterans showing us the ropes. Except for Allen Dulles, of course.'

'Wouldn't that make more sense, hiring more Dulleses?'

'The OSS had been targeted on Germany. Our enemy is the Soviets. OSS-niks were a definite liability if they didn't have Allen's dedication. So we asked SIS for help. They sent us the Englishman in 1949. He was with me nearly four very productive years. And now I've asked for him again, on the Cuba matter.'

'Christ.' The Vice President looked even more unhappy than usual. He stared at a finch trying to settle down in a tiny pond of crickwater, there to shuffle its wings clean. Without thinking, Nixon shied a rock at the bird and watched it fly deftly out of harm's way. 'Nasty little cocksucker.'

'We also,' Angleton added as what he hoped would be a sop, 'have a young man in Havana who used to work for the casino interests. Highly trusted by Meyer, I might add. If any of our people could spot unrest, he would.'

'Meyer Lansky? That shit? On our payroll?'

Something more than malice seemed to snap behind Angleton's thick-lidded eyes and falcon stare. 'I believe you paid your first visit to Meyer right after the war? When you were looking for business as a fledgling lawyer in California?'

He smiled, a gesture more hostile than a frown would be on his bony face. 'Your FBI file shows something like eleven or twelve visits to Havana in the late '40s and early '50s. Your later intervention with Lansky to forgive gambling debts of Congressmen and Senators is also on record.'

The smile died slowly as Angleton remembered what it had cost the CIA to pry the Nixon dossier loose from the FBI, its hated rival. Only an operator like the Englishman could have wangled it, being trusted by both sides, even now, after all the rumours about him.

'Hoover told you that?' the Vice President huffed.

'Hardly. Nor did he open up the early pages of the dossier, where you applied to be hired by the FBI.' He illustrated hole-card strength by not even bothering to remind Nixon that his lifelong connections with mobsters had led Hoover to turn him down for employment. '"Too dodgy to work for the FBI,"' the Englishman had reported. '"But okay to be Vice President."'

A finch, most likely the same once since birds rarely learn a lesson quickly, returned to the tiny pool. Nixon reached for another stone.

'Imagine,' Angleton said then, 'the losses Meyer has sustained since the revolution succeeded. It does shrink the cash he can contribute to political candidates,' the CIA man continued. 'As for his many partners, I wouldn't want any of them that angry with me.'

The Vice President's face grew puffily pink, then red. He let the stone drop, got to his feet and took a few paces to limber up his legs. 'Fuck innuendo. Is that what I came here to listen to?'

'Just the usual DC gossip. We've all been wondering why you have made yourself flagbearer for the Get Castro people.'

Nixon nodded, dodging sideways. 'It's a crisis. Ike won't let us use US troops. Any invasion by CIA mercenaries has to have two things or it fails.'

Angleton, his body poised bonily on a rock like a basking stork, nodded in agreement. 'Air cover and a great uprising of the Cuban masses.'

'I'll deliver the air cover,' Nixon told him. 'You deliver the goddamned uprising.'

'Not I,' Angleton assured him gently. 'Our English cousin.'

'Can he?' Nixon stopped and kicked a stone in the direction of the finch. 'Isn't that hanging too much on one tired Brit prick?'

'An extremely valuable agent,' Angleton went on. 'One of the very few authorised to liaise with both the CIA and the FBI.'

'So valuable you haven't mentioned the miracle shit's name.'

'British Intelligence won't like me identifying their former Washington chief of station. All their top people pretend to be under deep cover. It's schoolboy games. They're called C or M, quite like the James Bond stories. Our man uses several aliases. He's now called Piers Plowman. He's also called Giles Galveson.'

Then he told the Vice President Plowman's 'real' name and spelled it for him. 'Yes, I did,' he told me that afternoon during visiting hours at Walter Reed's Maternity Wing. He had brought flowers and a tiny card inscribed 'to what might have been. Happy Next Baby.'

He sat there with his homburg on his lap, his bird-of-prey eyes sparkling with malice. 'Odd nickname, Kim.'

'Not as odd as Tricky Dick. Nixon is a notorious grudge-bearer,' I commented. 'And also the party's 1960 candidate for President in November next year.'

'Not bloody likely.'

'Nobody to have as an enemy,' I added.

'Only,' his hawkish eyes snapped brightly, 'if he becomes President.'

Chapter Fourteen

'Feelbi?' I repeated. 'For sure?'

'Feelbi,' Ramos assured me.

He had come in the hour before midnight to my home.

That is, the tiny slum apartment of Maria Sanchez where I slept on the narrow living-room couch. Her bedroom remained empty. I kept it for her alone.

Some things on this island go on forever, despite a war between Cuba and the United States that was edging towards open declaration. The only non-combatant zone lay at the eastern point of this famous Pearl of the Antilles, the US Navy base at Guantánamo.

My mother was completing another tour of duty in the scrubbed and shipshape brothel there. No longer was she House Virgin, of course, but on this tour she was subbing for the madame, who was back in Miami on vacation. My mother was, after all, in her thirty-first year and, unlike those who let themselves go to fat and premature middle age, she still commanded a very high price.

'But it's a whole new leaf, Victor,' she told me. 'Rita and I have discussed it in much honesty, like a mother and daughter. I take only US Navy officers, no swabbies, and Rita's little tape recorder lies under the mattress. Who knows when one of them wants to talk?'

So far she had sent home three tapes for Ramos to pass along to what the Navy called Comint, Castro's fledgling intelligence network. She also sent me her weekly earnings which I banked. Yes, the Sanchez clan had gone respectable. What I got from Comint was peanuts, what Angleton paid via Feelbi more than made up. With my mother's earnings we would soon have enough to install hot water.

'We give Feelbi a long leash,' Ramos explained. His scrawny, earnest face, behind heavy-rimmed spectacles, had the morose look of someone to whom nothing peculiar is alien. 'We know he is CIA but there is a hands-off order.'

'Why?' I had run out of rum after half an hour of drinking with Ramos, who bored me. 'Are we hoping to turn him to our cause?'

Ramos' shoulders wrenched sideways in his skewed vision of a shrug. It was not clear why a CIA man merited hands-off treatment. But it was clear that Ramos was for sure in the dark.

'And what cause is that?' he asked, hoping to stir up some

talk. It struck me that boring people must always create conversation. 'While Fidel walks a tightrope, so does our cause,' Ramos added.

'He wants – we all want – to go it alone, without help from the Russians and the other Iron Curtain people.' I made a small, bitter, laughing sound divorced from joy. Was that the way true laughter sounded? We Sanchezes, with our bank account. Did respectability sour laughter? 'As if a land so small could face an enemy so huge as the Yanqui,' I threw at him, 'without help from outside.'

'The Russians count on that.' Ramos put on a wise squint that made him look more like an owl than usual. 'They know that all they need is one unforgivable sin committed by Uncle Sam.'

'One? The Yanqui commits dozens.' In my mind's eye I saw the empty bed in the next room, a bed on which I would never sleep, nor would any other man. It was Maria Sanchez' private bed, where she could be herself and alone. Beds were to her places of business, of humiliation, of surrender, of strange acts too disgusting to remember. One place had to remain sacred to her privacy, her own bed in her own apartment.

'One big act of violence,' Ramos droned on, 'and the Russians will be invited in like the second coming of El Salvador himself.'

'What do they want with my poor Cuba?'

'What? Ninety miles from Uncle Sam, ballistic missiles can reach any state in the union?' Ramos produced a snicker, wet and disdainful.

We fell silent for a long moment. Then, mostly to head off another outburst of conversation from Ramos, I got to my feet. 'So where does Señor Feelbi fit into this fairy tale?' I yawned.

Ramos glanced at his watch and stood up, slowly, as if not quite trusting his centres of balance. He fumbled in the right-hand pocket of his much-washed blue Levi's where on some models a tiny watch-pocket has been sewn. From it he removed a single leaf of cigarette rolling paper, thin as a sigh.

'On your next report to Angleton, insert this as second or third item, casually. Comprende?'

Even espionage, I saw, is made dull by Ramos. Although he was probably right about the Russians, biding their time to jump in and take over. It was too bad espionage got so boring. The thin paper bore pencilled notes on Castro troop movements, numbers of men, locations, all lies. I repeated the message, tucked the cigarette paper in my mouth, chewed and swallowed it.

'Bueno.' Ramos stuck out his gnarled hand. I had never asked him how a man so young, barely a year or two older than I was, had done so much permanent damage to his body. He resembled the survivor of a major catastrophe. Was that what had turned him into such a bore? But, of course, in the Movement, one didn't ask such personal questions.

Things were moving so fast, here in Havana and in all the other cities of Cuba, that one had no time to consider the personal side of life, nor the interest to spare from hard, daily problems. This was especially true of Rita and me.

We wanted to live together. Her parents had offered us a bedroom. A bedroom meant we had to get married. My mother wanted a big church wedding, of course. The Melendezes couldn't spare that much cash. If Ramos was a dull spot, the rest of life was constantly choked with problems.

Rita's father's and grandmother's tobacco fields had gone up in the world. Fidel had smoked Melendez cigars for much of his life. This had helped Rita rise in his administration from a mere enthusiast through small jobs to head of publicity. As a result, we were marked people.

Marked, that is, by crews of street assassins.

When I let Ramos out we checked the narrow slum street in each direction. Earlier in 1959 Havana had not been safe for Fidelistas. Too many survivors of the Lansky organisation remained on the darkened streets, darker than ever because of frequent power failures.

A known Castro revolutionary could be found badly beaten up, or kicked to death, often with mafian improvements like testicles sliced off and tucked into the mouth. Being in the Melendez family did nothing for your personal safety. Would you believe, there was even a plot to kill Fidel with an exploding cigar?

Who were these backstreet bandits? The money came, of course, from the CIA. But the men were people like my old team, Luis and Cruz, husky young guys with no conscience. Yes, it was Luis who killed Manolo's daughter that New Year's Eve. But I was the one who created the cover-up and funeral that kept the crime under control. In the eyes of the law I am as guilty as Luis.

Yes, I admit it, the Lansky hoodlums roaming the streets of Havana should long ago have been flushed into the harbour. Pimps. Pushers of horse and Mary Jane. Junkies who'd kill for a dose. Hustlers who serviced men or women. Recruiters of young girls. The girls themselves. Hit men. Pit men, including croupiers and security bosses. Accountants. Back alley doctors for syph, clap, abortion and pussy clinching. Bag men to convey small bribes to politicians. Couriers to convey big bribes to Zurich. Crooked lawyers. Fixers. Ward heelers to produce big voter majorities. Colonels and Generals to order strikers and protesters machine-gunned. Death squads of moonlighting cops hooked on killing. Torturers. Bankers.

What a metropolis, all of them on El Pequeño's payroll. And never forget the hijo de puta who collected his skim. How long ago was that? Fifteen months? And now Lansky's scum might well try to ambush and murder me.

I don't mean to blame. I thank God for Rita, even now, so many, many years later, as I thank God for my mother and my children and my grandchildren, all fourteen of them. But you must admit that for a young guy just eighteen to move upward so quickly as a double agent nearly to the age of twenty and still remain alive and happy . . .!

As a reward for staying alive, I had noticed lately that fewer Lansky kills had occurred. Finally, these alley assaults stopped. How do I know? One of the endless – and boring! – number of errands I ran for the CIA was to monitor this violence and provide body counts. The last time I'd telephoned the cut-out number in Miami I'd heard a curious thing.

I waited in a telephone booth for the return call from

Langley. Under Lansky Havana's phone system was nothing one could count on. Under Castro . . .! Whoever I spoke with – rarely Angleton, more often bored subordinates wearing only first names – on hearing that the back-alley attacks had stopped, mumbled something like:

'They're shipping the heavies to Happy Valley.'

'To where?'

The voice, which used the name Nick, produced a faint, dull chuckle. 'Never mind, Chico. Hasta luego.' The line went dead.

Chapter Fifteen

Then it came back: Happy Valley!

I stood at the door of my mother's bedroom and tried to visualise what she was doing at this very moment. Asleep, I hoped, but I could remember from my own childhood that officers were a different breed of pig from enlisted men and didn't need to return to quarters till they damned well pleased.

Usually once a week they'd stage an all-night orgy. The code word for it was Happy Valley. Four or five of them would get very drunk with some of the girls and end up in a squirming mass of naked bodies, sucking anything that came to hand.

It didn't take much brainwork to see that Happy Valley gave cover for anything. With a girl for each of them, plus the ready excuse of too much booze? Next day brought blissful memory loss. Such bisexual frolic was winked at by the Navy brass. Even a child could see that.

But one Saturday, waking with deadly hangovers, the young officers found one of them strung up, buggered in gang fashion and left to hang with a bleeding rear. He had wriggled his way out of bondage, he thought, but only to the point where a leather thong choked him to death.

All officers below Lieutenant Commander, involved in

Happy Valley or not, were confined to quarters for a week. The brothel was subjected to a week-long steam-and-ammonia whetstone scrubdown that removed paint from as far back as World War I. The Commanding Officer wrote the dead man's mother:

'Dear Mrs Armbruster, it is with great regret that I burden you with the saddening details of your son Hartley's heroic passing, a brave and innocent victim of covert enemy action in an undeclared war to keep our hemisphere free of the pernicious cancer of communism.'

Then it was back to business under new rules: one officer, one whore, no orgies. That restriction held for at least a month before the next Happy Valley.

I stood in my mother's bedroom doorway and stared down at the small bed. You had to hand it to her, a tough little bird in a grim world. How soon could the respectable Sanchez clan save enough for her to quit Guantánamo? Did she actually want to quit Guantánamo? Did I actually want to move in with the Melendezes?

Rita wanted her father to give Maria a job out west as bookkeeper at the tobacco plantation. Maria had been less than overwhelmed by the prospect of a dull, workaday job counting cigars for Fidel to smoke. Nobody knew how long it would take Fidel to normalise the island. As for earning hard currency, the US embargo on Cuban cigars was killing the whole industry.

The telephone rang. My mother was one of the few people in the slum to have a phone, installed by El Pequeño so that he could summon me at any hour.

'Number Seven. Half an hour,' a bored voice said in English.

Ay, que lagrimas! I slammed down the phone. It was now after midnight. I was to meet Rita at the Gatita Negra. This would delay me. When was a Cuban so cursed with slavery to the clock? Where was the easy-going style of Havana?

Number Seven was one of ten telephone booths at the Central Railroad Station down near the docks, almost across from the house where José Martí was born. The CIA liked it because these booths were in constant use by ordinary people.

The crowds that milled around promised some freedom from eavesdropping.

Two things destroyed that strategy. One was that, after midnight, there were no crowds or ordinary people. Two, I had reported the booths to Comint several months back. They were bugged twenty-four hours a day by Castro agents like Ramos. Nevertheless I stepped inside Number Seven and waited for an incoming call from Langley.

Angleton's voice was not as bored as the first caller. I heard the prissy sibilance of a professor giving a lecture. I unloaded minor matters and included the misinformation contained in Ramos' cigarette paper.

'Um, Nick tells me you and he spoke about the street violence?'

'Yes, we did, sir.'

'And he mentioned a destination? A certain . . . place?'

'Yes, he did.'

'I'd like that name forgotten.' A pause at Angleton's end. 'You may think this routine. But it was a major mistake. Nick has already paid for his carelessness. I want the name forgotten, is that clear?'

I grinned at the telephone. 'What name, sir?'

'Good boy!' The line went dead.

I headed off for the Gatita Negra, remembering: *they're shipping the heavies to Happy Valley*. Not hard to remember. And now, impossible to forget.

1 March 1961

Chapter Sixteen

Speaking as a woman who never frequents the place, the Tavern on the Green is an unplanned, ungainly, sprawling place at the western edge of Central Park. In March the great park playground of Manhattanites and their muggers is at its most forthcoming, a rich mixture of new green shoots against the black silhouettes of winter, rapidly growing camouflage again.

Although I don't think of myself as a New Yorker, I have lived there off and on long enough that I wouldn't be seen dead in the Tavern on the Green. I wouldn't call it tacky, certainly not by the standards of Demopolis, Alabama, anyway.

This particular three p.m. an unlikely visitor appeared, a small man, neatly garbed, with a younger man ten paces behind him. The place seemed empty to the short man whom no one in Manhattan would dream of calling the Little Man. Here on his original home turf Meyer Lansky was known as the Genius.

He wasn't often here these days. He spent most of his time near his major project, the retaking of Cuba, in a quiet retreat in the Hallandale area of Miami Beach, a place not far from the Art Deco Section.

But when he needed help he was still the activist graduate of Murder, Inc. who saw to matters personally. It was easy to see why.

There is a momentum in human affairs that we all understand, a matter of timing. The longer Meyer allowed Castro to rule Cuba the harder it would be to dislodge him. If neglected too long, the corrupt little island of yore would begin to look positively sleek with honesty and hard toil.

'Midge,' he had told me over a drink the evening before at the Oak Room of the Plaza, 'I needed a kind of miracle. A kind of . . . you know, like a . . .'

His lizard eyes stared into his cup of black coffee. Over the years his face seemed to have drawn to a point as his nose grew larger. 'When two things come together. A coincidence!' he almost shouted, overjoyed to find the word.

He glanced around the Oak Room crowd to see if this outburst had been noted. He went on in his usual undertone, silky and hard to hear. 'I found it.'

'The coincidence.'

'You remember how I never did get to pay what I owe Joe Kennedy?'

'The President's father?'

He was silent for a moment and seemed to be chewing, as if eating a memory. 'It goes back to Prohibition days. Guys died. Old Man Kennedy I will live to send to hell. Then my debt is paid.'

The slow-burning fire in his eyes winked brighter, then disappeared. In a very calm voice he added, 'So you can figure how I feel when the son sits his butt down in the White House.'

'Meyer, my mind isn't as fast as yours. You hate the father *and* the son? Isn't that a pretty big load to carry?'

His face split horizontally in a grin. 'All alone, sure. But now I got somebody else.' His eyes darted around the room, again. 'A whadyacallit? Ally?' He almost grinned the bottom of his face off. 'Sorry, doll, but if I told you who hates Jack Kennedy worse than me, you'd never believe it.'

His secret remained secret the next day when, forsaking the slightly classier Oak Room, he entered the Tavern on the Green with his bodyguard. They spotted a young man called Vince.

'Through here,' Vince muttered, his lips barely moving in a totally deadpan face. The young man with Lansky stood in the doorway while Vince led Lansky to the corner booth. A nattily dressed man with guileless eyes and a sharp nose got awkwardly to his feet.

'Wie gehts, Meyer?' They shook hands with very light finger pressure.

The dapper Lansky, gypsy-skinned from months of inactivity in Miami Beach, produced a wry smile. Frank Costello shot back the thick pleated, gold-linked French cuff on his left wrist and examined the diamond-crusted gold watch there.

'Shit. He'll be on me any minute now.'

'Where? Here in the park?'

'They kind of cordon off the Sixty-sixth Street transverse up to Seventy-second. The bastard takes no chances he'd be recognised.'

Lansky placed his tiny hand on Costello's sleeve. 'Frankie, I'm not here for the guy you're meeting. I need a real persuader. Nixon keeps blowing smoke up my ass, promising action in Cuba. While he looked like making president, I played along. Now I need somebody to goose the little vonce good and hard. Capish?'

'I'll get you Mickey Cohen? He poured more sheeny gelt into Tricky Dick's run for the White House than the mint at Fort Knox.'

Meyer's dark eyes looked hurt. 'Since New Year's Day of '59 not a cent of Cuban profit. All the cash we poured into Nixon for the 1960 election, blown. And who do we get? Momser Attorney General Bobby Kennedy busting ass.'

'He's sure got the shivs out for Hoffa.'

'And Marcello.' Lansky's voice dropped. 'Carlos wants to hit Bobby.'

'Not a bad idea.'

'He's got the brain of a gnat. It's Jack he needs to zetz.'

'Hey, do you think big, or do you think big.'

'Meanwhile I have every don in the US on my back. Why me?'

'Because Cuba was your patch, Meyer, your lay, your scam. Life is strictly whaddya done f'me lately.' He glanced at his watch again and got to his feet.

Costello picked up his soft taupe Borsalino from the oak table and fitted it carefully on his head. 'You know how it is

73

this high up in the environment, Meyer. You and me, we can never cop a plea for mercy. Either we produce or . . .'

His voice had gone up slightly so that when Lansky responded in his quiet tone it stood as a kind of rebuke. He eyed the two young bodyguards at the far end of the room. 'Nu, Frankie, why do you and I try to keep our guys civilised?'

His lips barely moved so that Costello had to bend over to hear. 'Level with them, Frankie. Say Meyer reminds them we were all wild men once. But now we don't have to be. We let our money do the hard work. And we make ten times as much paying the politicos to break the law for us.'

The heavier mobster chuckled. 'I'll pass it on.' He nodded to the young man called Vince. 'Avanti, cugino.'

'Oh, but listen, the guy you're seeing right now? Don't pass on the hit Marcello has in mind.'

'Do I have to be told?'

'Or my idea he should hit big brother instead.'

At Seventieth Street, after a short walk, Costello headed east into a wooded area, Vince followed. The south-curving inner road stopped them. Packs of cars rattled past. The two men waited for a lull and crossed to the other side where a cinder bridle path ran between overhanging trees, new leaves beginning now to appear.

A young man in a dark grey suit stepped out from behind a tall maple. 'Mr Costello, sir? This way please.'

Deadpan as always, Vince watched his boss, since Lucky Luciano's deportation the man who ran New York City crime. A short porker in a pale white fedora, brim turned up, pug-dog face set in a grimace of dudgeon, bellied into view.

A cheek muscle bulged on the right side of Vince's impassive face. The two walked on alone, neither bodyguard following. Vince turned away, thunderstruck.

Marrone! He felt he'd been promoted from button man to caporegime. Like having a hundred grand stuffed in his pocket. Just by having an eye for faces.

But who couldn't recognise, even in the park, even ten yards away, the face and figure of J. Edgar Hoover?

Chapter Seventeen

As the Sixty-sixth Street transverse runs east towards the Zoo it passes a rather run-down set of buildings belonging to the New York City Police Department. I often suspect they're left in such disrepair because the cops loan them out to authorised spooks.

Two nondescript dark grey Ford sedans sat shielded by a row of squad cars from passing traffic. Puffing slightly from the walk with Costello, Hoover slid inside one of the Fords. He turned to the man sitting in the rear seat of his car. 'Let's find us a place that sells drinks. Har,' he added as a kind of laugh.

'Quite. I had no idea you bigwigs grubbed your own worms.' The English accent was pure Cambridge, a touch tired, a bit brusquely superior.

'That was no worm. That was a snake.' Hoover grimaced, intending it as a smile. His driver and companion, Clyde Tolson, a tired man his age and height, mimed a smile but said nothing.

Hoover barked: 'What sort of game is Angleton up to that needs your help?'

Philby produced a look of pleasant innocence. 'My lips are sealed. If you tell me it's Cuba, I'll deny it.'

'Har. Why should I take the word of a guy who nearly did time as a commie spy?' He produced a deep sigh. 'I envy you lone wolves. You have no idea what us civil servants go through. I suppose you know I hit retirement age in the next few years. Mandatory retirement.'

'In the next few years,' the English voice repeated with a slight upward question at the end. 'During the second term of Jack Kennedy?'

Hoover jerked his thumb at the Englishman for the benefit of Clyde Tolson. 'Who said Limeys are stupid?'

'No love lost between you and young Kennedy?' Philby mused. 'But perhaps he can waive your retirement?'

'Perhaps pigs can fly. A guy exists who can do me a favour. If I don't let him know it's a favour. Clyde, let's go find some bourb.'

'Most kind.' Philby's soft face looked hungover. He wore a tan Burberry raincoat, unbelted and unbuttoned. 'Problem is I'm due out at Idlewild Airport.'

'Meeting somebody?'

'Catching the evening flight to Paris.' He showed them a stuffed briefcase. 'Rather a last second decision.'

'Clyde, radio for two escort cars, fore and aft.'

'Most kind.' A pause. 'Did this unnamed informant have much to offer? Besides a way of solving the Kennedy problem?'

'What gives you the idea it's a trade-off?' The director of the FBI produced a kind of indrawn grunt. 'These talks are my way of reminding him his whole life depends on me.'

Philby gave one of his supernal smiles. 'Somewhat the same as my relationship with you?'

Hoover's square, angry face began to distort and grow red. But what came out was a snorting laugh. 'Har. You're not dealing with that passel of patsies running the CIA. The only reason I re-established contact with you is that Angleton did. Cuba's off limits for me.'

'Did you ever let that stop you before?'

'Clyde, leave the sumbitch off right here.'

The plain grey Ford swerved to the corner of Fifth Avenue and Fifty-fifth Street. There was a long pause. Then Hoover guffawed loudly. 'Just kidding. A little test.'

'You give it to all your men?'

'Har.' Hoover's face resumed its look of high dudgeon. 'Just Limeys!' He and Clyde Tolson cackled as happily as schoolboys.

Chapter Eighteen

New York to Paris is easy. I did it now and then for the *Times*. Paris to Prague, in those days, was not.

It required a change of plane from Paris to Vienna, and a second change to get to Czechoslovakia. As the aircraft crossed the Moldau and reached approach level for landing, the passengers could see below them the famous span of the Charles Bridge.

It had lured tourists for centuries. On this brisk, sunny morning, strollers and groups of schoolchildren moved from one niched statue to another. High above them loomed the Castle with its busy bureaucrats who ran one of the most technologically advanced satellite countries of Eastern Europe, often used as adjunct headquarters for the over-crowded Moscow Centre.

Gleb Vasileyevitch Khsovko had been Harold Adrian Russell Philby's case officer almost since college days in Cambridge. They had met as journalists during the Spanish Civil War.

'If anyone can assess the judgement of this officer,' he assured his superior, Colonel Krachmalsky, 'I am the one. In sickness and in health – '

'Till death do you part,' Krachmalsky wisecracked.

I picture him as being of Gleb's age, approaching forty, and also dressed in civilian clothes. The two men leaned against the brownish granite railings of the bridge, conversing easily in colloquial English with adequate British accents. From time to time they glanced at their wristwatches.

'But, Gleb,' the colonel complained, 'this conspiracy is so . . . so grandiose.'

Gleb shrugged. 'What would you have said, Kolya, back in 1950 if someone told you a leading comrade of the Politburo would stand before the Supreme Council and denounce the entire regime of Comrade Stalin, dotting every i and crossing every t? And, moreover, end up as Premier of all the Russias?'

Krachmalsky made a face. 'But your friend Harold is no Khrushchev.'

'No?' Gleb lifted one hand and began ticking off fingers as he spoke. 'The moment Lansky brought Batista back to power Philby began reviving his old Washington affiliations. The moment Castro triumphed he was able to plant inside the CIA a conspiracy to invade Cuba. Listen:

'One, they believe it is their own brilliant idea but, two, it can only fail and fail miserably . . . costing them millions and us not a kopek . . . while, three, it is guaranteed to smear shit all over the Kennedy administration and the two stainless young brothers who run it . . . and, four, seat Castro even more firmly in Cuba's saddle as the defender of the people . . . and undermine in advance for all of Latin-America any future proposal of goodwill Uncle Sam might try to sell . . . and give Castro a horrendous and powerful excuse to call upon his friends, worldwide, meaning us . . . and hand over to us in the name of Cuban security the unrestricted licence to install whatever long-range missiles we deem useful in protecting our Cuban allies and dominating the land of the free and the home of the brave . . . from a base just offshore . . . and what is more, Kolya, to set up for the CIA and have accepted in the highest places of the American government *a model, a pattern of illegal clandestine work which routinely commits treason* against its own people and its own country's best self-interest and – '

'Enough!' Krachmalsky was grinning now from ear to ear. 'But how can your miraculous genie guarantee this tidal wave of subversion?'

'Think like a Brit. In British public life there are two fundamental facts: secrecy and fagging. Secrecy is their god. Leaking secrets is their vice. Searching out secret-tellers is their chief sport. And – '

Gleb watched a troop of schoolgirls in their teens move slowly past, the wind lifting their uniformed skirts. I imagine in those days the Czech schoolgirls dressed very plainly. Nowadays they are stunning little vixens. I have seen them.

To distract himself, Gleb glanced at his watch again. 'Angleton is Harold's fag. Figuratively he cleans Harold's boots by licking them daily.'

The colonel stared at him. 'But – ?'

'It goes back to 1949. Harold heats up Angleton's suspicions and sends him endlessly searching for a phantom army of NKVD agents stealing CIA secrets. More time is spent investigating inside traitors than any other activity. He is destroying the entire agency in the name of inner security.'

'But surely Angleton isn't British?'

'He's far worse. He's a Yankee Anglophile.'

A man in a battered tan Burberry raincoat, bareheaded despite the March wind, approached them, smiling pleasantly, an overstuffed briefcase in one hand. Gleb gave him a big bear hug, pounding his back vigorously.

'You . . . I . . . you've gained weight, old man. Travel agrees with you.'

'All those lovely rum drinks.' The newcomer turned and extended his hand. 'Good morning.'

I have wondered about Krachmalsky's eyes. I think of them as pale blue, the angelic but inhuman colour of the sky. They watched the newcomer reflectively.

'Your dossier shows how long ago you came to us. It shows such a strong, early dedication. It shows such a great faith in the power of history.'

The newcomer examined the departing schoolgirls and a young couple embracing each other across the way. One can never be too careful, can one? What's easier to set up than a pair of lovers?

'It is far too complex for a quick sketch. I have been perfecting this masterpiece, and the skinny hawk at the centre of it, since I arrived in Washington ten years ago.'

The man in the Burberry let his eyes shift sideways again to the couple, who were now kissing. As one, the three men turned and walked off along the Charles Bridge back into the heart of Prague.

Chapter Nineteen

My Havana has always been a big city for rumour. Rumour is the same word in Spanish and English so I get it double in my genes. Hanging out at the Gatita Negra with Rita would give anybody an overdose for sure. But me, in those days, I loved all of it.

All during the spring of 1961 the rumours were about invasion. Don't argue with me that it didn't make any sense, Uncle Sam invading Cuba. But that didn't stop people from arguing.

I'm a Cuban. I don't run from arguments. They are proof that you're alive and kicking. Rita would join me late in the evening, bringing along a few Fidelista co-workers from her department, Publicity. They would explain to me how crazy it was to expect invasion.

You learned everything at the Gatita Negra. People told me that the Yanqui was collecting a large force of men and training them on a coffee finca in Nicaragua with the code name 'Happy Valley'. It was hard not to laugh, since I knew how such a code name was chosen, in honour of the bisexual games of Yanqui navy officers. I knew now why the 'heavies' were going there.

They would tell me who had been seen in Happy Valley, people I had known in the gambling casinos and brothels of Havana. People imported from faraway places like Indo-China where the sadists of the French Foreign Legion enjoyed torture and murder. Where runaway Gestapo killers took advantage of new, legal victims.

They mentioned squadrons of Yanqui aircraft like the A-26 attack plane that had been relabelled the B-26 attack-bomber. They had a specialty, these relics of the second World War. Their low-stall speed made them ideal for low-altitude bombing to soften up objectives like landing beaches. Then they could strafe to finish off any of the living.

I would tell these people all this was proof for sure that Uncle Sam was itching to overrun our poor little island once more and once more make us his slaves.

'Wouldn't dare!' Rita said, her huge dark eyes producing that great smouldering look, as if banked camp-fires kept her cauldron seething. 'Wouldn't dare. Uncle Sam knows that people fight to the death for their own land. Uncle Sam remembers the Indian tribes he massacred and how they fought him. Uncle Sam remembers Custer!'

'Geronimo!' a weedy young man called Bernal cried out.

We all broke up laughing. We were too young to stay serious very long, even Rita who was very sincere about her beliefs. She knew I worked for Fidel but took CIA money. It didn't bother her because she knew my heart was with Fidel. She knew he could count on me to keep the faith with him and betray the CIA whenever possible.

Yes, this is a position without honour. It is immoral, I know. And all sorts of depraved, even freaky behaviour is expected of such an immoral person. But not Rita. Only the night before, in bed, I was sliding into her, nice and easy, the slow style the girls at Guantánamo called hombre commodo or easy rider.

What we both like about commodo is that it can last for an hour because it isn't the fiery hot fucking of intense lust. It is a considered meeting of two people, one sure of erection, the other sure of a series, a whole train of orgasms. Not an express, a local that takes its time.

'No, not tonight.' Her voice was soft, not commanding. 'I am in ovulation, guapo. Guaranteed we make a baby.'

'How bad is that?'

'Not bad. Thoughtless. To bring into this mean world, trembling under cliffs of avalanche, a helpless baby.'

'A baby with your face? A good deed.'

'You like my looks?' She rolled over on top of me and wiggled her glorious ass in my face. 'Good enough to bite?' I could feel her hot mouth clamping down on me. No more a considered meeting of two people. More like a killer attack of genitals on mouths and vice versa.

You do remember we had then known each other a year

81

and a half since that first night when she learned the mysteries of sex. I remember asking her – weeks later – how it was that . . . a delicate question, you understand. How it was that nothing had broken or bled.

I remember her quick, natural answer, with a shrug: 'Bicycles. Volley ball. Cheer-leading. Compared to my mother's generation modern girls are tomboys. We lose it long before some macho male thinks he's split it.'

Immoral? This is a convent-bred girl. She no longer attends church, of course. I would suppose very few Fidelistas still attend church. But this is a girl raised by nuns. The wonder of lust never explains itself. My mother could explain it but, of course, we have never had such a conversation and never will. Let's face it: my mother, too, was raised by nuns.

Later, as we fell asleep in the sixty-nine position, I dreamed we were rich. The Sanchezes had so much money we could buy off Uncle Sam. We could afford anything. We were drowning in riches. I awoke, choking for air, Rita's lovely luxurious muff smothering me.

Sitting in the Gatita Negra, arguing with her and her colleagues, I would suddenly remember her in bed and my mind would go blank, my argument trail away into silence. 'La Gatita Negra has his tongue,' one of them would jeer.

'Not so.' Rita would kiss me. 'I have his tongue. I own it.'

So all these smart people, far more intelligent about the world and its politics than an hijo de puta like me, would convince themselves that Uncle Sam was afraid of what the world would say if he attacked our little island.

'It has never stopped him before,' I argued. 'Playing the bully? He does it very well.'

But, they would explain, as if to an imbecile, that that was before radio, television, before Fidel, the big man who stands up to him with bravery and honour, before what happens in one out-of-the-way place becomes known a second later in every corner of the globe.

'The Yanquis have only to attack us and all of Latin-America would be up in arms,' the weedy one explained.

I had no use for Bernal. He sniffed after Rita like a dog smelling female heat. Well, who hasn't had that carnal feeling? But this Bernal was too badly brought up to hide his feelings.

'All?' I yelled at him. 'All what? Uncle Sam owns our nearest neighbours. Their governments exist on Yanqui hand-outs. Their armies are trained by Yanquis and armed with Yanqui weapons. They harbour anti-Cuban invasion forces. All of Latin-America? What a stupid idea. When Uncle Sam farts, all of our nearest neighbours shit.'

Ramos, the security agent who looks so much older than the rest of us, is sometimes on my side but mostly on theirs. I found out why he looks so wrenched out of shape, so ugly. The Lansky/Batista police hung him by chains to hot water pipes. With truncheons they spent a long time breaking all his limbs while scalding skin off his body.

This was routine torture. Lansky made sure not to hear about it, but the police? Honestly, I must say that most of Batista's police joined up *because* they were given a licence to do such things. Many thousands provided these sadists with their fun, some to live, some to die. But Ramos' case was different.

The crew that worked over Ramos started by chewing his burned skin as if it was pork cracklings. At first they dared each other. 'Hey, this pig deserves it!' Then they started to enjoy it. 'Where is the salsa?' When a mobster controls a country, you get a very sophisticated police force.

'Big Bic,' Ramos announced. He kids me which, I think, means he likes me. This I can do without, for sure. He is a hero of the Fidelistas but can you imagine having a pet cuttlefish or sting-ray?

'Big Bic is an expert on Uncle Sam. He has psychoanalysed the machismo of the United States. This is the curse of being half Yanqui.'

'Leave him alone,' Rita responded. 'Just because he is better looking than anyone at this bar, he doesn't have to take abuse.' She picked up my hand and kissed my palm half a dozen times, lingeringly.

'Excuse me,' I corrected her. 'I am better looking than anyone in Havana. If Rita loves me you loafers must listen

83

closely. The Yanqui knows many tricks. His favourite is cutting off his own nose to spite his face.'

But did they listen?

Chapter Twenty

In the basement of our little house in Alexandria, Virginia, my husband Jim keeps a full-sized billiard table. What he plays mostly is rotation pool, a dead giveaway of a misspent youth. But, oddly enough, for two people our age, as well as our guests, pool is quite a pleasant sport.

I'm no match for Jim, but he doesn't at all mind beating me incessantly. He is able to do that because he understands what I never can, which is the necessity of thinking ahead.

You know what it's like? You have a clear shot at sinking, let's say, the six-ball. The seven-ball is way over there. You want to send the six into the side pocket with a gentle stroke and make the cue ball rebound to a place where you have a clear shot at sinking the seven-ball.

This is how one sweeps a table, being smart enough while sinking one shot to set up the next. It's an elementary version of what chess players do. Jim's mind registers where the next ball is and how to hit the cue ball properly. I constantly rush forward to a shot without preparing for the next because I can't get it through my head that knocking balls around requires thought.

'Yes, the next shot and the one after,' he explains. 'A real pool player can think five, six shots ahead.'

Working away at the year 1961 in my memoirs, I suddenly realise that life is a game of pool. Life is won by those who think ahead. Life is a series of setting up what is to follow.

For instance, once Colonel Krachmalsky admired Kim's strategy about Cuba, it was only a matter of time before Station Moscow gave the go-ahead. Back Kim went to Washington, DC. Within another fortnight, the whole town was talking invasion.

That's the nature of a closed-off company village. Mark something top secret, restrict access to a handful of people within the CIA. It becomes such a juicy rumour to monger that it's all over town in a few weeks.

I'm not saying some things aren't truly secret. It has always been rumoured, down through both Democratic and Republican administrations, that no matter what the core intelligence outfit is called – OSS, CIA, NSC – there is an inner, secret group that is counted on to do the real dirty work.

In fact I once met a man I was sure belonged to it. He was a former Marine captain who asked to be called Sam. He was assigned as a military attaché to our embassy in Mexico City. But we met at a party in Kingston, Jamaica. In the way men do, Sam spun a whole web of gossamer bullshit about his own importance. Hints, nods, the usual.

We had reached the can-I-phone-you stage. Of course Sam could phone me. He was too good looking to let a little gossamer keep us apart. I gave him my number at the local *Times* bureau and you would have thought it was the local leper hospital.

'You're not a journalist?'

Those were just about the last words I ever heard from Sam. But I had heard enough to place him in that shadowy group called ISA, the ultra-secret Intelligence Support Activity that handles most assassinations, disappearances and other capital crimes Uncle Sam wishes to have happen.

ISA's been around a long time, staffed mostly by action types like former Marines or Green Berets, lads trained to obey orders but postpone thinking about them until long afterwards. If then. I imagine the CIA had recruited some for the Cuban invasion, if only as instructors.

As for the thinking behind the invasion, if all one wanted was to discomfit and denigrate Uncle Sam, that part of Kim's thinking would be more than enough. But invading Cuba also had an extra appeal to Station Moscow.

It brought the Castro regime well inside the bear-hug zone and turned a philosophical ally to a dependent client state. Let's think of that as the six-ball. Ker-plop.

Then another pool player took over from Kim. Once the

invasion was launched, and failed, this second person master-minded sinking the seven-ball. A third was waiting to take control of the white ivory cue ball and make absolutely sure the black eight-ball went down to defeat.

Why three players for one game of pool? Now, in my dotage, I have begun to realise it wasn't a planned thing. There was no conspiracy there, as we understand the term. There was simply a fateful succession of opportunities. You'll see what I mean.

The morning after I figured out how they dropped the eight-ball I got to my office at Defence a bit early because we had booked a small briefing for 0900. I don't have a very grand office, being without military rank, but high civil servant status. However, it is a corner office, although the pentagonal shape makes all corners obtuse. Is that a joke?

Anyway, I can make room for half a dozen folding chairs in a semi-circle around my wall chart area. This was to be what's called a 'soft' briefing, meaning for feature background on women's pages and the like. Well, if the United States isn't at war, I suppose all our briefings are soft.

In any event, I was to take them through a very short session on changes to current plans for repatriating US ser-vicemen and their families stationed abroad, more of a human-interest story than anything else. My assistant is a WAC sergeant called May Beavers and she was late.

May is black, almost as tall as I am and tilted towards the sexy side of feminine beauty. She has brisk short black curls. So do I this year, except that they're white. Quite striking. I inherited her with the job and we hit it off at once. May is just thirty years old, divorced, no kids but a social life that would exhaust Caligula. I supposed her tardiness indicated a late night.

I found the folding chairs and set them up myself, moving small tables this way and that to allow any demon smokers a place for an ashtray. I don't have to let smokers smoke, but if my job is to keep them friendly to Defence, what is a little ambient-smoke lung cancer for a true patriot?

Moving a small table I found gummed under one leg a piece

of my own note paper. It's from one of those small yellow-paper pads that has stickum on the back. I brought the pad from home because Defence doesn't do ephemeral things like stick-on notes.

This was in my own handwriting, a memory-jogger to Sergeant Beavers, and it read: 'MAY: PLS GET ACCESS CODES FOR BAY OF PIGS COMPUTER FILES.'

There shouldn't actually have been any. The Bay of Pigs invasion was entirely a CIA operation. But it depended on covert support from the US Navy and Air Force.

In the normal course of my work as a spokesperson there was no reason for me to access such material. I had told none of my superiors that I was writing memoirs of that long-ago era. It wasn't that I didn't want them to know. It was that the thought of telling them had yet to cross my mind.

But the fact that the note ended up trapped by its stickum under a table leg indicated that Sergeant Beavers, or someone else casually leafing through my paperwork, had taken a special interest.

I would imagine it rang no real alarm bells. When a 1961 matter surfaces thirty-five years later, it's not alarming. Everyone connected with it would be either retired or dead, and Defence's major concern is protecting its rear. So interest in such a long-ago event would not be alarming. It would be considered historic. Nobody gets alarmed about history.

So I didn't get alarmed about finding the note.

Chapter Twenty-One

I'm the first to admit that American intelligence work has not been a rock of security or a hotbed of efficiency.

I'm not one of those alumnae who continue to lavish praise and wonder upon past employers. Most of us, upon leaving the CIA, speak no good of the past but, out of patriotism, speak little evil.

Insiders of any kind who know the ropes, pitfalls and gross

foul-ups, tend to take refuge in vague smiles when grand-children ask the nearly always embarrassing questions they do. When you read published memoirs of tattle-tale veterans – Kim Philby's own account is a typical example – you learn what a fine line separates most intelligence systems from a Marx Brothers comedy.

'A funny one?' Jim asked, before dinner.

'The later ones were thunderously unfunny.'

'So was the CIA. How'd you recruit so many dodoheads?'

'That's not how it works.' I held up my glass for another splash of martini. 'Intelligence people aren't any more stupid than normal folk. Lord, no. It's just the nature of all humans to make mistakes fifty per cent of the time.'

'Is that what airlines call "pilot error"?'

'When did any airline ever admit such a thing?' I fell to remembering. When you're in the fiery flush of youth, mar-tinis get you up, out and half way around the earth. When you're, ah, more mature, martinis start you remembering.

'I will admit,' I said at last, 'that in the case of the CIA you'd have to call it wrong seventy-five per cent of the time.'

'I always said you were generous to a fault.'

'But the reason is that the CIA, almost from the beginning, was heavily computerised. When you have electronic help, you can easily break records for wrongness.'

I sat back and stared into the middle distance. 'The other half of the reason is called James Jesus Angleton.' I smiled at the Jim I married. He already knew how I felt about the Jim who called me his cousin.

I don't think you could find anyone disagreeing with me on Cousin Jim's ability to hamper, confuse, head off, wrongfoot and otherwise misdirect CIA activity. And all in the name of ferreting out insider spying by mole agents.

'All those boy's club mysteries,' I muttered, more to myself than aloud.

The hallmark of intelligence work is secrets. They are also humanity's most outstanding weakness. Secrets make you one up. Secrets let you lord it all over some poor slob who doesn't know the secret you know. Secrets authorise you to build your treehouse, club together, pull up your rope ladder and go 'nyah-nyah' at outsiders. Secrets are the juiciest pleasure there ever was.

When it came to the Bay of Pigs invasion, a sliding security scale was created in order to know whom you could holler nyah-nyah at. We fell into these categories:

In the loop and privy to all documents

In the loop but restricted to certain documents

Out of the loop but officially cognisant of the operation

Out of the loop and never instructed on any phase of the operation

In on everything but able to deny knowing (reserved for high-up administration officials at the Presidential level)

The last category was: Midge Boardman.

As a journalist I did not qualify to be told a damned thing, even Castro's shoe size. Quite the contrary: my occupation put me entirely on an enemy basis. But as Angleton's pet female contract employee and putative cousin, I was constantly downloaded with data I had no wish to know. Also, Lord help me, I fell into the added job of being Cousin Jim's go-between with Meyer Lansky.

Yes, the world's smallest mobster was actually considered an ally in all this. His was perhaps yet another security category: outside all loops but owner of the battleground.

Our aim was to oust Castro. Period. To dress this up as a counter revolution, we had collected a group of unknown, quarrelsome, fractious 'Cuban leaders'. None of them represented anything except what you get when you scrape the bottom of a particularly mucky barrel.

In particular, none were connected with the entity that so recently owned and ran Cuba. We call it the mafia but there is some doubt that Meyer represented that entity since he headed no family of the Honoured Society.

'All camouflage,' I told Jim, waving my martini glass about. 'There has never been anyone, in or out of the mafia, who could draw a table of organisation. There never will be.'

'Are you talking to me?'

'Thinking out loud. Old folks do it. About Meyer Lansky not fitting into some niche of the mafia organisation. Unless you think of him as their broker, banker, financial advisor and portfolio manager.'

'Midge, would you believe I hardly ever think of him at all?'

'You see, it was all that hot money from drugs and extortion and gambling and stolen goods and other rackets.'

'The stuff they had to launder?'

'Launder for use. Meyer was the one it came to for use. Invest this here. Bank this there. Meyer made all those decisions.'

'Meyer, huh? Another ex-beau of yours?'

We are talking now about a very brief period in our national history to have caused so much grief. It begins in early spring of the final year of the Eisenhower administration, 1960, when a totally secret and largely self-appointed group called the '5412 Committee' presented Ike with a paper: 'A Program of Covert Action Against the Castro Regime.'

It gained flesh when, on March 10, a full National Security Council meeting met to consider bringing 'another government to power in Cuba'. We used to talk that way, we superpowers.

We had talked that way about Iran, if you recall, protecting all that oil by destroying the Mossadegh government in favour of a shady Shah on a throne we had to invent. We had already done the same thing in Guatemala and would later do so in Chile, without even the excuse of oil.

We really thought this was what the US was placed on earth to do, undermine and destroy governments we disliked. It took Vietnam to shake our faith that destroying what we disliked was no longer a productive part of our manifest destiny.

As for destroying Cuba, within a week, being go-for-it Americans, we'd convinced Ike to OK the idea. He put his tricky Vice President to work probing Castro, then on a goodwill visit to the US. It's hard to believe, after so many decades of enmity, that we at first welcomed Castro and he welcomed the chance to explain his regime to us.

Clearly we were faking it. No idea if Castro was, too. After

Nixon and Castro shook hands, as the Vice President later admitted, he became 'the strongest and most persistent advocate' of liquidating Castro. The power of a single handshake! Fake, of course, since his feelings actually dated from the night Castro took Cuba from Lansky.

All through the long hot summer Nixon pushed the various bureaux and committees to accelerate plans for invading Cuba. His timetable allowed no rest. It wasn't just that Meyer was nudging him mercilessly. Come November, when he ran for President, Nixon wanted a 'strong' Cuba position.

Come November he was narrowly defeated. Unless you had been in on it, you had no idea what a shock this was to the corporate powers that run America. A young, good-looking Catholic womaniser in the White House? What were the Goddamned, lint-headed, mouthbreather voters thinking of?

What, indeed. The 1960 election was our first true television ballot. The voters weren't thinking at all. They were choosing star power, charisma, moondust, sex appeal. It wasn't an election, it was a Neilsen rating.

Nevertheless the powers that run America have agendas with which even an ignorant new president cannot be allowed to tamper.

By April of 1960, John F. Kennedy was being hand-carried through Nixon's invasion, unaware of who had done what to whom. White House records show many visits from the man he'd defeated, visits that probably curdled Nixon's partisan heart, but visits that had to be made if the President was ever to get off his butt and OK the Cuba invasion.

The two men loathed each other, then and thereafter. But what Kennedy shared with the man he'd defeated was a hunch that liquidating Castro would be seen by American voters as a 'strong' move.

Call it a year, more or less, a year between the decision, under Ike, to invade and the landing, under JFK, on Red Beach. A year of bureaucratic in-fighting, of people looping in and out of loops, of utter lack of secrecy so that Castro knew everything about the invasion except, perhaps, its precise starting time.

As a CIA contractor, I wasn't allowed to keep a personal diary. But a *Times* reporter had to keep notes. Even in those olden golden days, my management required note-saving because we never knew when one of us would be called on to stonewall a judicial or congressional inquiry in order to protect a source.

More to the point, before our bosses would defend us and save us from jail, we had to prove to them that we hadn't made up the offending news item. Only our notes could prove our innocence. So you can believe we kept them very safe.

When someone in a bureau would return to New York, he or she would carry back to West Forty-third Street everyone's notes sealed and labelled. That was the only reason, I can assure you, that I still have those notes.

When I arranged recently to pick them up I was shocked to find that they filled three corrugated cardboard cartons of the size movers used for crating books. That made them all but unusable, unless Defence gave me a month off to sort through them.

'That was a very friendly act,' I told Jim.

'Are you trying to wheedle another mart?'

'I am not wheedling anything. Just remembering how you helped with the notes.'

'That was rather nice of me.'

The biggest advantage to marrying a retired gent is that they have spare time. Jim volunteered to index the whole thing on a disc. Thanks to him I relived the years it took three men to sink the eight-ball.

Chapter Twenty-Two

That year of 1961 a joke made the rounds in Manhattan. Convinced he could get a job with NBC as an announcer, a man got an agent to put him up for audition. But NBC never agreed. Months passed. The ambition became an idée fixe.

Finally his luck shifted. NBC scheduled him for an audition. His agent waited outside, petrified with hope. When the man emerged, his angry face gave away the result. 'T-turned d-d-down! The antisemitic buh-buh-bastards!'

The joke always reminds me of Meyer, not in the years of this story but when, later in life, he tried to con Israel into accepting him as a permanent resident. You can picture him coming out of the unsuccessful hearing:

'Turned down! Just because a man's a murderer?'

The *Times* had assigned Spanish-speaking me to a Miami story about the amazing number of Cubans living there, most of whom had emigrated under Lansky, not Castro.

I had put up not in Miami but South Miami Beach in a darling, scabby little Art Deco hotel. Palm trees separated us from the gradual slope of the beach into the Atlantic. The offshore breeze had permanently bent the trees towards land, as if they had decided all the excitement was onshore. This included the architecture.

In 1961 Art Deco was not yet the design icon it later became. We had no idea what the hell it was, anyway, until we realised it was the hideous 'modernique' our parents had scorned before us. In any event, only the façade of the hotel was 1926 Art Deco. The inside was plain-piperacks poured concrete.

After a day of interviewing Cubans along Calle Ocho I came back late to find a message signed 'M' and a telephone number. 'Midge Who?' a woman demanded.

'Boardman.' I could hear her repeat my name in a softer voice. Then a man came on the line.

'Welcome to South Beach,' Meyer began. 'How about a plate of cholent?'

It had taken me a second to place the voice. 'No thanks. But a nice pastrami on rye wouldn't be sneezed at.'

We met in a motel café with booths, one of which seemed to have been permanently reserved for Meyer. 'Was that lady who answered the phone the new Mrs Lansky?'

'Whaddya expect?' he muttered. 'I should wait for you forever?'

My shriek of laughter drew everyone's attention. The moment they saw who was sitting with me they carefully

93

turned away and feigned intense interest in their barley-and-mushroom soup, corned-beef-lean-on-rye and Cel-Ray tonics.

After we gave our order we sat in silence. His curious eyes, small, dark, reptilian, looked me over feature by feature as if I were an inner tube with a leaking patch or two. I had been letting my hair grow back since the miscarriage and discreetly touching out the few grey hairs now making their appearance early in my life.

'Working for Angleton agrees with you, doll.'

'I had the vague idea you might have stopped off in DC on your wanderings.'

'Me? Why?' His voice had a quiet, silky tone.

'It's the place to be these days if you're, um, interested in Cuban history.'

'I got a fella looking after my Cuban interests.'

It's impossible to approximate Meyer's Ukrainian version of Manhattan speech patterns. He still glottalised his ls. A word like interest got smoothed to innarest. 'There' became 'they-uh', a pattern he shared with the Bostonian patois of the Kennedy family.

I had written Meyer down once, for my favourite prof at Vassar, Dr Domandi. He examined it carefully, tried pronouncing it and shook his head.

'Goyische kopf, bubelah,' he twinkled. Then he carefully tore it in bits and disposed of it. 'And don't ever do that on paper again, Midge.'

Sitting across from Meyer now, a worrying thing happened. I am not in the habit of making supermen out of short hoodlums. But he seemed to have woven some sort of electromagnetic web around us, lines of force that locked our minds together.

No sooner had I thought about his pronunciation and that of the Kennedys, without saying it, than Meyer's mind picked up the loathesome syllables.

'Besides, I don't like the class of bigshots in Washington these days. Bad enough to have a Kennedy in the White House, but an insult to call that little vonce Bobby an Attorney General.'

'Who mentioned the Kennedys?'

'Tricky Dick Nixon's my man.' He paused as the waiter delivered my sandwich and Meyer's bowl of rice pudding, swimming in milk.

'I guess the Prohibition era's just history to you,' he said then.

This time I carefully controlled my urge to shriek, either with shock or laughter. That kind of remark makes life worth living, like a friend of mine who once confessed to me: 'I don't like birds. They're so . . . inhuman.'

'Afraid so,' I said in a mild voice. 'But not to you, of course.'

'Hey. We wrote it. Me, Ben and Charley, we wrote it.' He spooned the rice without much interest and I realised that he'd already had dinner, probably prepared at home by the lady with the demanding tone of voice. Something unspiced, low in fat, high in fibre, short on calories, therefore invincibly goyische dreck.

'Talking about the past is not my game,' he went on then. 'But that doesn't mean I forgive and forget. Not on your life.'

Truly, it took a mind-reader to cope with his mind-reading. I tried my luck. 'Something about the Kennedys you haven't forgiven?'

I started on my pastrami. In tenderness and finesse of flavour, in subtlety of pepper zest, it beat anything a New York deli could offer. I realised this was a cut they must keep just for Meyer and his guests.

'Forgiven?' He produced a small, huffing snort of derision. His voice had been in his usual soft tones. Now it sank almost out of my hearing. 'This goes back to 1927, doll. Charley and Ben and me, we had a thing running all over the north-east.'

He sighed heavily, gave up playing with his pudding and took a cautious sip of his heavily creamed coffee. 'The way it worked in those days, somebody with money would finance a shipload of booze. Lemme tell you, you had to stand in line, waiting to invest.

'It was a favourite low-risk game for a tight-assed hypocrite like Joe Kennedy. Once he paid, the ship'd cross the Atlantic and dock – always at night – in some schmendrick little New England harbour town. By morning it'd be unloaded and on its way.'

He pushed the coffee away as somehow unworthy, too strong, too cool, too something. 'A convoy of trucks would be heading south from the harbour town to make deliveries in the Boston area and further south.'

He fell silent for a long moment. 'Your trucks?' I prodded.

'Joe Kennedy's trucks. With whatever gelt he could spare from creaming Gloria Swanson's behind, he woulda financed the whole operation: whisky buy in Ireland, ship hire, crew, stevedores, trucks, local cops, everything. Cost him a very serious bit of change. But once he unloaded it to wholesalers like us, he'd be a lot richer than if he'd put the same dough in utilities or streetcar franchises or railroads.'

'Ah.' I nodded knowingly. 'I see a lonely transfer point. A rendezvous. Don't tell me he fell for it?'

Meyer's face puckered in a leprechaun way, corners of the mouth turned down, eyebrows high. 'We're talking about a country road where all the trucks had to pass. But on board the convoy for guards we're talking real Irish donkeys.'

'You mean they didn't take kindly to being hijacked?'

'Hey, there are rules, doll. A guard in that job is supposed to have some judgement. If positions was reversed, our guys would've known not to start a fight. Our guys, if they see they're outnumbered, they're supposed to let it happen. What does it get you shooting each other?'

'How gentlemanly.'

'Nothing to do with gentlemanly. Nobody wants a lotta bodies and blood. It forces the cops to get up off their knees and start finding perpetrators. The next thing, headlines. Nobody wants headlines, not us, not even that donkey Joe Kennedy.'

'His guards resisted. Is that what went wrong?'

'They came out shooting when they hit our ambush. Like it was World War One and a Half. Typical Irish. By the time it was over eleven guys lay in their own pools of blood.'

He laughed, another of those tiny snorts of his, but his eyes danced with malice. 'You think it's easy hijacking booze that's covered with blood? You think retailers liked buying it?'

He paused and his eyes brightened appreciably. 'But it was

Kennedy himself, miles away, who nearly bled to death. For months the widows and families pursued him, demanding their blood money. That damned fool had recruited Irish and they weren't taking no for an answer.'

'Poor Joe Kennedy. The nerve of him, protecting his shipment. No wonder you've hated him all these years.'

I should have known better than to use sarcasm.

Chapter Twenty-Three

You think you know someone, even someone you see only now and then. You think you have figured out what makes him tick, how close you can come to treating him like just another human being.

But you can't. Because he isn't just another human being. He's barely human at all. His deepest centres are those of a predator of another species. He separates his contact with humans into only two categories: toadying agreement (rolling over on one's back, all four paws in the air) or outright attack.

Sarcasm was obviously an attack. His breathing quickened. His small head seemed to retract, or his shoulders bunch up, to protect the vulnerable neck artery. His eyes narrowed for sharper focus. If he'd had retractable claws they would have extended, quivering for blood.

'Watch that mouth,' he snapped, like a gut-string exploding in two.

'I beg your pardon.'

He took a long, deep inhaling breath. Slowly he let it out to calm himself. When he spoke his voice was no longer tight with rage.

'Don't ever take that Kennedy bastard's side. There was nothing nice about the bastard. You weren't even born when he was busy in England, trying to get them to surrender to Hitler instead of fighting. And when their government kept on fighting he got some of the Limey aristocrats to help him help Hitler.'

'How long have you been such a Jewish warrior?'

'My father taught me one thing. In this world, the way of a Jew is hard.'

'Then you ought to understand about the Irish . . . 800 years of bad blood against the Brits.'

He squinted at me. 'You're not Irish. I had you checked out once. You're Dutch. Don't stick up for the Micks, OK?'

'I sympathise with the Irish . . . and the Jews. So, don't blame Joe Kennedy for being Irish.'

His eyes narrowed again. When he spoke the words were spat out. 'And I shouldn't blame his two snotty rich-kid sonny-boys for being Irish either, right? The two he trained to hate guys like Lansky and Luciano. So that the first thing a know-nothing punk like Bobby does in charge of the Justice Department . . .'

He paused and for the first time I noticed he'd grown short of breath. It was an affliction that grew worse as he aged. But he had only to keep calm and avoid thinking about the Kennedys to breathe easy again.

'The second he's in charge,' he went on angrily, his thin, disembodied voice like a ghost's cry, 'he's trying to get even for a convoy of Prohi booze. You think I kid you? Old Man Kennedy drummed it into all his kids: above all, he would tell them . . . get even.

'So Bobby starts rewriting the Bill of Rights and the Constitution and the whole megillah of Federal laws. Give the little vonce four years in power and we'll have as much civil liberty as the Russians.'

I patted his tiny hand. It was shaking. I had to decide: was I watching a man who could give Stanislavky cards and spades, or was I watching a first-class schemer breaking down in paranoia?

Either way, I was tired and ready for sleep. The fact that I listened to him now and then should not lead anyone to think that I liked him. He was, at bottom, a nasty type, only prevented from reverting to his original profession – contract killer – by the fact that he was now a name the police knew too well.

He was, in short, the personality type I had been bumping

up against all my years in journalism, self-thrusting, socio-pathic. The kind, in short, that if I'd been a man I would have taken a punch at.

I almost grinned: the picture of me hitting Meyer Lansky. But I was taller and younger. What – besides common sense – was stopping me from telling him what I thought of him and throwing my coffee in his face?

Listening to his preening outcries against injustice had only been funny at first, like Prohibition being history. Now they seemed crazed attempts to make him seem more than the mobster he still was, more the sort of person on whom the *Times* might do a grudgingly complimentary piece.

'Graduate of a hard school, Mr Lansky is not one to minimise violence in the history he helped write. Now retired to a small South Florida beach house, he spends his leisure time walking his tiny dog, chatting with old friends in a nearby park and like most senior citizens, remembering what he would never have called the "good old days".'

And invading Cuba, I added silently. My fit of aggression had calmed. I no longer wanted to destroy him. But I still had words. 'Not only a Jewish warrior, you're a civil libertarian?' I thought a faint look of chagrin crossed that gypsy face. 'Meyer, you have to relax. You stress yourself out this way.'

'Don't I know it?' he complained. 'Haven't I delegated the stress? Isn't that what Nixon's supposed to be doing for me?'

'On Cuba. But he already tried knocking off Jack Kennedy and blew it.'

Meyer's small head, with its commanding nose, nodded slowly and then came to such a motionless stop that he almost seemed to have stopped breathing. 'For Kennedy,' he murmured in that soft ghost voice, 'I have somebody else.'

And addressed himself silently to his rice pudding.

'Anyone I know?'

He looked up, spoon in mid-air, milk dripping from it. 'Anyone you know?' He shook his head, as if laughing at me. 'Who wants to know, the *Times* or Cousin Jim?'

'Me. Just me.'

I could swear he was tempted. It told me something he hadn't meant to reveal, that enlisting this other person was a master stroke he enjoyed so much he really hated to let it remain secret.

I had poked a bit of fun at him. He wanted me to know he was a man of far higher accomplishments, real ones, not simply buying a used paper bag like Nixon to help him regain Havana.

'I know Angleton's worried Kennedy will welsh on our deal about Cuba.' His dark eyes tried to gimlet mine. I avoided his glance. 'Tell him not to worry, doll. There are big people in this world who hate Kennedy even more that I do. A guy like him just naturally pisses people off. Unnastand?'

Our glances met finally and locked. Something big. Something Machiavellian. Something Meyer was dying to brag about. But didn't.

He was trying to find out, by mind-reading, if I knew to what he was referring. If another of my sources had somehow tipped me off. Like everybody in the spook business I exuded an air of deeply profound clout, unlimited network of contacts and supernatural thinking ability. It's a trick blondes have a lot of trouble with.

Like the rest – leaving out Kim Philby – my façade was mostly bluff. Any clout I had was laid upon me by the hands of Cousin Jim. This, by the way, is what makes women so much better at espionage than men. In our ordinary everyday lives we already magnify our meagre advantages and minimise our flaws. A girl with narrow-set eyes and thin lips who has learned with make-up to make the eyes seem wide apart and the lips lushly bee-stung, this girl is ready for anything.

Anything but being mind-read. It's an unsettling process of double bluff and Meyer had been playing it all his life against Sicilian professionals. Someone, he had hinted, whose hatred of Jack Kennedy was lethal. Someone, moreover, in Meyer's camp, or perhaps only in communication with Meyer.

And then it came to me.

Chapter Twenty-Four

I ask you, amigo, in those days, how did you get from Guantánamo to Havana? They are five hundred miles apart, but in those days for sure on separate planets.

First you conned a US Navy plane to take you to the Bahamas or Jamaica. Then a civilian plane flew you to Havana. Call the whole trip a thousand miles simply to get from a Yanqui-controlled naval base to Fidel's capital city.

My mother had started the journey this morning, early. She arrived at last in Havana by sunset. In mid-April our sunsets are spectacular. All this not to miss my twenty-first birthday party.

Rita had planned something so big she had to warn me of it in advance. Havana was already very tense, expecting God knew what from Uncle Sam at any moment. A big birthday party was not what Havana needed, but . . .

She got permission to rope off a corner of Parque Lenin, where everyone goes with the kiddies on weekends. It is a wooded place just south of the city, not far from the airport. She wanted them to keep open the ferris wheel and rides. But Cuba was not only wracked with fears, it was also in the early stages of galloping poverty. Our idea of enduring all these presents from Uncle Sam was to stop smiling.

Well, tell me, what did we have to smile about? Never mind what my intellectual friends told me. I knew we were about to be invaded. By now I even knew where and passed it along. Fidel had already sent battalions on their way south to the Bay of Pigs. They'd be there in less than a week.

We knew he had stopped sleeping. We heard he lived on black coffee and fast catnaps. Never mind that we had almost no real army or air force, just young men in training. And that they had yet to reach their Bay of Pigs destination.

So here I was, welcoming a hundred friends to celebrate

something for which I couldn't work up a smile. Conscience? Never for one moment think that Victor Sanchez felt uneasy or guilty about serving both the Yanqui and my own people.

In my mind spying for the CIA was what paid for it all. It gave me dollars, advance information and the ear-hole in which to feed misinformation. Until tonight, I moved easily in my own skin.

Rita had had them put up a tent. Inside, at one end, she and my mother were putting together the meal. They had half a dozen friends helping. At the other end a trio – the boys from the rooftop of the Hotel Nacional – were treading their way through the 'Malagueña', slowly enough for people to dance to it.

The younger ones had no idea of what to do with Lecuona's soulful music, but it stirred them nevertheless. The old timers smiled dreamily and knew exactly what to do, intricate but relaxed steps.

I breathed in deeply and the smells of dinner entered my soul. To hell with Yanqui invasions. A load seemed to lift from my heart. You must realise that, raised as I was, I seldom if ever ate my own mother's cooking. But tonight, for a cold dish, my mother had made enchila de cangrejo, a very spicy crab salad. It smelled equally of the sea and of a tart, lemony mayonnaise.

On two alcohol burners she and some friends were warming a great tureen of arroz con gris, rice with dark beans. It had a basic, earthy smell of primitive farming that came down to us directly from our Arawak ancestors, a cuisine invented long before the white tastes of the conquistadores.

And above a charcoal brazier Rita and another girl turned over and over puerco adado, cuts of pork marinated for days and now filling the park with the hot, delicious smoke of broiling, fatty meat. Another Arawak throwback. The hunters have returned in victory. Soon we can sink our teeth into the kill. Yes, it may be human flesh but, what the hell, it's marinated.

I watched like one under hypnosis. It was as my mother often remarked, Rita was like her daughter. They and the other women moved back and forth in a very small space without interfering with each other, as if for sure they had been doing a malagueña together all their lives. They didn't speak; eye gestures were enough.

Now the musicians – these were middle-aged guys, in their 40s, who couldn't be counted on for the new tunes – broke into the Dizzy Gillespie 'Tango Havana'. It wasn't much without Dizzy's elevated trumpet, but the soprano sax gave it that high, nervous shriek and got people out on the dance floor, twisting back and forth in the only tango Cuba can claim.

Because Rita and my mother were the planning-ahead kind of women, this was not just Big Victor's Twenty-first Birthday. It was also understood that my mother would have a heart-to-heart talk with Rita's parents about an accounting job in the western tobacco plantation. She had been avoiding this for some time, mainly by not returning to Havana. Now she had let herself be trapped.

People had started arriving around eleven. Now it was after one in the morning, just starting. Four times I had refilled the punch bowl with my own daiquiri made the old-time way of old dark rum, lemon juice, new white rum, raw cane syrup and Añejo rum, which is half-way in age between dark and white.

In a great tin laundry tub a chunk of ice stood as an island amid chill water around which bobbed icy bottles of dark Mexican Dos Equis beer. I had found, in a deserted storeroom at the Nacional, some Dewar's Scotch El Pequeño had not had time to take with him.

It pains me to report that some of my own countrymen, offered this or daiquiri punch, chose Scotch whisky. The drink of the enemy. In just that way, as the Yanqui fought his cold war with the Russian, he became enamoured of vodka. People!

Since Rita had handled the invitation list, we had a large group of young Fidelista bureaucrats to offset the more elderly 'first families' of Havana, those who hadn't panicked in early 1959 and escaped.

Now those families were split between Miami and here. Those who lived among the Yanqui wrote constantly of gold on the streets. Every now and then someone in Havana would be lured at great risk to the mainland. There, even with the support of relatives, they would find real capitalism, which offers you the freedom to grow rich or die trying.

By now a return flow of refugees was coming back. In Cuba they could lie around on the beach and never starve. In Miami they had to work a sixty-hour week just to stay alive in lowly minimum-wage jobs. Only those with burning ambition stayed with the Yanqui and tried to make the Yanqui dream work.

As the birthday boy, I did what I usually do, remained a moving target. I moved around, said hello, joked a little and moved on. People would grab my arm and hold me from leaving them. One o'clock became two, then three.

It was nice, in a way. It meant they liked me. It meant they had no idea of the double life I led. Or, if they did, approved of it. For some it meant Rita had an influential job and they wanted to butter up to her through me. Who cares?

Listen, there is no point in pretending that human nature under socialism is that much different from human nature under any other government. Nor can I swear that for sure the purpose of every birthday party must always be social. But, most of all, it doesn't spoil my enjoyment to tell the truth about something.

Can you imagine if I had been one of those hypocrites who talks big? 'Yes, indeed. My sainted mother? She is administradora grande, head manageress in a big leisure centre. Where? To the East. Where to the East? Say, look who just came in! Pardon me, will you?'

No, I am sure everybody knew where Maria Sanchez worked. By now she was famous. And she looked terrific, like Rita's smaller, older sister. If you look like Maria Sanchez nobody cares what you do for a living.

Ay, what an evening. What a night. Four o'clock came and went.

Was it the food? The idea that we were dancing on the rim of an earthquake Uncle Sam would soon explode? Was it being among all the people who loved me? Daiquiris as our ancestors made them? Scotch as the Yanquis drank it? Being with the two women I loved? I was floating with happiness.

'Big Bic,' a tall girl demanded, 'that cannot be your mother. She is your little sister, yes?'

This girl hung out with the weedy guy I didn't like, Bernal. Estela was very thin but not plain. By which I mean she had a good figure but a very slender one. When she danced with Bernal she made him look the kinked shrimp he was.

Right now, though, Bernal was dancing with Rita. She had a faraway look in those deeply black eyes of hers. Was she bored or intrigued? You would never know. It was the fashion, in Havana, as almost everywhere else in the world, for young people to dance with an I'm-not-here look on their face.

Saves a lot of trouble, that look. You can, for example, like Bernal, keep brushing against Rita's great, lovely breasts, exciting the nipples beneath the thin pale orange knit blouse. I know what I'm talking about. Doing this even to an iceberg will cause a meltdown. But in Rita's case the word is volcanic.

'Look at that piojo!' I glared in Bernal's direction.

Estela swung me towards her as if we were already dancing . . . and we were. 'He spends his life making me jealous. We must give him something to worry about.'

She thrust into me, a direct slam of her pelvis against mine. It is easy for a female to deliver but painful for a male to receive. Still, what part of sex is without some pain? She was just tall enough to excite me front on front, bony enough to get through any layer of clothing to the dark, waiting flesh beneath. She was doing to me what Bernal was doing to Rita. People!

I could see that Rita's face was no longer in its where-am-I mode. I pushed Estela away from me but this only gave her the space to launch another frontal attack. Now Bernal was watching us.

This time I edged sideways and started to remove myself as one half of a couple. Estela threw her arms around me and gave me a great, open-mouthed kiss, her teeth hungry to chew my tongue. There is no mistaking the start of such a kiss. The movies have perfected every nuance of it.

I prised her loose and went to the punch bowl. Bernal came striding up.

'I saw that.'

'Pardon?' I swung around to meet him but the daiquiri in my paper cup spilled across his eyes. There is nothing half-way about that much rum and lemon juice in your eyes. 'Oh, sorry! Sorry!' I began mopping him with a paper napkin.

Rita arrived laughing. She dipped a cup into the punch and offered it to Estela. 'Next?'

There was a shout of laughter and then, suddenly, it mounted to a roar. I had no idea we were that funny. My mother, who had started towards us, stopped dead. Like everyone else she was staring out the entrance of the tent.

Fidel walked in.

Alone. Without Raul or Che, but with two bodyguards a few yards behind him.

In those days . . .! Ay, que lagrimas, in those days his beard was black as sin and his big frame walked in a military strut. He grinned a lot in those days, in those tense days, his cigar clenched in the corner of his mouth. Since then I have seen that beard go grey and the strut debased into a painful shuffle.

Bernal was sponging his eyes and whining: 'Que paso?'

My mother walked forward and stood before Fidel. 'Wel-come to my son's birthday,' she said. She was carrying two cups filled with daiquiri punch. She handed him one. 'Salud! Y viva la revolucion!'

Fidel's eyes brightened. He lifted his glass. 'La revolucion.'

'La revolucion,' a hundred voices shouted.

He threw back his head and finished off the daiquiri. He looked awful, truly used up, big bluish bags under his eyes. So the rumour about not sleeping was true. There was also a rumour that the CIA had paid the mafia to assassinate him. The one I liked best was that he was actually a Russian double. The real Fidel had died in Moscow.

Now, the real Fidel was standing here looking like he hadn't slept in a month. It didn't stop him from going at once to the best looking woman in the place, Rita, and brushing her hand with his beard.

He turned slightly to look at me, as if asking permission.

We had never actually met face to face and so, like millions of Cubans, I had the feeling he didn't know me. It seemed I was wrong.

'Big Bic,' he murmured, in a voice almost as soft as El Pequeño's. 'I am pleased to meet you at last.' Then he turned away and his voice roared like a lion to drown out the trio and the people crowding closer for a look.

'People of Havana!' he shouted. 'A special night! Tonight . . .' His eyes snapped with sudden mischief. 'Tonight . . . no speeches.'

With that he took my mother in his arms. The soprano saxophone moaned the three notes that begin 'Siboney', high, like a surprised howl of sexual climax. The accordion and guitar swooped down in broken syncopation, flooding us with our own music. We all danced.

The sky in the east had gone a pale pearly colour. We kept dancing.

When later I tried to remember everything, it seemed to me he had only been with us five minutes, if that. And yet he had found time to join me for a moment as I stood with his bodyguards, passing time.

One was Ramos, not my idea of a bodyguard for even a minor rodent, but politically savvy. However, the other was carrying a magnum pistol. He was my old sidekick, Luis.

Amazing, no? When he killed for El Pequeño he was a vicious hit man, mowing down innocent knife-wielding girls. Now he was guarding all our hopes and dreams of happiness. But he was still the same Luis, very fast on the trigger, to whom I may have owed a piece of my life.

'They tell me Manolo is in Miami,' he said. 'He has a whole new family of daughters, they say.'

'So much the worse for the American dream. They will get rich or die trying.' Fidel joined us. With movements of his eyebrows he signalled that he wished to be alone with me. They left.

'One thing worries me, Victor.'

'Only one?'

The cigar in his lips was a Melendez. I knew the aroma. If I smoked I would smoke this Melendez, a panatela, long and thin, from Rita's family business. But my mother forbade me ever to smoke and, somehow, I never got the habit.

'Victor,' he went on, 'it is unbelievable that we already know their beachhead. We even know what they don't, that their landing craft will run aground offshore because the Bahia de Cochinos waters are too shoal. Cuba is an island with a dozen better landing places.

'Put yourself in my shoes, Victor. I am facing a Goliath who knows I have only a slingshot and some stones. Now Goliath taps his forehead and says: "hit me right here."'

I started to speak but he pressed the palm of his hand on my chest. I didn't look around, but I knew he and I were the tallest men in the place.

'What is more, Victor, this is no simple Goliath out of the Bible. With bombers and Marines and naval artillery. No. This is a Goliath with the atomic bomb.

'I can pull back my arm – ' He cocked his right arm like a baseball pitcher, high and far back, his eyes squinting over their big dark pouches as if to read the catcher's signs. ' – and before I can deliver a stone to his forehead, the stone, Little Cuba, plus Little Jamaica and Little Key West are blown to slime that glows in the dark.'

Around us people were dancing a fast meringue. They paid no attention to either of us. Dancing is important. Dancing well is more important. And being seen to ignore the maximum leader of your nation, in order to dance perfectly, is the most important of all.

I was afraid to speak because I knew he was telling a part of the truth. I could argue. I could say the Yanqui wouldn't atomise Cuba, so close to US soil. But who was I to make such promises?

Now his hand on my chest became a finger prodding me. 'So tell me Victor of the twenty-first birthday, why must I believe you when you say Bay of Pigs is the one, the only, the unique landing place?'

Nobody told me when I started this double agent business that a man could back himself into such a tight corner as this. I thought it would be as easy as having affairs with several women at the same time. You simply had to keep physically fit and not let them feed you too many duplicate meals.

But this was deadly serious. If what he said made sense, Victor Sanchez was for sure either incompetent or a traitor to Cuba.

Near the entrance to the tent, watching Fidel's probing of me, the two bodyguards were joined by the Englishman. He had filled a large glass with my daiquiri punch. I don't remember having invited him and for sure Rita hadn't. She considered him a bad influence on me.

But, hey! Sometimes the hijo de puta gets lucky. Called street smarts.

'Let me say just one thing,' I told Fidel.

'It must be a good one thing, Victor. Don't disappoint me.'

'The one thing is this. You believe the CIA created this invasion, which is true. But who was it lit a match under the CIA? Under Angleton?' I nodded in the direction of the entrance. 'It was the Englishman. Am I wrong?'

'Keep talking.'

'And if it was the Englishman, ask yourself one question: does he want Uncle Sam to win or lose?'

Over their dark pouches of exhaustion his eyes half closed, then opened quite wide. 'You mean – ? Who he represents?' His mouth opened and stayed open, the cigar holding in place by sheer strength of saliva. Then it snapped shut as he glared hard at me.

The meringue had ended and suddenly, around us, couples paused and murmured quietly to each other. Dozens of pairs of eyes shifted this way and that, passing Fidel without landing on him. Cubans have a sense of cortesia even more delicate than their sense of timing.

'I am just a low-level amateur agent,' I said, trying to keep from my voice any sound of begging. I was quite sure my life was on the line but I knew that not showing it was my best, my only, defence.

I remember Fidel as basically a kind person. We all do. But we are all mistaken. No leader is kind. When a leader feels threatened – and at this moment all of us did – he can order the firing squad in a split second. And often did.

'I take Yanqui dollars, lots of them,' I went on. 'I take your pesos, which you never pay me. You know my heart is with Rita, with Cuba and with you. Tell me: with whom is the Englishman's heart?'

Fidel watched me for a long time. His was a high beard. It came up to his cheekbones. To have his eyes staring at you out of this thicket of bristling, curling jungle was a terrifying thing.

I prayed for the band to begin something, anything, 'Yanqui Doodle', for sweet Jesus' sake. Something to lighten the moment and ease Fidel's vengeful heart. There is fear facing one's enemy. Facing someone who begins as your friend and comes to distrust you, there lies death.

The trio struck up an old style version of 'La Cumparsita', a tango everyone enjoys. Fidel grinned at me like a cayman, as if saying: 'You just saved your ass by the thickness of a flea's whisker.'

He gestured to the three men in the entrance. The bodyguards started towards him but the Englishman began to leave. 'Los tres!' Fidel shouted.

When they arrived, the Englishman nodded politely to me. His breath had that same essence of dead sugar cane stench, a mixture of molasses and hydrochloric acid.

'Comrade Feelbi,' Fidel began. 'Visitor from faraway friends on the other side of the earth. I believe Uncle Sam follows a bad plan. Has he been badly advised on purpose? Is Cuba to be a way of humiliating him for the world to see? Is this our fate? Are our sons to die for this?'

'La Cumparsita' stopped with a triple rap. The silence was frightening. I watched the Englishman's drink-softened eyes. They seemed to grow stony, as if frozen. But never once did his posture stiffen, tensed by Fidel's demand.

'Can it be doubted?' the Englishman asked in that offhand way, as if discussing the weather. I considered his answering a question with more questions a sign of how experienced he was in such tight corners.

'Is there any other reason for my being here, Comrade?'

Then he turned towards me. His dark blue eyes glinted like lapis lazuli cufflinks. 'Guapo and I,' he said, 'did not invent Uncle Sam's thirst to conquer Cuba. That already existed. All we have done is misdirect him every step of the way. Tell me, Guapo – '

The god of tight squeezes was choking my throat. I swallowed hard. Whatever I told Fidel would be misleading because the Englishman was being misleading, making me his co-star when I was only his go-between. They were all waiting for me to speak. If I knew Luis, his trigger finger was itching to settle the matter in his normal way.

That was when the bombs began to fall on Havana.

'Bay of Pigs, eh?' Fidel shouted at us, his eyes hot with anger.

They sounded right on top of us. Big, crashing explosions. I put my hands to my ears and searched about me for damage, dust.

Fidel whirled about to leave the tent. In his anger he seemed eight feet tall. 'I see you two later.'

Off he dashed at a loping run, his guards after him. In his wake the explosions began again. They seemed closer.

It was six a.m. when the B-26 attack bombers arrived. They were US property but repainted to resemble Cuban Air Force planes, attacking Havana's military airfield at San Antonio de los Baños. This lay not directly on top of us in Parque Lenin but perhaps a mile or less to the south-west.

They came in low to avoid radar – we had no radar – and dropped a pair of bombs, bu-boom! Then with their fixed, 50-calibre machine-guns they strafed.

There is nothing more demoralising than being on the ground as a plane howls in, machine-guns spitting at you. You watch the bullets hitting in a line until they finish in your stomach. It is a technique perfected by the Nazis in the Spanish Civil War. That's why we use a German word to describe it.

After a moment the B-26s turned. Back on path they dropped another pair of bombs, bu-boom, and strafed more people. Multiplied by however many aircraft. this kept the entire southern part of Havana buried in dust, noise and death.

Being a military base, San Antonio answered back with the deadly four-barrel ack-ack guns made by the Czechs. Although it was all deafening, none of this was important because it was not the invasion.

'That, Handsome, comes in a few days,' the Englishman explained to me.

We were alone in the tent. Everyone had fled north into the city, including Rita and my mother. We remained because we knew Fidel would come back to find us. If we were gone we would be thought to have tried to escape. From him.

'Not the invasion? But a good imitation,' I remarked.

'These B-26s and several more have a disinformation mission. They are supposed to end up, dear boy, in Miami for refuelling and more ammo, carrying papers that identify them as Cuban Air Force defectors.'

'Whose idea was this?'

He almost blushed. 'Need you ask?' he said modestly. His breath, only faintly deodorised by overpowering amounts of lemon and rum, created a danger zone I kept trying to avoid.

'Suppose they are unmasked?'

'Cuba is a small nation. Its supply of qualified pilots is smaller still. Identify someone and his history is public knowledge. They will be unmasked ten minutes after they land in Miami.'

I shook my head. 'Fidel finds it impossible Uncle Sam is so stupid.'

'In the land of the blind, the one-eyed is King.'

'What's that supposed to mean?'

He stared down into the dregs of a drink, swished it about and swallowed it. 'America has blinded itself with devil-hatred. Anything the devil does must be opposed mindlessly, automatically, immediately.'

'And you . . .? You are Satan One-Eye himself, eh?'

'Please, old man, spare my blushes.' He got up, yawned, stretched. 'Only one man is going to be more upset by this fiasco than Dear Old Jim Angleton.'

I listened for more explosions. But they had stopped for good. 'Who are you talking about? El Pequeño?'

He gave me a small smile, as of a professor whose pupil has given the right answer. 'He is a patriot, a champion of capitalism. He sincerely believes his country will return Cuba to the Lansky empire. He has paid out a lot to make it happen. He will be hopping mad.'

'And what about us? Supposing, Comrade Feelbi, you and I have been disinformed, too? Suppose the landing at Bay of Pigs is a lie we were supposed to tell Fidel?'

He stared at his wristwatch for a long moment. 'Dear me, look at the time. Let me be the last to wish you a happy birthday.'

Fidel did not get back to us until very nearly noon. By then, having talked to the soldiers who had defended San Antonio de los Baños airport, having listened to the conflicting radio reports from Miami, he had for sure figured out what the Englishman had already told me.

He returned to Parque Lenin, driving his own Jeep and looking, if anything, more seedy and exhausted than he had at six a.m. 'Four dead,' he announced, indicating the rear seats of the Jeep for us to occupy. Behind him, Ramos and Luis arrived in a second Jeep, bristling with armament. 'Four dead to so cleverly disinform Uncle Sam yet again.'

'A high cost,' the Englishman agreed.

'You global plotters,' the bearded man rumbled, 'you present such costly expense accounts. I will admit,' his smile slashed a down-dropping sabre cut in his beard, 'that when I heard the bombs and assumed you were lying about Bay of Pigs, I felt relief. No more Feelbi. My heart lightened. No more Kremlin over my shoulder, always eager to help.'

The Englishman's smile was done much better, firm, sincere, amiable. You felt that behind those dark blue eyes lived your true friend. Whatever global power he carried was all directed in your favour. Of course, he had no beard to distort this impression.

'Why are you so touchy about having a superpower for a helpful friend?' he asked politely.

113

'If you must ask the question you could never understand the answer.' Fidel's hand went to a breast pocket of his combat jacket, feeling for a cigar. His hand drew out, instead, a long empty brass shell casing that one of the Czech ack-acks had probably thrown into the air.

'My cabinet and I,' he indicated Ramos and Luis with a sarcastic nod, 'have been wondering what to do with you two . . . especialistas. I must say none of us still trusts you as we did before. On the other hand, you have not yet been found to have committed real treason.'

'Innocence,' the Englishman murmured, 'is simply the state of not having yet been caught.'

Castro's laugh rocketed out of his beard like a projectile, sending him into paroxysms of coughing. When he had calmed down his beard still emitted vaguely benign signals.

'Here is your fate, camaradas. I'm giving you this Jeep. Its markings will help you. Ramos will give you proper documentation. Luis will provide you with arms and ammo. You will leave – ' he glanced at his watch, 'no later than one p.m. today.'

'For where?' I asked.

'Guapo! Where else? For the Bay of Pigs.'

Chapter Twenty-Five

We reporters are supposed to notice everything, even though our editor might delete it from the story. The palm trees along Ocean Drive, for instance, bend sharply away from the Atlantic. It's as if they just couldn't get enough of the beat-up Art Deco buildings.

In those days, the early 1960s, this was mostly a slum that had once been grand. Back in the mid-1920s, during a period of affluence before the Crash, people in the garment industry sent their elderly parents to winter in South Miami Beach. The design cliche of that era, battered and worn by the '60s, is today facing a post-pre-modernist new century entirely spruced up and neonised.

In all three eras, '20s, '60s and '90s, the sea breeze was brisk as it swept inland, moaning in the clusters of palm leaves. For this April in 1961, it was also damned chilly.

I had a perfectly good telephone in my warm hotel room and, in fact, an even warmer phone booth in the lobby. But as my mother taught me: a thing worth doing is worth doing well. So I walked, head down against the incoming winds, to a breeze-cooled booth some blocks away and dialled my direct-line connection to Cousin Jim Angleton.

Early this morning the local TV news people had gone insane and broken into regular programming to announce the invasion of Cuba. Maps! Historic sound-bite refreshers! Talking heads! Right on Florida's back doorstep!

Dissident pilots of the Cuban Air Force had taken sanctuary, fresh from bombing raids on their own air fields and their own aircraft, as well as their own comrades at Havana and Santiago de Cuba.

I wasn't in the security loop that knew *exactly* when Cuba was to be attacked, but it seemed premature to me. Also, it seemed eerily unCuban for buddies to start blasting the hell out of each other. About a girlfriend, OK. But about politics?

'Hello?'

There is always a faintly New England schoolmarm tang to Cousin Jim's voice. I do get the instant feeling of reporting to a maiden aunt. But that give-away-nothing greeting had already told me I had the right man. 'Cousin Jim? What's up?'

'Midge? I should be asking you,' he temporised. 'You're closer to the action.'

'So is Meyer and he's flummoxed. And angry.'

'He's got to get it through his head,' Angleton almost snarled, 'that we are not in business solely to pull his chestnuts out of the flames. We have our own agenda just as he has his. When they overlap, or coincide, ours takes precedence.'

'I think he always knew that. He's quite patriotic. But when I talked with him this morning I got a very cool reception.'

'Is he bothering you?'

'Not at all.'

'Because if he gives you any – '

'Cousin Jim, I appreciate your chivalry. In any event, I have my air ticket for Havana, leaving at two p.m. today.'

'I forbid it!'

'The *Times* is sending me.'

'Don't the fools read their own pages? They've blown our state of secrecy. Was there ever a time when clandestine work was so hard to keep clandestine? According to the *Times* the President and his close advisors are tied in knots – not over should we invade but over when. What gives the *Times* the right to betray state secrets . . .?'

'Shocking.'

'Shocking to send a woman into the thick of it.'

'Well . . . not just any woman.' I glanced out the side window of the telephone booth. A short fellow with the look of an acrobat stood with his back to me, away from the wind, lighting a cigarette but close enough to hope he might overhear something useful.

'Cousin Jim, do you have anyone tailing me?'

'Certainly not.' His sibilance crackled in my ear.

'Think hard.'

'Surely, my dear, one would not lie about such an important matter.'

The acrobat lit his cigarette and turned back into the wind. Gleb Khsovko was the name, Tass was the game. I relaxed. 'That's all right then, Cousin Jim. I'll phone you from Havana, yes?'

'Please be careful.'

'What, no last-minute "please stay in Miami"?'

He chuckled frostily. 'I know you headstrong Boardmans. Tell you one thing and you do the opposite. Besides, if the traitorous *New York Times* hands me a free agent in the hottest part of the action, so be it.'

I shivered, as if he'd run ice-encrusted fingers over my bare shoulders. He was a frozen old maid, but the business he was in was even more frigid. I hung up and opened the booth door. Immediately the breeze blew through my hair and I started to shiver again.

'Next?' I called.

Gleb grinned at me. 'Charming capitalist colleague, you look chilled as winter potato.'

'So would you if you'd been talking to my boss.'

'Then ... some hot coffee? Drop of vodka? I have never known an April so cold,' he sighed, 'except back home.'

I sighed. 'I suppose you're on my two p.m. flight?'

'Naturally.' He held out his hand as if to take my arm.

'Don't you have a call to make?'

'I have already tried. My – what is name of one being called? If I am caller he is callee? – callee is gone. Nobody knows where. Callee has wanished in Jeep. Hi-ho.'

'Hi-ho.'

'Is off to vork ve go.'

If we were the seven dwarfs he was clearly qualifying for Dopey. Don't ask: I felt fully Grumpy. He took my arm and we strode towards the nearest coffee shop. And the next invasion.

Chapter Twenty-Six

One day a woman can for sure beg a man never to leave her. She can't live without him. Then let him be called to war and she can't wait to pack him some sandwiches and send him on his way.

Was that unfair to say? It wasn't a war Rita was sending me off to. It was the defence of my mother country against an invasion.

'Do you know what that means, the medallion on the front licence plate of the Jeep?'

'Something about Fidel?' I guessed.

'You are driving *his* Jeep. All Cuba will know it. In the eyes of Cuba, you will be Fidel. Victor, never have I been so proud of you.'

'If I grew a beard, when the Yanqui arrives he can also mistake me for Fidel and ... bu-boom.'

I was a little angry with her and with my mother, who had taken the same patriotic line. However, they had also packed the back of the Jeep with bottles of rum and those little cheese sandwiches dipped in egg and fried like Cuban toast. More than enough for two men, except where was the Englishman now that I was ready to go?

'I have cables to send, old man, and to receive. You start. I'll get a lift and meet you there.'

'Or find a pilot to fly you there?'

'Not a bad idea. I've some strings left to pull.'

'Or sprout wings and fly yourself there.'

'Don't be cheeky, Guapo. I said I'll see you there. Does that sound as if I'm scarpering?'

'If that means turning tail . . . yes.'

'Cheeky bit of crumpet.'

'What is crumpet? You have been calling me crumpet since the day we met.'

'Crumpet. Ah, well, it's a sort of muffin, plain, with big bubbly spaces that sop up melted butter. Delicious with tea.'

'You call me this?'

'Erm.' He was blushing. 'Erm. It derives from the phrase "tasty bit of crumpet" and it's usually said of a young woman. And it is usually cut down just to crumpet. As in: erm, I sniff crumpet. Or, erm. . .'

'You call a man this?'

'Why not? Nothing sexist about Old Kim.'

I was happy to get rid of him. The English! My mother often told me that when British sailors put in at Guantánamo, there were orders to keep them out of the brothel. She never knew why but much later, thinking about my childhood there, I realised the British sailors had very little cash to spend, compared with the Yanquis. No sense looking for deep reasons; cash usually is the answer to most questions.

There is a small staircase, five concrete steps leading up to the front door of my mother's building. She and Rita stood there, waving and blowing kisses as I shifted the Jeep into low gear and drove off through an audience of neighbours.

All right, a performance. It would have been better if I'd found some military things to wear. As it was, I wore a pair of suntan trousers and a much washed olive T-shirt. In my earlier life, as a collector for Lansky, I'd looked very sharp, wide-bottomed slacks, big bronze-riveted belt, a vest of Paisley satin and sometimes a short, pinched-waist jacket. So, I suppose I had got as far from that image as I could as the neighbourhood cheered me off.

The way south and east out of Havana is today a national highway that leads through the centre of our beloved island. If you look at a map you see how wide and narrow we are. It may only be thirty miles from north to south in most places. East to west it must be 500 miles or more.

But in April of 1961 there was no highway. Fidel's gift of a Jeep was smart. Nothing else would have gotten me to the Bay of Pigs except, perhaps, one of those big prime mover six-wheel trucks the Yanquis sold us years ago.

In 1961 I was driving mostly through wilderness. There were shacks now and then by the side of the road because it is in the nature of poor countries for people to have to live as close to a road as possible. But the next step of settling the land – a village, then a town – didn't exist for most of the way.

Matanzas is the name of this area. It starts on the north shore with the hard-currency coastline that stretches from Mariel in the west, through Havana and Varadero Beach. Today, thirty years after, at new resorts and the Marina Hemingway leisure centre, the Yanqui dollar is king.

Today, even though we banned prostitution in 1959, our cute little jineteras patrol the dollar area. They are the only Cubans who have seen a steak, or even a grape, in several years. Fidel tells us they aren't forced to prostitution but do it by choice. Anyway, Fidel brags, our AIDS rate is the lowest. That, at least, is true.

But in 1961, as I bucketed along the roads, some only gravel, there was no dollar ghetto on the north shore. As I travelled south I watched the land gradually drop away to sea level. And below.

By the time I drew near the southern shore I was deep in swamps.

There is now a national park on the Peninsula de Zapata, a total swamp with filigree incisions, bayous and narrow boating creeks. The Zapata is ringed by keys, reefs and tiny islands often under water at high tide. To the east an almost north-south bay, narrow as a dagger, slices up into the marshland.

It is called Bahia de Cochinos, Bay of Pigs.

Hardly more than a wider channel into a swamp, it divides the southern shore of Matanzas into Western Zapata Swamp and its Eastern counterpart. On the eastern edge of the Bay sat the small village of Playa Giron. It existed even then although Playa Giron in those days was only starting its life.

Fidel had decreed that it would be a holiday centre for all of Cuba but especially for amateur fishermen, taking their family on cheap outings. Cabins and camping locations were already being built. A modern road surface led down to it from what is now the Guama Heritage Centre.

And, of course, today's Playa Giron includes the Bay of Pigs Invasion Museum. Why not? We didn't launch it, we repelled it. The glory is to us. Why not celebrate it with a museum that gives Cuban kids a heritage so different from the one Lansky left them with the dollar-jineteras?

But this afternoon, as the sun began to sink at my right hand across endless square miles of sea-level swamp broken by thin bushy salt-grass clusters, there was no invasion, no glory. Not yet.

But what temptation to second-guess that great mistake of Uncle Sam! To wonder how it was that in Washington, where the brains of the hemisphere were supposed to live, there was no surveyor, no geologist, no naturalist, no one at all to point his finger at the map of the Bay of Pigs and say:

'Mira! Water too shoal for anything but a rowboat. Mira! A few workers and militia already encamped here for the beach resort project. Mira! The Bay of Pigs constantly in Fidel's mind. Mira! Outside the island shelf a series of impediments, problems, disappearing islands, and endless hassle of obstacles for manoeuvring the trawlers and freighters bringing in troops. Here one cannot land a rat's ass. Anywhere else would be better.'

When you are in a flat landscape, the sun disappears as if two giant fingers, damp with spit, pinched off a candle flame. The silence rushed over me. The hard rattle of the Jeep, the street noise I was used to in Havana, the long roaring trip by motor . . . all of this fell back into the coming night.

I switched on the Jeep's headlamps but saw they had been altered for combat conditions so that they gave only a narrow beam of subdued light. So be it. Up ahead no young women were waiting in my headlights to flag me down. It is only now, three decades later, that the idea of fucking a woman comes to mind.

Up ahead I saw a few trucks parked under some trees. What seemed to be a cold drinks stand sat alone near the shallow wetlands. As I watched, a lonely electric light switched on. But to someone who has seen very few signs of civilisation in a day of driving, this sign of electricity was welcome.

I parked by the drinks stand. My butt had been pummelled all day by the curved metal driver's seat. Now I moved slowly with giant steps, trying to ease cramps and twinges. Signs advertised cold drinks, clams, crabcakes and fish soup. In this deserted landscape, a wall telephone hung bright and new.

'Felicitationes,' a boy remarked, sarcastically. 'You look like a rooster with a crippled cock.'

'Who insults me?'

The boy appeared behind the counter. Dressed in overalls and nothing else, he had longish, rough-cut blond hair, which puzzled me. A blond in this place?

He seemed in his late teens, slender but not bony like most boys. With one complicated movement, he lifted himself up on the counter, dropped his legs over the front and crossed them, holding on to his knees like a bathing beauty. He began scratching his crotch. He had small, beautiful bare feet, arched and pointing.

I realised he was a girl.

The hair was bleached, I figured, but found out later I was wrong. The face, without make-up, might have passed as a very young boy. But now those sweet curves and indentations had begun to advertise what sex they belonged to. No true breasts yet, but there was the faint suspicion of a very light lipstick colour.

'Guapa,' I said, 'something cold for a thirsty warrior.'

Chapter Twenty-Seven

'It rained all day the night I left,
  'The weather it was dry,' Gleb sang to me.
  'Sun so hot I froze t'death;
  'Susannah, don't you cry.'
  'Oh, Susannah!' I joined in, 'oh, don't you cry fer me,
  ''Cause I come from Alabama with my banjo on my knee.'

I suppose I have always had a weakness for the name Susannah. By two p.m. Gleb and I had finished a half-litre bottle of Moskovskaya vodka, not the green label, but a 100-proof version issued for export only to journalists, diplomats and other KGB agents travelling abroad.

It was now two o'clock but we were not at Miami Airport waiting to board our Havana flight. It had been cancelled. So had all other Havana flights. Airport and Pan-Am personnel had no explanation. Most of us needed none since the Miami papers had all reprinted the *New York Times* stories of the last few days which clearly indicated:

   1. A secret CIA cabal existed to get around Congressional oversight, sidestep Executive branch wariness and trash Constitutional restraints;

   2. A mercenary army of Cuban 'patriots', mostly former Lansky employees, was steaming closer to a landing in Cuba;

   3. A wobbling President Kennedy, not knowing which way to throw the tiger whose tail he grasped, made the mistake of asking the Chiefs of Staff for advice;

   4. They swore the invasion would succeed because all of Cuba would rise up and support the freedom fighters;

   5. These were an invisible army of US spooks, bagmen and ISA assassins waiting in the shadows to set up a new 'free' Cuba by hook, crook or napalm;

6. Many reports of internal uprisings by Cubans were not backed up by any physical signs of such rebellious locals.

On the second half-litre bottle, Gleb was trying now to reciprocate the 'Oh, Susannah' lesson by teaching me, in Russian, a song by which his mother had lulled him to sleep. My Russian was non-existent but Gleb's sketchy, drunken, sentimental translation provided a repetitive phrase about Mom's almond cookies.

We had started our drinking in the lobby of my Art Deco hotel until the singing began. Pained glances from the staff induced us to repair to my room upstairs, a rather nice front suite with a grand view of the beach and the palms.

Here we used the telephone to order food. It arrived about four or five – the narrative grows hazy – more pizza than any two people could ever eat.

'Ah, God, how I wish for New York City!' Gleb cried. He cried a lot. Almond cookies turned him teary. Now Manhattan pizza started his sobbing again.

'So thin, so fine. Not too much tomato. A plethora of cheese. Ah, God, the pizza of New York City.'

I did a few alcoholic moments on Manhattan Jewish food, mentioning in passing Lou G Siegel's restaurant where I had first met Meyer Lansky.

Gleb snorted to clear his upper respiratory tract of tears. 'Rank amateur.'

'Meyer?'

'Compared to Kim.'

I considered the comparison. 'I know you think highly of Comrade Kim.'

'Excuse me. Not high-lee. High-esssst.'

'You must stand in line for such idolatry. Jim Angleworm heads the queue.'

'Anglebaum. Anglewurst.' He started chuckling at his wittiness but in a moment the chuckles became sobs. 'It can do no harm,' he managed to mumble, 'to remark on the gullibility of Angleturd.'

'He buys Kim one hundred per cent.'

Gleb managed to shift back from sobs to chuckles again. Great tears washed down his cheeks as he smiled. I knew for a fact that by now he had to be crying pure Moskovskaya.

'He buys Cuba,' Gleb informed me. 'He has convinced them all that Kim's scenario is real. You have heard of a folie à deux? This is a folie of the entire covert operations section. They all believe exists a real liberation movement and invasion force and the transubstantiation of wine and bread into blood and flesh.'

This left us both speechless for quite a while. He began rubbing my legs, which are the longest part of me and require, or at least could benefit from, long, intensive friction.

In the morning . . .

In the morning I awoke alone to the sound of Atlantic wind moaning inland through bending palms. The little fellow had left. I vaguely recall it was getting on for daylight when I felt him ease off the bed and splash cold water in his face. Then I returned to sleep.

Now I saw by my watch, lying on the floor by the bed, that it was past nine a.m. and, well, and I had to, well, be up and doing. Finding out things. Phoning things. Being a correspondent, a spook, all that. But first some women's work.

No, I hadn't managed to fumble in a diaphragm. Yes, we seemed to have been at it quite a lot. These little fellows amaze one. First, that they're not at all daunted by tall women and, second, it does seem to spur them to supernatural feats of performance. My current husband, whom I hadn't seen in many weeks, was a big, tall galoot who considered once a week as about all a wife deserved.

I will say this about Moskovskaya. Its hangover is a small one. But it lasts all day. I found it almost impossible to do my Cousin Jim's work or even to make legible notes about the many, many things Gleb had babbled at my breast. He had, in point of fact, blown the whole Cuban adventure as sprung full-blown from the brow of Jove-Philby.

The Why Girl, with the help of Moskovskaya, had produced an espionage coup to rank with the highest efforts of the greatest spies. True, I had left it to the last second. But there was still time to put the brakes on the roller-coaster and save Uncle Sam from chaos and humiliation.

My hand produced a fine tremor that turned my penmanship into the anxious scribble of an electrocardiograph pen. Um, sorry, you have six minutes to live.

It took me an hour to produce even a brief memo for Cousin Jim. The text of it would not please him. It made clear the CIA had been cruelly hoodwinked by Kim. He had conned the Agency into doing a very thorough job of trashing Uncle Sam's standing in the Caribbean.

It stood poised to put Fidel squarely inside Khrushchev's loop. Then, within a year, missiles based ninety miles offshore.

CIA Charge into Ambush. Castro's Intimate Allies.

Gleb had waxed particularly lyrical about the inspired choice of the totally useless Bay of Pigs as a theatre in which to dramatise America's demon-driven will to suicide.

I put it all down, shakily but readably. All I had to do now was get to my favourite phone booth and read the news downline to Angleton. And kiss my career as a spook goodbye. Because it was clear, even to a novice like me, that Cousin Jim's fatuous Anglophilia had played right into the KGB's hands.

In years to come, trying to piece together the embarrassing self-wounding called Bay of Pigs – and the other monstrosities that flowed from it – other names would become central. But the original impetus had come from Angleton. Whatever he did from 1961 on, his colleagues would see him as the greatest enemy the CIA ever had.

Prince of Secrecy, High Caliph of Illegal Adventure, Chief Perverter of Constitutional Safeguards. One day a new chief would ask him to leave. Quietly. That would be the one and only punishment meted out to him by a nation he had damaged as severely as a knife thrust into the bowels.

'Every single CIA decision,' Gleb had bragged, 'has been a mistake created by Kim. And you ask me why my opinion of him is so high?'

'You're his duty officer, I guess.'

'Case officer.' He blinked at his own drunken daring in

explaining so precisely how he stood with Comrade Kim. 'Since before the war,' he added, proudly.

I frowned now, remembering that confession, and added it to my memo to Cousin Jim. I couldn't suppress this report. It would sink my career. In the time-honoured fashion of bureaucracies, they would shoot the messenger. Me.

But, as hideous as it would be for Cousin Jim, he had to know that it would end in missile bases targeted all over the US. It was important that he be told just how long –

My frown deepened. I dug in my purse for my diary-calendar. Flipping the pages I carefully counted days since my last period. Right. I had started ovulating yesterday. Or last night.

Oh, Susannah, oh, don't you cry for me.

Chapter Twenty-Eight

In the middle of the night, Terry got restless. That also sometimes happened to Rita. She would wake me up by teasing me into an erection she would then proceed to demolish, slowly. But Terry was not at all like Rita.

Growing up as I did, I have seen every kind of female body. Rita's is my absolute favourite, entirely feminine, with breasts that resemble her buttocks in their sweet melon-like richness.

Terry was another type in every way. Physically, she was slender and boyish, underdeveloped, with long calves, no hips and breasts one had to take almost on faith.

But all of her was made very carefully, quality work, with well placed bones in her cheeks and ankles, masterful carving of toes and fingers and lips and ears. After her physical beauty, spiritually . . .

Somewhere along the line, perhaps back in Ohio, perhaps in her home state of Massachusetts, someone had convinced Terry she was a goddess. Once that happens, as we know, the rules for goddesses are different.

It didn't matter that she dressed in one-piece overalls whose shoulder straps barely covered her nipples. Or that a fine layer of pinkish dust produced small crumbs in her crotch and armpits, tiny pearls of sand and sweat.

Nor did it affect her role as goddess that her Spanish was really bad, ungrammatical, mispronounced. Quite the contrary. Her role was to be the golden idol before whom men knelt, prayed and – as long as they were on their knees – pleasured the goddess all night long.

This she now indicated at well past midnight by waking me with words. 'Victor,' she explained, 'Terry's horny again.'

Janet Teresa Peabody left Ohio State campus at Kent, as far as I could tell, with a dozen other undergraduates who had volunteered to spend the summer of 1960 'helping Fidel with the harvest'.

I don't believe they were part of the Vinceremos group which came down later from the States, older pro-Fidelistas with well-developed skills. The 1960 group were unskilled kids. Their assignment was chopping cane, something a goddess does not do.

Terry convinced a boy named Kevin to escape with her to Havana and throw themselves on the US consulate there. They accepted a hitch from a melon farmer who abandoned them in the town of Aguada de Pasajeros, east of the Bay of Pigs vacation area-to-be.

There they had fallen in with half a dozen construction workers their own age. 'We got started with resin from Jamaica, by way of Grand Cayman,' she reminisced. 'Real good hash, made from ganja.'

'And then the Caymans people brought in horse,' I suggested.

She had a habit of lying absolutely motionless in a kind of artist's model pose. A model, that is, posing for a statue of a goddess. You have no idea what it's like to watch a live body that mimics alabaster that way. Not even a blink, a twitch, nothing.

'Horse and coke,' she agreed at last. 'We really turned on those boys. We had a real business going. My uncles would be real proud of me.'

127

'Uncles? Back in the States?'

'One's a banker. The other runs a machine tool factory. The Navy's his big customer.' She frowned slightly. 'You could say I was America's Number One Real Ambassador to Cuba. Number One Real American Fan of Fidel. Bringing them the latest high-tech products.'

'Your family keeps up with you?'

A scornful laugh, more of a low, moaning complaint. 'My folks got divorced the year I left for Cuba. My brother OD'd himself. Nobody even invited me to the funeral.'

'So it's just you and Kevin now?'

'One of the construction guys decided Kev was cutting the coke too thin. He and Kev had a real knife fight. Kev really lost. Out here in the boonies,' she explained airily, 'such things really happen all the time. By now, I figure crabs have eaten Kev.'

Her eyes widened as if previewing a shocking bit of behaviour to come. 'And I have really eaten that crab.'

'And the boy who knifed him?'

'Took off. Really vanished. His grandfather owns the drinks stand. I work for him. It's no real fun putting out for a real elderly person. He spends all his time running the Cayman traffic. I spend most of mine really getting it up for him.'

She had by now switched on a brilliant 100-watt bulb over the brass bedstead. I watched her naked body. It contorted, I think without her knowing it, into the swaying poses of the ancient sculpture of India, where all the goddesses look like Rita.

Then she got out of bed and walked around the rickety old frame house, switching on electric lights until the place was a blazing beacon luring seamen into the shoals. At each lamp or fixture she would pause and pose, pose and pause, silently, not looking at me, sure of the effect she was having.

I had no idea why I was weak enough to be lying here cheating on the woman I would always love for the rest of my life. Cheating on Rita with a tow-headed Yanqui tramp who wasn't worth one of Rita's pubic hairs.

'And the language,' Terry said then. She raised her arms over her head and struck a new pose in the lamplight. 'Really!

I mean, why does he expect me to speak real Spanish the way he does? I can't tell you how happy I am to put out for a real American like you.'

'Soy Cubano,' I snapped at her, angry at such ignorance.

She came back to the bed and stretched her legs out wide to show me the cornsilk blondeness of her muff. She began playing with herself as she watched me watching her.

'You can't be real Cuban. You Cuban boys go for gigantic titties.'

'How would you know?'

'It's the blonde hair. It has to be.'

'Is this some sort of audition?' I asked her.

'If so I'm flunking you.' I slid sideways off the bed and started to rise to my feet.

'Nobody escapes,' she cried. 'Eat!'

She launched herself at me, crotch first, sitting down hard on my face as my head hit the floor. Far away, as if in a dream muffled by her thighs, I heard what could have been an explosion. Then more.

Hot salt piss flooded over me. Shells began to howl past overhead as if the house had been electrified for target practice. An instant later a mortar shell howled insanely through the roof and exploded.

She was flung off me, dripping urine and spurting blood.

The house blazed with light and flames. Her rag-doll body split at the pelvis as she crashed into the wall. Arterial blood pumped out of her ripped throat, ebbed, failed. I blacked out.

I came to looking up at the stars. The roof had been torn away. Tracers hissed by overhead. In the distance 50-calibre machine-guns stuttered. Mortars coughed to the left near the water. Their shells exploded to the right by the trucks.

She had covered me with so much blood I had no idea if I was actually wounded. After a while, feeling myself, I realised Terry had died shielding me. She hadn't planned it that way. But as the first mortar round destroyed the house, this Yanqui daughter had saved my ass.

Number One Yanqui Ambassador to Cuba. First casualty of the Yanqui invasion.

I got to my feet, remembering the telephone I had seen in the drinks stand. I stumbled out into a night that shouted and stank of heavy explosives. I tried to see where I was.

Nothing looked right because the houses had all been flattened. A round of tracers started to cut me in half. I dropped on my belly and wriggled across an open space. The drinks stand looked as if a big hand had pushed it sideways into the sand.

The telephone on the wall now lay in the sand. Oigame! a dial tone. I waited as tracer bullets sparked past. By their light I managed to dial a toll-free number pasted on the inside windshield of Fidel's Jeep. It rang. Mortar shells crashed. It rang.

'Castro aqui.'

'Victor Sanchez aqui.'

'Speak louder.'

'Sanchez, at Bay of Pigs. It is as we promised you. The landing is on.'

'Now? Where are you?'

Somewhere towards the beach I heard a man's voice, amplified by a bull horn. He was shouting hoarsely in English. Another man, further away, shouted back in Spanish. They continued to howl at each other, a dialogue of confusion and babel.

'Playa Giron. I can't see much. No airplanes. Only mortars, machine-guns, sub-machine-guns.'

'No airplanes?'

'No airplanes.'

'Victor, amigo. Call back in half an hour. Every half hour.'

I hung up the phone. I sat there for a long time, using sand to rub her piss and blood from my face, my neck, my shoulders, arms, belly, crotch. Emptying herself on me that way ... deliberately? In panic? I was never to know. Everything smelled of Terry, her own musk, the pinkish pearls her body generated. But she was gone for good.

In a moment I would have to find my way back to her body, collect my clothes, do something with her corpse, something ... something that was a memorial to her death. Because, listen to me. For sure, if we had both died, Fidel would still be sitting alone at his telephone, waiting.

She had come to Cuba to help Fidel. Finely-made Yanqui goods, eager to help. It had taken a year but, in the end, she helped. And now he expected me to call again in half an hour. He must have thought I had a bullet-proof dugout for the telephone. Nothing would be here in half an hour, including me.

Chapter Twenty-Nine

Jim and I, in our pre-Alzheimer twilight, are devoted to eating places in Alexandria, Virginia, or Georgetown, where the chef produces unusual, but not bizarre, food and the patrons speak quietly while a CD player works its way at minimum volume through chamber music. Make mine Mozart.

Susannah, who shares a Sunday meal with us every month or so, has always been an ideal companion. That was before she gave birth to Tanya, who is now a Terrible Two. *And* a brunette.

'You were never a Terrible Two,' I told Susannah the other Sunday as Tanya began moving from table to table, giving the men great simpering smiles of unsubtle sexuality while carefully treading painfully on the ladies' toes.

'Tanya! Come back here!'

They are both tall for their age, a heritage from me. As for their fathers . . . When Susannah took her little girl to the toilet, Jim patted my hand. 'Don't you think she's ready to tell us who the father is?'

'No more than I am to reveal to Susanna who her blood father was. Fortunately she did have a legal father. By getting killed in Vietnam poor Emory relieved me of any awkward confessions.'

'And the Russian?'

'Kim died in 1987 but Gleb was younger. I was told he was

dead and I've accepted it as true. But there's no corpus delicti. What do you suggest? I dun him for Susannah's dental work?'

'I suppose you could make queries among your spook pals.'

I glanced around the room. Spook pals, indeed. We were out in the Maryland countryside on a beautiful spring day. Of the eight tables inside I could identify the people at six. Of the six, three I would classify as spook pals.

'Fair-weather friends. You can sense they feel their territory is being invaded. A place like this,' I told Jim, 'has to be careful who it lets book a table. Being with Defence and showing the face on TV now and then qualifies me for a reservation. But if it were based on my old life most restaurants would set their fiercest attack rats on me.'

'Paranoid,' Jim remarked, shaking his head. 'I covered this town since before the war. I say you're imagining things.'

'You were never a clandestine.'

'So?'

'A different set of rules governs us. Or, worse, no rules at all.' Tanya came at me like a firebolt from Hell, ramming into my lap and jerking the tablecloth almost hard enough to spill water, wine and the works.

I knew – I didn't have to look about me – that every damned eye in the place had registerd this Terrible Two atrocity.

'Gamma!' she shrieked. 'I peepee!'

The two tables who didn't know me were grinning. The six tables containing spook pals preserved that false po-face that tells you they not only heard the child, they deplore her and you and the dress you're wearing. Worse, they are petrified with fear that you will come over to them and strike up a chat.

'Amazing, isn't it?' Susannah said loudly, dragging her child off my lap. 'They say the Great Stone Face is up in New Hampshire somewhere?' Her voice had risen to room-filling level. 'But it's RIGHT HERE.'

'Tanya,' Jim said, getting to his feet, 'I saw a sandpile outside.' He grasped her hand and hauled her off for a tour of inspection, nodding politely here and there to people he knew.

'Coward,' I muttered.

Susannah watched him leave. She has my long body, arms, legs, neck. She has a completely different face, very broad with prominent cheekbones. No, not Russian. She is some kind of Dutch throwback to the first Boordmaans.

'You're not going to be stupid, are you?' she asked with a big, bright smile for the audience to see, 'and pick a quarrel with Jim and get a divorce? I want you to stay married to this one, yes?'

'Yes.' I glared at her. 'He's only the second man I ever wanted to stay married to.'

'You're not going to remind me about magnificent Dr Domandi at Vassar.'

'Wonderful, lovely man.' A telling pause. 'And your choice?'

'Certainly not the idiot whose DNA you see unravelling so disastrously in Tanya.'

For some reason this threw us both into deep laughter. 'What I like about our arrangement,' I said then, 'is that my daughter is really and truly my daughter and nobody else's.'

'Yeah. Exactly my sentiments. Isn't that Cory and Sam in the far corner?' She had put her hand over her mouth to foil eavesdroppers.

'Yes it is. And over by the bonsai it's Ginnie and Max. And neither pair of them has done anything but faint frigid nods and chill smiles.'

'People whose children's birthday parties I attended?' Susannah asked.

'They're all retirees. I suppose they don't want to be reminded of the bad old days. Least of all Bad Midge. I did something totally out of bounds.'

'Whatever it was, you're godmother to one of their kids, as I recall.'

'Susannah, to hell with them.'

'What a town.'

'What,' I agreed, 'a town.'

We parked outside the Pentagon which is just as busy a place on Sunday as any other day. I left Jim with Susannah and Tanya while I showed my pass and got myself upstairs to my office. I wanted to pick up a report I'd left behind. It was a bit of a surprise to see my WAC sergeant May Beavers busy at her desk.

'May! How enterprising of you.'

She looked more attractive than usual. She shoved some papers in a vinyl holder and rammed it in her large handbag. 'Just finished.' She got to her feet and gave me a big smile. 'See you tomorrow, Ms Boardman.'

She was gone, only the clack of her high heels growing distant on the long stone highway of a Pentagon corridor. One of those unsettling things happened, an episode of pre-cognition. Do you ever get them? You're walking along a street and someone you haven't seen for a while comes into your mind. And then, a moment later, she rounds a corner in real life and comes towards you.

I had that pre-cognition staring down at May's neatly squared-off desk book, pencil container, two-hole punch and faint sprinkles of fingerprint powder.

Well, Lord, you'll say, not pre-cognition at all. How would the average person know what fingerprint powder looked like? There are two kinds, light with finely divided particles of aluminium powder mixed in, and dark, with micro-granules of graphite.

The top of Sergeant May Beavers' desk is the normal piece of battleship grade grey vinyl. It shows light and dark powder equally, I suppose. The one might pass as face powder from a compact. The other . . .? Well, try pencil-sharpener shavings, the greasy black part.

At her desk, for some reason, May had been dusting something for fingerprints. Depending on what it was, the prints could be photographed – not a good idea unless you had everything set up in a lab – or lifted by applying pressure-sensitive tape.

Why, yes, since you ask, there was a bit of it rolled into a ball at the bottom of the sergeant's wastebasket. You could see she wasn't a real pro, just someone hastily seconded into clandestine work. A real pro would have taken the bit of tape with her. Or swallowed it.

I picked at it and finally managed to separate and unroll the three-inch square. Yes, indeed, fingerprints, the black-powder kind, but too messy to be used. She'd lifted a second set and taken them with her.

Whose? Lord, not mine. No profit in producing yet another tired impression of the Boardman pawprints. They are on file all over Washington. Someone I'd seen lately? Or borrowed something from? Or what?

It really didn't make sense. The only thing to be noted was that someone was preparing some sort of dossier on Midge Boardman. May had been asked – ordered? – to do the ground work.

When I got back to the car, not carrying the report I'd stopped off to collect, only Susannah noticed. 'Didn't need it, after all?'

'Need what?' I asked.

Her face went blank. She settled back on the seat and gazed out the window. 'Virginia is so beautiful this time of year,' she said. 'Don't you think?'

Did this have anything at all to do with Bad Midge and the disgraceful episode of rule-breaking way back in 1961 as the Bay of Pigs fiasco was starting, and ending, all within forty-eight hours?

I suppose, to understand what I had done back then, one would need to know all the rules of what is called agentcraft, by which spooks operate, live, die and are judged.

The rules are endless. Often they are made up to cover a specific problem that will never again occur. Let me refresh your childhood memories of the fable called the Emperor's New Clothes.

Two con men convinced the Emperor they were master tailors. They hit him with a huge bill for raiment so shimmering with value that it was invisible. When the Emperor showed himself to his subjects, everyone was amazed.

'But, look,' cried a child, pointing his finger, 'the Emperor is naked.'

Thus, the Only Rule of intelligence work is simply: don't give the con away. Don't blow the whistle. Admit nothing.

Keep up the side. Protect the team. However it's expressed, this is the Only Rule.

Intelligence keeps the fable very much alive, even now when we have lost our main partner, the Russians, in this grisly paso doble. What both CIA and KGB hacks did was to inflate each other. When your enemy is great, you gain stature and an equally cushy budget.

So the chief work of all intelligence units is to keep mum about being naked as jaybirds. We voters nod sagely and marvel at how good our people are to hold such a clever adversary at bay. No one points a finger and cries, 'The Emperor is naked.' Too many political reputations, too many heavy-industry jobs, depend on never pointing.

That may be one reason Defence hired me as a spokesperson. Of course, there has never been a single drop of love lost between Defence and the CIA. A matter of conflicting budgets and mutual distrust.

So having years before gotten CIA hopping mad did me no harm later with Defence. Not just as a token female, but as someone who could speak for Defence without once acknowledging that there is actually no enemy from whom we need to defend ourselves.

But I wasn't always so clever. That April, standing for hours in the Midge Boardman Memorial Phone Booth on South Miami Beach, feeding in endless amounts of small change while the incoming breeze howled past, I did something so stupid I can hardly believe it myself.

I pointed the finger and cried: 'The Emperor is naked.'

It began when I smoothed out the piece of hotel letterhead on which I had written down every damaging detail Gleb had babbled to me of the Philby plot to bankrupt US reputation in the Caribbean and place the infant Castro regime in the crushing embrace of the Bear.

I dialled Cousin Jim's private number. It rang for quite a while but I knew he had to be there.

'Yes' he finally answered, his monosyllable peevish.

'Midge here. I'm afraid I've got some bad stuff from Sovint. We've never had this product before.'

'Where . . . are . . . you?'

'Oh, still in Miami Beach.'

'Then you are totally ignorant of what has been happening off the south coast of Cuba?'

'That's just the point. What I have to report may change your. . .'

The line went dead.

I found enough change to place the call again. This time his 'Yes?' was more than peevish. You could call it pissed-off. 'I have to read this, Cousin Jim. Can you switch a recorder into this line?'

'If it will get you off the line any sooner.' I heard a click. 'Go ahead.'

'Subject swears the entire project was created by KGB agent Harold Kim Philby over a period of years. Subject swears KGB object is to secure Cuba as missile base by frightening Castro into closer alliance. Details include making Castro think only Soviet Union can protect him. Subject also – '

I heard the click again. 'Am I still recording?'

I got a dial tone.

Having run out of change I trudged back to a camera store on Ocean Drive and got the man to change a ten dollar bill. Back at the booth, I got Cousin Jim again. This time it rang without being answered. After thirty rings I hung up and tried again, hoping I'd been calling a wrong number.

No. The second time I let it ring forty or fifty times. Well, if things were happening in Cuba, he might have been called away from his desk. I waited ten minutes and dialled again. Still no answer. I took a walk back to the hotel. No messages.

Station Miami, the CIA office, had a telex system like the ones banks use, absolutely secure and untamperable. All of us contract spooks had been told we had the right to use that telex if we couldn't get through by phone. But I don't believe any of us were told how hard it was to convince Station Miami we had a right to anything.

I got there about ten that morning. A three-storey office building off Flagler, it had an entryphone that showed three tenants, none of them CIA, of course. I rang all three bells but nobody answered. Then I went across Flagler and used the telephone booth there.

I dialled Angleton very carefully. This time a woman picked up. 'Crown Dry Cleaners. Good morning.'

I cursed, hung up and dialled again, even more carefully. 'Crown Dry Cleaners. Good morning.'

This time, as I hung up, I wondered why Angleton was fending me off. Now, wait. This wasn't as stupid a question as it seems. I knew the news I was bringing implicated him.

But either you're a patriot or you're not. If something you let happen leads to enemy missile bases just off your nation's shores, you cannot cover up. No, I'm sorry, you cannot. Even if it puts your own butt in a sling, you have to ring the alarm bells.

You don't protect the team, you protect your country. You point the finger. Cry havoc. Call off the dogs of war. Cut your losses. Abort. Abort. Abort.

Well, does that begin to tell you how naive I was in those days?

Chapter Thirty

I was born Cuban, but that didn't mean I knew all the answers.

I tried to find a mirror in the destroyed house, now burning, its electricity still on, a mirror to know what a man looks like who has had a woman explode all over him.

Who gave her life for his without intending to.

I found no mirror and staggered out to the Jeep. There I asked myself: why is this a combat vehicle when the driver has no protection at all? Someone back in World War Two decided this was a combat vehicle. I was born too late to know why.

I jumped in, started the engine and backed out of a great pile of rubbish that had once been the drinks stand. In the rear-view mirror, as star shells lit the sky, I could see a man like me, but only a slice of him, eyes, a nose. I swallowed and tasted her again.

The invaders had yet to land. I could see, from the place where tracers came, that they were bogged down in the shoals of the bay. I had the crazy idea of sitting here behind some palms and watching them arrive in the early morning light. I would know most of them.

A parade of pimps, porno studs, male hustlers, arm-breakers, bunco artists, con men, failed croupiers, the whole arsenal of Lansky bravos.

I wouldn't know the rest because they didn't come from the gutters of Havana. Some were mercenaries the CIA never failed to recruit, fellows who lived for torture and loved killing.

But some, poor luckless bastards, were young aristocratic scions of Cuba's richest families, the ones Lansky had fattened like geese with profits from every kind of vice. These families, mostly resettled in Miami, had dues to pay. So, as always, they let the younger members of the family take the strain.

And some were the saddest of all, true patriots of democracy whom Fidel had passed by. Who had then been recruited by the CIA to provide non-Socialist political cover for the adventure. Who had believed the Yanqui promises and were now about to pay the price of gullibility.

I switched off the engine because I thought I could hear landing-craft motors. In the sudden silence someone far out in the ocean, perhaps on a trawler or freighter or US Navy sub-chaser, sent a signal rocket arching high into the sky. It was bright sulphur yellow.

It made everything stand out so sharply. I could even see the place beside the ruin of the drinks shack where I had dug a grave I knew was too shallow. I had found a cross formed by two pieces of wreckage.

With a nail I had scratched TERRY in the wood. If I ever got out of this I would find one of her uncles and tell him what had happened. A girl made with such care deserved more than a shallow grave on a foreign shore. If I ever got out.

Behind me came the sound of engines. Trucks in the distance, moving slowly without lights. Ahead of me, on the water and the water's edge, machine-gun fire opened up again.

It was hard to guess. It sounded as if Fidel had roused some of his cadet soldiers, who were arriving in trucks. It sounded as if the invaders had spotted them. This is how blind men must spend all their lives.

But then the cadets opened fire. Ay, madre! I was in the centre of instant hell. This unprotected combat vehicle of mine was for sure located right between the two forces.

I kept backing away, my headlights switched off. Finally I backed on to the east-bound road that led away from Playa Giron. I swung about and headed away from the shooting. To the east I could see the same pearly grey I had seen the night they bombed Havana airport and Fidel had stopped believing me.

He did now.

In an hour, less, they would be fighting in dawn light. I wondered whom it would favour. I wondered whether the local people had arms and would rally to the cadets. I wondered when the airplanes would start their bombing runs. Their strafing.

Up ahead I saw a kind of makeshift filling station where vehicles as well as boats could buy fuel. I pulled into the concrete apron by the pumps and filled the Jeep's tanks. A young man in his underwear shorts levelled a rifle at me.

'Que paso? You must pay.'

I nodded to the Jeep. 'The vehicle of Fidel Castro is thirsty.'

His eyes went wide. A woman came up behind him and then six or seven children. He lowered the rifle and examined the front licence plate of the Jeep. 'Fidel is here?' he asked, eyes wide, searching the bushes.

'In spirit. Soon in body.'

Two trucks came roaring in, braked to a halt and released twenty young men in various stages of military dress. A slightly older man – he may have been twenty-one – wore an olive drab shirt with a gold bar on its epaulets. 'Who owns this Jeep?' he demanded.

'Lieutenant,' I said, pointing to the telephone number on the windshield. 'Find a telephone and call this number. Fidel answers himself.'

'You take me for a fool?'

'Find a phone.'

Back in the garage part of the station a coin phone hung on the wall. The lieutenant felt in his pockets for a coin.

'No coin!' I shouted. 'Toll-free!'

He dialled the number slowly, solemnly, the way a priest fusses at the altar with the wine and the host before the communion. I saw his face jerk forward, his mouth open wide.

'Si! Si! Soy Teniente Avilar aqui.'

I took the receiver from him. 'Victor Sanchez here. The cadets have arrived.'

'And the aircraft?' Fidel demanded. His voice sounded as stretched as barbed wire. 'Have they started bombing?'

'No aircraft. None.'

'How can they hope to win without them?'

'Right now, no aircraft. None.'

'Bueno. Give me back to Avilar. Victor, I depend on you. Call me back in half an hour.'

The young lieutenant took back the telephone. Then he scratched in his shirt pocket for a pencil and began scribbling on the stucco wall of the garage as Fidel dictated instructions.

I felt terrific. I looked and smelled like sewage. But for him to say he depended on me . . .

Somehow I would have to stay alive at least another half hour.

Chapter Thirty-One

Lord, what a day. I barely made the noon Eastern DC-9 for National Airport in Washington, DC. By two p.m. I was headed by cab to CIA headquarters at Langley. I got there at two-fifteen.

The lobby guard looked at my pass and, rather smoothly, didn't give it back. He came out from behind the counter. 'This way, Miss.' He picked up my suitcase and escorted me to a waiting room. Having confiscated the pass he then confiscated the suitcase. He looked inside my handbag, returned it to me and left.

'I have an appointment with Mr Angleton,' I said, just before he closed and locked the door.

An hour later a woman guard brought in a paper cup of coffee to which whitener and sugar had been added. 'This'll take a while, honey,' she remarked.

'I take it black, no sugar.'

'Better make do with what is.'

She smiled nicely and locked me up again. Naturally I didn't drink the so-called coffee. At five o'clock I began to hear the characteristic shuffle of time-servers sweeping their desks clean, loading up their briefcases and heading out to the parking lots.

At six, a man in a business suit let himself in. Neat, with a short haircut, he looked like one of those very alert Marine captains usually assigned as assassins to ISA. My glance flicked over him, looking for an inside holstered gun. If you sit long enough in a windowless room ignoring a cold cup of coffee probably dosed with truth drug, you begin to have weird thoughts.

He smiled in almost as friendly a way as the woman who had brought me the drugged coffee. 'You're free to go now, Mrs Emory.'

'I don't suppose you can tell me what this is all about?'

He had left the door open. I could see outside to the lobby area. No one was at the desk or counter. We were alone. 'Not as such, no.'

Phrases like that ought to get awards for Major American Obfuscation. As a people we can't seem to just say 'no'. But I was no longer mad enough to start screaming at him. 'Not as such what?' I asked politely.

He did have a small spark of feeling. He chuckled, as if I'd made a joke. Probably a college man. 'I am assigned to drive you home, Mrs Emory. Is that all right?'

'If you show me a driving licence.'

This time he actually laughed. 'Why, certainly.' He produced a Maryland licence for a Major Murray Higgins.

'I usually rate a captain. Thank you.'

'Least we can do for Major Emory's missus.'

No awkwardnesses. He was not treating me as an enemy agent bent on blowing up the joint. He was one-to-one with another major's wife. Us service people stay buddies, right?

He produced my suitcase and mumbled something that sounded like 'sorry about the pass'. You know as well as I that Marines never mumble. He didn't need to ask where I lived. He got me there twice as fast as the cab which had brought me. He offered to carry the suitcase upstairs for me and I declined.

This business of 'I was powerful enough to lock up in a windowless cell for half a day but weak enough to have a big strong major carry my suitcase' had, by now, started to affect me like a torn hangnail.

When I got upstairs I went to the window and watched him down at the kerb. He hadn't gotten back in the car but was standing by the driver's door, waiting, his eyes lifted to the level of my flat. Oh, of course. I switched on a lamp. He got in the car and drove off.

I opened my suitcase. It had been expertly searched. Nothing was missing. But everything was subtly shifted to let you know what had happened. Now for the funny part. I had spent the flight recopying my original bill of particulars from Gleb, trying to make them look more respectable than the product of a Moskovskaya hangover.

This clean copy I carried in my handbag so that when Patriot Jim asked for details, Patriot Midge could hand them over without delay. The old, half-scribbled original had been packed inside the suitcase. It would have excited suspicion at once. Hastily scribbled stuff always does.

Whoever had searched would have found it at the very bottom of the clothes. But when I opened the bag in my rooms, the original draft, on hotel letterhead from South Miami Beach, was neatly centred on top of the clothes.

Had they xeroxed it? Of course. They wanted to be sure I knew I was the absolute centre of their attention.

I hugged my arms, shivering. April is still chilly in Washington, despite seasonal signs like cherry blossoms and such. I turned on the radiators but they responded feebly, as always.

I opened my address book, found Cousin Jim's home telephone number and dialled it. It rang only twice. Then a woman said, 'Crown Dry Cleaners. Good evening.'

I hung up and the shivering started in earnest.

Chapter Thirty-Two

My Havana has always been a beautiful city. We have endured everything, corrupt leaders, gangsters in supreme power, Yanqui invasion, Yanqui starvation. We are still for sure a pleasure to look upon.

As a slave-pen of Spain, we even endured Spanish nobility. Picture living at the mercy of these diseased apes dressed in gilded finery. El Conde de Bayona was such a hidalgo but I like to think the ape blood ran thin in his veins. He left behind a small palace.

Ay, que lagrimas. It is a palace of dreams. The courtyard is like the cloister of a monastery where only rich boys are sent. That I should end up there.

I had no way of knowing what would happen to me. None of us did. War is that way. We were short of weapons and ammo but, after a while, so were the invaders. And when the aircraft failed them . . .

But that's ancient history. They strapped my leg to two thick sugar cane stalks. With two other wounded men, he drove us back to Havana in the Jeep. He? Fidel did the driving. In his own Jeep. La verdad. Why not?

This was a week after the invasion. All of us had been wounded early in the game and hastily splashed with antiseptic. We traded stories about gangrene, blood poisoning, amputations. The usual stuff guys hearten themselves with. Fidel drove us back to Havana and the patio of the Palacio del Conde de Bayona.

How dreams come true: lose a leg.

No, only a joke. I still have my two legs. Ask Rita.

Here we recoverd, all three of us. If they play Dizzy's 'Tango Havana' we can still get out there and dance it. I figure our combined ages now total nearly two hundred years. And none of us will ever forget the Bayona.

We lay there on cots in the soft air of May. Palm fronds rustled over our heads. The whole patio was made up of arches on the ground floor and, on the second, a squared off balcony whose pillars repeated the arched pillars below.

Yes, of course, you can still see the Palace. We have made it over into the Museo de Arte Colonial, meaning the art of the Spanish colonization. Let me know when you're coming. I'll show you around the place. It's one of the few places you don't need dollars to enter.

But the Bayona stays with me for a different reason. Places where you have some sort of ceremony often stick in your mind. It was here that Fidel held the first Victory Dinner. You didn't know that the Bay of Pigs was a victory? Of course.

He held it a month or so after the invasion. June was very warm but the ballroom of the Palace had huge doors opening out on both sides, giving us whatever breeze there was. It made the candles flicker but it cooled us.

Who was us? First, me and the other two wounded men and our families. We stood for the hundreds who had died. We were all young, as they had been. Only one of us had any kids.

Rita had been asked by Fidel to plan the dinner. She set the tables in a U. In the centre sat Fidel and a few of his close aides. We living symbols of victory over Uncle Sam sat on the wing to his left.

On the right-hand wing a dozen people sat and gossiped among themselves. I only knew one of them, Feelbi. The rest were Russians.

Such were the acoustics of the old ballroom that we could hear everything the Russians said without understanding a single word. That was when I realised Feelbi barely spoke Russian. Nor did the Russians speak Spanish, naturally.

Nowadays, of course, many Cubans speak Russian and have no idea what the hell to do with this left-handed gift.

But my mother had taught me to be polite. After the speeches, after Fidel pinned medals on the three of us, after we all began collecting in little groups sipping a cooling after-dinner sangria, I made it my business to find Feelbi.

'So,' I said.

'So, you're not only a handsome bloke, you're one of the lucky ones. What in Christ's name were you doing down there among the mortar shells?'

'You bastard.'

'Don't get shirty with me,' he retorted. 'Because I never liaised with you? I never left Havana, you poor sod. I never intended to. How could I be earning my farthing if I'd left Havana just because Fidel told me to?'

'That's right,' I agreed. 'How else would you have pulled together this team of take-over commandos?'

The Englishman gave me that sweet, understanding smile of his. 'Dear chap, are you referring to these engineers, defence experts and missile scientists?'

'Is that what the KGB calls them?'

'And each one personally invited by Fidel to confer, consult and create a territorial defence net for Cuba.' He produced two small panatelas, the four-inch kind, and offered me one.

'Don't smoke.' I looked around me at the Russians, who seemed to have run out of things to talk to each other about. 'Who here speaks English?' I asked them in a loud voice.

Bingo. They all clustered around me, chatting away. What a wonderful dinner. Was the band setting up to play for dancing? What was the name of the medal Fidel had pinned on me? What was my army rank? What, not a soldier? How had I learned such good English?

They tended to be fairly squat, compact men. Feelbi and I stood half a head taller and Fidel higher still. We could eye each other across the shaved or crew-cut tops of their heads. We had reached the stage where they were pulling out wallets and showing me photographs of their wives and children. I brought Rita and my mother over and that was the end of their interest in me.

The Englishman moved close to me. 'Clever lad. They barely know a word of Spanish. But they will. Dear me, yes.'

'If they stay here long enough.'

He nodded. 'And they will.'

'You think?'

His smile lit up his face. 'They and thousands more. I haven't a clue what it takes to install and operate a major missile launching installation.'

I wanted to push the smile off his face. He probably guessed as much because he took a step back from me. 'You're worse than the Yanqui,' I said in a low voice. 'He hits and runs. You stay and corrupt.'

'Sorry, old boy, I don't stay. I'm off tomorrow. Forever.'

Because Rita's mother and father had come with us to the victory dinner, they asked my mother to stay the night with them. Rita and I had been married by a judge the day my bandages came off. That entitled us to one of the Melendez bedrooms. My mother wanted to sleep on the balcony in the moonlight. The night stayed hot and humid.

I couldn't sleep. The experience of sharing a Cuban victory with an advance pack of Russian agents had disturbed me. The experience of seeing the Englishman's special victory, and his escape soon to corrupt some other part of the world, kept me from falling asleep. Cuba was my whole world. For him it was only an episode.

On the balcony, in the moonlight, my mother was sitting up in bed smoking a cigarette.

'It will stunt your growth,' I teased her. 'You will never grow up as tall as me.'

'I was proud of you tonight,' she said. 'You stood out in that crowd as a real man, head and shoulders over the rest.'

'Over Fidel?' I winked at her. 'He is one tall Cuban.'

'Of course over Fidel. How could you think otherwise?' She glanced sideways at me. 'Why can't you sleep?'

'Problems.'

'They go with marriage.'

'Is that your only advice?'

'To solve your problems be like the Melendez family.' Her dark eyes sparked with the pleasure of saying something scathing about otherwise industrious folk. 'A socialist judge is good enough to marry their daughter. A priest? Well, who knows when? Maybe never. No problems for the Melendez family.'

I sat down on the edge of the cot they had made up for her. 'Mamita, that is how a cunt talks. They are nice people. You are nice people. Be nice.'

'You hear what my only child calls me?'

'A word you have never heard before.'

'For the place you came from.' She poked me in the ribs. 'What problems bother you, married one?'

'I introduced you to the spy Feelbi? He is leaving Cuba. His work is done. You saw that battalion of Russians? Fidel invited every one of them. He will bring in many more. For this we fought off the Yanqui mercenaries? We spilled so . . . s-so much . . . blood?'

All of a sudden – pow! – I was sobbing.

It came over me like a sneeze, one moment calm, the next tears streaming down my face, my gut shaking with sorrow. My mother put her arms around me.

'Guapo, Guapo, what is it?'

I couldn't talk. I shook my head and tried to get my breathing under control. I never cry, never. She lifted up my face by the chin.

'What *is* it?'

'A girl. At the Bay of Pigs.' My lungs seemed to fill with air. I was sobbing again. 'She died for me.' I felt everything coming out into the pale moonlight, as if this were the merciless light of day. I could see Terry's naked body, whole, beautifully made. 'She was on top of me when the mortar shell exploded.'

'You were lovers?'

Before I could speak she put her small hand over my mouth. 'A good girl? A whore? What happened to her?'

'She started out good. It's not that simple for foreigners. They have more choices than we do. When you have more choices, you can go very far astray. The shell blew her apart instead of me.'

'But your leg . . .?'

'That happened two days later.'

'And the girl? Her body?'

My breath was under control again. 'I buried her. I know how to behave. I know the names of her uncles back in Massachusetts. One day I'll get an address and write them.'

'She was Yanqui? Killed by the Yanqui?'

We fell silent. At the same time we both sighed. I knew we were both thinking of the same thing, Rita.

'Do I – ?' I paused for a long time. 'I can't tell – '

'Of course you can't.' She took my hand and moved it through the gestures of crossing myself. Then she crossed herself. 'Where is it written that a mother isn't authorised to forgive a sin?'

'But you're *not*.'

'I take it on me. I'm used to sins. One more sin for this old girl is nothing much.'

'You get a wholesale rate from the priest?'

'Priests understand the sin business better than we do. A volume discount is always possible.'

'And Rita?'

'Is fast asleep if you haven't wakened her with your tears.'

'I can't help it. Terry was killed for me.'

She nodded. 'It wasn't your time. She was sent to take your death because it wasn't your time to die.'

'That's crap.'

'No,' she assured me, 'it wasn't your time. It was hers. It won't always be that way.' She was hugging me very tightly now and in the moonlight her eyes were moist. 'Promise me not to do this to Rita again.'

'It was . . . I mean . . .'

'She is much smarter than you, your Rita. Don't let this happen again. You are not built for successful cheating. Comprende?'

'As if I would try again? What do you take me for?'

Tears ran silently down her cheeks. I had seen her cry before. She never made a sound. Only the tears betrayed her. 'A man,' she said. 'Just a man.'

What could I say? We sat there, hugging each other and after a while I felt better. She felt better. No more tears. You see, I never cry. That's why this thing hurt so much.

You say to yourself: he is making such a big thing of death? He who watched Luis gun down many for the greater good of El Pequeño? Who arranged many a funeral for those who stood in Lansky's way? He agonises about a whacked-out druggie who happened to be in the wrong place at the wrong time?

I don't know what to answer. If you saw someone pick up a beautifully made watch and smash it to splinters . . .

No, it was worse. My intellectual compadres like to insert a few words from the language of Marx. They, and Rita with them, talk about the Zeitgeist, the spirit of the times. I had met, in the person of Terry, the Yanqui Zeitgeist. To see that monstrous neighbour to the north destroy its own soul, spattering me with its debris, had been a bigger shock than I was ready to admit.

But there are other kinds of shock. I tiptoed back to the room where Rita was sleeping. Except she wasn't asleep. She was coming out of the doorway with a piece of paper in her hand. Had she overheard?

'Where were you?' she asked. Even half asleep those deep black eyes of hers could start my soul twisting.

'Speaking with my mother. She, ah, couldn't sleep.'

'And who can?' Rita asked, handing me the bit of paper. 'One of your Yanqui pests thinks he can telephone at any hour.'

I glanced at the paper. 'Number Seven,' Rita had written. 'Five a.m. sharp.'

Chapter Thirty-Three

I don't know where some of these CIA types get their basic training. To ask you to visit the railroad station telephone booths at an hour when no one at all walks the streets of Havana is for sure the work of an idiot.

But what do you call the idiot who goes to the phone booth anyway and waits for the call?

Curious, I call him. I hadn't heard from Angleton or any of his boys with first names for some time, probably since a week before the invasion attempt. Nor had Feelbi passed any funds from them to me. The Sanchez bank account was still skinny. But that was no surprise.

I assumed that after the big fiasco no one in Langley would even want to mention the word Cuba, let alone talk to any agents in place there. But, as for Angleton's blood money, I had come to depend on it, never a good idea.

The phone in the booth rang at exactly five a.m. 'Congratulations,' Angleton began in his prissy, s-hissing voice.

'Thank you. For what?'

'The victory medal. Very fitting. I only wish we could send you one of ours. And some day we will.'

'Just send those green paper medals with Ben Franklin's picture on them.'

'If it's money you need . . .' The silence grew awkward. Then: 'How hard would it be to get you up here?' he asked. 'There is a whole new strategy you need to know. And, of course, get paid for.'

'Up where you are? Quite a trip.'

'Get to Key West and we handle the rest.'

'For how long?'

'A week?' Angleton suggested.

'You know the big marina at Mariel? Fishermen put in there all the time.'

'Tomorrow evening, at sundown,' he picked up at once. 'The boat is called the *Vela*. A Mr Bravo will ask for Mr Tango. Goodbye.'

'You mentioned money?'

'A thousand at Mariel. A thousand at Langley. A thousand when Bravo lands Tango back in Mariel next week.'

'Dollars, cash. Hard currency is getting very scarce around here.'

'Does that mean yes?' Angleton snapped.

I walked back through the streets of Old Havana. I would say I walked with some lightness and speed. Money does that, have you noticed? The sky was lightening. The first of the old sweepers approached, brooms and carts clattering on the old cobblestones. He looked exactly the opposite of how I felt.

Up! I felt up! I had never been to the United States. I had never earned three thousand dollars for a week's work. Three thousand! I had no idea what the work might be or even where Langley, Virginia was, except near Washington.

I pictured it as a normal, tree-lined Yanqui town of the sort where TV sitcoms like *Leave It to Beaver* or *I Love Lucy* take place. Somewhere there, maybe just by picking up a telephone, I could get information for Massachusetts and an address for Terry's uncles.

It hadn't occured to me to ask what Angleton wanted with me that required face-to-face contact. I also didn't think Angleton might be looking to get even.

But that would take more than a week.

'I don't like it,' Rita said.

It was six in the morning. The sky outside had brightened so much that we had drawn the curtains, blocking off air. We lay side by side in bed, touching each other here and there, already too warm for anything closer.

'Three thousand is not to like?'

She shook her head. 'I saw the man only once. But I mistrusted him even so. He may have learned that you help Fidel. He means you no good.'

'You may be right.' It's always best with Rita to agree. 'But, on the other hand, he needs me. Who has he got in all of Cuba as close to Fidel?'

She wriggled closer to me. 'Through me you are close. Angleton must know that.'

'But after the Bay of Pigs I have a special place in Fidel's heart. Who was his eyes and ears for those crucial first twenty-four hours? Who kept finding telephones that worked? Who reported to him around the clock? How could he have led the defence so well without that?'

'You have the biggest ego in all of Cuba.' She took my penis in her hand. 'I am impressed by it. Not Fidel.'

'Only you?' I kissed her nearest nipple. 'That's enough for me.'

Holding on to me, she edged off the bed, making me follow her. 'We'll telephone him this instant.'

'Fidel? So early? Rita, my cock. Please.'

She pulled me up on my feet. 'Insomnia is what the Bay of Pigs left him with. He didn't sleep for a week, until we knew we had won. Now he can't sleep at all.'

We found bathrobes and moved quietly into the Melendez kitchen. I have always had a soft spot for this room because it's where I proposed to Rita.

She dialled a number, got nothing, re-dialled, got a wrong number, dialled again and again and ... got Fidel. She explained the offer I had received in very indirect language. We had no way of knowing if the CIA was able still to tap Fidel's lines. There were so many things we didn't know about how Cuba stood with America and vice versa.

When one country goes to war with another, there are rules. Especially when the war's over and there is a winner and a loser.

One signs a surrender. The other begins giving away amnesties, medical supplies, food, clothing, pocket money, educational material, a budget for a new government and more funds to make it work. It's very costly, winning a war.

But the Bay of Pigs wasn't a war. Cuba got nothing out of it but dead and wounded. The US lost prestige and a strategic missile site to the Russians. But it gained the right to boycott Cuba, place an embargo on buying its products, force other nations to do the same. This had no effect at all on the US economy but it hurt Cuba a lot.

In such a hazy situation, Rita explained now, would it be wise to send me north into the inner lair of the enemy?

I was standing beside her, my ear sharing the phone with hers. Fidel said nothing for a long time. I could hear background talk, as if he were repeating the gist of the matter to others.

Finally: 'Anyone else, no. Big Bic, yes.'

'I don't understand,' Rita responded.

'He is a gato dichoso,' I heard him say. 'He has been my good luck charm more than once. Let him go. Besides, he will pick up information we can use.'

'And if he isn't back in a week?' Rita demanded. 'He is my good luck charm, too, you know.'

As we know, all governments are slow-moving elephants. They take forever to make a decision and even longer to get it moving. I should have realised, when Bravo picked up Tango the next evening at Mariel, that someone had lit a bomb under the elephant.

First, *Vela*, the pickup boat, was one of those long, slim mahogany 'cigarette' boats the bootleggers used to use in the 1920s. Vela means sail but this was a powerboat supreme. It could out-speed anything on the water, even sub-chasers developed for the Second World War.

Speed was the password. Normally it takes three or four hours to get from Cuba to Key West, the nearest bit of the United States. The cigarette boat, double-ended, supercharger tubes honking like geese in heat, made the ninety-mile crossing in under two hours, prow nosing high out of the water, leaving almost no wake like a water bug treading the smooth inland sea.

We ended up five minutes from the Key West airport, not the one for civilians but one of the US Navy installations by the shore where, today, the anti-drug surveillance blimps float like tethered whales.

No one had spoken to me during all this. I mean, except for the opening question: 'Tango? Soy Bravo.' The pilot had treated me as if I was not there. And when he put me in the Navy motorcycle side-car there was no farewell handshake as a young Petty Officer in heavy goggles drove me off.

I had expected a seaplane. Instead they hustled me on board a Short Takeoff-Landing craft, again with only one man aboard. No Navy markings, just a civilian CAA number. If the captain of the cigarette boat was close-mouthed, this one was some sort of Trappist. No Bravo Tango. He sat me in the co-pilot's seat, buckled my safety belt and we were airborne thirty seconds later.

I expected to be airlifted to Washington, DC, but governments always hold extra aces face down. Instead, in the same time it had taken the cigarette boat to reach Key West, the

STOL-craft was landing on a postage-stamp-sized field in what I later learned was Goldsboro, North Carolina.

In the last rays of sun I got a glimpse of fields of tobacco plants with their big flapping leaves. As dark fell I was transferred to a station wagon and off we went. We would occasionally pass through tiny crossroads towns.

We were heading east towards the Atlantic shore. A little later – this was mind-bending – we passed through a town called Washington, but even a rude Cuban like me knew it had to be some other Washington.

Funny-named villages. Chocowinity. Mattamushkeet. At one point there was a fork in the highway. One sign lead right to Cherry Point Marine Base. The other went left to Wright Brothers Memorial at Kitty Hawk. But we were heading somewhere else.

When we got there about nine in the night I was for sure no wiser. We had been driving along a very high brick-faced wall topped by barbed wire and spikes. It seemed to me we'd travelled five miles or more when the wall was pierced at last by a gate.

It had a gatehouse and the gatehouse had a man in it and the man was holding a weapon I didn't recognise at the time. It was an Ingram M-10 sub-machine-gun fitted with one of those huge silencers like a stovepipe. Why did a gate guard require a silencer? Tact?

We spent some time showing ID. Even I had to produce something, so I handed over my driver's licence. It was only after the gate had been swung open for us to pass through that I saw the name of the place we were entering.

Kill Devil Farm, I later found out, actually was a farm, mostly sheep, cows, pigs and the crops to feed them. It stretched over low hills and gulleys hundreds of acres along the inner Atlantic shore of Pamlico Sound, protected by barrier beach islands of Ocracoke and Hatteras.

And guards with silenced Ingrams.

At about the centre of all this, on a slight rise that in daylight would give a view of most of the farm, stood a house that looked at first like Mount Vernon or one of those all-white Southern mansions dating back to Jefferson's time.

I found out later it had been built, on the site of the original Kill Devil House, in about 1947 or 1948 when the CIA was first empowered to go forth and do battle. Corinne told me.

She was a small, pretty young woman in a kind of all-white uniform. First she produced a cup of hot clam chowder, a ham sandwich and a huge cup of coffee. Then came an unusual twist: she sat with me, chatting, while I ate.

This was a welcome break from the strong silent types who had been hustling me across the map all evening. I felt I'd been shifted from being a package to being a human being. Or, another way to look at it is that I always did get along a lot better with women than men.

'Corinne,' she said. 'Just Corinne. I'm the chef round here. Chef and bottle-washer. You're Vic?' She delved in a front pocket of her uniform and came up with my driver's licence. 'Victor Sanchez. Such a nice, strong name. I do b'lieve we had a Sanchez in our family some generations back. Road agent, maybe.'

'Mm.'

She handed me my licence. 'Nobody told me you'd be so good-looking. I'm not coming on to you. I'm sort of like a nurse or a doctor. We deal with facts. It's a fact you're handsome. Nothing wrong me saying so. Such a strong mouth.' Her voice had what I now know as a Tidewater tang. Anything with an ou in it was pronounced ay-oo. Such a strong may-ooth.

'Hope you like Tidewater cooking. I do a lot of seafood's y'might expect. But I imagine you're used to seafood.'

'Mm.'

She was scribbling on a pad of paper now. 'Y'like buttermilk biscuits f'breakfast? Biscuits and bacon and eggs over easy? Soft yolks. If you're from Cuba, I can do you that lovely Cuban toast they make down there. And I know the Cubans are like any other Suth'reners. They adore grits. Am I right, Vic? Grits, bacon, big ole knob've butter melting in the centre? How's it sound, honey?'

'Mm.'

I think it was the coffee. By the time Corinne had signed me in, fingerprinted me, taken front and side Polaroid photos

156

and driven me to a nice little hunting-lodge cabin some miles away, I was out of it.

She had such nice hands. Undressed me. Tucked me in like a baby. Petted me some. Turned off the light. Closed the door. Locked it.

No coffee produces that kind of caffeine. Soft, dreamy caffeine. I didn't wake up until noon the next day.

I wish I hadn't.

Angleton had promised me a week. By the start of my second week I knew I was his prisoner. Yes, for sure in a country club, but locked up like any other con. He was pretending to debrief me but he was really trying to learn what my loyalty was worth.

We weren't in cells. Each of us had his own cabin or cottage. Mine was roomy. I could take walks. A stray cat wandered by so, as long as I fed it, I had company.

Two cabins away, a good twenty-minute stroll, lived a Russian KGB colonel who had taken a lot of risk to defect. Angleton was sure he was a plant. The colonel was under daily interrogation, trying to prove that the secrets he had brought with him, secrets the CIA badly needed about the working of the KGB and the GRU, were the truth and not, as Angleton was sure, disinformation.

In other words, both our brains were being X-rayed. That's always dangerous, but only for us.

Instead of a cat, Krachmalsky had found himself a ewe and her lamb. Or they'd found him, considered his cottage theirs and wandered in and out. From this you can picture a rather nice life. If it weren't for the questioning.

Soon enough I resented the questions and the weirdos who asked them. Krachmalsky was used to interrogation. It was part of his life but it had never been part of mine.

The interrogators would arrive at my cottage after lunch. I was never sure if Corinne put something in my food to make me co-operate. She would deliver a hot meal in an insulated aluminium box. An hour later Chet and Mel would knock politely.

Chet was small, intelligent, in a striped T-shirt and faded

blue jeans. Mel was big and used to play football. They were very formal. They shook hands, politely asked if they could sit down at my table. From that moment on their eyes kept meeting, as if they shared a very deep secret.

They would pack up the lunch plates, store them in the aluminium box and put a tape recorder on the table. In those days recorders were big things with two reels. Whatever the interrogators did required a sideways glance between them. Whatever I said was followed by more eye work.

'. . . heard from Mr Lansky since then?' Chet would ask.

Everybody had a title. Mr Lansky. Mr Sanchez. Only Mel and Chet were first names. For the first week I played their game, answering politeness with politeness from, say, two in the afternoon to around five or six.

No pressure. No raised voices. But after a week the exchanged glances got to me. I began to feel that either they were crazy or I was.

'. . . part of Guantánamo Naval Base were you quartered when . . .'

Angleton could keep me here for years, like Krachmalsky, if he felt the urge. He could call me a defector, mole, anything. It didn't have to make sense. He was answerable to nobody. That meant these loony-birds answered to nobody.

This was CIA-land. This wasn't the United States, with its so-called Bill of Rights. This was a separate country and – like most parts of the world – no rights at all. And run by insane people.

'. . . little better idea of this thing you call skim, if . . .'

The deadpan courtesy, the Mr Sanchezes, the breakfast ordered as I liked it, the little typed menu choices I could elect to have Corinne cook, the freedom to wander, even the freedom to yack with Colonel Krachmalsky . . . all of it was meant to disguise the fact that I lived in an illegal dictatorship, sort of what I thought it felt like to be an inmate of a crazy house.

Anything could happen here. It was another planet. A place where an illegal invasion could be planned. Where illegal troops could be raised. Where Caribbean drug money bought weapons and ammo for more illegal operations.

'. . . night of the Bay of Pigs we understand you . . .'

By the middle of the second week I was plotting my escape from the Chet and Mel Show. It makes me smile. In my wanderings I found that Kill Devil Farm was perimeter-enforced by three concentric lines of defence, some bricks and mortar, some high cyclone fencing. And all barb-wired and Jeep patrolled day and night.

'. . . a reporter for Tass called Gleb Khsovko, also known as . . .'

I had an idea who this Gleb was. I'd seen someone like him with the Englishman, off and on. Was this the kind of garbage these two maniacs wanted? But what could I have told that they didn't already know?

'Short, nice looking fellow?' I tried out.

Chet's glance at Mel carried so much heat I thought they'd hit pay dirt. 'How well did you know him?'

'No way. I'm not even sure we're talking about the same guy.'

'You said he was short? Small?'

'Yeah.'

'Small enough to fit in a fifty-five-gallon steel drum?' Chet asked in a nice, polite voice.

'Huh?'

'You know.' Mel's voice was rougher but still polite. 'The kind the boogies fix up to make music with little wooden hammers?'

'The kind they ship chemicals in,' Chet went on, 'or crankcase oil.'

I shrugged. 'Why would I know if he fitted in a can like that?'

'Because,' Chet said, as if lecturing to a class of one, 'when somebody goes missing in the South Miami Beach area, he usually shows up months later when his body decomposes enough to generate lighter-than-air gases.'

I nodded politely. 'Finally comes to the top?'

Chet's smile was so wide and so joyless that I thought he might be in pain. 'He comes to the top very deceased and dead.' His glance started darting this way and that, Mel, me, the tape recorder. 'As skipper of one of those fifty-five-gallon drums.'

Mel nodded furiously. 'They usually put pig iron it it for ballast but it sometimes slips out.' His eyes danced sideways, too. 'Brake drums off old trucks, they're more reliable as ballast.'

'Is that how he was found, in one of those drums?'

Mel frowned. 'Hey, Vic, we ask the questions.' He sounded unhappy that he'd been forced to say something that wasn't one hundred per cent polite.

Chet cleared his throat. 'Don't get us wrong. We aren't tying you to anything, Vic.' His glance grew very conspiratorial, checking dark corners of the room for eavesdroppers. 'It's your tie with Mr Lansky and his tie with guys who stage that kind of take-out. I mean, can you blame us for asking?'

I had to laugh, or tried to. 'This Khsovko guy is connected with El Pequeño?'

'Wait. Hold it.' Mel whipped out a spiral-bound notebook and pencil. 'That's going to be hard to get off the tape so let me write it down. OK? P, E, K? Or Q?'

'It's just a nickname. The Little Man, we called him.'

I found I was starting to yawn. Uncle Sam's powerful but insane interrogators, terrors of the earth, were sleep-producing. The second week crawled by. I tried trading info with Colonel Krachmalsky. He was a together kind of guy, hard to shake, as they'd found out.

'Khsovko?' His voice went up. 'Gleb Khsovko? Is that what they called him?'

I nodded. 'They didn't actually say he was dead.'

He turned away but I had seen his face. He was biting his lower lip. When he turned back to me his voice was harsh, as if produced at great cost. 'They put you up to this, didn't they?'

'No way, for sure. I thought he sounded Russian, so I'd ask you.'

'You thought he sounded Russian. They didn't tell you he was Philby's case officer? Is.'

'Him again. He's everywhere.'

'He's in Beirut.' It was the one time I saw Krachmalsky

really upset. His voice rose. 'Gleb's in a tin can and I'm in purgatory. And you're the third one to have worked with Philby. He's fucked us all.' Krachmalsky looked to be hurting. 'Please. We'll talk tomorrow. Soon.' He turned away. After a while I left him.

Corinne would bring meals in the same station wagon that had brought me to Kill Devil Farm. I worked out three ways of rapping her over the head, gently, taking the wagon and crashing out by a side gate. The guard there, with his Ingram M-10, might not be too hard to run down. But I didn't want to hurt Corinne. But I wanted out.

There was no landing field, even for a STOL-craft, but there was a helicopter pad behind the mansion. I heard a small Lynx-type chopper set down and ran to get a look at it. Angleton got out.

At a stooped trot, carrying a beat-up black leather lawyer's briefcase, moving like a bird of prey looking for mice, he disappeared in the direction of my cottage, ducking, bobbing, ready to pounce on another of Philby's ghost moles.

A third week was facing me. Back in Havana Rita and my mother were bitterly regretting this adventure. It was true I had been handed a thousand dollars, ten hundred-dollar bills. But if I escaped now I was forfeiting the rest.

The helicopter pilot went in the back way to Corinne's kitchen, probably for a snack or a leak. I slipped inside a tool shed only twenty yards from the chopper. Through its Plexiglas bubble I could see the inside of the cockpit. There was barely room for three people.

But, then, there didn't seem enough room for him to have tucked the Ingram M-10 between the two seats. But he had. It made all the difference in the world to me. I picked up a wrench in one hand to pretend I was a mechanic, I could see that the Ingram's silencer was already screwed in place.

That's what I like. A nice silenced getaway. Walk out. Hide in the cockpit. Hold the Ingram on them till they lift off.

My brain was working so hard it hurt. A hijack would convert me from a victim to a perpetrator. They would have an excuse to issue shoot-to-kill orders. I would have no one to blame but myself.

On the other hand I had protection as long as I kept Old Jim by my side. They wouldn't shoot him to get me.

My head ached with questions. *Think!* We'd lift off and go where? The Lynx couldn't take us back to Cuba. And Cuba was the only place I could be safe.

Keep thinking, Big Bic! Was hijacking the chopper the best idea in town? No, just the only idea. Come up with something else.

But, then, we Cubans are such impulsive guys, anyway.

Chapter Thirty-Four

On the *Times* a girl knows she's in trouble when they transfer her to general assignment.

I had had a nice beat, the Caribbean, filled with invasions, scandals, revolutions and such, loaded with contacts I had painstakingly made over Lord knows how many rum drinks while practising my Espagnol. But after I had a five-minute discussion with the *Times* health insurance lady about pregnancy leave, some lever slipped off its cog and alarm bells rang.

The more cynical would, I suppose, have added that when James Jesus Angleton drops you, he earnestly desires that you are also dropped by the whole world. Luckily for me, although at its highest levels the *Times* stooged for the CIA and every other governmental snakepit – as did each and every other major newspaper in America – lower down in the hierarchy rather decent people ran things.

'You wouldn't like . . .?' Mac's head began shaking negatively, '. . . the women's page?'

'No, Mac. I'm hooked on hard news. How about doing backgrounders on the Bay of Pigs and other Cold War disasters?'

He looked acutely unhappy. Mac is one of those editors who really gets into the role, eyeshade, sleeve garters, pencil behind the ear, the works. 'What about . . .?' I could see his glance desperately running up and down my curriculum vitae. 'Sports?' he suggested.

'You got to the part about me playing basketball for Vassar?'

'Sports,' he repeated, 'just a trial assignment.' He was one of those people who believe that the more you say something the more it begins to take on objective reality.

And there may be something to it, after all. I found myself assigned to do a feature story on the spring opening of the racetrack out at Jamaica, in Queens. A sunny day in May. Who's complaining?

I had never before visited a racetrack. That made for a funnier feature story. As I dawdled here and there, eyeing the horses and jockeys and betters and touts, I realised I was getting as much eye action as I was giving.

There is a point in early pregnancy when you begin to flood with excess hormones that speak non-verbally to the opposite sex. Your complexion glows. Your eyes melt lissomly, whatever that is. Your breasts enlarge. Your shape grows more feminine, but does not yet balloon. I'd already been through this with Susannah One two years before, only to have it crash-land in a miscarriage.

Everybody from teenage exercise boys to elderly touts in their two-tone shoes and well-chewed cigars shows you he thinks you are the cat's pyjamas. But whereas female cats need to go into heat to jog the libidos of the male, humans demonstrate their talent for confusion by starting the process of courtship when it's already too late and the bun's in the oven.

So it was no great surprise to feel someone slip his arm in mine and murmur, 'Doll, you're looking good enough to eat.'

I turned to issue a tart rebuff but saw that the man's head was considerably lower than mine. 'Meyer, don't tell me you've got a piece of the gee-gees, too?'

'What ain't I got?' he demanded. 'If the great American public wants to gamble, a patriot gives 'em what they want.'

'I'm a patriot. I want something in the third race.'

'Stay out.'

I squinted at my scratch sheet. 'I don't see such a nag.'

'Stay Out is the best horse in any race.' He squeezed my

arm. 'Good to see you, doll. For a while there you were right at the top of my shit list, together with your CIA schmendricks. Then I found out they hate you. So I love you.'

'The air cover. I know.'

'Air cover has to come from a president of the United States.' Meyer's sallow face darkened slightly. 'And when did a Lansky ever get a square deal from a Kennedy? From the beginning, Ike had OK'd air cover. He knew without air cover it was risky. Now we know it was impossible. But air cover never came.'

'You're saying Jack Kennedy nixed it?'

'Hours before D-Day. Fumfered, fiddled and finally fucked up.'

'He welshed?'

'And you know we don't let a welsher get away with welshing.' Meyer shrugged eloquently. 'A welsh is the same as a double-cross. That's the way hotheads like Sam Giancana out in Chicago see it. He's sharing a lady friend with the President so you have to think he's got high access. He says there's only one punishment for a welsher.

'That's how Carlos Marcello sees it down in New Orleans,' he added. 'He's been hounded by kid brother Bobby for a year now, so he'll jump at any excuse for action. Who can blame 'em? A deal is a deal. Only a Kennedy wouldn't know that. Rotten double-crossers, the whole family.'

'And how do you see it?' I asked him.

'Me, I'm a man of peace. You know that. Peace and business. But I can understand a hothead, too. You know,' he added in a suddenly lower voice, 'what we're talking here is supposition.'

'Only make-believe,' I quoted.

'Exactly. For a guy, no matter how hotheaded, to want to pull off such a thing, he has to have protection up to the maximum.'

'Expensive,' I commiserated.

'Money don't enter it, doll. This kind of protection is beyond money.'

He led me up a long flight of stairs along one side of the bleacher seats. He was puffing when we got to the level where the club lounge provided a bar, a restaurant and a shoulder to cry on for big-time losers.

'Good to feast the eyes on you, doll. I know you had nothing to do with the double-cross over air cover. Angleton I'm not so sure of. I hear he has cut you out of the Agency.'

'Nothing wrong with your ears, Meyer.'

'Two daiquiris,' he told the bartender, 'with my own rum. You got Myers rum, boychik?' This was apparently an elderly joke. But it made the bartender grin insanely.

'Yes, sir, Mr Lansky, sir.'

As we sat down I said, 'You're drinking?'

'It's the only thing eases my ulcer.'

'And makes it grow.'

He shrugged again. 'A guy my size? I'm *all* ulcer.' He chuckled grimly as the bartender himself brought the drinks to our table. He had stuck thick orange slices in each daiquiri. 'Your daily vitamin C, Mr Lansky, sir.'

'You're a good boychik.' He passed the bartender a hundred dollar bill. 'Keep the change.' Meyer's strange, gypsy eyes moved sideways, checking out the people in the club.

At the far end a tight enclave of young men in suits of varying shades of grey surrounded two men, one short and nondescript, the other a pug-dog little man hard at work making check marks on his daily scratch sheet.

'We have another celebrity today,' I said quietly, 'besides you.'

'Who? Clyde Tolson over there?'

'No, his driver, Mr Hoover.'

'We don't speak,' Meyer told me. 'And never in public.'

This curious construction only bothered me for a moment. In my new, hormone-enriched life, I was no longer worried about logical progressions. 'I'm expecting after New Year's,' I told Meyer. 'She'll be a girl.'

He made his small gambler's eyes go as wide as he could. 'Mazel tov. Major Emory's a lucky guy.'

'Thanks.'

'Also a real Houdini, engineering this from all the way over in Vietnam. He's still there, isn't he?'

'No more mind-reading, Meyer. Please.'

'I figured as much. A girl could do worse than have me watch over her in such a situation. Keep hubby nice and sweet. Make sure the gonnif who knocked her up keeps his commitments.'

'There aren't any.'

Meyer nodded. 'This was once a play down on Second Avenue at Tomashevsky's Yiddish Art Theatre. Called *Seduced and Abandoned.* Molly Picon played the girl but she didn't have an Air Force major to fall back on.'

'Meyer, cut it out. Things happen.'

I could almost see the wheels rotating inside his head. I didn't think he kept that much track of me but the impregnation had been accomplished on his home turf, South Miami Beach. Watching him was like watching the symbols flashing in one of his one-armed bandit slot machines. The moment they came to rest it was as if sirens went off.

'April on Ocean Drive!' His voice was tight with triumph. He glanced around to make sure no one had overheard. His face went very dark, as if choked with blood. 'Oi, vey.'

'What's the matter?'

'We got an expression in Yiddish, gurnischt hilf'n? Nothing will help, it means. However, one thing I can do.'

He reached across and removed my daiquiri from me. 'The little girl will thank me for keeping you off the booze, doll. Boychick!' he called to the bartender. 'Take this away. Squeeze instead the lady a big glass of OJ, got it?'

'Yes sir, Mr Lansky, lotsa vitamin C.'

Meyer seemed about to tell me something. Then he changed plans, glanced at his watch and got to his feet. 'Gotta run. Stay healthy.'

He backed away from me, gave me a smile and disappeared in the direction of the men's room. The bartender brought me about a pint of orange juice. In Meyer's absence, I drank my daiquiri instead. Surrogate fathers solicitous of my health tend to give me the pip. Besides, Meyer knew something he wasn't telling me.

I went back over the scratch sheet, looking for a horse's name that would make good copy. You know, a nag called

Lucky Lady or Close Shave or Bottom Dollar. The first race was fifteen minutes away.

I was due down at the betting windows to meet up with my *Times* colleague who normally covered the sport of kings. He was going to take me through a few races, pointing out details. I would have to rely on him to identify the cast of characters as well, the trainers, owners and such.

'Can't say I think much of your social life,' a voice informed me.

I looked up to my left to find one character I already knew by name. Mr Hoover moved much more lightly on his feet than I'd expected. 'You don't approve of mobsters?' I responded. 'You don't know what you're missing.'

'Har. I don't miss a helluva lot,' he informed me. He emitted a grunt as he sat down at my table. 'You two were having quite a gabfest.'

'We hadn't seen each other since before the Bay of Pigs.' I finished my daiquiri and started on my orange juice out of sheer nervousness.

'Then you had plenty to jaw about.'

He had a kind of derogatory mien that seemed to find everything not to his liking, including things that hadn't even happened yet. This had advantages for a man in his line of work, especially if he made daily contact with the individual players of the criminal world. Since he rarely did, it also worked on his own employees.

It was a stance, an attitude of pre-judgement that seemed to say: 'whatever you do, it's wrong and I know it.' I had never before or since run into such cast-iron sureness. It had great power because it was anchored in a completely different subtext: 'whatever I do is right, so give up.'

'Bartender,' I called. 'Bourbon hi-ball for my guest.'

'Who pays for it, the *Times* or Sissy-Boy Angleton?'

'Cousin Jim? I haven't been on his payroll for some time.'

I watched the action behind his little piggy eyes. His question had been a test. He knew Angleton had dropped me. The whole Christian world knew Angleton had dropped me. He wanted to make sure I'd admit it. Can you believe a man at the summit of the law-enforcement establishment relying on such schoolboy thinking?

'Then thanks for the bourb.' He gave me another of his 'you're wrong' stares. 'Angleton's got his hands full now, anyway, right?'

'Doesn't every successful bureaucrat?'

'You know what I mean. Thanks to him, the Cuban welcome mat's out for the Russkis.' He watched the bartender deliver his hi-ball. 'Without you being his favourite cousin any more, what're you doing to make up the deficit?'

I frowned. 'Beg your pardon?'

'Don't tell me you can make ends meet on what the *Times* pays you?'

'It's a decent salary. Almost.'

'Added to what Major Emory sends home from Vietnam. I understand these so-called "instructors" Kennedy is sending there get combat pay.' He sipped his drink delicately, one pinkie stretched outwards. 'But when the baby comes . . .'

I flashed him what I hoped was a killing look. 'I suppose you have someone in the *Times* health insurance office?'

'Har. That is a real naive question.'

'It wasn't a question.'

'I was going to offer to help,' he said then. He made his small eyes look guileless. 'What're friends for?'

'I had no idea the Bureau hired out contract workers.'

'It sure doesn't. What the Bureau does is provide another kind of security. Freedom from getting found out.'

'Found out?'

'I don't have an idea in hell of how long Major Emory's been in 'Nam. Could be he got there, say, some time in January at the latest?'

'Around then, yes.' His subtext came to me so suddenly I blinked.

Ours is a society that pays special homage to certain women, particularly widows and pregnant females. Men defer to such women, help them, advise them, do special favours for them because, being widowed or gravid, they are at an obvious disadvantage.

It is, therefore, quite common that often the same men also

168

bilk, cheat, steal from, rape and otherwise loot such disadvantaged women. This is ordinary jungle law. Any woman who forgets it, even for a moment, pays dearly for her lack of caution.

A blonde has her own weapons, smiles, laughter, giddy eye moves. But brunettes have to lay it on the line.

'Why, you nasty, blackmailing little son of a bitch!' The words were out of my mouth before I could control them. 'What on earth won't you stoop to?'

He burst out laughing. I can't hope to describe the sound. It had a stifled, plugged-up quality as if each time he unleashed it it had to break itself a whole new anal passage. 'Then we have a deal. Right?'

'What sort of dirty work did you have in mind?'

'A bona fide cousin of Angleton gives me possibilities, even when he's banished her. First, I want you back on his payroll. That won't be too hard. I can give you a few titbits he'll be happy to get. Then you go back to work.'

'And spy for you?'

'Not just for me. For domestic tranquillity.'

'You'll keep Emory believing he's the father of my baby? How could you guarantee such a thing?'

'You still don't get the bargain, do you? You work for me. Or I make sure Emory learns about the Russian.'

He finished the rest of his bourbon and got to his feet. 'Now, *that*, I can guarantee.'

Chapter Thirty-Five

When I was a kid in Guantánamo, scraping for a peso here, a peso there, there was a time when all of us smoked grass. I mean all day.

It's what musicians do all night. There were five of us, eleven, twelve years old. When we woke up late in the morning we'd roll and smoke even before we took a leak.

Where'd we get the money? Who said we had money? We

begged grass, pickpocketed it, rolled drunks for it. We even earned a little cash doing gopher runs – you know, 'Hey, Chico, go fer this, go fer that' – and actually *bought* a bag or two.

As long as I think back to that time, that's how long I can't figure out why we did it. Grass makes everything move slow. That's why musicians use it. The beat comes to them so slowed down they can improvise like geniuses. It seems to them they have all the time in the world, thanks to grass.

But kids? Always hustling. Half-starved all the time. Why did we try to make time stand still? What we needed was something to make it fly past so we could grow up.

That's what I was thinking as I hid in the tool shed near where the Lynx copter was waiting. Everything was ready for my big scene. The Ingram M-10 was waiting in the cockpit.

Trying to make up my mind. Waiting for Angleton. Looking for the pilot to return. That's when time started to drag as if I'd been hitting the grass again.

And then it was too late.

The kitchen door swung open so slow it could've been the door of a bank safe. Beyond the doorway, hiding inside, the pilot moved in such a slowed-down, funny way, I knew I'd hit a couple of tokes of Mary Jane.

Then I saw why he was moving so slow. Behind him, the short guy, Chet, held an automatic pistol to his back, jammed in so hard I could only see the butt of it. Chet's face no longer looked polite. It looked crazy. He was chewing his lower lip and talking at the same time.

Behind Chet the big guy, Mel, held another automatic, muzzle down at his side. They were staring out wildly into the sunlit landscape of Kill Devil Farm, all rolling hills and faraway firs. It was obvious to me they were watching and waiting for Angleton to come back.

And then what? Weren't all these guys on the same side? OK, they were goofballs. But not enemy agents.

Slowly, a black thing appeared in the distance. I could see him. Like a hawk, like a raven, like an undertaker in his black clothes, his sharp, beaky nose, his skeleton's arms and hands. He was moving in a fast walk back to the chopper.

As they saw him, the three men retreated further into the kitchen and slowly closed the door. Who was good guy? Who was bad?

I stepped outside the tool shed and started walking directly towards Angleton. He saw me at once, raised his hand like a preacher and gave me a welcoming wave like 'hello and bless you my son' sort of thing.

I met him at the door of the Lynx's bubble. He stopped and frowned. Where he stood he hid me from the men in the kitchen.

'How are you, Victor?' he asked. The words seemed to come out of him with big puffs of air in between. 'I . . . was . . . at . . . your . . . cottage . . . looking . . . for . . .'

As far as I could see we were outnumbered and outgunned. They had the added advantage of the layout. It was against any success on my part. Between me and them stood Angleton and the pilot. We had only one advantage and I wasn't sure it'd work.

I had put one arm behind me and lifted the Ingram M-10 from where it was, between the seats of the copter. The fat stovepipe silencer was the size of one of those cans of tennis balls.

'Put that down, for goodness sake.' Always the schoolmarm.

'Mr Angleton,' I said. It seemed to me my words took forever to leave my mouth. 'In the kitchen behind you Chet and Mel have gone apeshit. They are holding guns on your pilot. You tell me who is for us and who is against us.'

His face, usually bone white, went grey. His falcon eyes glared at me like yellow flares. 'This is impossible. All three men are trusted p – ' Words stuck in his mouth.

'Hands up, Mr Angleton,' Chet called. His voice grated harshly, the buzz a knife blade gets when the whetstone rubs off a jagged bead of steel. 'Hands up, Mr Sanchez.'

The sun shone down brightly on us. In God's greenery everything was peaceful, soft-edged, restful. You really hated to leave such a world, especially for good.

I hoped I was right: they didn't know I had the Ingram yet. I hoped they didn't know it was silenced. OK: go.

'When I say to,' I told Angleton. 'Drop to the grass. Start crawling away. Understand?'

'I understand I'm in the crossfire if I don't.'

'Smart thinking.' I nodded and smiled. 'Drop!'

It was Bay of Pigs all over again, but in total silence.

The skinny Angleton fell like a stone and started churning up grass as he crawled away. I let off a burst of three at hip level.

Because my Ingram was silenced, they had no idea what was happening until Mel – big guys are real sucker targets – lurched sideways with a shattered elbow and knocked Chet off centre.

I got Chet in the thigh just as he started shooting. The whole thing took half a second. Maybe a whole second. But in my mind it went on for hours.

The pilot had hit the grass when he saw his boss do so. I ran forward, checking the two interrogators and picking up their automatics. They were both in a lot of pain.

Angleton came scooting over to us. 'Harry?' he demanded of the pilot, 'what the hell is this, Harry?'

'They found me in the kitchen and marched me out here. They have the girl tied up in the cupboard.'

Angleton knelt by Chet's side. 'Premature burnout? KGB field agents? What possible excuse can you – ? You know you're going to have to tell me some time, you stupid people.' He glanced at the pilot. 'Get on the copter radio and call an ambulance. I want these two patched up and talking a blue streak.'

I went in the pantry cupboard and untied Corinne. 'Oh, good,' she said. 'I was hoping it'd be the good-looking one.'

'What did those hombres expect to do? Improve your cooking?'

She massaged her wrists where the rope had cut in. 'It's not an easy life. They start to crack, some of them. And then, you know what life in the Company is like.'

'I don't, for sure.'

'Temperamental? Nervous? There is always some kind of

palace revolt. Some top level honcho is always going up in smoke and trying an inside coup. This is probably my fourth in, say, six years.'

'And your last,' Angleton muttered from the doorway, 'if you keep talking freely to every Tom, Dick and Harry.' He gave me a grim look. 'Victor, I've been trying to make you into an assassin. That was the purpose of your stay here. I see you already are one. I expect I owe you my life, you young devil.'

'I expect you do, plus two thousand bucks.'

Chapter Thirty-Six

The doctors have tricky ways to calibrate the nine months of pregnancy. They speak of trimeters and other learned arrangements. My system is simpler.

There are just two stages: your period of maximum sexual appeal to the opposite sex and, once you start showing, your period of being a public freak.

By July of 1961 I had joined the freaks. So it was particularly appalling that the Kennedy clan chose this moment to invite me to a glamorous Rose Garden party.

This was *the* social event of the summer, complete with dancing till – as it turned out – four-thirty in the morning. Camelot with a vengeance! Although the year had been chock full of private social encounters between Jack Kennedy and a series of attractive young women, this would be one of the few major public events that included his having the first dance with his own wife, Jackie.

To have attended in my sexpot stage would have been the achievement of a lifetime, a triumph, a rhapsodic victory, a personal best, a grand opportunity. To show up with a big belly rated zero on the joy meter.

I nearly sent regrets. After a lot of string pulling by Hoover, the *Times* had returned me to Washington, DC to handle Latin American news that surfaced in the nation's capital. I had written Cousin Jim and asked for an appointment, mentioning 'some material I've come across that you must have'.

By July he had let time elapse to indicate that he was still unhappy with me. Then there arrived the Rose Garden invitation. It was signed in JFK's name by one of the social secretaries. But I knew it had been sent by, or because of, Angleton.

It couldn't have been generated by Hoover. By mid-1961 the Director of the Federal Bureau of Investigation was so high on JFK's hit list – and vice versa – that Hoover couldn't even have wangled an invitation for himself.

We journalists are, I know, an exaggerating bunch of gossips. Otherwise our readers would fall asleep. But when I say that Kennedy and Hoover hated each other, it is not hyperbole. What's more, both men were activist enough to do something about their hatred.

In JFK's case, he loathed the anal closet-queen personality that brandished such infinite blackmail power, in his case as far back as World War II. At the same time, helplessly randy, he kept giving Hoover more blackmail power by a series of affairs that peaked during the summer in the serial fucking of Marilyn Monroe, mafia mistress Judith Campbell and quite a few other targets of opportunity.

It was Jack's command to his Attorney General, Brother Bobby, that Hoover's power be broken within the Justice Department by exposing him as the mafia's inside protector for nearly forty years. Then he could be ignominiously dumped.

In Hoover's case the hatred had sharper urgency. Being dumped was clearly to be his fate. Born on the first of January, 1895, Hoover would reach the age of seventy on the first day of 1965. He would then face mandatory retirement.

A president as popular as JFK, elected in 1960, would easily win a second term in 1964. If friendly towards Hoover, or sufficiently cowed by blackmail threats, a president had the power to waive mandatory retirement. JFK had already done so for Admiral Rickover as he reached seventy. Would he for Hoover? No way.

He'd rather die first.

Worse, from Hoover's viewpoint, Kennedy was already clearing out, by forced retirement, long-term public servants who had proved disloyal or incompetent or a combination known as die-hard Republican. Allen W. Dulles had resigned the CIA. U.E. Baughman had quit the Secret Service at the age of fifty-five. Reading Kennedy's heart-felt expressions of regret on these occasions, one could taste his joy at freeing himself to hire his own men.

Rumour had it he and Bobby already had standing in the wings a specialist in combating organised crime, ready to replace Hoover. The man was on salary and ticking away like a taxi meter.

Better yet, he was actually *inside* the FBI and already understood its arcane standards of behaviour. He was Courtney Evans, the Bureau's least-used executive, since he was in charge of fighting organised crime. It would be Bobby's pleasure to elevate him to the directorship.

Some of my more ghoulish colleagues in the *Times* bureau felt the feud was resolvable only by a duel. 'I can hardly wait. J. Edgar's been doing target practice in the basement FBI range. I understand he can drill Jack's right eye at fifty paces.'

'Well, we can't let Jack choose his favourite weapon,' another literate, respected journalist told me. 'Otherwise it'd be sodomy.'

But all of them were adamant that I should not tender regrets for the Rose Garden do. Andy, younger than the rest, made the ultimate sacrifice. 'I'll take you myself. I'll even dance every dance with you. Did you know I did my pre-med in obstetrics?'

So I had my hair done.

I think it's time for me to explain that Hoover made me privy to nothing. What I knew of his manoeuvres had become common knowledge among Washington journalists. But what we had pieced together was appalling.

There was an FBI the world saw and an FBI not even the FBI knew about. Mainly this centred around illegal wiretapping.

The law said no agency could eavesdrop unless it had a

court order signed by either a judge or, in the FBI's case, a higher-up within the Justice Department. This law the FBI broke a hundred times a day.

These illegal adventures were reported in codes, one called LEGAT, another ELSUR (electronic surveillance) and AIRTEL, a transmission system. They ended up in only one place, Hoover's own hands. They were not filed anywhere within the FBI. Nor did Hoover share them with any FBI person except Clyde Tolson.

This backdoor intelligence channel, steered by Frank Costello's tips, concentrated on the activities of Meyer Lansky, Carlos Marcello, Angelo Bruno and other mafia capos and dons registering anti-Kennedy fury and issuing threats of revenge.

Well they might. JFK's close election win seemed to trigger anti-mafia activity even before the Bay of Pigs betrayal. On December 16, 1960, Bobby had been appointed Attorney General. On December 19 the Electoral College named Kennedy victor, 300 votes to 219. But Jack had yet to be sworn in. That would happen in late January of the new year.

Nevertheless, on December 28 Bobby moved to deport Carlos Marcello. That fast. And thus began a reign of terror mounted by the Kennedys against organised crime, with a success rate far above anything the FBI had accomplished under Hoover's forty-year hobbling. Why were Jack and Bobby so determined to defeat the mafia?

The frustration of reading the minds of dead men. Only one clue is obvious, the fact that their father, Joe Kennedy, grew rich investing in illegal booze during Prohibition. This made organised crime a skeleton in the sons' closet.

The money had bought them women, paid their college tuitions, funded their political campaigns and bankrolled their lush life styles. These would be skeletons in any politician's closet. But why did the Kennedy sons feel so sensitive about it that, to cleanse themselves, they took steps that inevitably led to their deaths?

On the other hand, as Meyer pointed out to me once, they had no idea they'd *have* to die for such hubris.

Prior to the Rose Garden affair, ELSUR and LEGAT

recorded more than twenty specific assassination threats. Most came from Marcello, but Bruno was not far behind, nor were mafia stooges like Jimmy Hoffa and the don of Buffalo, Stefano Magaddino. They started out wanting to shed Bobby's blood. But now Meyer's idea was catching on; some were targeting the President of the United States.

That life is entrusted to the Secret Service, not the FBI. Hoover's responsibility was to report the illegally-recorded threats to the Service. He didn't. He sat on them.

'Lord, I have no idea,' I told the very tall gent from State Department Intelligence. He had latched on to me in the Rose Garden, pleading a long-time friendship with my absent husband.

'But there actually has to be some reason for this elegant bash,' he insisted.

The orchestra under its colourful tent was playing its Latin-American numbers. It had already gone through its old-time Glen Miller repertoire.

'Well,' I gagged, 'Hoover's birthday is January 1. So this must be Tolson's birthday, right?'

He snickered. 'Tolson's born in May, actually.'

I had been drinking quite a bit, but he'd had a head start on me.

'What a lovely rhumba,' he mooed in my ear. 'Care to?'

He turned out to be a peachy dancer, perhaps the best at tonight's party. The weather was the usual late July Washington mix of humidity and heat, as if it were the capital city of a banana republic.

Jack Kennedy, of course, danced hardly at all. He was not trawling for what he called pussycat tonight. All business, three people stood behind the President, feeding him names as we came up to say hello.

This informal kind of reception line was, if not a Kennedy invention, certainly raised by him to a high art. He always looked for ways to implicate people as pals or allies. Nothing was better than having them drift over and press the flesh, no big thing. Real cool. Jack Kennedy was young but, Lord, he was the slickest politician since FDR.

The next time the Latin rhythms came around, I sat it out. Jim Angleton and I perched awkwardly on the edge of a round dry fountain. I pictured us as Beatrice and Benedict or Kate and Petruchio, one of Shakespeare's warring couples who cannot fall into each other's arms until the last act.

The fountain's centre spout had been turned off. Enough publicity had featured the Kennedy penchant for tossing people in pools to make the press man, Pierre Salinger, touchy about any body of water deeper than a puddle.

'I'm supposed to hand over the goodies I promised. Maybe we can have lunch next week.'

'Goodies?' His schoolmarm's voice emitted suspicion. 'Some scandal from the *Times*?'

'No.' I made my voice sound ashamed and miserable. 'Cousin Jim, I have been put up to this fandango by that arch rat Hoover. He's got something on me.'

'What, you're to spy on me?'

'I'm to ingratiate myself first. Then I'm to play fly on your wall, I suppose. He might want me to put rat poison in your Cream of Wheat.'

'All-Bran,' he corrected me. 'Do you have any idea how badly you damaged me, Midge? That memo of yours!'

'Never meant as a memo. Notes for when I could give you a report, face-to-face. But you never let me. And then one of your inside snoops latched on to my notes.'

He frowned. Together with his falcon's beak and sulphurous eyes, the frown made him downright scary. 'Tell me the source for all that guff about Philby.'

'I'm not sure I should break his cover.'

'It's the only way I could ever forgive such a hatchet job.' He turned to face me directly. 'The only reason I wasn't dumped like Dulles is that there had to be somebody with hands-on experience. The minute they find a replacement, I'm dead. Something's already happened down at the f – ' He stopped.

'Down at the farm? Kill Devil Farm?'

'Never mind. Who gave you that Philby stuff?'

I watched his face. His long-term romance with Kim Philby could only be excused by the fact that even SIS in Britain had been unable to make an accusation stick. They'd had to let Kim waltz out of their hands.

'You remember that nice little man from Tass, Gleb Khsovko?'

Angleton gave me a pained look. 'That won't work, Midge. You know I can't verify anything he told you.'

'Why not?'

'Because he bobbed up dead in Miami Bay. One of those torture-to-death interments in a fifty-five-gallon drum. Lansky style, if not actual guilt.'

Bastards! All of them!

Hoover knew. Meyer knew. Playing me for a patsy. Everybody knew but me.

I wasn't in love with Gleb, Lord knows, but I liked him. I liked him being my baby's father. Oh, Susannah, oh don't you cry for me.

'Were you two having an affair? Is that why he talked?'

'Gleb had worked Kim in the NKVD since the end of the Spanish Civil War. A life for the Tsar. Try laughing that off . . . Cousin.'

Now, decades later, with Teddy out of the running, there is very little point in wondering which Kennedy was the better man, Jack or Bobby.

Sometimes, of an evening, Jim and I talk about them. But it's more than a little heart-breaking to disinter bullet-riddled corpses when our memories want to play back the times when both men were vitally alive.

That night, in the Rose Garden, each Kennedy played his role in soldierly fashion, whether it was the result of planning or the natural pecking-order discipline of two sons in a large family.

Travelling light, Bobby had no staff people to identify for him the other players. But he was agile and daring. Because he wasn't the President of the United States he could say and promise things the President couldn't.

Yet – and this was the clever part of it – he carried enough clout on his own that you believed he spoke for Jack and that alliances he forged were iron-clad. Where Jack was pinned to the Presidential receiving role, staying in one place to favour his back pains, Bobby kept in motion, manoeuvring, agile as an acrobat and just as fast.

'You're the, um, Caribbean lovely,' he told me, giving me his Bugs Bunny grin. 'I remember your great story about the night Batista fell.' Then, abruptly, as if I had slapped his face, the Irish eyes weren't smiling. 'You're also one of Lansky's ladies.'

'If you mean do I know him, do we speak now and then, the answer is yes. Otherwise being called a Lansky lady is a form of insult.'

His eyes darted from one part of my face to another like Jimmy Cagney looking for a fight. I couldn't tell if he was testing or just dishing out rudeness. 'So it won't come as any news,' he added, 'that Meyer Lansky is a bigger enemy than his prat-boy, Nixon.'

All of a sudden we had nothing to say to each other. Drop-dead remarks do tend to do that. I couldn't help but notice that after an evening of pleasant chat I was for the first time facing open hostility.

'Are you one of these accurate observers,' I asked, 'who can't be swayed by facts because your mind is already made up?'

'About Lansky? Yep.'

He paused. 'About you?' This time that Bugs Bunny grin with its big buck teeth was neither friendly nor goofy. 'We have you with Angleton, who couldn't run an invasion of an ant farm. Bad as that is we can live with it. But your Hoover connection makes you an enemy.'

'Of yours? Don't flatter me.'

'That pug-dog faggot thinks he's got the world's biggest file of confidential dirt.' Bobby's eyes narrowed. 'He ought to see ours on him.'

'*I* ought to,' I corrected him. 'Give me a look at it and let the *Times* win me a Pulitzer Prize.'

'How far'd you think you'd get?' He gave me an appraising look. 'Hoover's isn't a war you fight in the press. Or the courts. This is a back-alley fight. You gouge, cheat, ambush, kick nuts. And so does Hoover.'

'Against you? Your brother? Your family?'

He nodded. 'When we called off air cover at the Bay of Pigs we violated the Eleventh Commandment: Thou shalt not doublecross the mob.'

'Meyer has a thing about your father, but I guess you know that.'

'I'm surprised Hoover hasn't leaked that one yet. He's been leaking everything else, including money the mob paid to elect Jack. As if they didn't cough up millions to Nixon.'

Like a pair of boxers, we both paused and checked each other for superficial wounds. I got the strong feeling that the only way to get this man's respect was to land as many punches as he did. 'Hoover wants me spying on Angleton,' I said then. 'He didn't mention spying on you.'

He gave me a sideways, testing glance. 'You're already in the crossfire. What you need is friends, high up.'

'As high as Attorney General?'

He took hold of my forearm with strong, very warm fingers. 'You're an honest broad. You don't cover Justice or Defence or Treasury or State. Nobody there has peed in your ear. You have an assignment nobody connects with the big boys. So the big boys choose you to deliver all the messages.'

'And what would I deliver to Hoover?'

The corners of his mouth grimaced tensely like a squared-off trap. 'Tell him we know he's suppressing info he should pass along. We can protect ourselves, now that we fired Baughman from Secret Service. Tell Hoover we know how he operates. How he can stand back, look the other way and let something happen.' The contortions of his mouth had grown frightening.

'Tell the traitorous little pissant that if his mafia pals think he's given them a licence to kill, they're in for a shock.'

'You really think he's done that?'

'He's told them: the fix is in, right from the top on down. Every eye in law enforcement will look the other way. Do it, boys. This is your green light.'

'If that's the case,' I argued, 'why haven't you cut him loose the way you did Dulles and Baughman?'

'Not that easy. Hoover runs a slave society of blackmailed

police chiefs, newspaper columnists, TV producers, all sorts of child-molesters and masochists shouting his praises. Doing his dirty character assassination for him.'

'Then any message I deliver from you is so much chin-music.'

This time he didn't grin. 'Just tell him Bobby says . . . Bobby says the telephoto shots we took at La Jolla came out just great. Can you remember that?'

'It sounds like it was swiped from a Raymond Chandler epic. And he's supposed to go all wishy-washy, sink to his knees and beg for mercy?'

'You paint a terrific picture. J. Edgar on his knees before a woman. What a switch.' He gave my arm an affectionate squeeze. 'It was back in May, at Clyde Tolson's birthday retreat out in California. Our guy had a long-focus reflector lens. It gets you so close you can smell the KY jelly.'

'Sounds like just the message to get the messenger killed.'

'Listen, I warned you this was back-alley warfare.'

'But you didn't warn me I'd be stupid enough to say yes.'

When the Latin-American music came around again, I was dancing with my date from the *Times*, Andy. A nice boy, he wouldn't remain in print journalism much longer. He would soon become a smooth, believable TV anchor man.

'What, not a rhumba?' I asked. 'Not the favourite dance of osteopaths and accountants from Fairfax County?'

The band was playing a slow, terribly seductive, percussive tango, featuring a high cornet solo that loosened the wax in your ears. 'A slow tango. Do you know the steps?' I asked.

'Let's fake it.'

'You don't fake the tango.' We danced for a while, me leading. I'd heard the tune before, usually much faster. Minor for most of the chorus. 'Tango Havana, played like horror movie music.'

'Hey, I'm impressed.' He had caught on and taken over the lead. That was why, when he bent me over backwards, part of my lower back gave a deep, soulful bwang! and went into spasm.

He rushed me off the floor and tried to rest my bottom on a

chair. 'No!' It was Jack Kennedy's voice. 'She has to keep standing.'

The President of the United States of America took me in his arms. The pain in my lower back was so appalling I couldn't speak. His arms folded under my armpits and he lifted, very slightly.

Our eyes were on a level with each other, engaged in something so sexual it exceeded any pain the sex act could produce. The tango orchestrated a moan, a howl, sinister and scary.

'How's that?'

'Mm. Sexy.'

He kept me slightly off the ground for a few moments more. What this was doing to his back I had no idea. But I could feel the Presidential erection. The tango mimed a long, slow screw, necrophiliac in its mounting terror. JFK's glance remained locked with mine. 'Girls always say yes to Bobby.'

'I already did. You guys get your signals straight.'

Carefully he released one hand from supporting me. He patted my belly. 'Not guilty, your honour,' he murmured.

Tell me, Why Girl, why oh why does a notorious swordsman, who happens to be the President, send a female heart as curmudgeonly as mine into cardiac arrest?

'Angleton's butt hangs by a thread,' he murmured. 'That memo of yours has made the rounds of every spook in the District. It finally got to me.'

'Lord, it doesn't make any of us look brilliant, letting Kim Philby invent American foreign relations.'

He smiled charmingly, his hand massaging my spine where it bifurcates into buttocks. Just, in fact, where carrying Susannah had started giving me backaches.

'Don't quit now,' I mumbled brokenly. 'Nobody told me you had magic hands.'

He gave me a reassuring grin, not the kind his brother had used. 'Remember, Midge,' he murmured, 'life's tricky. I'm the magician who just saved your immortal ass, so life's less tricky. Andy, keep her upright a while more?'

Andy took charge of my lifeless body. We continued to listen to Tango Havana. It had no words I knew. Words popped into my head anyway. Havana is death. Anything that touches Havana touches death. Plague city I have touched, sipped, eaten. Giant sepulchre. Ay, lagrimas.

As I hung there, all I could think of was that they'd all touched Havana, Hoover, Philby, Angleton, Gleb. Gleb?

'Miss Boardman?' A liveried chauffeur stood there. 'Mr Robert Kennedy's compliments, ma'am. The limo's waiting.'

Oh, wait! Hold on! Terrifying things happened. Nobody knew it, not even Andy to whom I was babbling. Tango Havana mourned on. Its moves were:

One: I sat down on a chair. Thunk!

Two: I started to sob. Tears spouted.

Three: I wailed, 'Life's tricky. Gleb knew that.'

Four: One of the White House press girls brought me a wad of Kleenex.

Five: Everybody understood. Back pain's a bitch. Poor Midge. Fifth month, is it? Have to get her home.

'Do you need a doctor?' the press girl asked. She was called Kathy.

Poor Gleb. 'Tortured him,' I told the girl.

'She says it's like torture,' she told Andy. 'You must've injured her back, you klunk. Let's get her to the limo.'

Amazing. People hear what they want to hear. I could've stood up on a chair, grabbed the band's microphone and sung the Tango Havana:

'Now hear this! Cha-cha-cha.

'Lansky had Gleb tortured to death.

'All of them are in cahoots.

'Lansky, Hoover, Angleton. Arriba!

'All of them want Jack and Bobby dead. Olé.'

'Honey,' Kathy told me. 'Try to relax.'

I could've yelled into the mike. 'We're doing the Tango Havana. Having fun? Say something, you bunch of implausible nincompoops!'

I was lying on a canvas sling. Andy and the driver were fitting me into the back of the world's largest, blackest, shiniest Fleetwood. A motorcycle cop roared up as escort. Kathy held a paper cup of cold water to my lips.

Such a sweet girl. What could I do without her? So comforting, one's own personal angel of death. Did Gleb have one, too?

'Relax, Ms Boardman. Everything's going to be al-l-l right.'

Chapter Thirty-Seven

I'm ashamed to admit it. A Havana boy like me, trained by El Pequeño, and for sure I didn't see what was coming.

But, then, neither did Angleton – to his dying day – and he'd been in business with Lansky a lot longer than I had.

They were brain-washing me at Kill Devil. One-time code pads, cut-outs, safe houses, clear channels. They were making an assassin out of me. I asked if Rita could come up and visit. You know the answer. She was in so tight with Fidel they wouldn't let her dip her toes in US tidewater. She was a dangerous alien.

It was a weird time. She wasn't so dangerous that I couldn't mail her my paychecks. Or pick up a phone and talk to her. But then, the relations between the US and Cuba have always been weird.

Also, I think they didn't want her with me because she would have guessed what was about to happen.

After a month learning the Agency's Silly Tricks Bible, I was free to return to Cuba via a stopover in South Miami Beach.

'Tell Meyer hello,' Angleton murmured in one of those voices that he believed he would later be able to deny.

In Miami I stayed clear of the swarms of Cubanos, many of whom would wonder what the hell I was doing in the US. I picked one of the few taxi drivers who was a white cracker – they call themselves conches, pronounced conks – and had him drive me to the Beach.

'Where does he eat dinner?' I asked. 'It's almost seven o'clock.'

'Eats who?'

185

'The Little Man. Don't come on innocent with me, Paleface.'

He frowned in his rear-view mirror, a middle-aged, saggy guy with women's tits. 'Try this joint,' he said, coming to a stop at the Singapore Motel. It boasted a small café.

'Is that a promise or a hope?'

'Cheese, the fare isn't even a fiver. Wha'd'y'expec' f'y'moolah?'

'And if I added another fiver?' I showed him a ten-dollar bill.

He took it. 'The guy eats dinner at home. The only time he's in this joint is when he's having coffee with a pal.'

'I'm a pal.'

'You look more like a male hooker.'

I locked his throat inside my crooked elbow and removed the ten-dollar bill from his greedy fingers. 'Being a cabby means you don't have to watch your mouth? Is that it?'

'Hey.' He was choking. 'Gg.'

I got out of the cab, dropped the bill in the gutter and walked inside the café. The girl behind the cash register seemed also to be the joint's sole waitress. She might have been the chef, too.

'Do me a big favour?' I asked.

'For love or money?' Her face was starting to light up. It must have been a slow evening so far.

'Call Meyer. Say Guapo is waiting to buy him a cup of coffee.'

She gave me the mere start of a stuck-out tongue, turned and picked up the wall telephone behind her. She slipped in a nickel and dialled a number.

'It's Belinda at the Singapore, Mr Lansky. Somebody called Guapo?'

She listened for a moment, then turned and looked me over a second time. 'Yeah, moderately handsome.' She nodded and hung up.

I produced another ten-dollar bill and slid it across to her. 'That's for the moderately. Let me have something nice and cool and keep the change, Belinda.'

She was slowly caressing her right breast, small but

shapely. 'They named me after a cigar. Cool, you said? Cool this isn't.'

'I was thinking more of something to drink.'

'You forgot how to suck?' She sighed unhappily. 'If I give you a lemon Coke does that mean I never see you again for the rest of my life?'

'What sort of contract is that? What does a thirsty guy have to do around here, Belinda?'

'When do you figure your cup of coffee with Mr Lansky will finish?'

'Are all you Beach broads this oversexed?'

'Guapo, you ask a lot of questions.' She made me a long lemon Coke, choked nine-tenths with ice the way they do in the US.

After a while a small mongrel dog of occasionally Pekinese background arrived, followed on a leash by a small man of pure-blooded Ukrainian provenance. We went to a booth in the back of the café.

'Looking fit,' El Pequeño said in his thin, quiet voice. 'Good-looking guy like you, he's smart to keep fit.'

'You're pretty fit yourself.'

'Fit like shit. My insides are busted up.'

I looked him over. It had been a while since the last time I'd seen him, January first of 1959. He looked older than he needed to. His skin had gone, at the same time, darker and more pallid. But somebody was keeping him well dressed, very natty in two-tone brogues and a blue-white seersucker blazer.

It being Florida, he wore no tie and showed his neck was as crepy as a turkey's, as if he'd originally been a fat guy with a thick neck, much shrunken now. He might have been sleek, but never fat. Now he had this sort of wattle that moved out of synch with his neck, lagging a beat as his head swung to one side or the other.

He reached into his jacket and brought out a cigar. 'Enjoy,' he said. 'It's got the right band on it.'

I could tell without checking that it was a Melendez. 'I don't smoke,' I confessed.

'Too bad. But not essential.'

I listened for the rest but it didn't come. 'Essential for what?'

'Let me explain, Guapo. Angleton knows he has to broker any assassination attempt through me.'

At Kill Devil, once I became a trainee, not a suspect, I got to hear assassin secrets, among them the forty-three crack-brained dreams being analysed for assassinating President Kennedy. Mel and Chet had been merely an earlier loony contingent. You understand this was all so that JFK could be *protected*.

But to hear that Angleton had advanced to the level of brokering such a kill through the mafia struck me as completely evil. 'How did he get to be the target?' I asked Meyer, hoping I didn't sound shocked.

'You have to ask? Who brings the bastard down gets a combined joint reward of five million dollars. In cash.'

'Whose cash? His own government's?' I was starting to froth over with anger. The poor bastard Kennedy had been in office a year and he already had a price on his head? Not from the Russians, from his own spooks? Luckily I kept my trap shut.

'Not a lot of gelt,' El Pequeño mused, 'when you figure it'd open Cuba again.'

The pause was even more shocked on my side. 'Five mil . . . to ice Fidel?'

'None of that is going to stick to my fingers or yours, Guapo. We are middlemen. You're Angleton's cut-out. I move between Sam Giancana, Carlos Marcello and the law guys who are set to turn a blind eye. But before you return to Havana, you have to have a reason, a watertight excuse, for popping back and forth to the States. Get it?'

'No.'

He picked up the cigar again. 'Tell me what you see here?'

I grinned. 'It's a Melendez short, shaped like a stogie, the size your pal Feelbi likes.'

'See? You already have the knowhow. You ask your father-in-law to fill you in on the tobacco types, claro, madura. You already know a panatela from a perfecto. To you a cigar's a smoke, right?'

'It's something else?'

He almost laughed in that terribly quiet way of his. 'Just like a beer or a snort of alky is a drink, right?'

'It isn't?'

'Guapo, you are too innocent to live. From 1918 to 1933, a shot of hooch was the way we ran America. The secret . . .'

The hairs at the back of my neck started to bristle. It was coming to me but Lansky wouldn't deny himself the pleasure of making me look stupid.

'In this great land of ours,' he muttered softly, 'well-to-do schmuckolas need to puff up their image on cigars, the way they buy a Caddy or a hand-made London suit and shoes or an eighteen-year-old nafke with giant tits.

'In 1959, these guys were perfectly willing, and able, to buy a single Cuban supremo of well-known brand, protected in a cedar box or an aluminium tube, for anything between ten and fifty bucks. They would open it up in a restaurant so their business prospect or some doll could see how rich they were. True?'

Even the Melendez name, barely known outside Cuba, could produce such a flashily packaged smoke.

'You mean to tell me,' I began, 'that the whole Bay of Pigs disaster was staged so you guys could make Cuban cigars illegal?'

'Of course not.' When he smiled his teeth had a dark look, as if he had been chewing on raw meat. 'It's only a by-product, Guapo. Embargoing cigars makes one of these ego-building cedar-boxed numbers worth at least two hundred a throw. Maybe more.'

His smile looked even bloodier. 'Just a by-product. Like the whole aerospace defence industry is only a by-product of hating Russia.' He dipped into his jacket again and brought out a business card:

'CARIBBEAN TOBACCO CORP,' it read, with addresses in Miami, Los Angeles and Dallas. At the bottom right was printed 'Victor Sanchez, Director of Sales'.

'You're serious?'

'Right now,' he told me, 'what we're stealing out of Castro's warehouses, smuggled into the States, produces a weekly turnover of nearly a million bucks. We clear more than half as profit. If you can make an under-the-table deal with Fidel to help us bust the embargo, we quadruple our take overnight.'

This man's reading of the minds of others was always scary. His instinct for the crack that widens to a chasm was always supernatural. He had every right to believe that Fidel would go for such a deal, maf or not. It produced hard currency for Cuba, thumbed its nose at Uncle Sam and kept the mystical reputation of Cuban tobacco alive.

I pocketed the card with my name on it. 'So tell me,' I asked then, 'why can't Angleton see that by making Fidel a partner, we guarantee he stays alive and well?' The look he gave me said I'm-ashamed-of-you clearer than words. Obviously, Angleton knew nothing about the cigars.

Belinda arrived with two coffees. Holding them behind El Pequeño's head out of sight, she mimed squeezing a squirt of her milk into each cup. I have rarely run into a non-professional girl as goofy as this one.

'If you want more milk,' she told me, setting down the cups, 'just ask.'

Chapter Thirty-Eight

In early winter, Washington, DC can be lovely. Yes, I was back in Walter Reed Hospital's maternity wing. Lord, yes, this time I produced the real Susannah. As a reward I had two visitors at the same time.

Emory, my second husband, was tall and, being a combat pilot, slender. I am old-fashioned enough to believe that one speaks no ill of the dead.

This was autumn. The following February Emory was being ferried by copter to the Tan Son Nhut airbase, not even as pilot, just another passenger. Off we go, into the wild blue yonder. Flying high into the sun.

Guerrilla fire did the whole chopper with a heat-seeking

missile launched from one of those shoulder-held bazookas. Down we dive, spouting our flame from under. At 'em, boys, give 'em the gun.

Some Headquarters clown, not thinking, sent home with Emory's dogtags the cruel shard of shrapnel the size of an exploded baked potato that had, I think, done him in.

Susannah still has it, mounted on a wooden base, sitting on her mantel with the tags nailed into the base. Well, if you were only a couple of months old when you had your last glimpse of your Dad, even shrapnel is something.

Emory was never a great talker, so he made my second visitor sound downright gabby. 'Thousands of things to relate,' Cousin Jim Angleton was saying, 'which I'll have to save till Major Emory gets a Triple-A Security Clearance.'

'He's OK,' I vouched. 'I mean, we're letting him get shot at.'

'Yes, I take your point,' the skinny, beaky Angleton agreed, his eyes hooding slightly as if signalling to me. Having said that, he lapsed into ordinary Langley gossip, who'd been promoted, retired, divorced.

'Somehow nobody ever gets married,' I pointed out.

'The job is hostile to normal family life.'

'Ha,' contributed Major Emory, USAF.

'Some people have no idea how severe hard security has to be. I had a fellow down at Kill Devil recently who asked if his wife could visit him.'

'He's not cut out for covert work, obviously.'

'You remember Victor?'

Angleton picked up his felt homburg from an adjoining chair and got slowly to his feet like a skeletal set of fire ladders. 'I'm off, Cousin Midge. Major, a great pleasure meeting you.'

He held his hat over his head and tipped it, then turned and left with that forward-leaning slope of his, as if moving on to the next embalming patient.

'Funny man,' I said, merely to make conversation. 'You want to stay for Susannah's next feeding?'

Emory wrinkled his nose. 'It gives me the hots, all that tit, loaded and firing.'

'Really?'

'When are they discharging you?'

'End of the week.'

'Can I get my hands on the wet goods then?'

I had never before heard him describe my sexual apparatus quite that way. I imagine it was something he'd picked up in 'Nam bordellos, along with God knew what else.

'They tell me,' I said, 'that women go quite off fucking for some months after giving birth. I wonder why?'

'Ha.'

I was still living in the same second-floor flat. It was big enough for two adults, but not when you added a newborn baby. There was no second bedroom, only a wide entry hall that took Susannah's crib. I must say I thought she was a marvellously co-operative baby, sleeping through the night after only a few weeks. The same couldn't be said about Emory.

He seemed to have (a) girl(s) in Washington. At least somebody called him now and then and left one of those cryptic 'Ask him to call his office before three p.m.' messages. Since Emory's unit was in 'Nam, he couldn't possibly have a local office. Just a local girl.

Her (their) existence had no effect on his libido. I imagine a fellow with Emory's self-esteem wouldn't worry that Susannah's entry only marginally matched up with his last visit to my bed. By the same token, however, he wanted to make damned sure my next foetus was his. Too.

'There,' he grunted, pulling out and off in a single sideways roll.

He reached for some Kleenex and carefully wiped down his penis and testicles as if they were made of non-rustproof metal. As his erection died he took a fresh Kleenex and began slopping out under his foreskin. I got an unpleasant picture of the kind of infections he'd had to protect against. Or was it just normal Air Force hygiene?

This was two weeks after Susannah arrived. As an after-thought he tucked a Kleenex in my vagina. 'I just planted bouncing baby boys. I'm locking those little burglars in. OK?'

Did I say he was taciturn? Sometimes one wished for total muteness. The only reason I remembered mattress remarks as charming as that was because, in an odd way, Emory seemed to have had a sort of premonition of multiple impregnation.

On Susannah's first birthday, the following autumn, I had twin girls.

Re-reading these notes now, so many decades later, I see that I still haven't forgiven the poor man. That's about all I can work up to, pitying him for an early and violent and useless death.

We live in fame, or go down in flame. Nothing can stop the Army Air Corps.

What I was left with was his service pension and a private insurance policy. That, plus my *Times* salary when I returned to work, and Cousin Jim's regular freelance payments, put me in the privileged position, for those days, of being a single mother who could afford a nurse, then a nanny, then baby-sitters. So, in a way, Emory did right by me, and his daughters, after all.

Rest in peace, old mattress warrior. Your death did nothing to forge peace in Vietnam. Nor did it bring a war-drugged nation to its senses, not for so many more years. Nor did it save more youngsters from being fed into the fire of combat. But it did remove from J. Edgar Hoover the blackmail weapon he held over my head.

He and Clyde were sipping bourbon and buying me a dry martini at one of Hoover's Washington hangouts. He changed them regularly, as he should have done, so that anyone wanting to assassinate him would first have to know where he was.

And, believe me, assassination was in the air. Castro's was spoken of openly. Bizarre attempts, often pinned on mafia stoolies, were freely discussed. Secretly, attempts on the lives of the Kennedys were a regular rumour.

'This is what I like,' Hoover said, his pugnacious, mean little face settling into dull-eyed rest as he smiled at me across the table. 'A pal, a co-worker, a helping hand, *without*

I need to clobber you with blackmail. Just plain ordinary fellowship.'

My head was shaking from side to side long before he ended his encomium to friendship. I had recently had my hair bobbed in that short, black, sleek mop-top look. You remember Louise Brooks in the 1920s. It even looked good with that single narrow lock of growing white in the bang over my left eye.

'No way,' I stated flatly. 'If ever I drank a farewell martini, this is it.'

'Har. Foolish girl.'

'No girl any more. Mother of one with two on the way.'

'All the more reason you need help in high places.'

Suddenly I was boiling mad. 'Exactly what your buddies, the Kennedy boys, promise. High places? Not high! Low! Poisonous slugs, lurking in pond scum to suck the blood out of their next victim.'

'Motherhood sure hasn't smoothed you down.'

'Not as long as people keep conning me with kindness. Is there a sign tacked to my back that reads "KICK ME"?'

Hoover glanced at his bosom buddy, Clyde Tolson. 'Clyde, wha'd'we do with this mouthy broad.' He turned his tiny eyes back to me. 'You see, you're an investment. Maybe you don't realise what we've put into setting you up with the Kennedys, with the Angletons, the Lanskys.'

'You? You set me up for the Kennedys. But the rest you lucked into and now your luck is saying goodbye. What's the line? Luck be a lady tonight? A lady should do you the favour of letting you know she's leaving. Bye bye.'

'You're saying it's possible to work for the *Times* and still be a lady?'

I frowned at him. I could feel an electric urge in my thighs to get up and walk out. But the martini was only half finished. 'Explain that remark, please?'

'I have stuff a reporter would die for. But she'd have to earn it the same way you have been, by feeding me Kennedy info.'

'You're right. No lady'd do that.' I finished the martini in one ladylike swallow. 'Um. Yes. All right. Tell me.'

'You tell me, are we working together or not?'

'Well.' I saw the waiter arriving with two more bourbon hi-balls for the boys and one great frosty martini for the girl.

'Well,' I asked, 'whoever said I was a lady?'

'Har.'

Chapter Thirty-Nine

Nobody can tell me that under Fidel my Cuba grew sleepy and tortoise-like. This for sure happened in other socialist lands. In fact, we now know the Marxist work ethic – we pretend to work, they pretend to pay us – sent many a country into a long snooze.

But they didn't have the advantage Cuba did: the implacable hatred of a giant superpower ninety miles away. Giant but with the petty mind of a gnat.

'A gnat,' Fidel grumbled.

His intelligence goons had met me at Mariel the instant I got off the speedboat *Vela*. They were not interested in this overpowered vessel of capitalism. In action they moved like kidnappers. I was glad to see that socialism hadn't slowed them down. All they wanted was to hustle me to Fidel's office and plant me in a squeaky chair across from his cluttered desk.

'No,' he corrected himself. 'A gnat has wings. The Yanqui has the brain of a body louse.'

He got to his feet and took a few paces towards and away from me. Many observers had reported that, for a Cuban, Fidel is quite tall. Well over six feet. When he paces, the floor shakes more than slightly. To have him also regard you closely with those dark, sad eyes is an additional weight.

'Fidel,' I said, 'we are not up against just Angleton. If that were the case we only had to call on your great friend Feelbi, who owns his immortal soul. No, we are once more up against El Pequeño.'

'*Your* great friend.'

'Employer, yes.' I sat silently for a moment, wondering how

195

much I should tell Dr Castro – as he was now called – and how much had to wait for a second meeting.

I had heard stories that as Yanqui pressure grew Fidelista hit squads emerged from the slime like toxic fungi, targeting not just spies and terrorists but, inevitably, ordinary dissidents, people who were honestly and a bit openly against the government. What I had to tell Fidel could be considered extremely anti-Fidel.

So there might be a midnight encounter with a hit squad and . . . no second meeting. 'Fidel, let me report some CIA plots against you.'

'They have been trying to poison me. This I know from an old girlfriend they paid to try it.'

He laughed softly and I joined in. The island has three major products: sugar cane, tobacco and former lovers of Fidel.

'This is a sabotage campaign called Operation Mongoose,' I said then.

'Ah! And I am the cobra they send the mongoose to attack?'

'They plan to torch all our cane fields before harvest. There is a second phase after they have destroyed Cuba's biggest money crop. They will intervene in the world sugar markets and depress the price. In other words – '

He waved his hand before his face impatiently, as if brushing away cigar smoke. 'Next point.'

'Next point: tobacco.'

'More torching?'

I noticed him feeling in a breast pocket of his olive-green combat fatigues. The mere mention of tobacco does that to smokers. It reminds them they are smokers. They begin to reach here and there, fingers searching for their next smoke.

Meanwhile his gaze grew distant, a knight of the Round Table questing for the Holy Grail. He finally found a working-man's cheroot which needed no cutting to prepare it. He lit it and sent fragrant clouds of smoke at me.

I shook my head. 'No torching. El Pequeño is black-marketing cigars stolen from Cuban warehouses. The market for contraband will pay four times the old prices. Much more as the embargo bites deeper. He wants a legitimate undercover deal with you to sell him cigars, spit in the eye of Uncle Sam and earn much hard currency.'

He stopped pacing, stopped smoking and stared down at me as if I had handed him a scorpion on a saucer, but a cute one. Just for the effect of it, I placed the business card Lansky had given me in Fidel's big hand.

His frown had always been intimidating. His close scrutiny had been fearsome. But now his grin, as if about to chomp off a finger and munch it down, scared me speechless.

'Guapo, guapo, guapo.' He shook his head as if trying to deny the existence of Victor Sanchez. 'Where would el revolucion be without you?'

I produced a small shrug. 'You have no idea for sure how temporary our great victory could be if Angleton crazies get their way.'

He drew down the corners of his mouth and his whole beard signalled disbelief. 'You consider the Covert Action people out of control?'

'Lone wolves. They eat each other. I lived for weeks in their lair. A government all their own on the dark side of the moon.'

'You are mistaken.'

He sighed heavily and marched back behind his desk. When he sat down the room shook a bit. He puffed smoke for a moment. It gave me the peculiar feeling that inside his head he was thinking so fast it caught fire.

Then: 'Never underestimate two things.'

He stopped for such a time that I thought he'd put out the fire. But no. He held up one hand and reduced it to thumb and forefinger. 'First, never forget, I am sitting at this desk courtesy of the CIA. We like to think Comrade Feelbi created the Bay of Pigs for the greater glory of the Soviet Union.'

He swung sideways in his chair and stared off into space. 'But, guapo, you know how loosely we held Cuba in 1959 and 1960. Nothing could have strengthened our hold on Cuba more than being attacked by the Yanqui.'

He let go of his thumb and held his forefinger. 'Second, never forget that the CIA is an arm of the US executive, the President. To kill me is called "executive action". This is not

197

just code. Assassination must be ordered by the executive. Never assume it goes off on its own, out of control.'

He brandished his forefinger at me as if giving me the up-yours sign. 'Everything the CIA does bears the approval of the man in the White House, whoever he may be. Do you understand?'

'Yes, I see.'

Fidel requires the same handling as my Rita. One always agrees, up front. Later one shifts to a truer position, one that accounts for all the facts, the shades of grey, the contradictions.

I mean, think of it: Angleton had no idea Lansky would be making great profits on the Cuban embargo. How would he know the man I was sent to assassinate I would first have to link with the cigar business even more than he already was? And keep very much alive?

I suppose to be a true leader, one must learn to ignore contradictions. But from my lower position on the totem pole, all I have seen of life is cross-currents, tangled motivations and the interweaving of treacheries. Was it up to me to taint my leader's purer view with such pollution?

'I must tell you what they were doing with me at their internment farm.'

'Transferring large sums of money. Your Rita reports the CIA has made you filthy rich.'

'They were teaching me how to murder you. Forget poison. Let me merely mention guns, grenades, rockets and mortars.'

I watched his tongue moisten his suddenly dry lips without once disturbing the position of the cheroot. 'And that doesn't mean they don't have half a dozen girls looking to slip cyanide in your daiquiri.'

He winced.

'Or hydrofluoric acid in your condom,' I added.

His beard seemed to retract in agony as he began puffing smoke like a locomotive on an upgrade. 'Or anthrax spores in your water supply.'

He stared for a long time at me, as if sucking truth from my brain. Then he got up, came around the desk and pulled me to my feet by my shoulders. My creaky chair cried out.

He kissed both my cheeks. The short cigar, tucked in a corner of his mouth, managed to give me a fervid love-scorch on my ear.

'El revolucion. Its first hero,' my leader said. 'And the last honest man in Havana.'

Chapter Forty

I don't say Operation Mongoose didn't hurt us. But like all CIA operations it was mounted by Yanqui amateurs. They hired professional Cuban helpers and then wouldn't trust them in the pinch. It was exactly like the Bay of Pigs on a slower time-scale, first thrusting Cuban mercenaries forward, then betraying them out of sheer paranoia.

Or plain ordinary Yanqui racial prejudice. What do these spicks know? How can we trust these illiterate fuck-ups who talk funny? Most've'em have coon blood in their veins anyway. Better take charge and do it ourselves.

Taking charge you still need to take advice. To an amateur, a cane field in the dark loses its sharp outlines. In broad daylight anybody can tell if the cane stalks have already been chopped and carted off to the mill. This produces a lot of tall, useless leaves. But at night, if advised by the native experts that these are what you torch . . .

If you're sent into enemy territory to set fields on fire, that's what you do. Especially if the Cubans who advise you at night are by day the illiterate spicks on the payroll of the Caribbean Tobacco Corp. That was my little joke, using Lansky money to fund the anti-Mongoose brigades.

And, meanwhile, the Russians kept installing their missile bases.

Meanwhile, we cigar smugglers got a handshake from Fidel. How would it have looked to put the deal into writing as a legal contract? The handshake meant: Cuban intelligence will look the other way while you export every quality cigar in our warehouses. Just remember the briefcase of hundred-dollar bills once a week.

At Lansky's request, any perfecto or panatela six inches or longer, whether madura or claro tobacco, was to be tubed, screwed airtight-shut, profusely labelled and laid reverently to rest in an aromatic cedar coffin at least a foot long and perhaps four inches high and wide.

El Pequeño stayed in the US. I worked my ass off as his Number One deputy. It didn't take a genius to see that he was scared to show his face in Havana. Too many had died because of him, murdered when he ran Cuba or shot when he sent them to die at the Bay of Pigs. As long as I made sure we were rolling and shipping cigars worth several hundred each on the black market, he was content to remain out of sight.

To roll such a cigar requires special handling.

By this time my mother had agreed to a month's trial at the Melendez plantation and factories in the far west of the island. She would set the books in order, institute new accounting procedures and – since this was her basic expertise – take charge of supervising the young women who did the actual rolling.

'Anything as long as six inches,' she told Rita, the two of them giggling, 'is under my control.'

Never having seen a quality cigar rolled, and not being a smoker, it came as a deep shock when I finally visited the factory. You would have thought, considering how I grew up, that a roomful of women in their late teens and early twenties – I looked it up; they are called nubile – would have little effect on me. You would be wrong.

To begin with, the Melendez factory is a huge place, but only one storey high, like a low barn. Very inadequate ceiling fans manage to move the air around but, by and large, the huge halls are humid at eighty degrees and downright damp when the thermometer hits one hundred.

Men and women are strictly segregated. Mostly the men are old. Their sons till the tobacco fields. The fathers and grandfathers produce the cheaper cigars in mass quantities, packed in boxes or cellophane-wrapped in five-sided packets of six cigars each.

It's not a hand operation, more of a Detroit assembly line. And these are the original machines, introduced right after the turn of the century, noisy and prone to breakdowns. They require a special repair squad that does nothing else.

The women's hall is just as hot and damp. But the work is different. Not a machine in sight. It's the women who handle the six-inchers and make them stiff. Naturally a hand job.

The air is sharp with the odour of cured quality tobacco, like living inside a snuff bag. It is also aromatic with female musk. There is no machine clatter or female chatter, just a soft dovecote murmur of quiet voices. Tobacco scraps and dust lie underfoot.

Against the heat the girls wear as little as they can. Since no men are allowed in the hall, the women frequently go bare-breasted. Basketball shorts or cotton panties complete their wardrobe. Do you begin to see the effect on a man watching them from a peephole his mother showed him?

At Guantánamo the brothel women had a parlour where they might read magazines while they waited, or dance to a radio. But mostly they were off in their rooms with customers. Never could I remember seeing more than two or three in one place at one time.

Here thirty young women, mostly half-naked, sat cross-legged as they rolled the cigars. There is a lot of folklore about this work and the superstitions that require it be done by women. Originally only virgins did the work in the days when the Arawak Indians rolled their own smokes.

There may have been virgins in the hall the day I spied on them. My mother mentioned that she already knew some of the young women. They were alumnae of Guantánamo, as she was.

'Hard to know,' she explained. 'Women have ways of changing their hair and make-up. In any event, you can imagine we don't ask each other such questions.'

'Why not?'

'Don't be stupid.'

It was by asking stupid questions that I learned more about the operation. Cigar-makers sit cross legged for a reason which has nothing to do with virginity. To begin with, a girl will assemble shorter leaves or those accidentally torn in pieces during the long ageing process. This is filler but it is of wrapper quality.

They roll the mass into a cigar shape between the palms of their hands, compacting as they go along. Then, from the leaves on their table they will select several of the best and largest.

With great skill they will drape and wrap these super-leaves diagonally over the filler mass. To get it to hold together in this humid heat requires a slight touch of some sort of binding fluid.

Very slowly and carefully, the women roll the almost finished cigars over the soft, damp, velvety inside skin of their upper thighs. The tiny beads of sweat there, so close to the promised land, inches from paradise, exude the female scent so prized by the largely male smokers of cigars.

Like the tobacco leaves, this natural binding fluid is also aged. The rolled cigar is clamped in double wooden moulds to make sure it dries firm and within the proper measure for packaging. Only then is it ready to be cased and shipped.

Most men have no idea why they dote on the quality Cuban cigar. They just know that since the embargo and the start-up of rival factories in other parts of the Caribbean, nothing tastes like the true Cuban product.

Let me say at once that this thigh procedure is entirely hygienic. If, instead, the women licked the cigars with a kiss of saliva, diseases might possibly be transmitted. But decades of experience have proved that this use of a woman's sweet perspiration is quite . . . quite . . .

Obviously, you could not get away with acrid male sweat, could you?

My mother edged in behind me as I watched. I was speechless, maybe for the first time in my life. The sight of all those erect tan penises being lovingly rolled in pre-vaginal sweat . . . ay, lagrimas! The heated musk of thirty women hard at work. The acre of breasts, small and neat, big and overpowering, white, tan, black, each glistening with its central river of perspiration.

'Say something.'

'I can't.'

'You're in awe,' she accused me. 'I brought you up to worship the velvet of women's skin. Now these cats have your tongue.' She gave me a sharp elbow in my ribs. 'I'm getting you out of here. That much I owe Rita.'

'In a minute. No rush.'

'I find out the men raffle that peephole. The winner gets to sneak a look for as long as it takes him to jerk off.'

'Ten seconds?'

Laughing, she pulled me away along a corridor and out into the laser-hot sun. 'Some production, eh?'

'How did they run it before you? You are a natural supervisor.'

She searched my face for a long moment. When she spoke she had changed the subject completely. 'Guapo, you are working again for El Pequeño. Anything to do with that man is dangerous.'

'Yes.'

'They tell me you go back and forth to Miami all the time now.'

'Mostly New Orleans.'

'Why there?'

'It's a big cigar-making city.'

'So is Miami,' she persisted.

I shrugged. 'Lansky doesn't trust Santos Traficante, the clever Miami mafiosi. He once tried to muscle in on Havana. In New Orleans El Pequeño has a firm arrangement with Carlos Marcello. Stupid but reliable. Marcello's so stupid Lansky pays him off in cigars.'

'Ah. The specials rolled by black girls?'

'Is that his weakness? If he had to pay money the black market price is five hundred a smoke.'

We looked at each other in silence for a long time. I asked myself how she had ever raised me to some degree of being a human being. She asked herself how long the two of us would remain stuck on the underside of life, controlled by underworld spiders, mired in the flypaper of this cut-rate life.

How do I know what she asked?

Did I need it spelled out? Over the past few years, since I was a tough kid of eighteen running El Pequeño's errands of death, the Sanchez fortune had risen, if you measured that rise in money. Some day, thanks to criminals like Angleton and Lansky, we might even consider ourselves rich.

But that was such a long way off.

Chapter Forty-One

Towards the end of 1962, my twin daughters arrived. They almost qualified as Christmas presents.

Susannah wasn't too pleased to greet these premature gifts which ate up all my time. But, Lord, I was. They were clearly Emory's, dead in 'Nam, on whose insurance we were living. They helped salve my conscience.

One was named Jane, for Emory's mother, as he had asked. The other was Kate, for my mother. Not Katharine, Kate. Within a month, thanks to a good baby nurse, I was once more filing stories for the *Times*.

WASHINGTON
SPOOKS WALK
ONCE AGAIN

– by Midge Boardman

(Oct. 3 – Washington, DC) It's said real spooks never die, they simply get recycled. Whether this accords with the CIA's basic manual or not, the fact is ex-spooks certainly stir the Capital's rumour factory to new activity, especially now that we've spotted Russian missile launchers in Cuba.

As always, it's the 'why' that matters.

First missiles. Now the noted Kim Philby, redolent of 1950s double-spook scandals in British intelligence circles, but officially cleared by the prime minister of that era, Harold Macmillan. In Washington's current pre-nuclear prep for a pre-emptive-strike, such sightings excite attention.

Philby is remembered from the late 1940s when, as chief of British Intelligence in our capital, he hobnobbed with our own top security people.

The donnish Cambridge graduate now sports an American wife and a Beirut tan. He makes his headquarters there as correspondent for the London *Observer* and the authoritative *Economist* magazine.

Still, it was a bit of a shock to run into him at the Smithsonian last Sunday.

The rest of the story carried even less 'why'. No wonder it was yanked after the first edition. And, re-reading it now, I'm struck with shame. It's a malicious story designed to explode Kim's cover in Washington for the few days he was there.

Malicious but not vicious. I did wait till he'd left town before blowing the visit. But I had my reasons. One was that the new wife had been stolen from a colleague on the *Times* who'd thought Beirut was a safe place for him and his spouse to raise a small daughter.

The other was that Cousin Jim Angleton was mortally afraid of his own weak gene, Anglomania, and his well-known crush on Kim.

'Midge, must I tell you how many enemies I have in the Agency waiting for me to stumble?'

Again, I added, silently.

'Say it,' he responded in a bitter voice. 'Stumble again.'

We stared solemnly at each other. During the twins' pregnancy I had finally done what I should have done the day I first met Angleton. I checked our family trees. It took quite a bit of time because his had been deliberately expunged from most standard genealogical material. *Who's Who* was no help and the man didn't exist in official government documents.

I finally got at it through the Boardman side. Even then it wasn't positive proof. At the end of the nineteenth century, up in Peekskill, New York, one Peter Boardman had married a local schoolmarm named Letitia Angletonne, spinster of this parish.

Putative Cousin Jim, I knew, had been in bad odour among his high-ranking CIA colleagues not for the Bay of Pigs fiasco, still carried on the CIA's books as an unclosed case, but for his deliberate tainting of Sovint material being produced by KGB spooks who had crossed over hoping to win fame and fortune ratting out their old comrades.

Instead, as prisoners at Kill Devil Farm, they were all dying on the vine, dying of distrust and the sheer frustration of knowing you have something valuable to sell that day by day, like once-fresh fish, grows too stinking to command any price at all.

It's a funny business, intelligence. So damned much of it is based on luck.

I did run into Kim Philby at the Smithsonian. We did finish examining the exhibition and then retired for a drink at a popular District of Columbia watering hole called the Hawk and Dove. We had last seen each other when I drove Meyer to the Havana airport in the British Embassy's Jaguar that hungover January the First, 1959.

I have mentioned how pleasant Philby was to chat with, lightly. There was no other mode for him. Unlike most Englishmen, he truly liked women. But, no matter how one turned and shifted conversations towards more serious themes, he had the knack of keeping it light and in the end quite superficial.

Speaking as a journalist, I found it impossible to draw blood until I tried a personal attack. 'There's a man on the *Times* who's no great fan of Kim Philby.'

The Hawk and Dove was decorated in American Eclectic, alternatively known as Early Barn Sale, meaning framed photographs of someone's 1840s great-grandmother, pseudo-Colonial windvanes, milk cans and embossed tin road signs. I watched Kim do a full minute of minutely examining this tat-Americana before responding to my dig.

'No, I don't fancy I have a great many fans here in Washington. Jim Angleton hasn't rung me back. Neither has J. Edgar.'

He startled me by taking my hand and softly stroking my fingers. 'But I should think a feminist like you, my dear, would understand my wife's need to take control of her own life, even if it means divorce when one's child is quite young.'

'Divorce and abandonment.'

He let go of my hand. 'Not really. Custody was awarded the father but she has regular access. It's all perfectly in accord with the norm of these matters.'

'Hardly what I'd call – '

'Midge,' he interrupted me. 'Fresh martini?'

I frowned. 'Don't tell me we've hit a taboo topic. Don't tell me the way to divert Midge is another mart?'

'Taboo? I would have called it of questionable taste. Neither of us can claim to inhabit a high altar when it comes to marriages.' He waved over a waiter. 'Again, please.'

'For instance,' I persisted, 'as a man you might be more solicitous of the former husband's position as wronged party.'

'Up to him, sweet girl. Life's dodgy enough without one having to consider protecting the feelings of every Tom, Dick and Harry one scrapes across.'

'You draw the line where responsibility is concerned?'

His smile was sweet, tired but understanding. 'Midge, you're a novice where marriage is concerned. Two turns of the roulette wheel?' He took my hand again and I found myself gazing into those dark blue eyes.

'If you learn anything that way,' he went on, 'you learn life isn't a continuum. It's not a book, where events are connected. That means – '

'Don't patronise me, Universal Husband. I speak Higher Bullshit as glibly as you do.'

'Then you didn't carry Gleb's death over into Major Emory's death.'

A prize bastard, like the rest. 'Am I supposed to choke on my cud and ask incriminating questions?'

'Gleb was an old, dear friend to both of us, that's all. A drinking companion of many decades' standing.'

'And like any other drunk, he babbled.'

The new martinis arrived. Philby sighed. 'I was going to suggest a toast to someone dear to both of us.'

I picked up my chilled, triangular glass, shimmering with frosty droplets. 'Here's to Gleb, Moskovskaya's most popular field rep.'

He chuckled and touched glasses. 'Brava. It's the devil to make a joke out of a personal tragedy. I've spent my life trying to do it.'

'You've spent your life deodorising Stalin's rectum.'

'Precisely.'

The light talk had vanished. It was suddenly deep between us. Was he confessing guilt? Agreeing his life had been wasted? That all intelligence work was nonsense? Gleb had been his case officer, not his long-lost kid brother. There had been a backbone of steel to the Philby career. Was he breaking down into mush?

'If one has work to do,' he mused, his voice suddenly slower, 'one grows a casing around one's heart. If one has dedicated oneself to a vision, one requires some form of blinders to keep forging ahead.'

'Highest bullshit.'

'But true.'

'I hear the voice of someone who has quite ruthlessly followed his secret star for nearly thirty years now. It deserves medals and I hope you get them. It could never earn forgiveness.'

'Not for – ' His voice went scratchy. He cleared his throat. 'If forgiveness was my game, I could have bought it from a priest long ago.'

This was so true it silenced both of us. I turned my hand upside down, grasping his. 'Why are you here, you bastard?'

'It's what a foreign correspondent does. He travels.'

'Does the Cuban missile thing need fine-tuning?' My grip on his hand grew stronger. 'Are you here to issue the "Fire!" command? We're seeing all sorts of aborted invasion efforts. As of 1962 we've unleashed the Miami Cubans to start shooting up your freighters.'

'My freighters?'

'Two that I know of, the *Lvov* and the *Baku*.'

He lifted his martini and watched me through it, managing

to look clown-like, as if playing for a laugh. 'Lovely names. But not as lovely as Jane and Kate.'

'You are a fount of information.'

He glanced at his wristwatch. 'Cin-cin,' he said and drank his entire mart at one slug. 'I've a plane to catch.'

'Prague again?'

He frowned. 'No idea Gleb had been that indiscreet. New Orleans.'

It was my turn to check my watch. 'Mardi Gras isn't for months. Why New Orleans?'

Chapter Forty-Two

As a man who had survived El Revolucion, I tell you visiting New Orleans that October of 1962 was for sure like infiltrating an enemy camp under conditions of war.

The CIA's spy planes had at last discovered that Russians had placed missile bases in Cuba, targeted on the US.

Kennedy and Khrushchev were on the hot-line exchanging desperate threats and compromises before the warheads were loaded in the missiles.

The Yanqui man in the street – since he was brain-washed from infancy to believe his country would never make a first strike – was shitting in his B.V.D.s.

His nation, his family and his life were on the brink of becoming radioactive grease. Nobody told him that for every Russian warhead in Cuba – about thirty – there were twenty US warheads pointing towards Havana.

Wherever he was at that moment, probably Beirut, Comrade Philby must have been going about his business with a pleased smile.

I like New Orleans because it is so Spanish. It is for sure as Spanish as Havana. And, like anything Spanish in the Caribbean, it smells of buried treasure.

I don't mean French. The old, historic part of New Orleans,

where you might expect pirate treasure, was a Spanish colony and only got a coat of French varnish just before it was sold off in 1803 to the Yanqui.

I came and went, bringing big sealed footlockers of cigars and collecting bulky briefcases of cash. It was torture, that trip. I took Cubana Airlines to Jamaica. As a Cubano, I couldn't fly direct from Havana to the US even though I was on the patriotic Norteamericano business of Meyer Lansky.

I had to wait in Jamaica for a flight to New Orleans and a chance to show the very real US passport that El Pequeño had procured for me from the Department of Immigration. But the less you know about that the better.

This flight would land me not in the big international airport west of town but the tiny local one up near Lake Pontchartrain. And then I would become something special. I think I was probably the only tourist who knew New Orleans by being guided around town exclusively by whores.

Whores are good at uncovering buried treasure. They have a nose for it.

I saw the inside of luxury hotel rooms and their plush bars downstairs. I ate at famous places like Antoine's, entering the side door and asking for El Pequeño's favourite waiter and being seated in lonely splendour at the big corner Lansky table under the sweeping ceiling fan.

But that isn't travel.

'You must be Muñoz,' some slimeball would say, always with a knockout blonde on his arm. Muñoz was the name on my authentic passport.

'He must be,' she would coo. 'Nobody else is that good looking.'

'What about Cary Grant?' I would ask.

If the Little Man wasn't himself there to meet with me, a contact like this one showed up, always with a whore. He never understood my real reason for asking to dine alone with the whore though, of course, he felt sure he knew. But I never touched the women. I simply preferred a bought woman to one of Lansky's local pimples. Who wouldn't?

Also, it appeared New Orleans was in the grip of open

warfare between the Marcello family of the local mafia and Bobby Kennedy's Justice Department. Being seen breaking bread with a local stand-in for El Pequeño was a sure way to get my name noted and filed against a future arrest.

I have always wondered why, with the Kennedy plate spilling over with problems, especially Cuban ones, the brothers still had time to pursue their obsession with getting the mafia behind bars.

'Thank God you got rid've him, darling,' the blonde would murmur. 'He's nothing but bad news.' She would give me a quizzical look. 'You're not Cuban, are you?'

'Puerto Rican.'

'Because everybody's scared to death the Cubans'll nuke us in our beds.'

'*Your* bed should be reserved for better things. Uh, the guy who just left. He's not your boyfriend, is he?'

'Him? He's my, um, agent.'

'I knew you were show biz.'

It was not a good year for the mafia, here or anywhere else. Frank Costello was being deported. Jimmy Hoffa was being indicted. Bobby was trying once again to deport Marcello or put him behind bars. He also had him in court, on gambling charges, for running a wire service.

Angelo Bruno of Philadelphia was being hounded by the Justice people. In Buffalo they were fitting up Freddy Randaccio for a frame. Sam Giancana of Chicago, although he shared a mistress with Jack Kennedy and existed under the imprimatur and nihil obstat of Pope Sinatra, was being growled at by Congressional committees.

Was such activity worthy of nationwide publicity, the way the missile crisis was? Of course not. How could you ask?

One or two newspapers printed a small wire service story that for all of 1962 the Kennedys had indicted 101 mafiosi, while the FBI hadn't come up with one. Any sensible editor was too scared to make a big story of it. But a few had grown semi-bold because other articles whispered of Hoover's upcoming retirement. Still, I knew better than to believe what I read in Yanqui newspapers.

For forty years they had made Hoover a symbol of fighting

crime while, for the same forty years, he had done just the opposite, franchised the Costellos and Lanskys to build the most powerful mafia on earth.

'Jack?' the blonde would say. 'Would I love a date with a stud like Jack Kennedy? Not when I have you, sweetness.'

'You don't have me. You have dinner with me. It's a different thing.'

'Eat now. Eat later. I'm not hard to please.'

'Now you're talking dirty.'

'Aren't you the guy who's going to nuke me in my own bed?'

I ask you, does anybody ever listen? I would feed her something very expensive, some of those New Orleans seafood specialties with a thick broth and mussels galore, and a lot of Sazeracs. Her breath would begin to smell of the absinthe or Pernod in them. If the place had dancing we would dance.

When another customer might bring her quickly to bed, I would ask her for a sightseeing tour. It tickled her pride. I saw more of New Orleans than anybody else. The old Pontalba Buildings, down by the French Market. The LaLaurie haunted house on Royal Street whose perverted mistress killed slaves by torture. The Cabildo. The State Arsenal, called a calabozo. Jackson Square, with Old Hickory making his horse rear high. Where Storeyville gave birth to jazz before the US Navy closed it down in 1918.

I know whores. I know each of them enjoyed being treated as if we were on a date. And, let's face it, sometimes the girl would be very pretty. And bright. But I had promised my mother never to cheat on Rita again.

Then I would give the girl one of Lansky's hundred-dollar bills, tuck her in a cab and send her on her way. That was me, Luis Muñoz, God's gift to prostitution. I would walk back to my hotel, sieving my thoughts to remove any dark and dirty ones so that I might sleep the sleep of the pure.

There are towns in this world that breathe the dark side of life. I have seen some of them, like Napoli, a city of evil and woe or – be frank – my own beloved Havana. Such a town is New Orleans. It isn't the evil that lives in its stones. It is just something native to world-class ports through whose harbours have passed God alone knows what.

Carrying God knew what treasure. For sure. Where there is crime there is loot. Where there is loot there are banks. And where banks can't be trusted, there are deep graves, well-covered, unmarked.

In a town this old its typically Spanish buildings turn blank faces to the world and keep their secrets well hidden within central courtyards. But I knew I was passing by the true life of this corrupt, easygoing city. I knew that behind these walls with their cast-iron balcony façades lay truly filthy joys, satanic crimes, perverse self-indulgences ... and dark surprises.

It would have driven crazy a man with less will-power.

This night I got back to my room around one in the morning. Her name had been Stephanie and she had been a brunette, for a change, with long hair dark as sin, as dark as Rita's, but straight, a waterfall of blackness. The pout on her sweet face when she realised she was being returned by cab was a mix of hurt and curiosity.

I suppose I should have been flattered. But having grown up so close to women I learned not to pay too much attention to pouts and the making of eyes. I opened my hotel room door, closed and locked it from the inside.

That was when all the lights went on.

'Guapo,' someone said. 'When they said you hadn't changed, they were spot on.' Shock. I admit it. That voice. Feelbi.

'Say "missile base",' I told him, 'and up pops Kim.'

'Spare my blushes. Just a humble toiler in God's vineyard.'

I squinted to see him. He got up from an upholstered armchair by the balcony window and put out his hand. I could smell the absinthe on his breath.

'Do you still have that victory medal Fidel awarded you?' he asked.

I was slow shaking hands. That whole unpleasant evening with the Russians came back to me. They'd been only a small scouting party. My Havana was now crawling with Russians. The Bay of Pigs had been a year and a half ago. And now that the Yanqui knew what the Russians had built on our soil there would be no stopping them.

Every nasty bit of Feelbi's original blueprint was coming true.

Around Havana most of us were asking the question: by which H-bomb would you rather be melted down, Yanqui or Russki? You got some very funny answers, let me tell you. Cuban humour works overtime right at the brink.

I gave him a dead look, not a welcoming one. 'Don't tell me you're here for drinks and a cigar.'

I eyed a pitcher in which Sazeracs had been delivered by Room Service. It was almost empty but the room was filled with the peculiar bourbon-absinthe aroma of the drink, part burned sugar, part anise, entirely corrupt, a drink for ladies of leisure and their pimps, or maybe Cambridge graduates.

He smiled loosely. 'We can skip the cigar.'

'You couldn't afford one, anyway.' I grumbled. 'The stuff I carry is like gold. Only not as heavy.'

'This isn't a cash transaction,' the Englishman explained.

I suppose that was meant as an English joke. 'It's been suggested by a mutual friend that you might help me do a quick recce about this town and save me valuable time. It's been suggested that you are a New Orleans aficionado. I need to develop some leads quickly.'

'How does it stand between you and El Pequeño?'

He looked mildly surprised. 'Our money is good. So the relationship remains a working one. I don't need much. Just intros to the local pro-Fidel and anti-Fidel people. If I know the Little Man he's studiously cultivated clout with both sides.'

It took me a long time answering. There was no way of knowing how someone from such a faraway mountaintop as Feelbi was operating. His arrival in my hotel room was like the fall to Earth of one of those minions of Beelzebub that the priests scare you with, all leather wings and the choke of brimstone.

I knew such visitors from Hell had supernatural powers. A telephone call and they could bring down a torrent of plutonium, a rain of toads and the slaying of the first-born. I knew, also, the track record of those who had worked closely with Feelbi. To know why he was here I had to know where his masters stood with Fidel.

This required mind reading.

Did Sovint want Castro dead or alive? I figured: alive to enforce good faith on the missile bases. I figured: dead to be replaced by a Moscow-trained puppet. All Havana gossiped about such questions. Why hadn't I paid closer attention to experts like Ramos the Ugly and my own dear Rita?

'It's crazy,' I told him, 'how many people want Castro dead. Or alive.'

I suppose an expert like Feelbi could produce whatever expression the moment required. What surprised me was that he looked puzzled. It took him a while to reshape his expression. 'Alive?' he snapped. 'Certainly alive and well.'

But as smooth as they had trained him at Cambridge or wherever the Brits train traitors, that little hesitation and that quick pro-Fidel assurance told me there was another job on the fire.

The old buried treasure again. But without a map.

Well, a minute ago I hadn't even suspected a surprise. I'd just have to be patient. The map to the buried treasure had to show up. Eventually.

The next morning, after some telephone calls, he and I went down to the riverside where Dumaine crosses Decatur. The haze was still rising off the slow-moving Mississippi. Even this early barges and lighters were moving here and there, loading, unloading. I suppose for the river folk seven a.m. was midday.

There is definitely a romance to running water. I'd always felt it in Havana. It's the thrill of movement, of a flow that never stops, a life always on the move. What a shame I was wasting its romance on fools like Feelbi.

That made me a greater fool. Instead of behaving like a man last night and now treating Stephanie to a breakfast of chicory-tinted coffee and sugared beignets after a night of reckless lovemaking, I was standing at the outdoor kiosk of the French Market with this tall English menace nobody loved.

The nasty pimple of last night who had provided me with Stephanie turned up at seven-thirty looking unshaven, hungover and full of pus about being wakened early. He knew he had to take orders from me because Lansky owned his ass. And he knew I knew. But being a Louisiana Siciliano, he had to put on a tough show of being his own man, or pimple.

Finally, show over, he said in a hurt tone: 'I suppose they have that FDC bunch in mind.'

'Says what?' I prodded. 'Can't you tell my friend's a gent? He doesn't speak hoodlum.'

'Friends of Democratic Cuba,' he spat out. 'Remember them? They were buying trucks for the CIA's Bay of Pigs invasion. They have an office in town.'

'You're being jolly helpful,' Feelbi said. 'Can you think of any other group?'

'FPCC? Uh, Fair Play for Cuba Committee. They're on Camp Street.'

'That's your two groups,' I told the Englishman. 'Anti-Fidel and pro-Fidel.' I signalled the pimple that his services were no longer needed.

He made a production of finishing his beignet and coffee. When he left he wore a line of snowy powdered sugar around his mouth. Be a clown. Be a clown. Especially when you're trying to come on mucho macho.

After he left, Feelbi turned to me and poured a little more molasses-talk. 'Fast results. It's been a pleasure working with you,' he said. 'Maybe our paths will cross again.'

'The brush-off? You still have to find these two outfits.'

'Any competent cabby will do that for me.'

I did my best to give him a real, friendly, your-best-interests-at-heart Kim Philby smile. 'Do you really think when I get back to Havana and tell Fidel this story he won't want to hear the rest? I'm sticking with you, Comrade Feelbi.'

He made a face. 'Sometimes people fare much better not being so bloody well-informed.'

The FDC office was shut tight. A sign on the door, penned in ink, promised us it would reopen after Mardi Gras. But the

FPCC office on Camp Street was bustling. People came and went. There was even a waiting room of sorts with a few people lounging about reading left-wing magazines.

The Englishman handed over his business card so quickly I couldn't read it.

'What are you hoping to find?' I demanded.

'Maybe nothing. Maybe a needle in a haystack.'

I watched him for a long moment. Another hunter for buried treasure. It was odd the spell this city had over all of us, even now when the entire US was momentarily expecting to hear the air raid sirens that always warn too late.

A moment later a tall, balding professor type ushered Feelbi inside. Apparently his arrival had been expected. But not mine. I sat down next to a slight young man who was worrying his chin with the unclean nail of his right forefinger.

He had that restless, unfocused look as if he'd forgotten why he was waiting. For a second or two he reminded me of Terry. She had that same unfinished look as if she barely knew how she'd got there but had no idea where she was going.

It was a special look that I associated with the new dancing, where you hopped around and did awkward things with your arms.

I wondered if that was a Young America look. How did such a look come into being? You never saw it in Havana except on a dance floor. Nor Miami, for that matter. Mel, the fat CIA interrogator who, with Chet, had danced his way into a ruptured palace revolt, he had that I'm-not-doing-this look. Maybe they taught it in college.

But this young guy here didn't look like college to me. Nor did he resemble Terry except around the slightly unfocused eyes. His finish was too ordinary, too common, to resemble the finely-cut details of Terry's face, her toes, her hands.

As a goddess, she maybe had a right to that look. But this young man was ordinary stuff, maybe even sub-ordinary. Yet the look was the same. Not lost. To be lost you have to *know* you're lost. No, it's a look that speaks of something that lies ahead. Some event, some deed, somethng . . . about to be lost.

217

It made me suddenly start talking to him. I don't know what it was. Maybe I was trying to track back on Terry. Maybe I missed her more than I admitted. 'Is this the place,' I began, 'where you can sign up to go to Cuba?'

I knew the Yanqui government had cracked down heavily on student visas even before the missile crisis. But even now, I had heard, if you claimed to be a journalist you might still be allowed to visit my island. He had a vaguely student look that went with the soon-to-be-lost look.

But then he nodded very seriously, pompously, hinting that his presence here might mean other things too important to discuss. He suddenly lost the first look and resembled an ordinary asshole.

I suppose when you are one you must give yourself airs. Nothing people are all the same: they desperately act out being something. Heavy silences help. I got tired of waiting for more wisdom to drip from his chops. 'You trying to get to Cuba?'

'I'm quite a traveller,' he assured me. 'I been a lot of places. Cuba might get to be one, yeah.' As if being inflated by a monster air pump, his face grew fatuous and foolish.

'Me, I just go back and forth.' I confessed. He looked bored at hearing this. 'To Cuba, that is.'

His eyes showed interest, not easy for a face as uninteresting as his. 'Hey. Good for you. Havana's my main goal. I was born here but I been around. Shit, man, I been everywhere. Even lived in Russia a while,' he added, unable to sound in any way modest.

'How'd you manage that?'

'Married a Russian girl.'

'Is that all it takes?' I wondered.

His smile grew conspiratorial. He dug in a pocket of his much-washed plaid shirt and brought out a photo of himself holding a rifle with a telescopic sight and a hand-gun. 'It always pays to be ready for action,' he informed me in a voice rich with pride and a lot of self-esteem.

'Now that missiles come into it, right?' he went on. 'I guess maybe that's why you're here?'

'Is what?'

He touched the photo by pointing at the rifle. 'That your interest?' He sighed and shifted expressions on his fatuous face. 'I'm haunting this place, hoping they'd take me on.'

'Should be easy enough if you can call yourself a journalist. Me, I'm a native-born Cuban. Uncle Sam wants me the hell and gone.'

Over the self-satisfied smile, his eyes widened. 'No shit? You sounded like an American.' He put the silly photo away. 'I just got back to town. Living here with my uncle. He runs a book, Uncle Dutz.' One eye squinted, like a sharpshooter taking aim.

'Knows his way round N'awlins,' he said, dropping into the accent. 'In tight with Marcello. Most bookies are. So I sent for my wife and daughter.'

'The Russian wife?'

He nodded. 'Damned fool gets homesick. She wrote her consulate here saying she wants to take the baby back home to Moscow to visit her folks. Can you beat that?'

I smiled and nodded but said nothing because my heart had just done a lurch. I wasn't sure I could speak a single word.

I was filled with surprise and awe. Wasn't life weird? Even complicated answers can come simply. So simply at first you just don't realise what you've got. Sometimes the map to buried treasure dodges you forever and sometimes it just flops open on to your lap.

But for sure this was New Orleans and I had a right to expect a little buena suerte, some Spanish good luck.

Hey! Only one question, Camarada Feelbi. You lucky Englishman, answer me one question and I will hand over your needle treasure buried in a haystack. Ready?

How long did it take the wife's pitiful letter to go from the Soviet consulate in New Orleans to Station Moscow to Kim Philby in Beirut?

I stuck my hand out. 'Name's Muñoz,' I said. 'Glad to meet you.'

He pressed his cold, damp hand to mine. The word is clammy. But it was, for all that, a firm handshake, no tremor, solid, his aiming eye still squinted. 'Name's Oswald,' he told me. 'That's my last name.'

Chapter Forty-Three

A hundred years ago the House of the Rising Sun was a New Orleans brothel, one of the most famous in Storeyville.

Nowadays late-closing music places sometimes let you stand up with a mike and croon away, Japanese style, to a recording. The old House of the Rising Sun had been a pioneer in such self-entertainment.

The patrons were rich older politicians, cotton brokers, bankers and other scum. They would take a girl off to what was supposed to be a private room. But it had a wall of peepholes where, for a silver dollar, you could watch Mayor Crotchrot do nasty things all over P'ti' Amalie. Or sometimes vice versa.

The fact that Crotchrot knew he was providing entertainment didn't seem to matter, either to him or his audience. It was a mark of odd prestige, I suppose. It was that kind of era.

But the House of the Rising Sun I was in tonight was a different kettle of fish. First of all, it was a copy-cat without teeth or claws, second a seafood joint and, third, one of those nerve centres, like the Gatita Negra in Havana, where the elite meet to greet, cheat, repeat and retreat.

This was October of 1962, I think, and Khrushchev and Kennedy had still not decided whether to let us all live or die. This time when I arrived, shepherding my overloaded cases of Cuba's finest, I was met by El Pequeño himself.

'Guapo, this is Denise.'

'A pleasure, Mr Muñoz.'

'That's my father's name,' I corrected her. She was a platinum blonde, almost as tall as I was, which made of Meyer the poison dwarf he was. 'Just call me Luis.'

'Louise?' she asked, mimicking the Spanish pronunciation. 'That's not – '

'Call me Lou.' I nodded to our mutual employer. 'You picked this one for brains, right?'

'Brains,' he agreed gamely, 'and beauty.'

He got to his feet, having neatly left on his chair a stuffed briefcase. Now, at last, he was taller than the two of us. 'Lemme wise you up, boychik,' he said in tones so low I barely heard him. 'That shipment you just brought? We figured it at a street price of half a mill. You know what this missile crisis has done?'

I stared up at him. 'Boosted the price?'

An evil grin warped his small, pointed face. 'Doubled it, guapo. Nice going.'

Off he went towards a darker corner of the House of the Rising Sun where a table quite far from the band, and lit mostly by one candle, supported three drinks.

Three men sat there listening to the female vocalist crooning an old tune about 'I am just a little girl who's looking for a little boy who's looking for a girl to love'. Two of the men, more or less my age, looked almost like brothers, with that absent expression I had noted before.

One I didn't know. The other was the fellow who called himself Oswald. The third drink was being inhaled by an older man who really seemed to be listening to the song. He was Kim Philby.

El Pequeño stopped for a moment at the table and bent sideways to say something in Comrade Feelbi's ear. Then he disappeared in the mêlée. I watched him reappear near the entrance, locked in earnest whispers with two short, stocky men. I recognised one as Carlos Marcello, whose mafia cosce controlled the city and in fact the whole Gulf Coast.

You could tell he had responsibilities, Don Carlos. He wore a worried face and small, bright eyes, probably enhanced by a touch of eyedrop to reduce the drug-swollen irises. The other chunky man had bodyguard written all over him, or at least in the bulge under the left lapel of his jacket.

'Your boyfriend knows all the celebs,' I muttered to Denise.

'Mr Johnson?' meaning Lansky. The band finished the song. 'He's not my boyfriend, silly. Now, Mr Marcello is another story. Him I see now and then.'

'And the third guy, who sort of resembles Marcello? His brother?'

'Silly billy. He manages this place. He's Jack Ruby.'

Abruptly the female vocalist burst out as the band went into a fake Dixieland foxtrot.

'You so ugly!
'Man, you ugly!
'You some ug-a-ly chile.
'Now the clothes that you wear
'Are not in style.
'Y'look jus' like an ape
'Ev'y time you smile.
'Ooh, how I hate ya,
'Ya alligator bait, ya.
'You the homeliest gal I ever saw.
'You five by five,
'Box-ankled too.
'How'd they ever get
'A pair of shoes on you?
'Yo hair is nappy.
'Who's yo pappy?
'You some ug-a-ly chile.'

I turned to Denise. 'What kind of song is that?'

She made a funny face. 'Been hearing it all my life. Some-body told me they used to sing it in the old Storeyville cafés.' She hummed along with the music for a moment and then sang in my ear:

'They's a hunch on y'back
'And a wart or two.
'They's a curse on y'fam'ly
'And a spell on you.
'Yo teeth is yella.
'Who's yo fella?
'You some ug-a-ly chile.'

The band was doing all those Dixieland things, the trombone slides, the high, shrill clarinet noodling, the percussive blats on the cornet's upper register. But I had heard better music from electronic chips.

'Denise.'
'Yes, Louise?'
'Lou.'

222

'Yes, Lou.' She tucked her long arm inside mine.

'Where in New Orleans do they still play jazz?'

'Well.' Under her marcelled platinum-blonde hair, a dead ringer for photos I'd seen of Jean Harlow, Denise's forehead wrinkled. It was not a big movement but it was startling in the way it changed her face from the usual Yanqui blah to something a lot like a real person.

'My boyfriend's a musician,' she said at last.

'What does he say?'

'He says there hasn't been any real jazz in New Orleans since the old time black guys went senile.'

'Old-age senile? Or too much Mary Warner?'

'Silly, is there a difference? My boyfriend says the only jazz is shipped in from the north. Little trios and combos that play in the lounges of the big chain hotels. You know, the Hiltons and Sheratons and such.'

Meyer had long gone. So had Marcello. Both had disappeared during the Ugly Chile number, leaving the man called Ruby behind. If he really was the manager of the House of the Rising Sun, this fake replica of Old Time Sex, he had a funny idea of what a manager did. He seemed planted at the entrance like a bouncer, still daring the world to check the bulge under his lapel.

All the way across the room the Feelbi table had added yet another young man. He was hard to tell from the other two. They were all slight but not small, unfocused without looking sleepy. Something other than their age seemed to give them a family resemblance, but I couldn't figure out what it was.

Nor could I figure what Sovint's top schemer was doing here, wasting his valuable time. As if he'd heard me, Feelbi got up and went into the men's room. I excused myself and followed him in. He was using the right-hand urinal. I opened up in the left one.

'Da svidanya, tovarich,' I said. In Havana we all picked up these useful bits of Russian in case any of us were put in charge of pressing the red buttons on the missile launchers. It absolutely did the trick as far as I was concerned. It made him jerk sideways and irrigate the floor.

When he saw who it was, he burst out laughing. 'You. Don't tell me I'm bog-trotting next to the busiest prick in New Orleans.'

'Who told you that?'

'The pick of the Marcello stable? Yours for the taking?'

'It's not the way it looks. And you? What're you up to with all those would-be Cuban tourists?'

His smile was angelic. 'Guapo, it's not the way it looks. Let's just say I'm doing a bit of personality testing.'

'If I knew what that meant, would I be any wiser?'

He shook off the last drop and zipped his fly. 'I'm more or less freelance now anyway.' He went to the door and started to open it. 'A man on as many payrolls as you surely understands the virtues of freelancing.'

'As a personality tester?' I zipped up and prepared to follow him out.

He shook his head. 'Give me two minutes head start. These three young lads are under heavy FBI surveillance. At least one of them is actually on Hoover's payroll. You don't need to be tied in.'

'You mean the Bureau haunts a den of evil like this one?'

'Ah, youth.' He shook his head as that sincerely friendly smile played over his lips and eyes again. 'When are you going to learn, Young Guapo? If it's evil, J. Edgar franchises it.'

'Communist propaganda.'

'Does that make it false?'

He got his two-minute lead time as I stood there trying to make sense of what he was hinting at. Heavy thinking is hard for me. I admit it. It was enough to give me a headache. When I returned to Denise, Feelbi's table was empty.

'Listen,' I began diplomatically, 'I got a headache.'

I moved a folded hundred-dollar bill across the table into the palm of her hand. 'Let's find you a cab to take you home.'

No sign of regret. She examined me coolly and then applied the same look to the hundred-dollar bill. 'I had a feeling you were too good looking to go for girls.'

'You got it, Denise. No hard feelings.'

She giggled, feeling under the table for my crotch. 'Every

little squeeze,' she sang softly, 'seems to blister Louise. What makes you think I don't service girls?'

'My God, of course you do. But not tonight. Let's go.'

Chapter Forty-Four

Going back is always the hardest part, even for a guy who knows Havana like his own face.

The briefcase I pick up in New Orleans must be placed in Fidel's hand and nobody else's. If this were a normal transaction it could all be done in the light of day. But there is nothing normal about it. Fidel doesn't want anybody seeing what happens. It would take endless explanation. And being in the midst of an about-to-be nuclear holocaust made it even worse.

Normally I fly from New Orleans either to Jamaica or to Mérida, in Mexico. I do this in the daytime and choose almost full planes because I want company, carrying so much in twenties, fifties and hundreds.

On the next leg of the trip I duck my Luis Muñoz passport and become Victor Sanchez again. I have to find either another day flight, this one to Havana, or I have to hire a light aircraft. There are very few choices. I often end up with shady characters who usually fly drugs. I arrange to be met at the other end by Fidel's guards.

On this leg of the trip my enemy is someone who knows why I go to and from New Orleans. El Pequeño has not tipped off my itinerary and payload. My employer is a bad man but he has never been known to cheat his partners.

But around him roost some of the meanest buzzards in the Gulf of Mexico. My only protection is that Lansky is not into drugs, where the buzzards eat each other. Not yet. But this is hardly a guarantee of any kind.

This particular return trip was typical, except in the way it ended. Early in the morning I took a Mexicana Airlines BAC 1-11 to Mérida. The US immigration people were checking passports very closely to see that no Cuban missile-carriers got through.

Mérida lies on top of the Yucatan peninsula directly south of New Orleans. Tilt the 1–11's steering a degree or two eastward and – if it wasn't for the Yanqui embargo – the flight could land at the same time in Havana.

I spent the rest of the day trying to find my last leg. The atmosphere was tight with fear. The Air Cubana flights had been cancelled. Cuban immigration didn't want any aircraft with potential saboteurs landing at Havana. Nor did they want Cuban skies choked with passenger flights when the Yanqui missiles arrived.

No help there. I checked out the other airlines known to schedule a Havana flight but because Air Cubana wasn't flying all other flights were overloaded. Any that went on from Havana were being denied overflight routing by Cuban traffic control. A mess.

You might think, considering the mission I was on, that Fidel could exercise some governmental influence and order at least one Air Cubana flight to be up and running. But you must remember that I was a spy in wartime: my own government would have to deny me if I were caught.

By afternoon I was talking to private pilots. This got to be scraping the barrel's bottom. Now, you know me. You know that if I strike out, totally, nobody with an aircraft who had the time to take me, for sure somebody was worsening the odds against me. You would smell a trap.

You would start to feel like a clay pigeon who will soon be blasted into flying chunks. Somebody phasing out the small-time pilots? It couldn't have been too hard.

Can you picture Mérida in those days, before the big tourist invasion of Yucatan spruced up the place? A fifty-dollar bill would've taken any freelance pilot out of circulation and given you change. Even if you had to bribe dozens, what was that compared to hijacking the 300,000 dollars I was carrying?

A bodyguard? For me? What good would that have done? Bodyguard loyalty cost about 200 dollars a day to buy. Double his fee and he'd bring you my head in a hatbox. Dry ice? No extra charge.

Do not insult either of us by suggesting local police. They existed mostly as cut-rate discounters in the bodyguard business. Of course, you might live through being bodyguarded by corrupt police. Minus your teeth, thumbs and toes. Hard to tell.

It was long after sundown when I ran across Boyd Cromarty. Desperate was no longer the right word for me. Anguished, squeezed, back to the wall. No wonder I cultivated this third-rate mid-forty drunk. Daiquiris were my weapon.

I have heard Feelbi use a British expression: legless. Boyd had just fallen off a bar stool beside me in a place out near Mérida's small airport, a bar called Calcetin de Viento, which is that tube of fabric that flies in the breeze to tell its direction and strength, a windsock.

The sun had just gone down over the mainland at Veracruz. Boyd Cromarty went down much more noisily on the stool next to me. The Windsock makes a daiquiri the way I do. I was finishing my third. Boyd was finishing his ninth.

He was a short, trim type of man but with a daiquiri pot belly. He had Scots-Irish eyebrows, bushy and sandy, and a long upper lip. When he was soberer, earlier, he had bragged about having been cashiered from the Irish Air Force, whatever that may be.

On an earlier daiquiri he had also admitted that he was the owner of a Grumman Seacat, a useful small amphibian aircraft whose one engine drives pusher and puller propellers. It seemed to me it could easily carry one passenger and an overloaded briefcase.

'Absolutely. There is only the matter of the bank,' he added.

I know that phrase. 'You mean they have a lien on the plane?'

'I mean they have it padlocked not half a minute from here in Hangar Three.'

He was squinting now because he found it hard to see me through what was left of Daiquiri Nine.

Let's face it. I'm not a pilot but I did all the hard work. I dragged his legless body over to Hangar Three once it got dark enough. I jimmied off the three padlocks the bank had affixed to the Grumman: one on the cockpit door, one on the fuel tank and one on the dolly that put wheels under the Seacat's boatlike hull.

I'm also the one who found a ten-gallon can and a nearby fuel pump and slowly stole enough gasoline to fill the Seacat's tanks. It took hours but none of that hard work was amazing. What really mystified me was why I wasn't already being stalked by buzzards. I imagine it was because they knew the Seacat might be ready to fly but Boyd wasn't.

At five a.m. he awoke with a vile hiccup and flailed about him for a moment as if I'd dumped him in chill water. 'Whoosht! Who be you?'

'The fella who's paying you five cees to land me in Havana.'

Recognition was out of the question, for sure. But he surprised me. His pale, watery eyes blinked with a form of intelligence. We are used to a pilot having steely, steady, far-seeing eyes. Boyd's looked like a newt's awakened by flash-bulb. He took a deep breath. 'Right!' he snapped.

Picking dried saliva off both corners of his mouth, he sighed heavily, as if inflating his lungs for the first time in days. He combed his sparse, dishwater-pink hair with his fingers. Then the two of us wheeled the creaking wooden dolly and its load of aircraft out the side door of the hangar.

It led down an incline into a narrow, polluted inlet that connected with the Gulf. In the dark, growing light of the sky irridescent rings of waste oil looked pearly and terribly expensive to produce. On the other side of the inlet, perhaps twenty yards from us, something small went 'Pop!'

It took out the nearest side window of the Grumman's cockpit. Glass spattered us both. Cromarty stumbled in and began pumping gasoline, priming the fat engine that sat overhead. A moment later he pressed the starter and it caught with an ungodly roar.

I crawled in beside him and slammed the door shut. We were already moving downstream. Behind us they must have continued shooting but I couldn't hear them. Anyway, one of these macho marksmen who thinks a .22 Colt Woodsman is all he needs deserves to lose his quarry if it's as easy to hit as we were.

Boyd gunned the engine, a particularly noisy one since it drove two props via rachitic gearwork. 'Look at the barstids!' he exclaimed, sniffing mightily.

I think he meant two police cars coming towards the creek with sirens screaming full blast. Hard to tell who'd called them, my would-be hijackers or the bank that thought it had a lien on the Seacat.

'Soon's we reach the Gulf, Bob's yer uncle,' I thought I heard Boyd say.

'What does that mean?'

'Means we can start our take-off run. Uh-oh.' His hands were shaking.

Another police car was bearing down on us, howling like a coyote. It braked hard and uniformed men jumped out, one with a riot version of a shotgun but the other with something serious, a World War II BAR mounted on a bipod. He had it set up in no time.

I heard Cromarty gun the engine so hard the little seaplane seemed to jump forward. In a moment, although we were still running down the centre of the inlet, the rear of the pontoon seemed to rise slightly. As he adjusted control wheels here and there, his fingers shook badly.

A moment later we were skidding across the tops of waves. The Gulf of Mexico loomed ahead. Boyd lifted the Grumman's nose and 'rotated' us slightly. We were airborne. The engine's roar shifted to a high hornet's buzz.

I could hear the BAR stuttering angrily. Wrong weapon. It couldn't lift high enough to follow us once we were aloft. As our speed increased and we began to run ahead of our own noise, I could hear the sirens below, moaning in chagrin.

'Boyd, you did it. Heartfelt thanks.'

Chapter Forty-Five

If you ever wondered whether pilots were like other people, I can tell you this. Either they sit in lone splendour, nose for sure up in the air, fiddling with switches and small controls. Or, like Boyd Cromarty, they ask you to sit beside them and start pointing out interesting things below.

The most interesting was that we could already see Havana.

The flight was short. A commercial airline, fussing about under traffic-control orders, can make a forty-minute affair of the trip. But Cromarty would have us there much sooner.

The man who had gone legless earlier in the evening was now on his third swallow of Dominican rum. It seemed to have a wake-up effect.

'Tell me where to set down.'

We were already losing altitude. Below, even before six a.m. with the sun only discolouring the eastern horizon, much paler than the big moon overhead, I could see that we had already passed the last of the tiny islands that make up the Archipelago de los Colorados.

Below lay Mariel, the harbour from which Angleton's cigarette boat had picked me up and brought me back. I looked closer. In fact . . .

In fact the damned boat, the *Vela* or its twin, was right below me, its stern throwing off a great rooster fantail of spume. 'Make a turn to the north,' I yelled to Boyd.

He banked left. The *Vela* swung left. 'Now east again,' I said. As we turned, so did the boat below. I took it to say as plain as words: 'We are following you. Wherever you land, we will be your welcoming party.' That shows you how stupid one person can be, thinking he is the centre of attention.

'Get Havana air traffic control on the radio.'

Boyd Cromarty said nothing.

'The radio,' I urged.

He gave me that bleary-eyed Celtic haze of a look. 'What radio?'

'You cannot operate an aircraft without a radio,' I reminded him.

'Yes, but the radio can only be found in the vault of the bank.'

We were flying now at about a thousand feet over my beloved city of Havana. With every second the eastern sky grew brighter.

'That cigarette boat down there,' I pointed out. 'Where can we land quickly, before they catch up?'

He shrugged. 'We are twice, three times as fast. We can land where we wish.'

'Where there are a lot of people gathered.'

'Near water? At six a.m.?' he asked.

'Is today Monday?'

He stared at me. 'Does that matter?'

'There is a special baseball event for the children. Fidel is pitching the first innings.'

'Against children?'

'The game is between Cuban construction workers and Russian construction workers.'

'At six a.m.?'

'It's a whole day's outing. Schoolchildren come from all over the island by truck. They will be fed. There will be speeches. Jugglers. More speeches.'

'Sounds horrible. Where is it?'

'The beach at Santa Maria del Mar.'

He frowned. 'Such a public place?'

'It's a public event.'

'Well guarded?'

'I'm counting on that.'

'So they might shoot at us,' he suggested.

'Fidel's guards? You know they will.'

'So that makes two sets of people trying to kill us?' He had slowed us down to just over stall speed and was tracking the cigarette boat. 'Look down there!'

'The boat?'

'It's a bloody floating arsenal. You mentioned missiles?

231

Man, y'dinna see the rocket launchers?' It was the first hint of brogue I'd heard in his voice.

'Cromarty! You're right. They're a Mongoose team working overtime.'

'They're not after us at all, y'eedgit. They're after bigger game.'

I felt the Grumman lift as we began to gain altitude again. Boyd was handling the awkward craft as if he'd had a full night's sleep and had never heard of a thing called alcohol.

'Watch the barstids,' he suggested.

They were heading due east. There were at least four Mongeese in the boat, none looking up at us. We had passed Havana now and were heading over the new facilities at Santa Maria del Mar, white-sand beaches and well-watered greenery meant to give the local people a luxury seaside resort much closer to town than posh Varadero to the east.

The sun had broken over the eastern horizon. I could see convoys of trucks converging on the area. The focus was a temporary baseball diamond with hastily installed bleachers. Already the rows of seats seemed filled. But as more trucks unloaded, schoolchildren with their teachers began to take seats on the surrounding grass.

We could see a podium and loudspeakers set up in front of home plate. Naturally there would be a speech from Dr Castro before he donned his pitcher's cap and glove. Many of the children, travelling all night, would now fall asleep.

The cigarette boat had trailed behind us. It now caught up and paused offshore, rocking slowly. The four men lifted massive rockets into their launchers. Their movements were precise, team-like, very Yanqui.

Given the sight-lines from shore and the lack of pleasure boats in the sea offshore, it seemed to me we were the only people who could have seen what was going on aboard the Mongoose speedboat.

'It's a CIA ambush,' I announced.

Cromarty peered down through watery eyes. 'Those launchers are for 90mm. rockets, not your baby bazookas. They can fair make cockaleekie of the whole baseball field and everybody in it.'

'We have to stop them.'

Along the coast road from Havana a motorcycle escort led a very short cortege of black government sedans. The open phaeton was Fidel's. He was standing up, cigar in mouth, waving both arms to the trucks still arriving with students.

'Damned fool, in an open car.'

'We Celts like to live dangerously.'

'You're calling him a Celt?'

'And what else, with a Gallego grandfather from Galicia over in Spain?'

'Can we land on the water in front of the rockets? Can we block them?'

'Block them, hell. I learned a trick or two in the Irish Air Force.'

From the speaker's podium at home plate the crazy Grumman Seacat was easy to see. It probably looked like part of the festivities. The cigarette boat at sea level was quite invisible.

Fidel's phaeton sedan arrived at first base. The band struck up. I could see the horizontal rays of dawn sunlight flash among the sousaphones and cornets. I could see the drummers drumming. But I couldn't hear what they were playing. For all I knew it could be 'Take Me Out to the Ball Game'. Fidel mounted the podium and gave the children his biggest arms-skyward salute.

Cromarty banked and began flying away, out to sea, in the general direction of Key West.

'Hey!' I yelped in his ear.

'Dinna fash y'rsel'.' His Scots-Irish brogue kept growing stronger. 'One wee drap.' I handed him the Dominican rum. It wasn't the usual water-white stuff. It was a cocktail in its own right, dark amber and sweetish.

He uptilted and finished the last of it in one long gargle. 'To me,' he breathed in a voice choked with emotion, 'tis Mother's bleeding milk.' He squinted over our left shoulders and found the cigarette boat miles away. He squinted ferociously.

'Right then,' Boyd Cromarty said. He banked left and

gunned the engine. It howled up a hideous scream as we shot forward, dropping like a flung stone.

We were closing in so noisily that the men in the Mongoose boat swivelled around to see us. One aimed an Armalite at us. Cromarty cut the engine suddenly and the Grumman slapped down across the tops of waves, bucketing like a roller coaster. Fa-dum! Fa-dum!

Our single pontoon sank deeper in the sea. Shkruush . . . and our speed slacked as if brakes had been applied. I slammed forward, nose against the windshield. Cromarty seemed to be steering us by the backflow of props over our rear rudder.

An instant later we crashed into the back of the Mongoose. 'Ram!' Cromarty shouted in delight. 'Bam! Ka-runch!'

The long, light-weight, beautiful mahogany-veneered hull lifted high out of the water. Our momentum toppled it sideways. Instantly it went keel up. Everything in it that wasn't lashed down sank to the bottom. Can Mongeese swim?

Water was pouring into our pontoon from its bashed-in nose. My own nose, battered by the windshield, was bleeding.

'Prepare,' Cromarty said with great dignity, 'to abandon ship. Dinna fergi' the bluidy briefcase.'

Chapter Forty-Six

The last time an enemy got this close to the US, we only needed one horse and one rider, Paul Revere.

I know. A Boordmaan was there, or so the family myth states. But now all Washington – which seemed to us like the entire nation – went on twenty-four-hour alert. Our SAC aerial defence, our ICBM networks, our Distant Early Warning arrays, our U-2 sky-spy squadron, all on instant Red Condition alert.

Everybody from newspaper hacks like me to female attendants in ladies rooms acted out great personal reactions to stress, drank double our daily dosage and where possible accelerated our sex life by an improbably overheated percentage.

Illiterates kept their radios tuned to news broadcasts. Motorists switched from country-and-western to all-news stations. Never before did the six p.m. network news have such high audience ratings.

Me? Lord, if I'd been able to let it, keeping track of a one-year-old and two newborns would've used up all my missile crisis energy. But nobody let me get away with such an obvious cop-out.

What early in autumn had seemed more CIA paranoia turned out by late autumn to be the real thing. Our U-2s officially noted the next step in the Philby Bay of Pigs Plot: arrival and installation of Soviet missiles and launchers in Cuba.

By October 20, on a political trip to the midwest, President Kennedy was alerted that the state of readiness in Cuba had reached combat level. He stiffed Chicago, hustled back to Washington. Sweat started to pour.

Moreover, although the Russians hadn't yet installed the missiles' atomic warheads, the CIA reported that our nuclear death had been loaded and was on a slow boat to Havana.

U-2 pilots had watched Soviet Strategic Rocket Forces loading warheads aboard the freighter *Poltava* at Odessa, supposedly bound for Algiers but now steaming west across the Atlantic to arrive in the fullness of time.

This suggested that the Russians themselves were in no hurry to arm their missiles. Otherwise they'd have flown the warheads in. They probably figured they had time because they hadn't been spotted. How delightfully naive. The whole sky was an eye.

Now, over night, everybody knew everything. The dare, if that was what it was – the test of Kennedy guts and Khrushchev stubbornness – had been taken up.

Life took on sudden, frightening colours. I had brought sandwiches and coffee and Susannah in a stroller to Lafayette Park, behind the White House. We were meeting a 'source' – actually that nice press girl, Kathy, on the Kennedy staff who'd put me in a limo the night of the Rose Garden freak-out. She and I would exchange the kind of chitchat I could re-create as an exclusive leak.

After she played with Susannah for a while – at one, Susannah was walking and talking and hasn't stopped since – we both felt the same sudden clutching at our hearts. I was gaping at a statue of Lafayette, who had nursemaided us colonists in our infancy.

'I guess . . .' Kathy's voice drifted away.

'I guess this is all sort of futile,' I finished for her.

We stared at Susannah, too young to feel what had settled down over us like an opaque mist. And the longer we looked into those big, clear, witch-hazel eyes of hers, the more we saw the mushroom cloud that would be Washington, DC.

'I mean it's easy for me,' Kathy murmured, so as not to frighten Susannah. 'I mean I'm single and not attached. But you've got three. I mean it's not fair for you. I mean if I go, what the hell, I go. But . . . babies?'

The leaves were falling this late in October. The Earth was dying right before our eyes.

It finally got to Susannah and she began to whimper. So we dried our own eyes and switched on grins and played let's pretend. Let's pretend the men stop playing chicken and agree to behave.

'I know what.' Kathy looked away from me. 'Let's pretend we'll be here with all three of your girls a year from now. Having a picnic.'

I lifted my styrofoam cup of coffee. 'I'll drink to that.'

Personal plans got cruelly axed. In my new, slim condition, I had looked forward to another White House social. I was, this time, ready for any flirt the Kennedys had on offer. But all parties were cancelled. The phone lines between Washington and Moscow choked up first with accusations and denials while Jack Kennedy and Nikita Khrushchev measured what had happened.

Their own techno-generals, idiot-savant button-pushers of both the missile and the spy plane, had produced a full-frontal confrontation, a shoving contest designed to become a nuclear holocaust. *Why* did they do this? What *else* do generals do?

Now the politicians stepped forward. This always reminds me of the joke that quotes the three biggest lies in the world. It ends with 'I'm from the Federal government and I'm here to help you.'

First came the informal or secret polling of both nations' consciences, hurried and highly informal, as to how eager each population was to die. Preliminary answer: not at all. Instead of instant backdowns, this instead produced threats, counter-threats, step-downs, backings-off, face-savers and other male manoeuvres of overbidding before a noisy haggle.

Susannah, who's a mother herself now, just yesterday at Sunday lunch unburdened herself of an insight. Talking about the utter lint-head who had fathered Terrifying Tanya and wanted to compound the felony by marrying Susannah, she said 'You know, people get things right or they make mistakes. About fifty–fifty. Women know that. The thing is, men don't ever admit it.'

That was what lay between Jack and Nikita. Testosterone, festering among the military, had leaked down to the entire intelligence community. Even Capon Cousin Jim Angleton showed signs of being balls-driven.

'We simply cannot let them get away with it,' he explained to me in his office at Langley.

This was the same building where, on my return from Cuba with Gleb's complete but unacceptable exposé of the Philby Plot, I had been locked up for an entire afternoon as if caught purse-snatching.

'You mean Jack Kennedy cannot,' I demurred.

'Who do you think has authorised all the Mongoose strikes against Castro?'

I nodded in agreement. It has always been the CIA line that whatever they are caught doing, no matter how obscene, was originally authorised by a civilian politician elected by the American voters. A lot of the time this is quite true.

'So he and Khrushchev are seeing who can piss farthest?'

Angleton looked shocked. 'Cousin Midge! Motherhood has coarsened your tongue. Do you speak this way among your daughters?'

'Shit, no,' I murmured contritely.

We got down to what he wanted from me, not dirty words, dirty tricks. There were vast computer files inside the FBI, he said, based on illegal wire-taps and postal snooping among the Miami Cubans, that the CIA desperately needed. Hoover was withholding this, just as, we later learned, he was withholding from the Secret Service the Kennedy assassination conspiracy.

'In a nuclear eyeball-to-eyeball confrontation,' Cousin Jim explained, 'we need every help. The Bureau is sitting on enough blackmail to convince Khrushchev he's backing the wrong horse when he pins his hopes on Castro.'

I sighed unhappily. J. Edgar had never trusted me except when I was under his thumb. As a widow, I was now protected from his sleazeball blackmail. But the idea of wheedling from him the material Angleton wanted was quite bizarre. 'If he refuses access to you,' I said, 'why should he let a *Times* hack see it?'

'I'm not asking that from you.'

'Then what? You know the little porker is immune to feminine charms.'

Cousin Jim leaned forward across his desk and put his fingers in a praying position. He looked quite eager, malicious, a falcon zeroed in on live bait. 'My boffins,' he said in an undertone as hard to hear as the famous Lansky mutter, 'assure me they can hack into FBI computer banks any time they darn please.'

'Dear me.'

'All that's required is an access code and a password.'

'Is that all?'

'I don't propose to write your scenario,' he went on smoothly, 'but may I suggest you engage Hoover with questions that require access to his Miami files? Then you'll spot the necessary codes.'

'I've never seen him use a desktop computer screen.'

'Try it.'

'Cousin Jim, don't you understand the nature of such an interview? I have to ask sharp questions to get him fiddling with computer access. He's far better off just saying no. So he will.'

238

Angleton's frown was frightening. Malice gave way to something very like blood lust. 'And what about his leman?'

'I beg your pardon?'

'His catamite. His darling, Clyde Tolson?' He had grown dangerous in an instant. I had the feeling that what he had denied himself all his life, a good buggering, he loathed Hoover for openly enjoying. It was unforgivable.

But he had started me thinking. The Tolson name reminded me of Bobby Kennedy's message I'd delivered to Hoover that summer, a blackmail threat concerning his constant companion. Could Bobby help me now?

I found myself wondering how far female charms went with a Kennedy. Despite their reputation, I suspected, not very far. Like most Irish men, they seemed attracted to women as warm surrogates for masturbation.

'Maybe somewhere else inside the Justice Department,' I told Angleton.

He shook his head. 'We've tried that. Hoover's internal security is near perfect.'

'*Near* perfect?' I gave him my first smile of the interview. 'Then there's hope.'

One of the things people still ask me – since they remember I did know the Kennedys fairly well – is how two such busy men could manage so much daytime fucking. My first answer is always: what do you mean by so much?

My second answer starts them off on a whole new track: when your working schedule takes no account of day or night, why treat fucking as a high-priority activity? Schedule it at the same level as going to the john or putting out the garbage.

My third answer finally comes to grips. Rich men ignore other people's taboos. Remember the way Nelson Rockefeller died and you realise that time and place and partner are hobgoblins of the middle class. Rich men's arrogance gives sex the priority of a good belch.

But none of that post-priori musing prepared me for the arrival at the *Times'* Washington bureau of Bobby Kennedy. Everybody was out on their beat except me. Without help, trying to fend off Bobby was like a swimmer trying to avoid a hungry shark.

'I heard about your twins,' he said, sitting on top of my desk. He readjusted his crown jewels for a moment. Then: 'Look, basically I'm well-bred. I waited till you had 'em. But how long can I wait?'

'That was Major Emory's excuse, too,' I said. I got to my feet and prepared for flight. 'Otherwise how does a girl deliver twins ten months after her first birth?' No sense treating him delicately. 'Ask your wife. She'll tell you.'

'Leave Ethel out of it.' He gave me a glance he seemed to feel was carried by X-rays. 'Angleton says you won't play ball.'

'Not won't. Can't. He's asking a miracle.'

He gave me a Groucho Marx leer, eyebrows wagging as he examined my legs. 'So am I.'

I sighed. 'I know how attractive any child-bearing primate is to a randy Catholic lad. But don't get it mixed up with the idea of breaking into Hoover's computer.'

The leer widened. His two Bugs Bunny teeth seemed to be lit from inside. 'Look,' he began, 'put yourself in my shoes. I'm on the mafia's hit list and my chief law enforcement officer, Hoover, is in cahoots with them. It kind of broadens your perspective. If I could once broaden those gorgeous long legs of yours and – '

'And fall in never to be heard from again . . .' I moved several yards from him. 'Mr Attorney General, you must have some way of dodging around the Hoover barricade. Good God, you're his boss.'

He shut up suddenly and I realised this was his most sensitive spot because he was hiding something. He and his brother had to have designated someone inside the Federal Bureau of Investigation to take over when they dumped Hoover. He had to be Hoover's organised crime expert, Courtney Evans. Certainly they'd let Evans know, which made him, willy-nilly, their FBI mole.

'It isn't,' I said aloud, 'as if you're asking him actually to steal the damned files. All we need is access codes and passwords.'

'He? Who?'

'Who? He who cannot be named. Your man in the mask, Evans.'

'Is this some dream of your cousin Jim's?'

Years later, decades later, we think of the Kennedys as helpless victims of a criminal conspiracy and a corrupt bureaucracy. We think they suffered from their own naïveté and lack of experience. We feel the plotters struck too quickly for a proper defence.

We forget that they were two tough young street fighters with the highest power in the land over knights willing to rid them, as Edward dispatched murderers to Becket's cathedral, of troublesome priests. We forget that together they burned ruthlessly bright, attracting talented supporters as surely as a compass needle points north or a sunflower bends toward the sun's awful flame.

'It's not a dream,' I assured him. 'We're talking ten minutes work for Evans. And ten more minutes for Jim's boffins to open up Hoover's data files like a shucked walnut.'

'But first, right here, ten minutes for a passionate head job,' he said.

'Head? Go soak it.'

'I'll call it a downpayment.'

'You're offering me a head job?'

'I'm volunteering you. I bet you give great head.'

'Grow up,' I suggested. I put my hand on the outer door. As I did, it swung open and Andy came in. His eyes lit up as he saw me. 'Midge, I'm getting that CBS – ' He stopped, realising we had a witness.

'That CBS audition?' Bobby finished for him. 'Congratulations.' As he slid off the desk he concluded his rearrangement of the crotch area.

'Let's hope CBS is still in business next week,' Andy said in a rueful tone.

'And there's a country left for them to broadcast to,' I added on a similar note. 'Any good news?' I asked the Attorney General.

'Good news?' He gave me that toothy leer again as he moved out the door. 'You know the guy in the hospital? His doctor says, "I have bad news and good. Which would you like first?" The guy says, "Bad." The doc says, "You've got a week to live." The guy groans "Quick, the good news." The doctor says, "You know the night nurse with the big tits? I'm fucking her." '

Andy and I stood there after he had gone, staring blankly at each other.

'Tell me,' I said at last. 'With Bobby as Jack's closest advisor, do we have any hope at all?'

One of the things you learn in newspaper work is that when a plot fails you can usually find half a dozen conspirators willing to blame it on each other. Whereas when the plot succeeds, mum's the word.

By now the Cuban Missile Crisis had reached unbearable heights of real pain. The last week of October was ending. We were drowning in a game of Terminal Chicken: he who pre-emptively strikes first wins but goes down in history as a Bad Person.

But what if all history has ended, all books are incinerated and nobody is left to know who was bad? Where there is no planet there is no bad.

Finally, on October 28, Nikita broke. He promised to remove the missiles if Jack gave up any plan to invade Cuba. This got put directly into words two weeks later when Jack added one last jab: that the US wouldn't invade if Cuba committed 'no aggressive acts against the nations of the Western Hemisphere'.

At the time these were top secret documents. It was only much later that we noted that nobody asked Fidel about any of this, nor is his signature on any of these hasty but healing promises. When superpowers back down, small islands keep their mouths shut.

So ended the Philby Plot.

At least, it appeared so to someone as ignorant as I of the convoluted schemes a Philby could dream. I never had the chance to ask him whose original orders he was carrying out. His employer was the KGB, not the Soviet Army. But within

242

any secret police there are factions for hire as well as divisions whose loyalty is to the KGB and only the KGB.

What seems clear, with great helpings of hindsight, is that Philby underestimated the degree of iron in Kennedy's backbone. His original conspiracy was created and set in motion under Dwight D. Eisenhower, surely one of America's least testosterone-poisoned generals, but a general none the less.

The Bay of Pigs show invasion branded Uncle Sam a villain, thus helping Castro embrace Moscow's missile defence. Pointed directly towards a military stand-off, only nuclear war – the surgical, unmessy kinds fantasised by generals – seemed a solution.

Cheated of this, the Philby Plot seems, from today's vantage point, a failure. But we now understand that no Philby plot is ever quite that simple. Because it is designed to play on the weaknesses of a rather large cast of characters and entities – think how this one manages to link Lansky, Hoover, America's defence effort, Lyndon Johnson's crude energy and the mafia's cash flow – its outcome is delayed. It doesn't go off with a fizzle. Its subterranean rumble is only just beginning.

Cup your ear. Shh. Listen.

Chapter Forty-Seven

After Kennedy and Khrushchev had backed down we were left in a peculiar state: ready to die but reprieved. It was worse, if, like me, you had babies. You had expected to lose them.

Tensed to the limit, waiting for the pure blue sky overhead to ignite their body fats into shapeless blobs that glow in the dark, when you tried to return to normal thinking you suffered deep-seated suspicions, a state much like paranoia, where anything seems possible.

Anything, including altered states of existence. You questioned whether you were still the same person you had been.

Was anyone? People changed, all the time. How could you cope with them after they had altered themselves?

Let's not knock paranoia but, Lord, normal thinking points out that if *anything* can happen, there's a fifty–fifty chance of it being good news. Lydia Crake was it, short, plump, smiley and in her 50s. When I hired her she volunteered that her great-grandma had been a slave right here in Virginia and, what's more, had been a wet-nurse slave.

'Tending babies is in the Crake blood,' she explained.

Miles Arrow was my second piece of good news. He was a frail widower I knew to be ex-CIA. How many other kinds of people did I know? He leased me his two-bedroom lower floor in Arlington at a very low rent. Retired to his upper floor, he handed over to me the back yard, flower garden and a small wading pool.

'The twins still cry at night,' I warned him. 'That can get Susannah started. Quite a chorus.'

'Music to this old man's ears.'

Arrow had to be lying. Howling babies at three a.m.? Even if Mrs Crake soothed them back to sleep? Naive little mother, I didn't suspect Cousin Jim had a finger in the pie till he pulled it out and, with it, paranoia returned.

In the wake of the missile crisis, our breathe-easy period tested each step for landmines. Relieved of annihilation, we started examining lesser enemies.

That started the bad news. My idea of getting those FBI computer access codes Angleton craved was to let Attorney General Bobby get them from his Bureau mole, Evans. Perhaps because of some raunchy fantasies about me, the idea worked.

Cousin Jim loved me. Never had my stock rated higher in his book. Good Old Midge. The moment the CIA hackers began using this information, it triggered off some inner security formula. We deadlocked whatever the FBI hackers had planted inside their access codes, a brilliant last-ditch defence.

Bad Midge. I was summoned to the Presence. The eyes

burned orange-yellow. I was sure it wasn't cousinly hatred. But maybe I was wrong.

'If you're finished wasting my time,' Angleton began in a waspish buzz, 'let's return to the real world. There have been big changes. All the Fidelista cadres have shifted to New Orleans. And, with them, the core mafia cadre.'

He shoved an airplane ticket envelope across his desk. I opened it.

'To New Orleans? I can't go. My nurse isn't ready for it.'

'You owe me this. And it's hardly more than a day or two.'

'Why don't I believe you, Cousin Jim?'

'Why? None of the changes were cleared with me. I wasn't consulted when Santos Traficante put Miami Cubans on his payroll. Nor when they started running drugs. Nor when Lansky shifted to Marcello's fief in New Orleans. Any diaspora of criminals is worrisome. It disturbs the mix.' His eyes glared at me.

'Traficante is too smart for Meyer,' I explained. 'But Marcello is an ox.'

'Perfect to charge headlong into harebrained assassination efforts?'

I inspected him more closely. In paranoia everyone else seems crazy. 'Against Castro? Or Kennedy? Meyer's got them both targeted.'

He produced a delicate shrug, as of a bacteriologist watching the mis-mating of microbes. 'After that fiasco with the computer codes, you must make good, Midge. You must explain these changes. We need to know why Hoover's let Frank Costello be deported after decades of close co-operation. Is his new mafia contact Lansky? Is that why he's moved Courtney Evans to New Orleans?'

I sniffed. My private opinion of Evans – he may have been the one to lead us astray with those FBI access codes – was of an underused, underendowed man. No one to worry about. Why was Angleton bothering about Evans?

It gave me a dig under my lungs to realise, as I had on several occasions, that I was working for a looney. 'You have it backwards,' I pointed out. 'Hoover focusing Evans on New Orleans means we can forget about New Orleans.'

'Yes?' he retorted in a nasty tone. 'Agents heading for Cuba now leave from New Orleans. Cuba's *my* turf, not the FBI's.'

He stared at me with those eyes, those feral turf-defending eyes. Then he pulled out a vinyl folder with one single sheet of photocopied text. He surveyed it for a moment, as if it might contain swearwords unsuitable for feminine eyes.

'Why I still trust you, God knows. Anyway, a present from dear Kim,' he said, sliding it across to me.

'From New Orleans?'

'As it happens, yes. There's a verb Kim uses, to "suss out". British slang. He's sussed out something fascinating.'

I read through the text. The lettering was debased, as if re-copied dozens of times, but legible, even the opening chunk in Cyrillic characters. 'I assume the English text is a true translation?'

He nodded in a tired way as if routine spook-craft bored him as much as it does the rest of us. I read the text, turned over the sheet and read the continuation. What looked like a Russian identity card was included in the photocopy. The young man's picture was eminently forgettable, posing self-importantly.

'Why,' I asked at last, 'has the KGB spent all this space psychologising a dopey American misfit who defected from the US Marine Corps in the Far East?'

'Why? Because they assumed he was mine.'

'And he's not?'

'Harvey wasn't and isn't on my payroll. He does get postal money orders now and then. From the FBI.'

'Lee and Harvey are his given names. His surname is Oswald. And according to KGB shrinks, he's a prime fantasist, delusional thinker, burning to make his name somehow. Why is he on Hoover's payroll?'

'You see that note at the bottom? Oswald's wife wants to return to the Soviet Union. He, on the other hand, wants to go to Cuba. Hoover, like the KGB, assumes Oswald is mine.'

'Ah.'

'Yes, ah.' He got to his feet, instantly faking anger. 'Every-one accuses us of being our own secret government. You know we're not.'

'I do?'

'Come on, Midge. We cut corners. We blow smoke. But when caught we still have to account to holier-than-thou legislators. *He* doesn't.' His voice fizzed with frustration. 'Secret governments? That fat little pervert can close off an area the size of Texas and run it like Nazi Germany and account to *no one*!'

He paced furiously, head down, his skinny frame buffeted by interior stress I was beginning to think was real. The resemblance to a raptor deprived of his meat became absolutely scarey.

'Please sit down,' I urged. 'Are you saying Hoover's closed off New Orleans? Or Texas? And what does it have to do with Philby's gift of Oswald?'

'You're the *Times* reporter, Cousin. Big changes mean you dig deep. When you reach New Orleans get next to Courtney Evans. I think he's ready to spill.'

Looney-work.

Grab a Coke at National Airport in Washington. Sane but sleepless from all-night babies. In-flight chicken fricassee on rice. Nod off. Emerge at noon from New Orleans baggage claim. Take first cab. Doze on ride.

French Quarter. Not my hotel. Cab driver helps me inside. Nap.

Cracked bell tolls twelve times. I wake. Dark of night. Not fuzzy, everything distinct. Twelve bell-tolls. I seem to be naked.

Sprawled naked on a four-poster bed. Playmate of the Month. Beautiful handmade quilt is soft, comforting. Recognise the design: 'Sunflowers and Sugar Cane'. Ante-Bellum pattern.

Kidnapped by the Junior League? Women's Institute?

No. Remember? No blindfold. Nobody worried about being later identified by me. So. Mafia snatch. Back to sleep. Sleep.

They really have this thing diabolically worked out. In the morning, quite early, the coffee-coloured lady who brings me a dressing-gown to cover my brazen nakedness is a short, busty person.

'Mawnin'. I'm Clarice. I'm Lydia Crake's niece.'

Changes. The stairwell she leads me down is as curved as an attack of vertigo. They have me at the top of an old house. I watch my silver-like toenails showing beneath the dressing-gown hem every time I take a step down.

Dear God, she does resemble Mrs Crake. No way of knowing if it's true or a malevolent lie. But the suggestion that my three babies back in Arlington, Virginia, are in the hands of a mafia nurse is more than enough to keep me civil and downright obedient. But not silent.

'She told me her great-grandmother was a slave,' I offer.

We push through double doors into a dark mahogany dining room with a long table and huge armoires. It has the look of a Sicilian undertakers. I have the look of a pre-corpse. Too much sleep is too much.

They have but to drain me and pump in embalming fluid. That part is easy. If this woman is Mrs Crake's niece, I am already disembowelled.

She pours me coffee from a heavy silver pot. It reeks of chicory. I loathe chicory. Or is it laced with embalming fluid?

I thank her and sip the hideous concoction. It's amazing. Here I sit in a pre-death condition. In a pre-mausoleum of a prison. Someone has figured me out down to my silvery toenails and knows what buttons to press.

'That'd make her your great-great-grand-aunt, wouldn't it?'

'Who?'

'Mrs Crake's ancestor, the wet-nurse.'

Her eyes flash sideways to the doors that have remained closed. I recognise the look. It telegraphs the hope that someone in this haunted house will arrive soon and take charge of this gabby white broad.

Does that mean she's lying about being Mrs Crake's niece? Do they or don't they have a way of harming my girls?

By the curtained window stands a small secretary-desk, the lid open. A doll's coffin lies on it. Yes. A coffin for a doll on a pile of loose papers.

'I had a second cousin twice removed who was a slave,' I

248

continue, firmly launching into fantasy. 'She escaped to New England on the Underground Railroad in 1855. An ancestor of mine taught her to read and write and married her.'

'Wha-at?'

'They had eleven kids. Can you believe it? I tried to figure it out once.'

'Figure why they got married?'

'I figured I have one-thirty-second black blood in my veins.'

'Shee-yit.'

'No shee-yit,' I demurred. 'You know something? Most people passing as white have at least that much black in them. Often more.'

'Sometimes,' she came suddenly to life, 'one helluva lot more.'

The doors opened. 'OK,' Meyer Lansky said, making a sweeping, take-charge gesture with his tiny fingers as he entered the room. 'Stop annoying your cousin, Clarice. Get us some toast, OK?' He took my hand. 'Sleep agrees with you, doll.'

'I had no idea this mortuary was yours.'

Something about his popping in like a jack-in-the-box, something dark in his look, in those worrying eyes, made me shiver. I could feel it flash across my shoulders. This man was the worst news yet.

And much changed. He had assumed a deadpan look of authorised menace, like the Dybbuk Rabbi Löwe created to save the Jews of Prague. The change was almost visible, a mantle of would-be supreme authority.

We stared closely at each other, I searching for changes, he trying to establish hegemony. He gave me an icy smile. 'I admit it's got a kind of haunted look, this joint.'

'But it goes with the territory.'

His frown was meant to terrify. It only chilled. 'What kinda crack is that?' He fell silent till Clarice had left the room. 'One-thirty-second black blood. You'd've had that girl eating out of your hand in another minute.'

'Meyer. You know us brunettes. Harm my kids and I'll rip out your nasty little heart and eat it for breakfast.'

He shivered in mock fear. 'Your kids are OK. All you have

249

to do is behave, OK?' He fished in a pocket of his vest and brought forth a folded slip of paper. 'Here's Courtney Evans' local phone number. He's expecting your call.'

'Who set that up, Angleton or Hoover?'

'Lansky,' he snapped. 'Get used to it.'

Clarice brought in a tray with toast and more of the regurgitative chicory-tainted coffee oozing hot steam into the deadly room. The smell of it did something deadly to my brain.

Was I doomed to spend the rest of my life with a murderer, a low-end-of-humanity felon? To see that face always in mine? That perverter of life? That murderer of Gleb and a thousand more? That self-righteous bag of pus who was now making my appointments for me? Who had my girls in his nasty doll's hands?

I was taller than Meyer Lansky. Younger. Maybe even stronger.

I couldn't let this horrible place get to me. The moment we were alone again I was going to prove it hadn't gotten to me. I was going to pour steaming-hot coffee all over him.

And then I was going to bring the heavy silver coffee pot down on his head like a ton of lead. To reassert my sanity. And then . . .

It was a Gothic novel. Tosca with the carving knife. And then our heroine, barefoot in a dressing-gown, flees along the twisted alleys of the French Quarter and makes her way to . . .

'Yes, Lansky,' he said in a thoughtful tone. 'Learn to trust Lansky and your future's made.'

'Is that the purpose of this kidnap? To brand your name on my butt? To prove you're the top pimp on a mountain of dog shit?'

'Such a mouth! Just say I'm testing and you're my guinea pig.' He bit a small half-moon out of his toast. 'Clarice, the orange marmalade. Vitamin C.' He picked up the doll's casket on the desk. 'You got a fella these days, Midge?'

'Other than you?'

'These cigars are real nice. Take this one back to James Jesus Angleton.' So, a coffin for a dead bratwurst. My glance went beyond it to the pile of papers it had been holding down.

I could only see the top one. I tried sharpening my focus.

'You know what the black market price of this perfecto was during the missile crisis?' he demanded. 'A week ago this was selling for four hundred clams. The minute they called off the crisis it fell back to two cees.'

I stood up. He blinked. Now I could see the top sheet of paper quite clearly, a typed text with a copy of a Russian passport and the face of a fantasist with delusions of grandeur. Damn Kim! He'd sussed right.

Meyer frowned up at me. I could see my girls tied up on nursery chairs. I had the feeling he had no idea what was in store for him. Lord, at that moment I didn't even recognise myself.

The coffee splashed hot, steaming, stinking of chicory all over his face. He threw his tiny hands over his eyes.

I brought the pot down with one long curving stroke, as if felling a fence-post and sending it deep into damp ground. New Orleans stood on marshland.

Dead bodies couldn't be buried underground in New Orleans. They had to be walled up in mausoleums above ground. It wasn't possible to bury one's dead.

He started to fall, silently. On the floor he made a small, kinked shape at my feet. Like a shellfish in boiling water, he emitted a heart-breaking sigh.

First I grabbed the top half dozen sheets of paper. Then I dashed to the doors and tried to lock them shut. But these twin doors were meant to swing freely. Someone pushed the doors back at me, opening them.

Clarice I was ready for, the pot still clutched in my hand. Murderous Midge was ready for anybody short. But this one was tall. His shove scattered pieces of paper from my hands to the floor.

They were mostly New Orleans Police Department flyers for mobsters with Sicilian names. I looked up to see who had burst open the doors.

'Midge? Ay, lagrimas!' Victor Sanchez cried out.

'Guapo!'

Chapter Forty-Eight

Havana is shut down tight, thanks to Fidel. But, also thanks to Fidel, our Gatita Negra stays open. He must have so many agents spotted along the bar that it becomes for sure a better intelligence sweep than bugging people's telephones. Let's face it: Havana phones don't always work.

But Fidel has agents all over Miami, where telephones work perfectly. Somebody told me – at the Black Pussy, of course – that for every Miami Cuban waiting to slit Fidel's throat there are two Fidelistas stealing his bayonet.

I have given up that vulgar life. The last such thing I did was to carry El Pequeño to an emergency clinic that morning in New Orleans ... a million years ago. I barely made the Mérida plane but I am sure he got the finest medical care New Orleans can provide. At least that's what he told the CBS News team that afternoon.

'Me,' he said in a tired rasp, propped up in bed. His face was smeared with ointment. A huge white dome of a bandage guarded his head like the yarmulka the Pope will wear if he ever wakes up Jewish.

'Me, I'm a gambler. And a patriot. Castro agents ambushed me. They gambled with my life but I won.'

'I don't understand the deal,' Rita told me.

We were no longer using a bedroom at her parents' apartment. I could now afford our own little house. It is a sort of inside joke because we now live in one of the luxury cottages close to the Marazul Hotel at Santa Maria del Mar. It's a five-minute walk from where Boyd Cromarty sank the Mongoose boat.

Those fellows? To become a terrorist you must be good at many things, including swimming. They struck out for a far shore. That was where the police picked them up as they emerged from the surf. I think, by now, they know it would have been better to drown.

As for the deal Rita was asking about . . .

In the middle of 1963 — after six months of dream profits — the smuggling of Cuban cigars went sour. Competitors were growing Cuban tobacco all over the Caribbean basin. Lansky's lock on Cuban production turned meaningless.

Most of his customers were rich, ignorant show-offs who wouldn't know a Cuban perfecto from a twist of burning sisal. They were flocking in greed to rival products that looked the same and, for them, smelled the same. Anyway, he had another project he was working on for J. Edgar Hoover as well as a big investment paying off in Las Vegas.

That was when I suggested to Fidel we promote directly in countries which didn't honour Uncle Sam's embargo. You would be surprised at how many there were in 1963. At normal mark-up we make almost as much as on the illegal pay-offs I was risking my life to bring back in briefcases.

'The deal,' I explained to Rita, 'is what we businessmen call a royalty. A commission. Because we are a socialist land, it's small, one per cent. But it bought this place. It bought my mother out of Guantánamo. It bought me out of ever having to touch El Pequeño again. It even bought me freedom from the CIA.'

It's a real pleasure being married to a Fidelista socialist executive. Every morning a driver arrives from Rita's office about seven. We give him coffee and grits. He likes his grits with butter and honey. I like them with bacon. Rita cooks all this. Then she is driven to her work and I go back to sleep.

I haven't yet decided what to do with the Sanchez fortune. Sometimes I lie in bed almost till noon, thinking of what do. It overheats my brain. I go down to the beach and cool off my head in the surf.

'A rotten deal,' Rita told me.

She shook her head sadly, her big looping curls shifting lazily. 'A selfish, crass capitalist deal. The only reason Fidel did this for you is that you saved his life at that baseball game. Plain and simple.'

'And the lives of the schoolchildren.'

'Yes, all right, them too.'

'And for this act of heroism,' I said, 'money is an insult. You cannot buy heroism with money. Nevertheless, to make Fidel happy, I take it.'

We were lying in bed because this was Sunday. 'Ever since you got back from that last trip to New Orleans,' she said, 'you have been a different person.'

'Look at me.' I threw back the sheet so that she could examine my body bit by bit, which she likes to do. But it wasn't enough to sidetrack her mind. 'I am the same man, hair for hair, as the one you married.'

'No. Something happened that you never told me.'

'In New Orleans? Months ago? You expect me to remember?'

Now she was combing her fingers through my pubic muff for white hairs. 'You probably can't even remember her name.'

'Her name? Whose name?'

She found a grey hair and yanked it out. Has anybody ever done this to you? There are millions of nerve endings down there. 'Rita!'

'Oh. I think I see another.'

'Rita, I told you what happened in New Orleans.'

'Finding El Pequeño on the floor? Carrying him to the clinic? It's full of holes, Victor. Why did you run away? What did the police say? Who was his attacker? Why with a coffee pot? How did he get inside Lansky's house?'

You can see why my mother warned me never to cheat on Rita because I wasn't smart enough to get away with it. But neither am I completely stupid.

'Rita, querida, this is what happens when a big mafioso gets hit. He will tell the coppers nothing. And without him they are helpless to continue.'

She fell silent, absent-mindedly stroking me again. 'That part I can believe. But, knowing you, the part I can't figure out is where the girl comes in.'

'What girl?'

Instead of answering, she ran her leg over me and slowly hooked me between my legs. While I was congratulating myself that she had given up asking questions about New Orleans, she was kissing my pubic hairs to make up for yanking one out.

In a few minutes she rolled over and fitted me deep inside her. We settled in for a long, slow hombre commodo. In hot weather, even the ceiling fan can't keep you dry. By the time you've had enough the sheets are wet. While it is meant for the woman, for the man who can manage the long delay the final come is sensational. Twice as long as a regular orgasm. Three times. Who knows?

All I know is that when you have your own little cottage with a little bit of garden all the way around it, you can forget about neighbours. When you come you can shout, yell, howl as loud as you want.

We lay there afterwards in silence. I could taste Rita's perspiration. I rubbed her moist skin and licked the sweat off my hand. Then I began licking her damp body. 'That was extraordinary,' I said.

'I hope so. In a few months it will be a memory.'

'What?'

She nodded, her face suddenly serious. 'Victor, our first child will be born in six months.'

'Ay! Madre mia!'

'Si.' She rolled back on top of me again. Her breasts were shiny with sweat. 'So enjoy it while you can, guapo.'

Chapter Forty-Nine

I bought the house on the corner of Nineteenth Street in Arlington, Virginia, after Miles Arrow died in 1964. My girls grew up there.

Jim and I recently made it over into a double dwelling with two entrances. Kate lives in one apartment, Jane in the other. They are not identical twins but they seem to enjoy the proximity. Jane will be getting married in the fall. Of my three daughters, she will be the first to take the plunge.

I moved into Jim's home in Alexandria when we married. Susannah lives a few miles away, with Terrible Tanya and Mrs Lydia Crake. Yes! She claims to have only just reached the age of seventy. Since she helped me raise all three girls I am trying to figure out a way to blame her for Tanya, too.

This Sunday, after dinner, I made the mistake of telling Jim, in Susannah's hearing, that I'd finished the first section of these memoirs, Pre-Dallas. First she put Tanya to sleep in the basement on the billiards table. Sitting beside Jim on the sofa she read each of these pages as he passed it along.

It was midnight when they finished. I had been pretending to read the *Sunday Times*, but was secretly listening to the small noises readers make when they're pleased or puzzled. Now the three of us sat in silence, mulling over that very short dot of time I had described. Really. The five years from 1959 to 1963 were a mere split second in history: Castro Wins; Kennedy Loses.

'Why does it stop when Victor discovered you?' Susannah wanted to know.

'Why does it stop before Dallas?' Jim demanded.

I cupped a hand around one ear. 'Is that it? No well dones? No, Lord, I loved it? Will someone perjure themselves and call it enthralling?'

'Oh, it's great,' Susannah said in the absent-minded manner of one flinging a table scrap. 'Absolutely terrific. But . . .'

'Searing,' Jim chimed in. 'Riveting. Mind-boggling.'

I nodded. 'How about . . . "not bad"?'

'That, too,' he agreed. 'But I wanted you to take us to the Texas Book Depository Building on Dealey Plaza. To the Sixth Floor. To the grassy knoll where the crossfire came from. Or is that in the next instalment?'

'If you knew how hard it's been getting this first part on paper.' I retrieved the manuscript from Susannah. 'What does this weigh, a couple of pounds? It'll take a manuscript twice as heavy to continue the story.'

'But shouldn't we – ?'

'And that's without the Los Angeles murder of Bobby.'

'But we know who did that, Sirhan Sirhan.' Susannah got

up and tiptoed to the door that leads downstairs. She opened it a crack and listened. 'Who says two-year-olds don't snore?' She sat back down. 'OK, Midge. Give.'

'You said,' Jim recalled, 'that the KGB called Oswald a delusional thinker. Is that the same as an assassin?' He gave it the full fake Russian pronunciation, ahs-ahs-yeen.

'I wondered about that,' Susannah chimed in. 'How *do* you get some turkey so hyped up he agrees to shoot the President of the United States?'

For somebody used to thinking at a keyboard, talking is only second best.

'Cousin Jim Angleton spent years on Operation Artichoke. He dreamed of creating CIA assassins. He even claimed success. Sirhan Sirhan signed up in order to pay off the fourteen thousand dollars he owed LA bookies. A cheap hit. Shooting the president is such a common crime – like insider trading – there ought to be a minimum penalty fee placed on it.'

Outside our little home a breeze started up across the wide part of the Potomac. It wasn't a strong wind but it made tiny shuffles and moans in our shingled walls and roof.

'The technique had to be fail-safe with Oswald. The killers had to get clear without embarrassing all the lawmen with turned backs. I got most of it from Warren Commission documents. It seems there were two Oswalds. At least.'

'She's snapped,' my daughter announced, sadly.

'Like an old corset stay,' Jim added.

'What's a corset stay?' Susannah asked.

'The real Oswald,' I explained, 'was a confused twenty-four-year-old ex-Marine radar operator with foggy delusions about individuality and freedom. He saw himself as destined for greatness.'

'And the other Oswald?'

'Oswalds. Look-alikes with a similar frame and face. Somebody you might pick out of a line-up if the cops were leaning real hard on you.'

I had them, now. It doesn't take much to get an American interested in Who Shot JFK. It's been our favourite parlour game for thirty years now. But back in 1963, trying to raise my babies and keep off what I felt sure was the top of Meyer's hit list, the game was still brand new.

'Not that the other Oswalds would face a line-up,' I went on. 'Their job, in the months before November 22, was to lay a false trail all over Dallas.'

They were watching me closely. 'You know, making a pest of himself at the shooting range. One of them was a dead shot. He forced everyone to remember him because he had the show-off habit of popping out the bullseye on the next guy's target. And never forgetting to give out his name loud and clear, Lee Harvey Oswald.'

They stared silently at me. 'Same game plan with Sirhan. They prepped him at LA gun clubs, made sure everyone knew he was a noted shooter.' I watched both their faces register a shock of distaste.

'And whatever contortions the corrupt LA cops do by way of cover-up, however they frighten witnesses into silence, there's no denying Sirhan's gun held eight bullets, but twelve were sprayed at Bobby.'

'And the real Oswald?'

'We have documentary evidence the real Oswald was in New Orleans and then Mexico City, trying to get into Cuba. He used aliases. While he was doing this, and going broke, and returning to Dallas to find a job, other Oswalds continued to incriminate him.'

'In what? What had he done?' Jim asked.

'He was being *pre*-criminated for the assassination. By September 14 of that year, everyone knew the President would visit Dallas November 21 or 22. After the hit, when the real Oswald rushed out of the Depository looking shocked and guilty as hell, the cops were supposed to put two and two together and say: "hey, this is the show-off who's such a dead shot." Which they did.'

'After which,' Susannah put in, 'other Oswalds disappeared into thin air.'

'In other words, a frame-up?' Jim demanded.

'A patsy. And very easy to do. You didn't have to brainwash the real Oswald and make him into the killer. That might take months. You only had to target him as a dead-eye sharpshooter long before he ever got to Dallas.

'He arrived already set up as a fall guy to hang it on. Nobody would go looking for any other assassins. And J. Edgar's boys flitted about making sure any further investigation was either aborted or faked. Remember, Hoover had at least eighteen months pre-knowledge. You could call him a co-conspirator, if only for the way he kept his knowledge secret. As to cover-ups, he could be generous. He had what he wanted.'

'Kennedy dead,' Jim said. 'A year before Hoover would have to resign.'

'And Johnson in the White House owing Hoover his political life,' I reminded him, 'already pledged to waive Hoover's retirement.'

'How did he manage that?' Susannah asked.

'LBJ, through aides like Bobby Baker, was up to his eyeballs in mafia kickbacks and embezzlements so huge they rivalled the national debt.'

'I always thought of Johnson as an OK gent,' she said. 'Big on civil rights. With a better record on social entitlement than Kennedy ever had.'

I nodded. 'Where is it written that you can't get in over your head with the mafia and also be a good Democrat?'

We fell silent. Deep in the walls something moaned, a keen of mourning for a long time ago. Susannah shuddered. 'You have to do something about those shingles.'

No one said anything for a long time. The river breeze complained again, slowly, the sound a cat makes when frustrated at not getting its prey.

This time I shivered. Susannah came over and sat in my lap. She is almost my height, this eldest daughter, and no ethereal sylph.

'Midge.' Her voice was tiny. 'Listen, Midge, Jim, can we sleep over? There's plenty of room for me downstairs with Tanya.'

'Sure thing,' he said. 'It kind of gets you, all this remembering.'

'All those ghosts,' I added, like a fool.

There was a long silence, marked by another spectral moan.

'Midge,' she asked then, 'is ... um ... is Kim Philby still alive?' There was a funny child's note in her big, grown-up voice.

I hugged her hard. 'Dead. Guaranteed dead. It's that kind of night, is it?'

She shook her head. 'It's that kind of life.'

So, what remains is the ghost of Kim Philby.

I helped Susannah make up the basement couch as a bed. Jim went upstairs after kissing us all good night. Terrible Tanya stayed fast asleep even when we transferred her to the couch so how terrible could she be?

I wanted a nightcap martini. But, instead, I found my copy of Kim's own autobiography, a British paperback. I sat down with it.

Everyone who's tried cracking Kim's soft-looking, steel-hard British shell has come away crying 'enigma'. I don't buy enigma as an excuse, but even his four wives had never gotten through to his core. Knowing him in his high-glory Bay of Pigs days did nothing to help me solve the enigma either.

Finally, the Why Girl was ready to admit failure. Even my pet prof at Vassar, Dr Domandi, had warned me there was no why. When you're obsessed by the search for why, you ask questions of rocks, clouds, the wind. You pore over documents. You replay old taped interviews.

In 1988 the British writer-historian Phillip Knightley visited Philby in Moscow. He had earlier written a book about Philby's exploits. After some talk at Philby's large, but not grand, Moscow apartment, Knightley asked permission to snap a photo.

The paperback of the Philby autobiography I was holding had a foreword by Graham Greene, who had worked with Kim, and a more recent one by Knightley. It also had his snapshot of Kim.

I have glanced at that view for years. But only now, to try to tidy up my own mind and to have something more to tell Susannah, did I really study the photo. Just as I did, another ghost walked down the stairs. Did I jump? Damned right. But it was Jim in his pyjamas.

'It's two in the morning.' Sore note in voice.

I made a guilty face. 'That late? Give me ten minutes.'

But he stood there, watching me. 'There was something I didn't want to ask in front of Susannah. Why didn't Lansky have you killed?'

I laid down the Philby paperback. 'Lord, the damned coffee burns were superficial. And I wasn't strong enough even to give him a concussion.'

'But in terms of him saving face.'

'I was small fry. He had big stuff waiting for him. Helping Marcello set up Dallas. Other big partners like Charley Lucky. After he killed Meyer's boyhood pal, Bugsy Siegel, Las Vegas began to show a profit. How would it look putting a hit on some broad who'd banged you on the noodle with a coffee pot? Petty and cheap.

'Remember,' I added, 'Meyer and Charley were truly lucky. They began to cash in just as the cigar racket cooled off. And the drug racket had just started. Besides, only an idiot kills a *Times* reporter.'

Jim frowned. 'Nice company you kept.'

'About on a par with Angleton and Hoover and Philby.'

He continued giving me one of his heavy looks. 'I am just beginning to figure out the woman I married. You are obsessed with baddies. You're a conspiracy junkie.'

'Dead ones,' I pointed out.

His forehead stayed puckered. 'You know, I once met your pal Philby. At a party early in the war. Bebe Reboso threw this bash for his buddy Nixon to celebrate . . .?' His face went blank.

'To celebrate getting Nixon put in charge of rationing rubber tyres after Bebe had opened the biggest tyre recap plant in Florida.'

'That's my girl!' The frown faded. He grinned. 'One of us better have a memory,' he said, and started back to bed.

'Did you talk to Philby?'

'He was dead drunk. Lots of philosophical gabble. Meaning of life stuff. You know.' He left.

I know. I know my Gentleman Jim. Just like him not to ask a question like that in front of my daughter.

The real question he hadn't asked was whether Meyer and I had had — don't gag — a lover's quarrel. Whether Meyer had let me go because, after all, a man always forgives his mistress. Less gentlemanly interrogators have asked it often. Not in front of Susannah, however.

Amazing the number of Philby sightings. The man had been everywhere. Well, naturally, he would be.

I picked up the paperback and examined its cover. It shows Kim, seventy-six years old, seated at a cluttered desk. Behind him stand neatly filled bookshelves. An ordinary but businesslike desk lamp hangs over the clutter.

Kim looks tanned, fit, very much at ease, very *plausible*, everybody's grandpa. His white hair, parted smoothly on the side, reflects the sheen of the photo flash. His hands cannot be seen. He has rested them in his lap, below the surface of the desk. Hands are terrible tattle-tales, anyway. As for those other giveaways, the eyes . . .

Damn his eyes. Damn his snowy eyebrows that hide his modest, downcast glance from my eyes. I would want to see that spark of malicious excitement again, that hint that although he played a deadly game, the why of it never appeared.

By 'why' most people mean how much. If not executed by a secret police bullet, or sent sailing Miami Bay in a fifty-five-gallon drum, a top-level agent like Philby could end up in a Swiss ski chalet with a staff of servants. He will have made treachery pay big.

I doubt Kim got rich off the NKVD or the KGB. His devotion couldn't be bought. No fee would be too great for such loyalty. His genius as a plotter was beyond mere price. Even if he'd never done anything except Cuba, he deserved immortality.

He sits there in the photo looking utterly at peace with life. His face had broadened in old age, like a tom-cat's. In this snapshot he looks almost benignly monk-like. If there is a key to knowing Kim it is this photo. He made it so.

According to Knightley it was taken a few days before

Philby died, in May of 1988. Did he know he was about to die? The photo doesn't tell us that. It tells us something more important.

Just as death-bed evidence is superior to other kinds, under law, the picture a man poses for just before he dies must also be considered as carrying a message superior to any other he might have sent over the years.

No, it isn't a clue to why. Those clues lie elsewhere.

He has posed himself the way he wanted us to remember him, to celebrate and reaffirm his faith. To strike the pose that symbolised him and what he stood for. What he'd devoted his life to defending.

A large book lies open on the desk before him. He is looking down at the full-page drawing on the book's left-hand page. I had never before bothered to examine the drawing. It's Kim's face that draws one's attention. But there is another face he wants us to note.

Touching. It is a drawing of a plotter even more successful than Philby, an even greater manipulator. Baddies, did Jim say? Kim is looking at a portrait of Lenin.

The night wind keened softly in the shingles. Things passed, touching me with chill fingers. The fingers of dead baddies? And here I sit, glad as hell I don't believe in ghosts.

We all woke Monday morning a bit stiff in the joints. All except Tanya, who took the occasion to run shrieking through the house scattering cornflakes and spilling her orange juice. Twice.

'Gamma! More paper tow-wels!'

'I solemnly promise you,' Susannah said, 'this will never happen again.'

'You mean you're sending her to obedience school?' Jim asked.

'No. I'm never having any more kids.'

Jim whistled softly with relief. He handed me the first section of the just-delivered *Times*. Still making whistling noises he started reading what was left. I glanced at my watch. Seven a.m.

At Defence they'd assigned me the early Monday briefing,

as they often did, on the principle that grandmothers would have spent a blameless night before. Which was more than one could expect of the young sparks with college haircuts who usually handled Defence Department briefings.

'I'll give you two a lift home,' I said, getting to my feet.

'Tanks, Gamma. Gamma, who's man?' She was holding the Philby book in her orange-juice paw and staring at his face.

'One of Gamma's old flames,' Susannah supplied helpfully.

Jim looked up from his paper. 'Where'd you put the manuscript of your memoir?'

'Right-hand desk drawer. Why?'

'I'm getting it xeroxed. I'm having Larry Gelb lock it up with the rest of our papers.'

'Your lawyer?' Susannah asked. 'Is that wise?'

Jim thought for a moment. 'OK. A second xerox in our bank vault.'

'Better,' Susannah told him. 'Tanya, put down the book. Tanya, wash your hands. Tanya, we're leaving. Tanya, put that shoe back on this instant.'

So long did it take to get going that the morning mail arrived before we left. In addition to the usual litter, a large, heavy, important packet shouted for my attention.

It had been sent from Cuba with enough stamps to make sure you noticed it. Of course it had been opened, that was obvious. It had also been resealed oafishly. In my day we were a lot neater. A red string bound it all together, its knot sealed by a blob of bright red wax. Everyone clustered around as I hacked open with an inadequate paperknife the seam made by whoever in the US had intercepted it.

Under layers of paper lay a sheet of vellum as big as a college diploma and just as ornate. 'The citizens of the Republic of Cuba cordially invite you . . .'

It was slated for early January when they hold the Three Kings celebration. I had absolutely no desire to see what a run-down, poverty-stricken place we had created out of the once glamorous Havana. Nor did I yearn to sit through one of those all-day Castro lectures.

Nor, in a funny way I couldn't explain too well, did I want

264

to put myself back in Cuba, even for a day. A sinister feel pervaded my thoughts. Cuba wasn't *my* enemy but in this hemisphere it was still the major devil to whom the CIA sacrificed virgins. I stood there, staring down at the parchment-like invitation.

Jim reached out to rub his fingers lightly over the heavily embossed lettering. 'Um. Real engraving. Midge, don't go.'

'He's right,' Susannah chimed in. 'Trouble with a capital T.'

I felt relieved, not having to explain why I agreed with them. 'Well, in that case . . .' I tilted the whole packet into the wastebasket.

This time, when I got to my office at the Pentagon, May had arrived first and was already spacing out the folding chairs to make a semi-circle. She had pulled down the wall screen and set up the opaque projector.

It could be because of her figure, which is tall, trim but full-breasted, or the four-inch heels she wears. But Sergeant May Beavers is always a sight to behold for our predominantly male morning contingent of horny hacks. I sometimes wonder how some of them free up a finger to scribble notes.

'Morning, Ms Boardman.' Her voice was light and cheerful but her glance never got to mine. 'They haven't sent us the briefing pack yet. It's Sarajevo, I expect.'

'Or Kabul. Or Tbilisi. Or Havana.'

'Mm. We don't lack for trouble spots.'

'Lord, no. That seems to be the way we've arranged it.'

A frown distorted her smooth tan forehead. I could see that for her the idea that we Americans arranged our own agenda, that it didn't come down from Mount Olympus riding a thunderbolt, was a disturbing one. She'd had it before, because she was bright. 'You mean . . .?'

'I mean it's our list. Nobody asks us to put all these cities on alert. Most of them consider us a deep pain in the ass.'

Someone knocked at the door, then opened it, a corporal about twelve years of age who delivered the briefing pack to the only other uniformed person in the room, May.

He held out a clipboard and she signed it. Then he copied

her name and serial number off her chest badge. I could see the way the badge jutted out gave even a twelve-year-old trouble.

After he left she stood there, as if afraid to open the envelope. It would be pretty much as always, a packet of press kits, a one-page summary for Spokesperson Midge and some maps and photos for projection on the screen.

'You mean,' she repeated then. 'You mean if I chucked this in the wastebasket the world would still go on spinning?'

'Would it ever.'

This did not produce a smile. My remark, and her own, seemed to plunge her deep in Monday-morning gloom. Instead of opening the heavily sealed envelope, she put it on my desk and then sank into the chair reserved for visitors. She stared up at me, pain in her eyes.

'Sergeant Beavers? What's wrong?'

'Nothing. Why do you say that?' A long pause. 'Listen: everything's wrong.'

'Love problems?'

This time her silence lasted quite a bit longer. 'You have to tell me something, Ms Boardman.'

'Shoot.'

She winced. She actually did. 'Is there something nobody knows about you? I mean something bad? I mean . . .' Her voice died away. This time her glance was locked dead on with mine. 'I mean some national security thing I have been wasting my time snooping around looking for? Making phone tapes? Sifting your wastebasket? Lifting fingerprints? Photo-copying your personal mail?'

Our glances were absolutely glued to each other. I started to say something. But her word 'photocopy' had sent my hand to the telephone. I dialled home.

'Jim? That xeroxing?'

'It's done. It's delivered. We work fast around here. What's up?'

'I called to say I love you.'

'Listen. About Philby. I – '

'Later, Jim.'

I hung up and resumed what I can only call a soul-to-soul

266

inspection of Sergeant Beavers. She had a strong, broad-cheeked face, the kind that always looks honest. Her tight black curls reminded me of when mine were that springy and glistening with health and youth and ideals and common garden variety lust.

She and I had worked side by side for several years now. It is in the nature of American democracy that such black-white pairings at the executive level are not common. May and Lydia Crake. Period. The rest of the black women I know are casual acquaintances, nothing more.

'Sergeant Beavers. Who is putting you up to this?'

'Some handsome dude over at ISA.'

It had never occurred to me that in addition to all the tight-faced Marine captains and majors assigned to Intelligence Support, our secret assassination corps, there had to be black killers, too. Not to accuse May of racism, but seducing her might be that much easier if they shared a skin colour.

'What else was he putting to you. Never mind. Forget I said that.' I sat down at my desk and we resumed our impassioned study of each other's features. 'What's his name?'

'Daryl Gomez. Captain.'

'Cuban accent?'

A startled look crossed her face. 'N-no. I take him for a homeboy, maybe a Puerto Rican father.' One eye closed slightly in thought. 'What's a Cuban accent?'

'It's just that some of these ISA types are into projects that have nothing to do with official US policy. They can resign ISA, take home crates of thrilling weaponry and set up as private terrorists on hire to fat-cat Miami Cubans.'

Her head turned from side to side, negating the idea. 'If they had given the Castro job to ISA he'd've died back in the '60s.'

I mimicked her gesture. 'They did and Castro's still alive. How much did Gomez tell you?'

'Just that it happened before I was born. He's one of those keep-em-pregnant-and-barefoot types.'

'Mention Bay of Pigs?'

'He didn't say.'

Even saying the name of that long-ago bloodbath had a

depressing effect. I yearned for something to lighten this. A week ago Jim had read me a London writer with the improbable name of Sue Limb. Talking about self-righteous loudmouths she'd coined the phrase Bray of Prigs.

May wouldn't laugh at that. Right now, neither would I.

'How much have you given him?' I asked.

'Prints. Phone diary stats. Not much else. You don't get personal mail here.'

'And now you know why.'

She looked contrite and glanced away. 'I'm having drinks with this player some evening this week. What can I say to him?'

I smiled at her, hoping it looked reassuring. 'What would you want to say?'

But her face remained terribly grave. 'Ms Boardman, you know the Army. Your record follows you everywhere. All the good stuff. All the bad. This brother has his own service record to worry about. He only has to give me one bad mark and it blows my security clearance. They send me to some base camp where I show female recruits how to insert diaphragms.'

'I know. A Pentagon posting like yours is big time.'

She shrugged modestly. 'It goes with having big boobs.'

I patted her hand. 'And a high IQ, Sergeant Beavers. You just proved that part of it. Let's think. Naturally, Gomez is crazy about you?'

For the first time she smiled, slightly. 'Insane. You understand, these pro spooks don't ask questions, they just take orders. Somebody presses his buttons and he services me like a mad thing.' She sighed.

'So why spoil it?'

'What?'

'Keep feeding Gomez on scraps from my wastebasket. See how long that satisfies him.'

'Not long.'

'Try it. How bad could it be?'

This time the smile grew into a grin. Then she sat forward and examined me closely again. Her fingers went to her black

268

curls for a delicate scratch. 'I get the feeling you have had . . .
um . . . quite a life, Ms Boardman.'

I scratched my own curls, tight and white. 'It's still going
on.'

That's why the two of us were cackling wildly when the
morning briefing of hacks arrived. I hadn't even opened the
briefing pack yet. They stared at us in amazement but they
never did find out what we thought was so funny.

Jim takes afternoon naps. I don't. I usually put in a full day at
the Pentagon but when they have nothing for me in the
afternoon I slip away – the Army term is fuck off – and do
something else. Research at the library. Taking Tanya off
Susannah's hands. Helping Jane with redecorating her
apartment.

No. Not seeing an old friend. I'm beginning to realise I have
no old friends.

But I really hadn't slept well last night with all those
ghostly moans. So, yes, I went home for a nap at four p.m.
Jim was snoozing in the study. On the table next to the couch
he'd left a note: 'DON'T FORGET TO ASK ME ABOUT
PHILBY.'

I went upstairs and the next thing I knew I was doing a
tango with JFK. Yes, of course, Tango Havana, its piercing
high screech shared by two trumpets, Dizzy's and the new
Cuban genius, Arturo Sandoval. Jack's hand massaged the
small of my back where it starts to become buttocks. Amazing what grandmothers dream. Then it was six p.m. and I
could hear martinis being stirred in a tall pitcher.

I tottered downstairs, very slowly, to let the tango die
peacefully away. I know James Bond liked martinis shaken.
But he was altogether too Brit for words. Martinis are stirred
so as not to bruise the gin. That's folklore. Actually they're
stirred so as not to bruise the ice. Shaking dilutes them too
quickly.

I arrived at the door of the study. 'Novel idea for a wake-up
alarm.'

'If that hadn't worked,' Jim said, 'I'd've passed the cork
from the gin under your nose.'

We have our set routines, we old-timers, our liturgies if you will. I opened a foil bag of nuts and poured them in a bowl. Jim carefully pared off two bits of lemon rind. I reached up high on the top shelf for two martini glasses. You know, triangular on tall glass stems.

Jim bent each lemon zest until it spat a tiny sweat of oil on to the inside of each glass. Then he filled them two-thirds full and handed one to me. 'Confusion to the enemy.'

For some reason we both remained standing as we took our first sip. Then I found his note and handed it to him. 'DON'T FORGET TO ASK ME ABOUT PHILBY.'

We both sat down. 'It's all come back to me,' Jim said then. 'You know, if you don't chivvy yourself to remember, it all comes back, whether you wanted it to or not.'

'Spare me the vagaries of old-age memory.'

'But it's amazing how much comes back, even though it was a heavy-drinking evening. It was your memoir that got my memory perking.'

'About Kim?'

'You see,' Jim went on, 'Dallas was a major pay-off for only two of your principle players. It fulfilled the mafia's need to make an example of the guy who called off the Bay of Pigs air cover. Who hounded the mafia at every turn. And it made sure J. Edgar could stay in office after he hit the age of seventy.' He shifted in his easy chair. 'But what was in it for the KGB?'

I retrieved his note and held it up to him so he could read it: 'DON'T FORGET TO ASK ME ABOUT PHILBY.'

He sat for a moment, scrolling back through his celebrated memory. 'He was thinner and more aristo looking in those days. But still a very heavy drinker.'

'Aristo? Kim?'

'Well, maybe it was a pose.'

'His father was what they call an Arabist,' I recalled. 'No Sir or Lord. Lived in Arab lands. Married Arab wives. What we might call a wasted life if you didn't tag the title of 'Arabist' on it. Otherwise worth a few lines in Who's Who. I mean, look what a ne'er-do-well like Lawrence did when they added "of Arabia".'

270

'Whose reminiscence is this?'

'Carry on, Mr Memory.'

'There had been some routine English defector caught slipping over to Moscow,' Jim went on. 'Not Burgess and Maclean. That was after the war. This was something low level the Brits were playing down. Fella named Bigsby, Grigsby. After all, Russia was our ally.'

The martini was so delicious. Lord, I know how decadent and self-destructive that sounds. But, look, neither of us smokes. We keep fit. Give us our one pillar of light in this shabby, cold-hearted world.

'I asked him if he knew the fellow and he got very huffy. It seems Grigsby, the poor bastard, was Oxford and Philby was Cambridge. I didn't want to continue anything that boring so I started an "oh-look-there's-Charley-I-must-say-hello" bit when he shifted gears.

'"University is the only hope for a sodding great grind like Grigsby," Philby went on, sort of slurring his words. "No background. No family. Hideously wet. Just a bright young spark in a nation that abhors brightness. The weather. The architecture. The interior tat. The endless parade of royal, noble and commercially-knighted arseholes one's tongue must be prepared to lick clean."'

'Yech,' I said. I held my martini up to the light. It was mostly gone. Jim took it from me and refilled it. But then I put it down, struck by the realisation that Philby's thumbnail portrait of Grigsby was really a self-portrait.

'I think I did try to get away from him then,' Jim recalled. 'But as hard as it was to understand his Cambridge drawl filtered through alcohol, his message gripped me. I saw a vista Americans never suspect is there.

'"You must see," he kept saying. "To be bright is to want to rise above the grim toadying and make one's mark. To leave the world changed, *by you*. Not to piss away your years putting out the cat and taking in the newspaper. But to *change things forever*." He took a heroic breath. "So that the bloody world bloody well knows it was bloody you did it."

'Those dark blue eyes of his were so sadly sodden. That young face looked so alone. But determined. Kim Philby will by God make a mark on the world before he passes by.' Jim fell silent. 'The end.'

I heard a heavy sigh in the study. It was me. I found myself staring into my martini to see Kim's face, not the bright young man choosing treason as the mark he would make, but the old tom-cat smiling down on the icon of Lenin and knowing that he'd actually done it. I felt about me on the sofa for the Philby paperback.

'And that,' I said, 'was what it was all about? Someone denied kudos by a system of aristo swank and deadly amateurism?'

'Hey,' Jim exclaimed. 'I don't make these things up. I just report them.'

'Somebody too bright to be a patriot when being a traitor got bigger esteem?'

Jim sipped his martini. 'Britain's most notorious export is traitors. Something to do with their caste system?'

'Or the way they treat their sparks by smothering them. But it implies something we know isn't true, that the Russians knew how to treat them better.' I got to my feet, ignoring my newly filled drink.

'I suppose in the 1930s they had a better sales pitch, eh?' I said, glancing at my watch and starting for the kitchen. 'Or, none of the above.'

'Don't you mean all of the above?'

'In Kim's case it leaves out the single most important thing.'

'Which is . . .?'

'The sheer pleasure of making serious mischief.'

I finally spotted the Philby book. Someone had shoved it brusquely under a thick rug. We normally don't treat books that way.

In the growing twilight I turned it from front to back to catch a last glimpse of his seventy-six-year-old face.

Someone had taken a dark orange crayon and squiggled it all over the photograph. What a fate. Gamma's ex-flame, obliterated forever by a Terrible Two. Tanya had – effortlessly – done the job that the rest of us, including History, will *never* be able to do.

Chapter Fifty

We in Havana for sure celebrate a lot of holidays.

Now, in the 1990s, we no longer have the money to enjoy them as we once did, especially those of El Revolucion, with marching bands, colourful reviews and fireworks. But some are older than the revolution. The Three Kings is one of those.

It takes place just into the new year, just after the birth of the Redeemer, when the star of the east led these three wanderers to the Baby in the manger. It's very colourful. I have seen the Three Kings we hold in Miami, all flash and tinsel with women and girls dressed as nakedly as possible. Just, in fact, as it looked before Fidel.

In Havana, thanks to the Yanqui blockade, the Three Kings is more on the sombre side. This upsets Rita and makes her even more angry at Uncle Sam. She has handed over her publicity job to a younger person but she is still a consultant to Fidel on such matters. No salary, of course.

You should see her. She has not gained a single gram in all these years. Her hair is still as dark as a raven's wing, with that same bluish shine. She and my mother use the same hairdresser and, for all I know, the same dye.

Yes, my mother, Maria Sanchez is only seventy-three years old. Let's face it, it makes me just this side of sixty. Ay, lagrimas.

What? Of course. Children, grandchildren, the works. All female, if you don't count three sons-in-law. My entire existence has always been lived inside a blanket of women. If I had ever had a son or a grandson I wouldn't know what to do with the poor kid.

Well, maybe one thing: I would teach him how to live with women like his mother and grandmother. This is simple. Agree up front. Make the changes later. Take this Three Kings nonsense.

273

'Without political content,' Rita explained to me, 'Three Kings is a cheap, tawdry, vulgar religious hangover from the Lansky days. That's why I had them dedicate the parade to that glorious moment in the history of our revolution when my own brave husband fell down out of the sky to save the life of Fidel and five thousand schoolchildren.'

Can you imagine? Do you for one moment believe that I could have lived all these years in peace and quiet if I had spent my time pushing myself forward as a substitute hero? The revolution has only one hero.

'What did Fidel think of the idea?' I asked Rita.

'He is in Spain. He'll be back tomorrow.'

'He may have a different idea.'

'We have already mailed engraved invitations all over the world. Even to the US. Let the Yanqui attend. Let him see what some of his hired killers tried to do to us with their deadly rockets.'

'Rita. You amaze me. At your age and still able to stir up shit.'

She giggled. 'And that's not all I can stir up.'

I got going fast. You understand, all these years while my hair has turned white and I have assembled in my humidor-fridge some truly remarkable cigars to give my guests, I have not let myself get lazy or slow.

Life has not let me. Cuba's crisis has never let up. Not for one damned moment. Now, Uncle Sam no longer openly tries to invade us or burn our crops or assassinate Fidel. Now he starves us of the hard currency we need to buy essentials like oil. And to twist the knife, he flaunts his capitalist goodies in our very face.

Yes, a showcase of capitalism has developed along our northern shore, the shore that faces Key West, the shore with the luxury beaches and marinas. No US money was spent building it. Instead the money comes from Japan, is managed by Swiss hoteliers and built by Spanish work-gangs.

Here, if you have dollars, you can buy anything. Translation: no Cuban can buy anything.

Here, on our own soil, damp with our own sweat, only

tourists can live. Tourists and jineteras. These are young girls in miniskirts who prowl the north shore. Jinetera means a strutter, a prancer, one whose walk is a provocation, an invitation.

Fidel outlawed prostitution soon after he came to power. He frequently tells us that *if* there is prostitution it's done out of choice, not need. If you get the feeling he's off in dreamland making such a statement, he returns to earth by saying that, anyway, take heart: Cuban prostitutes have the lowest AIDS rate in Latin America.

Guantánamo continues as before, but Guantánamo is leased from us and not under our supervision. It and Melendez-Sanchez Tabaco, Inc. are Cuba's major producers of hard currency. What's left for the jineteras is the north coast, the dollar coast where, if a Cuban wants even the scent of a sirloin steak, that Cuban better be a whore.

And this is the shore where my dear Rita wants to stage this year's Three Kings fiesta, this shoreline so vulnerable to nearby Uncle Sam. In other words, precisely the place to play into the Yanqui hands.

I got to Rita's old office that morning, late, and asked to see the list of those who got engraved invitations. The event itself was pared down to an inexpensive minimum. But it would be held in the baseball stadium at Santa Maria del Mar and it had only one speaker. Fidel.

There would be a press conference and photo opportunity afterwards. That is – remember how vulnerable to sea attack this place was – if there would be an afterwards.

The one hundred invited guests were mostly press. These were marginally OK. Some were political – Canadian, Mexican and US legislators – and only semi-OK. But some were dangerous.

Hey, I love Midge Boardman. But she is still employed by the Yanqui government. That it isn't the CIA is only a fine point. And she no longer works for the *Times*. That justification is gone. But how could we know that she didn't work for Defence Intelligence? We couldn't. So why invite her?

You understand, Midge was impossible not to like. In those days. With her sophisticated kind of humour and her sleek society good looks. In those days. And the easy way she bridged the gaps between · Lansky and Angleton. Between Hoover and Kennedy. In those days.

Those days were gone, forever.

For Midge and me, they ended long ago in New Orleans when I spirited us out of town, blowing any credibility I ever had with Lansky. Midge and I looked like partners in the Coffee Pot Murder Plot.

I also knew, from our Miami agents, that to this day she remains under ISA surveillance. Those water-rats never forget, never give up. What an insane asylum is intelligence work.

What little smarts I still had told me to find a telephone booth.

'Is this Midge?'

'Who wants her?'

'I do. Yo soy Big Bic.'

She let out a scream. 'Guapo! Let me guess? You look even more beautiful with that thatch of white hair. Right?'

'Even more handsome. Only women are beautiful, Beautiful.'

'God, give me Cuban bullshit every time.'

'Who told you my hair is white?'

'I saw your photo the other day in a Mexican weekly. They gave you some sort of award?'

'Spook of the Century,' I explained.

'You'd be my nomination, too.' Her voice got crisp. 'Listen, this Three Kings invitation? Nothing personal, but I can't make it.'

I stopped talking for a long moment. 'Oh,' I said. 'That's too bad.'

'You don't want me, anyway. You must have some real celebrities to invite.'

'Sure.'

There was a longer silence now. I was glad she'd turned down the invitation. So why did this whole conversation worry me? 'Midge, que paso?'

'Nada, guapo.'

'Is somebody there? Can't you talk?'

This time she was the one who took her time answering. 'In a manner of speaking. I'm being tapped. Here's a name: Daryl Gomez,' she said then. 'Dark complexion. Late thirties? Good English. Cuban-inflected Spanish. Well set up, you know, fit and muscular and alert.'

'Not Daryl. Bernal Gomez,' I said.

Dear God, this time the silence tried to burn down the telephone lines. 'Bernal was somebody sniffing around Rita when we were young. I never liked the sonuvabitch. This is his son, also Bernal, in Yanqui Daryl. He emigrated to Florida as a boy and lived with his aunt.'

Midge gave a soft chuckle. 'I know he will audit the tape of this conversation. I'm trying to find out why he subjects himself to such dull stuff. I think he may have gone freelance with a wildcat ISA squad. There is always money among the Miami machos Cubanos for such nonsense. Any message?'

I cleared my throat. 'Why not? Escucha, Bernal. Thirty years ago Santa Maria del Mar took everything the ISA had, men, rockets, and sent it to the bottom of the Estrecho de las Florida. This time, we swallow you like a garbanzo. And spit you down the crapper.'

'Gee, I love cryptic messages. Wasn't it smart of you to phone me? Now that I've given you Daryl, can we call it quits for that New Orleans escapade?'

'Smart? Nobody calls me smart.'

'OK, lucky. Sixty years of luck, guapo.'

'Luck and friends like you.'

She paused again. 'You think it's worth moving the fiesta elsewhere?' A woman like Midge doesn't make such a suggestion lightly. You can expect that she knows how expensive such a move would be. And there was a tone in her voice that told me she had just put Bernal and the Three Kings together. If we held it where Rita wanted, we deserved everything the ISA could throw at us. 'You hear that, Bernal?' I asked the silent tapper. 'With a friend like Midge do I need enemies?'

'Sorry. I don't seem able to outgrow my curiosity.'

'Nobody does,' I assured her. 'We all want to know . . . how it all comes out.'

'But, Victor, you know what I mean.' Her voice got dreamy,

for an old lady. 'To sit in your rocker and stop wondering. Stop analysing. Let the whole shitty world go by. Good riddance.'

'That's no rocker. It's a coffin.'

We both had a cackle over that one.

'Just tell me one thing,' Rita demanded as we lay in bed that night. When you reach a certain age, what you do in bed is talk.

'Tell me how you found this out. Bernal's son. The ISA.'

'Your profession is publicity. Mine is espionage.'

'Victor!'

'What's important is that we have advance warning. We have a chance to hold the Three Kings somewhere else, where an attack by sea can't be made. Where we don't highlight that dollar shore with its hard-currency hookers.'

She was silent for a while because I was hitting hard on unpleasant truths. Unpleasant for a socialist, that is. Unpleasant to realise that Cuba's salvation lay in the wage-slavery of waiters, chambermaids, busboys, bartenders and whores. In serving a largely Yanqui market of big-boat owners, the same blofistas who used to adore watching Mojo shit and come at the same time.

Lansky's revenge had come full circle. Thanks to his Yanqui ally we had the brilliant opportunity once again to become the whorehouse of the Caribbean . . . or die.

'Any other location would look seedy, run down.' Her mind had already started repairing damage. 'There is no part of Havana that can be made to look as inviting as the north coast. As for the girls, we can ship them south for a week.'

'How does it look for the honoured publicity consultant to sponsor a fiesta celebrating her white-haired husband?'

'How?' A very big sigh came forth with all the glorious power of those magnificent breasts. 'Victor, no festividad featuring Fidel ever celebrates anyone else.' She paused and I could tell she was making a hard decision.

'Guapo,' she went on, getting me set for some hard truths, 'you know the way we are thinking these days.' We always meant Fidel. 'We are thinking of the old capitalist slogan: "if

278

you can't lick 'em, join 'em." We are certainly thinking of ways to reach a rapprochement without seeming to.'

'Fine. But not along the north coast.'

'The other motto is "best foot forward". Either we do this right or not at all.' She began contacting my chest, slowly, little touches of her fingers.

I have always followed a different slogan: what will be will be. If my elderly wife wants to seduce me for political reasons, why struggle?

Why try to explain the risks of a seaside locale, one that faces directly into enemy territory. A coast vulnerable to almost any aerial attack, rocket-bearing Stealth fighter planes, radar-invisible, coming in at a hundred feet over sea-level, arriving well ahead of their own sound waves.

She had begun rubbing and then pinching my nipples. In a minute or two she would be gently biting them. This doesn't excite every male but a lifetime of it has sensitised me to this kind of treatment. The girls at Guantánamo had done that to me as a baby just to see my tiny penis unkink. They knew better than anyone how directly connected are the nipples and whatever lies between the legs.

'Rita,' I said in a faint voice, 'if you think the presence of celebrity guests will keep the Yanqui from an attack, you still don't understand the Yanqui.'

'Guapo, the invitations have gone out.'

Her teeth closed down over nipples teased erect. The pain was absolutely gorgeous.

The only one who saw it my way was Ramos. Ugly, distorted Ramos. He now lived in a wheelchair in an old people's home along a part of the north coast where foreign capital had never been invested. Elderly cripples spent their days contemplating Miami TV from beds whose linen was in such short supply it couldn't be changed more often than once a month. If you were incontinent you had to wash your own sheet. If you could find soap.

I always spend Sunday morning with Ramos. I bring him seven perfectos from my humidor, the best, one for each day of the week. I know he gets other visitors because whatever data-storage has taken place over the years, Ramos' brain is still the computer that drives Cuban intelligence, or so he wants us to believe.

'Yes,' he said in a thin, weary voice. His big-rimmed spectacles looked gigantic on his skull-like face. 'I am familiar with the strategy. The risks, they claim, are worth it to showcase our north beach to the Yanqui capitalists.'

'Why not mail them a porno video?' I demanded. 'Cheaper. No risk.'

He gave a small hopeless twist to his wrenched shoulders. 'You always were our Yanqui expert,' he told me. 'The idea of the video cassette is exactly right. The US lives in front of its TV screens, as we do here in the old people's home. Send their press a video and a price list.' He made a small brushing gesture between the palms of his hands, as if dusting them clean.

'But since they have sold Fidel on this thing,' I went on, 'it is up to us, Ramos, to protect the fiesta from harm.'

'Not possible. Thousands of our people. Hundreds of foreign visitors. All that is needed,' his eyes grew sombre behind their thick lenses, 'is one accredited journalist with almost any kind of proper weapon, grenade, personnel rocket, time-bomb.'

I shook my head. 'We can weed them out. But what can we mobilise against a low-level air attack.'

Ramos was silent for a long time. Then his creaky voice began again: 'You say Bernal's son is now called Daryl?' I nodded. 'Do they stay in touch?' I nodded again. 'And the son is tapping Midge Boardman's telephone?'

'Midge believes it's not an official ISA project, just something funded by Miami fascists.'

'To whom the son was introduced by the father.'

'Ramos, this Daryl needs no intros. He is a true son of Uncle Sam.'

The shrivelled old man gave me a small smile that showed me he had at least been outfitted with wonderful dentures. 'What I am thinking . . .' He paused.

I have noticed, all my life, that when smart people begin to describe a thought to me they always pause. Is it so hard for them to expect understanding from me? Do they think I'm too stupid to think along with them? Why is this? I have grown sick and tired of being treated in this way, even by Rita.

'What I am thinking,' Ramos went on very slowly, 'is how to get around Midge Boardman.'

'Trick her? She doesn't need tricking. She's a friend. She gave me Daryl.'

Ramos' misshapen head slowly cocked to one side and his eyes, enlarged hugely in his spectacles, gave me a look, not pitying, not jeering. The look of one whose faith in humanity has never risen above total nil.

'Big Bic,' he muttered. 'When I believe a woman on the Defence Department's payroll is a friend, strap me in this wheelchair and send me over the nearest cliff into the sea.'

He was quiet for a long time. The usual will-this-idiot-understand-anything? pause. Finally, he came to some sort of conclusion. He showed me his dentures again and said: 'Pay attention, Big Bic.' His gnarled fingers felt inside the small knitted blanket on his lap. From underneath he drew out a book-sized lap-top computer.

'Ahi! The brains of Ramos,' I kidded him. 'Not Russian, I hope.'

He gave me a look. 'Japanese design. American chips. Made in Taiwan by girls with very slender fingers. She is married for the third time, yes?'

'Who? Oh, Midge. Yes.'

Ramos' twisted fingers did a bizarre little dance over the keyboard of the computer. 'James Q. Galton, magazine publisher. Correct?'

'If the machine says so.'

'Three daughters,' he read off the video screen. 'One grand-daughter. The address is on South Henry Street in Alexandria, Virginia. Ever been there?'

'Never.'

'Ever met Jim Galton?'

'Ramos, stop wasting my time.'

He closed the lid of his computer with a soft snapping sound. 'What is the status of the Luis Mūnoz passport.'

281

I only barely remembered. 'The last time I was peddling cigars in London I renewed it at the US Embassy.'

'When does it expire?'

'Early in the twenty-first century. You want me to go back to the States? You want me to make trouble for Midge Boardman? Forget it.'

'Not trouble. If she is, as you say, a friend, this is not trouble for her.'

'Then for who?' I peered at him. 'The husband?'

He hefted the computer. 'You realise that we have girls in your cigar factories whose fingers are delicate enough to assemble these machines?'

'Ramos, I asked you a question.'

'Our only production problem would be to keep them from rolling the chips on the inside of their thighs.'

'Ramos!'

'Or higher up.' He chuckled hideously and hid the computer away. Then he wheeled himself over to a telephone and began talking to someone called Paz about maps and aerial photos. It takes a person a while to realise he's been dismissed. I stood up.

'Sit down. No, not you, Paz. Bictor! Sit! You and I are not finished with each other. Not yet.'

Chapter Fifty-One

I am the only Boardman with a station wagon. Every few weeks, when I plan on going to one of the huge shop-or-die supermarket-malls, I see which daughter needs to do serious, life-threatening shopping. This day I snagged the twins.

Jane is blonde like her father and a mere shrimp at five-feet-eight. Kate is dark, like me, and manages to look quite normal, though six feet tall. Neither of them has much money to spend. Or so they complain.

We were in an endless market with fifty checkout lanes. You could be born at one end, buried at the other. New auto tyres, Sardinian whelks in extra virgin olive oil, half a steer, valid Episcopalian baptism – all there for the asking. From the entrance where Alcoholics Anonymous held open-air meetings, to the exit, where job counselling and cooking lessons were available, this market had replaced a whole city. Before we knew it, law courts and legislator's halls would serve us for our greater comfort and convenience and validate our parking tickets.

Two elderly adults should by rights spend a minimum on food and drink. Well, food, anyway, I told myself as I helped the boy load a three-quart fridge-pak of gin into the back of my wagon. One has no idea how heavy liquid can be.

But then he loaded what Kate and Jane had bought. True, one had a live-in fiancé and the other occasional boyfriends, but there was no reason to spend that much on gluttony. I was about to tell them this when I realised that this was exactly what they were expecting from their mother. They went off to find out what was playing at the movie theatre next door.

The young boy touched his forehead when I gave him a tip. 'That gemmin over there wan stalk to you,' he said in a Latino accent.

I looked twenty or thirty yards across parked cars, an ocean of them, the sun's heat sending up wavering layers of air from the hot roofs. My close-up vision is a wreck. My long-distance is hawk-like. Besides, I had already seen a photo of what Victor looked like these days.

Insufferably beautiful man, no facial lines, no facial fat. Just a sea-change in his hair to crisp white. As he approached me I shook my head from side to side. 'Do I win a cigar?'

He kissed my hand. We didn't embrace but the air between us started producing its own heat waves. 'You look sensational,' he said at last.

'Keep talking, guapo. How do I explain you to my daughters?'

'Come on. You must constantly meet old friends.'

'None who look like you.'

He considered this for a time. We both turned in different directions and very obviously surveyed the scene for lurkers.

A class lurker never lurks. 'Would Bernal Gomez handle this himself?' Victor asked, sotto voce.

We turned back to face each other awkwardly, like teenagers. I glanced at my watch. 'Victor, I'll introduce you as an old beau – my girls don't believe anything I tell them – and we'll all go back to my place.'

'Will Jim be there?' His dark eyes looked mischievous.

'You'll have a drink. We'll call you a cab. Everything will be calm and normal and totally middle-aged. Comprende?'

Jim hadn't made a daiquiri in years. But I don't think Victor cared. He had set out to be the charming stranger he guessed I'd portrayed in my memoirs.

'Memoirs?' Victor sipped his drink. 'That is a book I would like to read.'

'If I ever finish it.'

'You're in magazine publishing?' he asked my husband.

Jim frowned. 'Was. You've done your homework, haven't you?'

'Not me.' Victor winked. 'Ramos.'

Jane began paging through a fashion magazine. It may be hard for us to accept but even our most stressful conversation bores the socks off our children. Kate, who is a bit more social, gave Victor one of her wham-into-the-retina smiles, the kind that has encouraged more than one short man to make a fool of himself with her on the dance floor or tennis court.

'Girls.' I held up my car keys. 'Let's take you home and unload your stuff.'

Victor stood up and managed to look longingly deprived as his eyes followed their departure. 'Lovely girls,' he murmured.

'Lucky to have a mother who's also a transport manager,' Jim added.

When I returned only twenty minutes had elapsed but it looked very much as if there had been an argument, now quite patched up. How can you sense such a thing? The argument hung in the air in the form of hyper-hospitality. Jim was treating Victor like a long-lost younger brother and college room-mate.

For his part, Victor was drinking too much. Cubans drink, but usually at parties. The Anglo-Saxon ideal of quietly glugging oneself under the stool is not Cuban. I wondered if the argument had something to do with me. What else?

'I'm glad you settled whatever it was,' I offered.

'Jim wants to drive me back to my hotel,' Victor suggested, too smoothly. 'I'm happy with a cab. It's for sure one long ride to make twice in an evening.'

'Nonsense,' Jim responded.

Since driving Victor back into town was also nonsense, I saw Jim was determined to spend Midge-free time with Victor. As sometimes happens, even to a tranquil relationship like ours, I sat back and cold-bloodedly reviewed my life with Jim while the men talked further nonsense about the old days when American baseball clubs often did their spring training in Cuba.

Jim and I had been married six years. His first wife, an attractive blonde lady named Audrey, had died of cancer without ever having children. Six years ago, when I retired from the *Times*, they gave me a party we all still remember. It was there that Jim and I first met. We married a week later.

This is OK for twenty-year-olds. But when both the bride and the groom can – in Jim's immortal phrase – get into any movie at half price before six p.m., the world expects a more stately courtship.

Watching him now as he and Victor produced reams of throwaway man-talk I began to wonder if a mutual addiction to very dry martinis was enough. Yes, we also knew all the words to Gershwin, Porter, Kern. And we got on well in bed. And he was supportive and warm with my girls.

What else did I know about Jim? Did I need to know much more? He was a good man. Period.

Like Emory, he'd been in the Air Force during the Korea fracas, not as a pilot but in Public Relations. He'd gone back to publishing magazines and, by the time I'd met him, had sold off control to a conglomerate and put a huge golden farewell handshake away for a rainy day.

I had taken him as found, no locked rooms. He played pool every Thursday, lunched with the same cronies every

Monday. We visited his friends with country homes. Their wives and I all got along well without becoming girlfriends.

Both he and Victor got to their feet and turned ceremonially towards me.

There is always something watchable about tall men who have kept their figures.

'Victor, I had no idea you knew so much about American baseball.'

'Not me,' he demurred. 'The Navy guys at Gitmo. That's all they ever talked about. To me.' He smiled, as if those old memories filled him with nostalgia.

'And your family? How are they?'

'Rita and Maria are both retired. As much as two bossy women could ever retire.' His face went blank. 'But you never met them, did you?'

'Rita. Once. The first of January, 1959.'

He looked really stricken by nostalgia. 'Everything began that morning.' For a long time he was lost in thought. Then he came back to the present. 'Well,' he said, turning to Jim, 'enough of that, eh?'

'Right.' Jim went to the front hall radiator where we keep our keys to make any burglar's job less tiring. He waved car keys at me. 'Back in half an hour.'

'Nonsense,' I said silently. Instead I blew them both a kiss as they left.

There had to be a strong reason why Jim insisted on doing what he loathed, threading a car through evening traffic along the byways, bridges and arteriosclerotic tubing of the capital area. He would be gone an hour, sixty minutes of motoring hell he hated most, bumper-to-bumper, stop-and-go.

In six years we'd never had secrets. Why now?

Jim didn't get home until midnight. Somewhere along the way, he muttered, they had grabbed hamburgers, so his share of our dinner, derived by micro from a frozen package, was reassigned to the deep-freeze.

So was conversation. The authorities tell you never to refreeze food because it's dangerous. Re-freezing and re-starting conversation may be even more so. I had by now found any number of major flaws in my third and last husband.

When Jim finally started talking it was, as it often is, simultaneous with an outburst from me. I was undressing for bed and couldn't stay buttoned up, in any sense of the word, another minute.

'What the hell kept you so hellishly long?' was how it came out in what must be called an accusing tone, just as Jim began:

'That clown knows more about me than you do. He knows why I quit the Air Force and went back to publishing.'

'You mean I don't?'

'Whatever reason I gave you,' he confessed, sitting down in a low bedroom armchair and removing his shoes, 'the truth was that I hated having to liaise with ISA. If the bastards are so secret, let 'em skulk, not strut.'

'You had a run-in with ISA?'

'No!' He sounded peeved as hell. 'I avoided a run-in with ISA.' He began nursing an ankle. 'I've regretted it ever since. In those days I had a little clout as a goddamned chicken colonel. Now it's much too late.'

His chair was one of a pair, called slipper chairs, in which millionaires relax as body servants remove their slippers. I sat and my own body servant, Midge Boardman, now did the honours for me.

'It's that Three Kings fiesta.'

Jim looked startled. 'Did he tell you?'

'About Cuba I need very little instruction. Once before he had to defend that site from an ISA attack. What's he asking you to do?'

'It's done, dear heart. We done did it an hour ago.'

He gave me a ghastly smile. 'We went to a late-hours joint, the Sacred Cow. After a lot of silent-movies acting to make sure the world knew we weren't being watched, Victor played defector and slipped me a black plastic binder of maps, intelligence surveys, spy-plane photos, engineering charts, concerning two heavy-duty underground missile sites that bracket the Santa Maria del Mar area.'

'Didn't the Russians remove them years ago?'

287

'These two are invisible. Bungalows have been built on top of them. What looks like a basketball court hinges up and frees the missile for its flight. We were installing the same damned things, you know.'

'Where are these missiles targeted?'

Jim began removing more clothing, slowly, grunting as his joints rebelled. 'About where we're sitting right now. Greater District of Columbia.'

'To what end, for God's sake?'

'All documents were in Spanish. Victor called the hidden missiles a Domesday machine. He repeated it for any hidden microphones that missed it. Thus, if Fidel had to face another Bay of Pigs, he could retaliate. The documents detail what sort of threat might trigger off the missiles. If I saw it in a movie, starring George C. Scott, I'd giggle. When somebody shoves it under your nose in real life, you freeze.'

I was silent for a while. 'Why show this to you, of all people?'

'I wasn't the designated receiver. I was just a cut-out who would sneak the stuff to the CIA or the ISA or the Pope in Rome. As subtly as Victor slipped me the McGuffin, I slipped him a brown No. Nine envelope stuffed like a Christmas goose.'

'With real money?'

'Real counterfeit Victor had given me in the car beforehand.'

'To make himself look like a traitor to Castro? Jim, why did you agree to this farce?'

'Because.'

'Because? That's the kiddie excuse.'

He shrugged. 'He said the ISA had you targeted for a hit. He said this would take their minds off it for good.'

'He's wrong on both counts. But even if he were right, why would the ISA buy this stuff?'

'The loonier the tune, the more credible that some government yahoo has created it. Why does anybody in intelligence believe anything?'

I almost blushed, remembering dear Cousin Jim Angleton.

'Because if they don't, they're out of a job?' Both of us brooded over this jagged splinter of truth for a long time.

'Victor claimed,' Jim said at last, 'that with the proper window dressing anything looks believable. Incidentally, never patronise that Sacred Cow. They make rotten hamburgers.'

What with talking it over five more times, we didn't get to sleep till well past one a.m. Privately, I decided Jim had been touchingly worried about me, a fact Victor had played on like a burglar. Anyway the whole story stank. How could the ISA get excited about a folder of stuff they still didn't have?

The hell with men. I rooted down deep, deep in my subconscious for some REM adventures. One-fifty a.m. Hoarse, ragged shouting on a bullhorn!

Upstairs bedroom filled with retina-etching glare from searchlights. Pounding on downstairs doors, front and back.

'THIS IS THE DEA! DROP YOUR WEAPONS! COME OUT WITH YOUR HANDS UP!'

I could hear them breaking down both doors.

Jim jumped out of bed and went to the window. 'What the hell are you bastards – !'

A volley of sub-machine-gun fire, unsilenced, like the downpour of a tropical storm's fat raindrops. I hoped they were just firing warnings.

'Get back from the window, Jim!'

I reached for the telephone. No dial tone. They'd cut the wires.

Something smashed the window apart. Glass flew all over the bed. The choking stench of tear gas filled our bedroom. I started to weep.

Who the hell was I going to call, anyway?

Real Drug Enforcement Agency SWAT teams wear bullet-proof sleeveless flak jackets with huge capital letters: DEA. That's so you know which storm-troopers are illegally breaking and entering. Our bunch wore torn T-shirts and jeans, more like a squad of upstart teenage drug pushers.

After the bullhorn howling, silence. Nobody was talking,

showing ID cards or badges. The neighbours stood in their open upstairs windows in their nightgowns staring at us and nodding 'Didn't-I-tell-you-about-those-two?' looks.

We were hustled, pushed, slammed and shoved into the back of a station wagon whose windows had heavy-duty fencing welded into the inside frames, as if normally used to transport rabid rottweilers. We were handcuffed to each other.

After a while our eyes stopped tearing and I stopped coughing.

A fourteen-year-old guard wearing a Czech Scorpion machine-pistol glared at us. He hadn't mastered the cop trick of pretending there was nothing personal in order to hide his hatred. No, he loathed or feared us and wanted us to know it.

While he breathed heavily the rest of the squad looted the house. I expected they'd torch it but, instead, one got behind the wheel with a large bag of books. On top of it he laid a plastic binder of the sort Jim had described.

Reading matter is a favourite form of incriminating evidence. In a crowd, a lawman will single out someone with spectacles to club down since bad eyes mean reading books, therefore, guilt. Rule One: plant drugs or take books.

Off we roared into the night, no sirens or flashing lights. Alexandria is a very quiet neighbourhood. We like it. It's on the Potomac south of the District of Columbia, right on the Virginia line. You go due north along the Jefferson Davis Highway to reach the District.

But our book wagon was tearing due west along the Capital Beltway, US Highway 495 that rings the city. It curves right and north where it crosses the Henry O. Shirley Memorial Highway, US 95. No, I have no idea who Henry O. Shirley was, but I did once know a Shirley O'Henry.

The librarian behind the wheel had us illegally up past sixty miles an hour along a thoroughfare that should have been deserted this early. But interstate truck traffic thinks it owns the roads at these small hours.

The white, unmarked truck came up behind us so fast I didn't see it. It swung to the right-hand lane and spurted ahead, passing us on the wrong side.

'Sumbitch spick shitbag motherfucker,' the lad with the

Scorpion shouted. His spittle on the 'f' plosive spattered my forehead with saliva. I wondered if SWAT teams took AIDS check-ups.

The white truck swung into our lane yards ahead of us and clamped down on its brakes. Its rear lights burned bright red. We could hear its piercing brake-squeal. Then ours. All our throats closed over with fear.

The station wagon ploughed head-on into the truck's rear bumper. Deafening crash. Mad swerve. Sparks shooting out along the concrete roadway.

The two vehicles seemed welded in an intimate dog-love embrace. We skidded off the beltway, our speed down to about thirty. The grass slowed us a bit more.

Then the white truck ahead wrenched hard to the right. There was a sharp yelping noise as our driver kept pumping his jammed footbrakes. He grabbed wildly for the handbrake.

But we crashed, at about twenty, into the guard rail. And overturned.

Wouldn't you know it? Just at the interesting part everything went black.

Chapter Fifty-Two

Some day let me take you on a drive around lovely, old-style Alexandria, Virginia. It's a river town, elderly, relaxed, colonial in the old parts. And surrounded by airports.

I'm not sure which one I woke up in.

Neither was Jim. Our handcuffs had been removed. We were locked in a spacious tool cupboard near where aircraft took off and landed. Someone had ripped open Jim's right pants leg and bandaged his knee.

We found other superficial injuries that looked bad. But neither of us felt bad.

'If I could get to a phone,' I muttered, 'I could call Susannah and get her to shut up the house.'

The door of the tool cupboard made a noise. Jim picked up a huge monkey wrench, easily the size of a tennis racket.

'Miz Boardman?' It was the Latino boy who loaded packages at the supermarket. 'You 'member me, Miz Boardman?'

He produced a triangle of torn paper. On it someone had written 'Hangar Seven, 10:00.' I had a small-of-back pain, nothing hot tubs wouldn't cure. Jim's right knee wouldn't bear his weight. I gave him an arm and we two crocks limped along to Hangar Seven. I had stopped suspecting him of anything but believing Victor's con games.

We climbed into a Citation II with Mexican markings. A pilot traded very fast Spanish with the boy from the supermarket.

'Bye, Miz Boardman. Bien viaje,' the boy said as he left.

'Listen, fella,' Jim began in his best colonel's voice, 'you think – ?'

The pilot produced a deep shrug. 'You talk with Luis Muñoz.'

In my dotage I can't remember where I left my comb. But Victor's alias that day in New Orleans? To save me explaining it to Jim, Victor arrived.

'Midge, your hair! Not easy getting you out without getting you killed.'

Jim frowned. 'Not easy fobbing off those damned missile plans.'

Victor eyed the pilot. 'Por favor, amigo.' He waited till the man had left. 'He is, after all, Mexican, not Cuban. No business of his, right?'

'Does that make us honorary Cubans?' Jim asked.

'In a way. You have worked hard to make sure ISA has the plans. My flight plan calls for take-off in half an hour for Mérida. Then Havana.'

'Is that supposed to be our flight plan, too?' Jim asked.

Victor's face went suddenly grave. 'You have done my country a great service. I have no control over how you will be treated by your own country.'

'Badly,' Jim supplied. 'The only thing that will let us come back will be some sort of rapprochement with Cuba. In what would've been our lifetime,' he added with a fake grin.

'Is there a telephone nearby?' I wanted to know.

'I telephoned your *tall* daughter,' Victor said, smiling crookedly. 'The one with that smile that blinds you down to your back teeth.'

'Kate.'

'She said she would get over to the house. This was at five this morning.' He led the way to a corner of the hangar and handed me a quarter. 'Your own telephone should be repaired by now.'

I dialled. 'Kate?'

'It's Susannah,' she responded. 'Where are you?'

'Safe.' A tight silence as we considered the probability of eavesdropping.

'Stay there. The DC cops don't have a warrant. But they want to, um, talk. You two have put peaceful Alexandria, Virginia, on the map. Suspicion of harbouring books. Classical CDs.'

'Susannah, you and Tanya and the twins. We love you. Back soon!'

'Call it a second honeymoon!' she cried and hung up.

Thirty minutes later we were over North Carolina, overlying Kill Devil Farm.

'I hear,' Victor said, 'the place is up for sale. All the games are over.'

Jim gazed out of the window. 'What about your Domesday missile game?'

'ISA believes.' Victor brought out two cigars. They were short, cropped-end stogies. 'As long as they believe, they leave our Three Kings festival alone.' He offered the cigars. 'They leave Midge alone, for sure.'

'I don't smoke,' Jim confessed.

'I never did,' I reminded him.

'Me neither,' said Victor Sanchez. He gave me a baffled, beautiful look, handsome as ever. He handed the cigars to the pilot, who shook his head. 'Then for Jesus' sake give them to a friend. *Somebody* has to smoke cigars.'

I put an arm around Jim's waist. 'Susannah calls this our second honeymoon. Should we?'

'We never had a proper first one,' Jim reminded me. 'Plenty

of time to get home and face the music. By then, maybe the tune will've changed.'

'Meanwhile, amigos,' Victor promised, 'we dance the Tango Havana.'

Also by Leslie Waller
and available from Mandarin Paperbacks

The Banker

Woods Palmer is in at the deep end. He may be the new vice-president of the bank with the mightiest financial muscle in the free world. But he's up to his neck in political chicanery, industrial intrigue and internecine warfare of the competition.

There are no rules in the risk business. Just the players and the tricks of their trade – inside deals, political pay-offs, sexual blackmail, coercive pr, espionage, rumour . . .

Woods Palmer is gambling to win. With big money. And grit.

The Family

Woods Palmer found out how to beat players at their own game in *The Banker*. And proved himself a fast learner.

Now the chief of America's biggest banking empire, he has all the instincts, acumen and smooth authority of unmistakable power. But he has still more to learn – much more than the delicate webs of treachery, subordination and corruption which usually shroud big business.

This time Palmer's up against the pros who make no secret of big business. Or big crime. And shamelessly think nothing of violence, sadism and wanton murder.

Mafia Wars

Assaulted mercilessly by rival organisations like the Chinese Triads, Japanese Yakusa, ganglords and the South American drug cartels, ripped asunder by inner conflicts and scandals, the Mafia is more dangerous and powerful than ever. Now, one family is brilliantly placed to explore new situations world-wide – drugs, entertainment, international finance, and above all, political power . . .

A Selected List of Thrillers available from Mandarin

While every effort is made to keep prices low, it is sometimes necessary to increase prices at short notice. Mandarin Paperbacks reserves the right to show new retail prices on covers which may differ from those previously advertised in the text or elsewhere.

The prices shown below were correct at the time of going to press.

☐	7493 0942 3	**Silence of the Lambs**	Thomas Harris	£4.99
☐	7493 1091 X	**Primal Fear**	William Diehl	£4.99
☐	7493 0636 X	**Bones of Coral**	James Hall	£4.99
☐	7493 0249 6	**Squall Line**	James Hall	£4.99
☐	7493 0862 1	**Under Cover of Daylight**	James Hall	£4.99
☐	7493 1441 9	**Before I Wake**	Steve Morgan	£4.99
☐	7493 1396 X	**The Annunciation**	Patrick Lynch	£4.99
☐	7493 1376 5	**Fall When Hit**	Richard Crawford	£4.99
☐	7493 1427 3	**Glass Shot**	Duncan Bush	£4.99
☐	7493 0192 9	**House of Janus**	Donald James	£3.99
☐	7493 1125 8	**House of Eros**	Donald James	£3.99
☐	7493 1252 1	**Running with the Wolves**	Jonathan Kebbe	£4.99
☐	7493 0564 9	**Hyena Dawn**	Christopher Sherlock	£3.99
☐	7493 1323 4	**Eye of the Cobra**	Christopher Sherlock	£4.99

All these books are available at your bookshop or newsagent, or can be ordered direct from the address below. Just tick the titles you want and fill in the form below.

Cash Sales Department, PO Box 5, Rushden, Northants NN10 6YX.
Fax: 0933 410321 : Phone 0933 410511.

Please send cheque, payable to 'Reed Book Services Ltd.', or postal order for purchase price quoted and allow the following for postage and packing:

£1.00 for the first book, 50p for the second; **FREE POSTAGE AND PACKING FOR THREE BOOKS OR MORE PER ORDER.**

NAME (Block letters) ....

ADDRESS ....

....

☐ I enclose my remittance for ....

☐ I wish to pay by Access/Visa Card Number ☐☐☐☐☐☐☐☐☐☐☐☐☐☐☐☐

Expiry Date ☐☐☐☐

Signature ....

Please quote our reference: MAND